Shark Wars

AND

THE Battle OF Riptide

EJ ALTBACKER

RAZORBILL

For Mom and Dad

EJ ALTBACKER

RAZORBILL

RAZORBILL

An Imprint of Penguin Random House LLC

Penguin.com

RAZORBILL & colophon is a registered trademark
of Penguin Random House LLC.

First published in the United States of America by Razorbill,
an imprint of Penguin Random House LLC, 2011

Copyright © 2011 by Penguin Random House LLC

LIBRARY OF CONGRESS CATALOGING-IN-PUBLICATION DATA IS AVAILABLE

Razorbill ISBN 9781595143761

This omnibus edition ISBN 9781984836212

Printed in the United States of America

1 3 5 7 9 10 8 6 4 2

PROLOGUE

FOR TIME BEYOND MEMORY THERE WAS THE ocean and it was empty. Then the first fish, a shark named Tyro, was borne from it. Tyro circled the Big Blue's vastness and found he was alone. So he swam once more through the seven seas and with each stroke of his mighty tail created everything that lives in and under the waters. He chose several sharks to hunt with him and called these the First Shiver, positioning them in a Line from first to fifth, with himself as leader.

First was mighty Finnbarr whose descendants became the great white sharks; second was powerful Longfluke whose children became the bull sharks; third was the cunning Machiakelpi whose sons and daughters became the mako; Ramtail the Battler was fourth and his young became the tiger sharks; and fifth, but never considered last in the Line by Tyro, was Leynar the Magnificent, whose descendants would be the threshers.

First Shiver governed with one goal in mind: to protect its members, which numbered all of sharkkind, and to ensure their survival from one generation to the next. For many years, every shark and dweller living in the Big Blue prospered under shiver law.

But after a long life Tyro grew weary. He summoned his Five in the Line and told them that one day a great evil would threaten all of sharkkind and every dweller in the seven seas. When this day came, only a united First Shiver would be strong enough to defeat the evil. After this warning, Tyro gave himself to the Sparkle Blue, where his spirit swims the eternal current to this day. But after their leader was gone, those in the Line bickered and fought about who would be best to lead against the coming danger. In the end, the five sharks of First Shiver could not—and would not—agree, and so swam off by themselves to create their own shivers . . .

THE
REEF

CHAPTER 1

SUNLIGHT DAPPLED THE WARM WATER AS GRAY flexed his powerful fins, gliding to a stop in a thick kelp bed. He used to hide in this patch of green-greenie unseen when he was smaller, but now his tail poked out. Gray made sure it waved back and forth with the warm tide so it wouldn't give him away. He would have been spotted going to the shiver's main hunting grounds, so he had snuck away in the opposite direction toward the lagoon. Gray was a growing fish, but the council, and his mom, Sandy, wouldn't let him hunt unsupervised. That was just unfair. He was twelve years old! He was practically adult for any sharkkind. Almost, anyway.

Even though his name was Gray, he was more bluish on his upper half and white on the bottom, with what he thought was a really cool stripe down each of his enormous flanks. "Everyone's jealous," he muttered. Apparently Gray was big for a reef shark. And ever since he grew larger than Atlas, the old bull shark who was Coral Shiver's leader, every fin watched him with a mixture of curiosity and fear. Like I'm a freak or something, he thought.

Gray pushed that from his mind and concentrated on the task at hand. He'd get into trouble for sure if the council, or his mom, found out he was this far away from the homewaters. And so near the lagoon, Gray thought. But this is where the tasty, tasty lobsters hang out. He gnashed his rows of razor-sharp teeth, imagining the satisfying crunch of a nice, plump shellhead. The lobster that Gray was hunting wandered into the next kelp bed over, which was even thicker than where Gray was hiding now, but no problem. Many sharkkind didn't like swimming through greenie because they were afraid they would get tangled. But not Gray. He swam where he wanted, when he wanted. And today that happened to be in a kelp bed. Now where was that lobster? Being such a great hunter, Gray was positive the dumb shellhead didn't have a clue that certain doom was coming for it.

But suddenly his prey jetted forward, abandoning all stealth and gaining speed. The lobster somehow sensed his presence and made a break for the lagoon where Gray couldn't swim safely anymore, not since his growth spurt. This was a little annoying. Gray used the currents to mask his stalking to perfection! Or not . . . How did this little krillface know he was watching? The lobster whizzed toward the mouth of the lagoon, where the landsharks had built some sort of floating home. Gray's mom would be really angry if she found out he was this close to the lagoon. But he wasn't about to be seen by anyone except the lobster. "And ol' Lobby will keep my secret once he's safely in my belly," Gray said out loud as he gained speed.

"Watcha doing, Gray?" asked Barkley the dogfish, disrupting Gray's concentration and even startling him a bit. Just a bit, though.

"Can't you see I'm busy?" Barkley could be very annoying. But still, he was Gray's friend and one of the few fish that made him laugh. He was also one of the few reef mates that would still spend time with Gray after his enormous growth spurt the previous year. Most of his old friends got very jumpy when he was around. Gray wondered why that was for a moment, but then set about leaving Barkley in his wake.

"Trying to catch that lobster, huh? Listen to your older and wiser friend—this isn't a good idea." Barkley was born a month before Gray and brought that fact up whenever he could.

"I'm not taking a survey about what you think!" Gray groused.

"Hey, I just don't want to see you with your head stuck in a bucket again." The dogfish grinned, now swimming upside down and eye to eye with Gray. The memory still stung.

When Gray was a pup, he explored an ancient wreck of a landshark boat, a galleon, and got his head stuck in a *bucket* which was something humans used to carry stuff around in. It had been wedged on so tight Prime Minister Shocks needed to ask three of the octos from the octopus clan to pull the thing off. Gray was called "bucket head" that entire summer. He pretended not to hear Barkley's teasing and increased his speed, but his friend was annoyingly fast for a dogfish and kept pace.

"Seriously, Gray, Miss Lamprey hunts around here before class. If she sees you, she'll tell your mom for sure," Barkley warned.

Everyone who grew up near the reef was taught by Miss Lamprey. They learned not only about the world in which they lived, but also about the dry world above the water where the two-legged landsharks ruled. Gray thought learning about the *human* world—that's what they called themselves—was a big waste of time. But it did make things easier if you knew the words for things that didn't come from the Big Blue. Especially if you got your head stuck in a bucket.

"Miss Lamprey can keep her pointy snout out of my business. And I thought we agreed to never bring up the *incident* again!"

"Oh, riiight. Totally forgot. Sorry. Let's head back to the reef," Barkley said as he tried to turn Gray by pressing against him. Ha! Fat chance. That used to work, but now Gray was four times the size of the dogfish who nonetheless strained against his bulk. "Seriously, stop being such a flipper! We're going to be late for class!"

"I am *not* a flipper!" Gray told the dogfish. "I'm a total fin!" Being a fin was very cool. Being a flipper wasn't.

"Well, you're not acting very finny!" Barkley said. Gray butted his friend to the side and sped forward. "Hey! Come back!" shouted the dogfish.

"Eat wake, buddy!" The lobster had passed into the mouth of the lagoon. Talking with Barkley cost Gray valuable time. But it still wouldn't be enough time for his prey to make it home. Gray would show the shellhead who was the big fish in this patch of water.

He bore down on the lobster. Gray could feel the warm water whisking through his gills and closed his mouth so it wouldn't slow him down. He could smell the lobster as he closed the distance between them. So delicious! He ground his teeth in anticipation. Closer. The lobster disappeared momentarily into the fronds of kelp near the opening of the lagoon. There wasn't enough to hide in, though. Gray sped through the sparse greenie, opening his mouth for his strike when—whammo!

But it wasn't a good whammo. Not good at all. Gray had hit a hidden shelf in the lagoon bed. He could feel his dorsal fin in the exposed air *above* the waterline! The lobster turned and clacked its claws at Gray while shimmying and flipping its tail back and forth. Was the shellhead doing some sort of victory swim?! Impossible!

Crustaceans were just dumb snacks. It sure seemed to be enjoying itself, though.

Barkley cruised to a stop, hovering near Gray. "Wow, that looked painful. And dumb! Was it more painful than dumb, you think? Or the other way 'round?"

Gray struggled, thrashing his tail to free himself. But he was stuck. "If you're finished, I could use some help!"

"Fine, fine." Barkley quickly swam to the shallower side of the lagoon and pushed. This accomplished nothing. He swam a tight circle and tried butting Gray off the shelf. "You know, you might want to lay off the fatty tuna and go on a seaweed diet for a while. I've heard it's very cleansing."

"Shut your cod hole and push!" Gray yelled. They were far too close to the landshark colony. And humans had things called boats to move on top of the Big Blue. One time Gray came upon a human in a rubber covering floating by the bottom of the reef. He was chasing a group of mackerel and didn't notice the human until they were snout to snout. It carried a spine shooter, and sometimes those were dangerous, even to a shark as big as Gray. But the landshark dropped it and blew bubbles instead, waving its arms wildly, looking very fierce indeed! It scared Gray so much he swam away as fast as he could! Close call. But this was more dangerous. Fish of all sizes—even whales!—were caught and killed by humans from boats.

Gray thrashed even harder. With one final ram from Barkley at full speed, he felt the ledge crumble, then disappear. He was free! Gray rejoiced as his dorsal fin submerged and he angled for deeper water.

"That was a close one, buddy!" Barkley chuckled nervously. After a moment, Gray did too. Pretty soon they were both cackling like crazy fish. "Can you imagine what your mom would do if she found out?" Barkley trailed off. Gray was laughing so hard he didn't notice his mother floating off to the side, her eyes blazing. Uh-oh.

"I think I'm going to find out," Gray said to his friend.

But Barkley wasn't there, of course. The dogfish had wisely vanished. How does he do that? Gray wondered silently as his mother frowned, her tail swishing in short, angry strokes.

CHAPTER 2

"YOU'RE GROUNDED FOR A WEEK!" HIS MOTHER said in a clipped voice, the barbels below her nostrils vibrating with emotion. They did that when she got mad. And she was angrier than Gray had seen her in a long while. Even madder than the time when he had talked Barkley into cutting school and got stung by a jellyfish. But seven days and nights of not swimming more than a body length away from the reef bed? Ridiculous! Was he some newborn pup that needed to hide in the greenie? No! Was he a bottom-feeding muck sucker that rooted in the sand for its meals? Disgusting! And again, no! Being grounded was no way for a big fin like him to spend even one day, much less a week!

But Gray's mouth was quicker than his brain so none of these perfectly good arguments made it into the conversation. Instead he blurted, "Awww, Mommm!"

"You broke your word to me," she said in a quiet voice.

"I'm sorry," he whispered.

Gray felt awful. Everyone in Coral Shiver respected his mother, proven by the fact that she had been chosen to be third in the Line. Gray was proud of that. Knowing how dangerous the Big Blue was, any shark in the Line could be your next leader. Usually shivers ranked five after their leader. It was an honor even though their shiver was small and didn't even have succession to the fifth, like a real battle shiver, only to the third.

Atlas was leader, of course. Then there was Quick-eyes the thresher as his first and Onyx the blacktip as second. Onyx had these awesome markings down his flanks, almost like they were put there on purpose. But how? When Gray asked about the markings he got yelled at by both Onyx and his mom so he never asked again.

In a shiver, any shark could challenge for position, even for leader. But if you didn't have experience in the Line, you wouldn't be accepted as a contender by the full-member shiver sharks.

Since he was still technically a pup, Gray wasn't even a full member of Coral Shiver yet. "You have to earn the Line's respect before you can join as a shiver shark," his mother had told him when he was younger. Well, he hadn't earned any today.

"I know it's wrong to go toward the lagoon, but when I saw the lobster, I got so hungry!" Gray told her.

His mother sighed. "You're a growing shark, Gray. No one says you shouldn't eat." She looked him over from head to tail. He was now almost twice her length. "You just have to be smart about it. You have to do what's best for everyone, not just yourself. Even if that means you go hungry for a little while."

"I'm sorry," said Gray once again.

They entered the ancient lava vent, which was the entrance to the hidden reef and their homewaters. Landsharks lived in a floating base by the other reef, nearer to their shore. Ours is much nicer, thought Gray as he followed his mom's swishing tail down the secret path through the giant kelp bed. There was green-greenie, blue-greenie, and even yellow and brown-greenie. The greenie was long enough that it looked like just another giant seaweed bed from above. And if you didn't know where the path began while swimming in, you'd most likely get lost or hung up. Even landsharks stayed away because their boats got snared by the greenie that floated all the way up to the chop-chop. Crabs used their sharp claws to clip and trim the secret lane of the tangly plant. Supposedly. Gray had never actually seen them do it and didn't really believe shellheads were smart enough to follow instructions like that.

"Gray, the Coral Shiver homewaters are a special place," Sandy told him.

"I know that, Mom. I do live here."

Sandy let out an exasperated sigh. "That's not what

I mean. What we have here is different than many parts of the Big Blue."

Gray got excited. She was talking about the Big Blue in the way that meant open ocean! Would she let him go to the Tuna Run this year? He wasn't allowed last time because he was too young. They *had* to let him go this season! He couldn't help himself, and asked, "Can I go with you into the Big Blue for the Tuna Run? To see how it's different?"

"Absolutely not!" she said so sharply that Gray darted into the thick kelp. When he poked his head out, his mom sighed. She motioned for him to come out from the weedy bed. "I'm sorry I yelled. The open waters of the Big Blue are amazing and wonderful in places. But they can also be dangerous. Sharkkind and dwellers that make their home there aren't as nice as the ones here."

"Okay, Mom," Gray answered. "I'm not planning any trips away from the reef. I promise."

"You won't because you're grounded. And Barkley—come out here!"

Gray turned and saw Barkley hiding in the greenie. His eyes popped open as Sandy stared right at him. He nudged himself forward, smiling nervously. "Oh, here's the path! Silly me, I got lost. Hello, Miss Sandy."

Her eyes narrowed on the dogfish. "Hello to you, Barkley. Now, both of you get to class." And with a whisk of her tail she was gone.

"Grounded a whole week. Bummer," remarked the dogfish matter-of-factly. "By the way...told you so."

"By the way," Gray answered, "quit being a flipper."

Barkley led them around the main area of the reef. Most days at least one or two of the groups representing the different types of reef dwellers would meet about something or other. Anemones, starfish, sea cucumbers, jellies, tropicals, even shellheads, would speak with each other. Gray didn't know why. It wasn't as if they were smart like sharkkind. Most dwellers, or non-sharks, never spoke to sharkkind in general except when something important happened.

Even so, Prime Minister Shocks set the schedule so there wouldn't be what he called "unpleasantness" between groups that might make a meal out of each other. A group of urchins was talking with a cluster of brightly colored tangs. Gray knew these different groups each had their own hierarchy, even the shellheads supposedly, but didn't believe they could have anything interesting or important to say. They were colorful, though. He'd give them that.

Gray loved the riot of colors in the reef. Between the dwellers, algae, greenie, corals, mollusks, and plants, it was like an undersea rainbow. He saw a rainbow in the sky once, and it was a pale imitation of the undersea world. And at night the reef glowed even more spectacularly in places where the lumos gave off their pretty lights.

"Oh, I see a spot! Follow me!" said Barkley as he swam forward to claim an area near the front of the class and close to Miss Lamprey.

"What a sucker fish," muttered Gray. The dogfish heard and glared.

Miss Lamprey held class in different areas around the reef depending on what was being taught that day. Gray settled in, getting a few irritated looks from groups of angel and parrot fish whose view he accidentally blocked. One particularly annoying parrot fish went right through his mouth and yelled "Move it, wide load!" He almost told the parrot fish he wasn't fat, just big cartilaged, but he knew Miss Lamprey would make him repeat everything to the entire class if she heard. The fish swam around his eyes to be annoying before finding a new place a tail length away. Gray swallowed the urge to put the fish in its place by eating it. He was hungry again. Lately, Gray was always hungry. But he definitely didn't want to get into more trouble by eating a reef dweller.

His mother raised him to never harm anything that lived on or around this particular reef, just as every reef dweller did. There were exceptions, of course. The bottom feeders had their own disgusting ways of eating anything and everything, but sharkkind kept to a higher standard.

"It's not what we do here, Gray," she told him from his earliest days. "If a fish has color, find another. Silver or brown, gulp it down." That's what he learned when he was a pup. Or, even more of a pup than he was now. There was a difference between dumb fish that grouped together and mindlessly swam around (those you could eat) and the smarter ones who could hold a conversation (those you weren't supposed to eat). That's not to say any shark, being big or tough enough, couldn't eat whatever he or she wanted. But the decisions you made spoke to what type of citizen of the Big Blue you were. His mother said that sharkkind who chose to hunt intelligent ocean dwellers were more than bad sharks; they were evil. Gray thought it was worth the wait to find a cluster of dumb fish anyhow. There were always more of them!

Besides, breaking the rules carried consequences. One of Barkley's cousins, Hegger, ate a scarlet grouper when he and Barkley were little. Despite the name, a colored grouper was not a mindless, grouping fish. And this particular scarlet grouper lived on the reef. Anyway, Hegger was *accidentally* stung by an urchin the next day and almost died. Hegger swore it was a payback and he was probably right. Urchins were low down, poisonous sneaks who did that sort of thing.

The lesson in Miss Lamprey's class today was about current and drift in the open waters of the Big Blue. Gray barely listened. When was he ever going to experience that? Never. Gray allowed himself to float upward a bit to stretch his flippers.

"Umm, Gray?" whispered Barkley. Gray looked over

20

at the dogfish who smugly reminded him, "You're grounded, remember?" Technically he wasn't a body length from the reef bottom.

Gray grimaced and lowered himself. "Thanks, buddy. Who would have thought you could be so helpful with your snout so far up Miss Lamp—"

"Gray!" yelled Miss Lamprey, cutting him off. "Would you please stop bothering Barkley and pay attention?"

"Sorry, Miss Lamprey." Gray settled almost on the seabed. He sighed and couldn't wait for moonrise. This day was a total bust.

CHAPTER 3

THE CARIBBI SEA WHERE THE CORAL SHIVER reef lay was clear and calm when the moon rose. After class Gray and Barkley went swimming. At least, in the areas where Gray was allowed after his punishment. Tonight everyone was getting along, however, which made them exceedingly dull to watch.

"You want to see if those crabs are still fighting?" Barkley asked.

"Who wants to watch a couple of shellheads whacking and clacking over some snail carcass? Gross!" They swam in silence but in the general direction of the feisty crabs, there being nothing better to do. "I'd give anything to be out in the open waters with cold water rushing down my flanks. I'm the type of fin that needs action and adventure!" Gray told his friend. "But where do I live? The quietest reef in the entire *history* of the Big Blue, that's where!"

"Well it's about to get a lot less quiet." Barkley pointed his snout in the direction of a sea dragon whom everyone around the homewaters had nicknamed "Yappy." Gray didn't even know his real name. "I hope you're happy," the dogfish muttered. "You jinxed us."

Most dwellers wouldn't talk to others not of their kind unless they had some sort of business, or knew them well, or it was an emergency. But Yappy talked with *anyone* he came across, no matter if they wanted to or not. One time everyone thought that ancient Janprickle the urchin had died. Yappy started talking to her and wouldn't stop for an entire day. Nonstop. In a crazy way, it was kind of impressive. Just as Janprickle's fellow urchins were going to *honor* the old dweller in their way by eating her—yuck—she shook herself a couple times and joined the conversation. Janprickle and Yappy talked for another whole day! Not only could Yappy talk you to death, apparently he could talk you *out* of death, too.

And for some reason Yappy thought Barkley and Gray were his best buddies, so it was extra inconvenient for them to bump into him. Even in the weak moonlight, Yappy's bright yellow body made him stand out. He also had blue stripes along his belly and orange highlights on the tips of his weedy flippers and tail. These were supposed to help him blend into the greenie when hunting small crabs and shrimp. But between the nonstop talking and his very bright coloring, it was hard to imagine Yappy blending in anywhere.

"Keep swimming. Don't make eye contact," whispered Gray.

Barkley agreed wholeheartedly. "Nod and gnash your teeth like we're talking about something serious and maybe—"

"Hey fellas! Isn't the moon just gilly tonight? You ever wonder what the moon is made of?"

"Yappy—" Barkley attempted to get a word in edgewise.

"I heard if a marlin jumps at just the right angle when there's a full moon, he can spear it with his nose. Do you think marlins eat bits of the moon for fifteen nights, and it grows back the other fifteen?"

Barkley tried again, "Yap—"

"If they *are* eating the moon and not sharing, I say the council should get involved. I mean, who do those selfish, moon-eating morons think they are anyway?"

"YAPPY!" shouted Gray, blowing the much smaller sea dragon back a fluke length. This got his attention.

"Yes, Gray?"

"Barkley and I would love to hear your theories on marlins eating the moon, but we're doing some, umm, serious talking about . . . things." Gray glanced at his friend to jump in anytime.

Barkley was never slow on the uptake. "That's right. Important shiver business. Sorry, we can't tell you about it. Or we could, but then we'd totally have to eat you."

"I get it. My cousins in the Dark Blue are always up to super secret stuff about prophecies that could mean the end of the entire Big Blue as we know it! I can't tell you about that, either. Did you know my cousins are giants? Bigger than Gray even! They would just eat that drove of bluefin right up, I tell ya!" Yappy said as he rocked back and forth with the tide.

"Excellent!" Barkley chimed as the sea dragon opened his mouth to say something else. "Let's agree to keep our various secrets safe and swim away without any more talking, so we don't accidentally doom the seven seas." Barkley tried to shove Gray forward.

"Wait, what did you mean by 'drove of bluefin'?" asked Gray, suddenly very interested.

"You guys didn't know? The angelfish are sooo miffed. A double drove of bluefin totally stole a swarm of shrimp from them." Yappy pointed toward the far end of the reef with a back fin. "Never heard such foul language from an angel in my life! Shocking, really."

Gray fairly vibrated with excitement. A double drove of delicious bluefin was swimming around and distracted by shrimp? Near the reef? His stomach rumbled. That was two hundred fish at least.

Sharks counted fish groupings by cluster, drove, horde, shimmer, shoal, legion, and siege. Clusters were tens, droves were hundreds, a horde was in the thousands, shimmers were ten thousands, a shoal was one hundred to four hundred thousand, legions numbered at five hundred to nine hundred thousand, and a siege was over a *million* fish.

Gray had never seen anything larger than a lower shoal, and those were teeny-tiny krill. They really didn't count unless you could fill up on those ugly, shrimpy things. The older sharks in the shiver said that in the times of their fathers and their father's fathers the Tuna Run was every sixth moon and was always a double or triple siege. Gray couldn't even picture what two or three million fish might look like. And supposedly, a siege of bluefin was so fast and dense it could injure or even kill a shark. Gray was sure they were yanking his tail, though. How could a bunch of fish do that to a shark? Only by overeating, he thought, which was a chance Gray was willing to take if he got lucky enough to see a siege. If he ever even made it to a Tuna Run. But maybe he could have his own little Tuna Run right now!

"I do not like that look," Barkley said as he watched the smiling Gray. "Not at all."

"Let's go fishing!" Gray rocketed under and around several brightly colored coral pillars, scaring the heck out of the crabs, eels, and other dwellers trying to stealthily hunt on them.

Barkley struggled to keep up, panting. "Wait, stop!" Just then Gray did stop, reversing himself so fast the dogfish plowed into his tail fin. Barkley let out an "Ooof!"

"Quiet!" Gray told the dogfish. "Look."

There they were: hundreds and hundreds of big, fat bluefin there for the taking!

CHAPTER 4

"GRAY, THAT'S INTO THE OPEN OCEAN FOR SURE," Barkley said. "And you're grounded!"

"Oh, come on! That's still Coral Shiver homewaters." Gray nodded to himself, salivating. "And dumb fish are always fair game! Why, we could get in trouble for *not* eating them!"

Barkley smiled sarcastically. "I know the rules on what to eat and when to eat it better than you, megamouth." The dogfish tapped him on the belly with his tail. "By the way, have you gained weight since this morning?"

"Hey, I'm big cartilaged!" Gray said indignantly. "And if you're done insulting me ..." He waggled a fluke at the fish.

"Fine, Overbiter is on duty for shiver business. Let's tell him about the drove. We'll be heroes!" Barkley swished his tail happily at the thought.

Gray snorted. "Please! Overbiter is like a hundred and sleeps all the time. He can't swim fast enough to catch these blues. You don't want to make him look bad in front of everyone, do you?

Maybe embarrassing Overbiter wasn't Gray's main worry, but the lemon shark *was* half senile. By the time they explained everything to him, the bluefin would be long gone. Barkley hesitated as he glanced longingly at the tuna feeding on the swarm of shrimp. "I'd hate to embarrass him, I guess."

Barkley drooled a little and Gray knew he had him. "Let's get our fill, and then go tell everyone. We'll still be heroes!"

The dogfish flicked his fins up and down in agreement and flashed forward so suddenly it momentarily surprised Gray. He did not just do that! Gray sped up, overtaking his friend. He aimed for a plump bluefin but never got there. Two others accidentally swam into his open mouth just before he was going to strike, along with a load of shrimp! It caught Gray by surprise and he gagged. This would be a story told around the glowing algae pylons for years to come—Gray the big, bad reef shark chokes to death on dinner! An extremely large blue slammed into his throat, kicking in a reflexive swallow. I really should remember that spot on my throat, he thought to himself. But later! The combo of bluefin and shrimp was scrumptious!

Gray and Barkley laughed and ate. It was crazy! No sooner were they done with one fish than they each caught another. The pair tried to keep count of who caught the most but gave up; the bluefin were eaten so fast and furiously. Then, as all groupings did, the fish thinned and disappeared. Pretty soon only a couple of woozy shrimp were all that was left. Barkley listed to the side. "Ohh, I think I might have eaten too much. By the way, where are we?"

Good question. How long had they been feeding? Gray wasn't sure. The reef wasn't in sight anymore. In fact, nothing around them looked familiar. Gray couldn't even see the bottom. They were definitely off the reef and into the open waters of the Big Blue now. They would get into serious trouble if someone found out.

Gray was about to say something when he felt a prickle of electricity go up his spine, a fin flick before a gray-and-white blur screamed into view. This alarm system saved Gray's life at least twice when he was younger, once when a huge moray eel hiding in a crevice surprised him. It was a vague buzzing that set him on edge right before danger struck. He now knew it was a survival instinct, but Gray hadn't felt it for a long time, not since his growth spurt.

Just in time, with a stroke of his powerful tail, he was able to deflect a shark's headlong attack at his dorsal fin. It was a tiger shark and he was massive! Larger than Gray was, even!

Barkley was indignant. "What's your damage, jellybrain? We're trying to digest here!" He coasted in front of Gray protectively as the tiger carved a turn and rushed at them once more. It must have dawned on Barkley that being a motionless target wasn't the brightest idea because he dove underneath the gnashing jaws of the tiger. The big flipper only gave a halfhearted snap at the dogfish. He was plainly after Gray, since his size made him the main threat.

Well, he's got that right! Gray thought as he sped up. They were lost, probably in trouble, and now some flipper was trying to eat them! Enough was enough. Gray accelerated out of the tiger's way before slashing his own turn downward and underneath the attacking shark. The tiger lost sight of Gray for a moment and hesitated. It was all the time Gray needed.

"You lose," said Barkley from his hovering position above the momentarily confused tiger. Gray heard a satisfying "Whuufff!" as he rammed the shark in the soft underbelly by his liver. The tiger tried to turn but was momentarily paralyzed. Barkley hammered the dazed attacker next. Or he tried. Because of his small size, he bounced off like a sea horse against hard coral. Gray wouldn't let his advantage slip away, though. He bore down on the tiger, ready to rip a fin off with his razor teeth.

"Wait! Wait!" yelled the tiger. "I'm with Goblin Shiver, and you're dead meat if you touch me!"

Gray chose to ignore this, but had to come to an abrupt halt when Barkley swam right in front of his mouth! "What are you doing?"

"Saving our lives!" Barkley whispered before turning to the tiger. "Sorry for the misunderstanding!"

"Misunderstanding?" Gray sputtered. "He tried to eat us!"

The big shark recovered somewhat, and the chance to send him to the Sparkle Blue passed. Gray hoped Barkley knew what he was doing. The tiger wouldn't be easily beaten a second time.

"Listen to your friend," said the tiger. "This is Goblin Shiver territory. You don't have permission to hunt here unless Goblin, or maybe Gafin, give their say-so. And I know you don't know Goblin. So, do you know the urchin king?"

Gray understood little of what the big tiger was saying. "We need permission to hunt?" he asked, genuinely puzzled.

"Of course you do! I thought you were from Razor Shiver, poaching our feeding grounds," the tiger commented, watching Gray and Barkley for their reactions. "But I can see I was wrong. My name is Thrash, by the way."

"I'm Gray and this is Barkley."

"Where are you from?" the tiger named Thrash asked suspiciously.

"Coral Shiv—" Gray began, but Barkley cut him off immediately.

"A coral reef where we rested! But there were landsharks so we left. Now we're here. Nice to meet you!"

Thrash dismissed Barkley but swam around Gray, looking him over. "I thought you were a great white, but you're not. You're just a pup! Don't think I've seen a shark like you before. What are you, anyway?"

"I'm a reef shark," Gray answered proudly.

Thrash laughed. "Oh, that's good! Yeah, right, reef shark! Goblin loves a sense of humor. Sometimes." The tiger indicated the direction he wanted them to follow. "Come on, he's going to want to look you over."

Neither of them moved. "Look us over?" asked Barkley.

"To be a part of Goblin Shiver," answered Thrash. "We're at war with Razor Shiver and can always use another shark who knows how to fight. Whatever you are."

Barkley swam between the large tiger and Gray. "Actually, we're not real big joiners, Thrash. We're more rogue fish."

"Rogues swim alone," said Thrash with a hint of malice. "That's why they're rogues."

Barkley got flustered. "Sure, we know that, everyone knows that! We're a rogue *pair*. It's a new thing we invented. Again, nice meeting you. We'll be going now." The dogfish kept his voice low when he passed Gray. "Let's get out of here while the getting's good."

Gray followed, unsure why Barkley was acting so strangely but knowing deep down he didn't want to be involved with a maniac tiger shark that talked about wars and had almost eaten him a moment ago. "Yeah, rogue pair. That's us."

Thrash caught Gray's eye before he swam away. "You'll have to pick a side sooner or later, pup. Everyone will have to pick a side." With a chuckle and a dismissive flick of his tail, the tiger shark left.

"Let's go home," Barkley told Gray, who quietly followed his friend.

Their first trip into the open water had been a real eye opener, but not in a good way.

CHAPTER 5

"NO, NO, NO!" YELLED GOBLIN LOUD ENOUGH to attract attention all around his homewaters. He gnashed his teeth so hard he felt one break and saw it drift to the sandy bottom. A crab scuttled over and began probing the tooth to see if there was anything to eat inside it. It almost made Goblin laugh, but the situation was too serious to allow that right now. "We need to keep up *all* our patrols! Razor Shiver isn't going to rest and neither can we!"

"You're telling me what you want, and I'm trying to tell you what's possible," Ripper replied evenly. The big, battle-scarred hammerhead was close to insubordination. But then he ducked his head and added, "I suppose we could promote a couple of the pups into full shiver sharks to make up for—you know—"

Goblin took time to appear thoughtful. His mother, the shiver leader before him, had always told him to do this. "Good idea. Let them flex their fins a little. When I was a pup, I couldn't wait to get into the thick of things!"

It wasn't as if he was much older than a pup now, being just fifteen. For great whites, fifteen was physically mature. But some of the sharkkind that Ripper was thinking of were a little *too* young and weren't experienced enough to survive a real battle. They could be used for patrols and as an early warning system, though, which would free up his veterans for more important things. Not a perfect solution, but it would do for now.

Goblin stared imperiously at his Five in the Line. Ripper was his first, a giant hammerhead and the only shark who might be tougher than himself. Thrash, the tiger, was his second. Goblin's third was Streak, a blue shark who was small for her kind but made up for it in sheer ferocity. Churn was an oceanic whitetip and his fourth. Goblin had known Churn since the whitetip was a pup. Then there was his fifth: Velenka, a sleek, black mako.

Velenka was undoubtedly the smartest and most beautiful shark he ever met. Such big eyes. She could have been his fourth, maybe even third. She was invaluable as an adviser. Why the mako didn't make a move up the Line was puzzling to Goblin. Velenka hadn't even won her rank by combat, as was custom when a position in the Line opened. It was done by vote after Goblin's last fifth, Hawley, was found floating on the surface in the chop-chop three months ago. Hawley wasn't attacked by sharkkind; there were no bite marks. His corpse was grotesquely swollen as if he had died a week earlier. But Goblin swam with the thresher the night before he was found, so he knew that wasn't the case. He had trusted Hawley most of all, and the thresher worshipped Goblin like an older brother. It was a bitter loss, but that was life in the open waters of the Big Blue.

"What do you want to do, Goblin?" asked Velenka. The mako spoke more than any of the others even though she was only his fifth. It was a little odd, even presumptuous, but Velenka did keep things on point. The others waited for Goblin's answer.

"Can't you see I'm thinking?" He snapped at the mako, his bulk nudging hers out of hover. "Do you have a current you're late for? Someplace more interesting to go?"

"I didn't mean any disrespect," she answered.

"And that's why I'm not feeding on your carcass!" he yelled.

His shiver, now called Goblin Shiver instead of Riptide Shiver, had gotten their tails kicked by the bull sharks of Razor Shiver a day ago. They'd lost two soldiers and hadn't sent any bulls to the Sparkle Blue. Razor and his shiver controlled the best hunting grounds in the entire North Atlantis and also owned a prized territory for the Tuna Run. This annoyed Goblin. It was because of Razor naming his shiver after himself that Goblin had done the same. He would never admit that, of course. Razor Shiver weren't the only tough gang of sharkkind on the Western edge of the Atlantis, but they were the strongest today. Food was growing scarce, with fewer and fewer large groupings to feed on. Goblin and his shiver would stay near the muck-sucking bottom if he couldn't figure out a way to recruit more warriors and conquer new territory!

And to top things off, Thrash now swam in as though he was being chased by a prehistore nightmare with a story about a *pair* of rogue sharks named Gray and Barkley. And this Gray was a mysterious giant type of Sharkkind Thrash had never seen before! His Five in the Line and the rest of the full members of the shiver were looking at Goblin now, waiting for answers. His shiver sharks hovered listlessly behind the Line, speaking and joking in low voices with each other. At one time there would have been order, every mariner hovering in its own row, waiting for the leader's orders to be carried out by subcommanders. When Goblin was young, discipline and numbers were the mark of a true battle shiver. But now . . .

Everyone was always waiting for answers from him. It was what Goblin liked least about being leader. Sometimes he wished his mother were still around. She would know what to do, he thought to himself.

Goblin turned to Thrash. "You're sure they weren't just passing through? Maybe from the Sific Ocean?"

The tiger shook his head from side to side. "Nah, they mentioned a coral reef. I think they're from somewhere near shore. They were soft."

"Beat you, didn't they?" noted Ripper. Goblin saw that the tiger took the insult personally, but if Thrash got mad the big hammerhead could take care of himself. That's why he was Goblin's first.

"Who cares about a couple of yokels from the boonie-greenie who don't know anything about the Big Blue?" yelled Streak. The undersize blue was seething. "We lost Scrape and Jonquil to the bulls! Let's attack and even the score!"

Streak would want to fight no matter what because Scrape was her brother. But Goblin was pretty sure the blue didn't care one way or another that Jonquil was gone. He had just joined the shiver recently.

"Bad idea!" cried Churn. "We should take some time to regroup." The whitetip had almost been eaten by Razor himself in the battle and sported a ragged bite mark across the gills to show just how close he'd come to death. Churn was now one jumpy fin and would be for a while longer.

"Coward!" Streak yelled angrily. "Swim off the Line, useless! Go find a turtle shell to hide inside!"

Churn might be jumpy, but he was much bigger than Streak. Goblin was about to lose control as his third and fourth tried to eat each other! But then, the smell of an enemy interrupted the budding fight. Everyone looked over as a solitary bull swam close enough to be seen, but far enough away to retreat. Goblin's spine tingled with the sense of impending battle. He was about to charge the bull when Velenka spoke.

"I don't think he's here for trouble," she said.

"How would you know?" snarled Streak.

Velenka took no notice of the blue's tone but answered the question instead. "You know what an attack looks like better than anyone, Streak. What do you think?"

Streak calmed herself and watched the lone bull for a moment. "Okay, he's not on offense. But who is he and why's he here?"

"That's exactly what we should ask him." Velenka swam forward, drawing Goblin with her. "Maybe this has something to do with the two sharks Thrash saw?" The mako seemed happiest when she was puzzling something out. Or scheming. She once told Goblin that her hero was the legendary Machiakelpi, the mako who swam in the First Shiver and supposedly ruled the entire Sific after Tyro left for the Sparkle Blue. Goblin had to admit Velenka was a schemer worthy of Machiakelpi's reputation.

"Keep your place behind me, Fifth!" He took the lead. Maybe this shark was an opportunity. If it was, Goblin wanted the credit for leading. And it wasn't as though he would let Velenka meet the bull without him.

Velenka tried to keep her excitement in check but felt her spine tingling as they swam to meet Kilo. She knew that the bull would play his part and pretend they'd never met before. But could he play it well enough so that Goblin wouldn't sense something out of the ordinary? That was the question. That was why she needed to carefully control the conversation. Goblin might be dim, but he wasn't without instinct. You didn't stay shiver leader for long without good instincts.

And who was the mysterious giant Thrash had tussled with? No one else had noticed the large tooth lodged underneath the tiger's fin. Was it important? Its shape looked so familiar for some reason. Velenka had knocked the tooth free before anyone could see, and it floated into the darkness below. She didn't need Goblin distracted just now, not when she was setting her plan into action.

Velenka would send Thrash back in the direction the mysterious sharks came from to find their home. Perhaps Kilo and his bulls could be useful in this also. Always bend circumstance to your advantage. Machiakelpi taught that eons ago. Good advice, then and now.

"Maybe I should find out why this bull is here?" Velenka asked Goblin. "That way you can watch for lies when he speaks. Besides, why should this puny flipper talk to you, our shiver leader, as if he's your equal?"

Goblin nodded as they stopped a few body lengths from Kilo. "Good," he said quietly. "Do it."

Velenka smiled as she swam forward. There was destiny in the current! She could feel it!

CHAPTER 6

AFTER SWIMMING FOR THE REST OF THE NIGHT—
the sun was rising by the time Gray and Barkley got
back—they reached the reef. How had they gotten so far
away?

The worst part was the place was in an uproar. Gray
hoped in vain it wasn't because of them.

Of course he was very, very wrong.

Atlas led the Line, along with many other shiver
sharks, in a ragged, three-level triangle formation. That
was weird. Gray had never seen them do that. What did
it mean? They certainly didn't look happy, though.

"Gray!" cried his mom. "Are you all right?" She tried
to swim ahead of Atlas but was slowed by Quickeyes
and Onyx.

Atlas gave her a hard look. "Sandy, please." Gray's
mom nodded, and the Coral Shiver leader spoke again,
"Gray, Barkley—are you okay?" Quickeyes and Onyx

swam overhead, watching the distant waters. Why were they doing that?

"We are," answered Barkley. Gray quickly agreed with his friend.

"Now tell me exactly where you were, and anything that happened," Atlas ordered. Gray had never seen the old bull shark so . . . *commanding* before. Barkley told the story with Gray adding bits and pieces. Oddly, the more the story went on, the angrier Atlas and the others became. Except Gray's mom. She got scared.

A full council of all the reef dwellers was called. The sharks of Coral Shiver wanted to make the decision by themselves but were overruled by Prime Minister Shocks. Shocks would have probably let Atlas, Sandy, and the others in Line hand out Gray's punishment, but the other reef dwellers demanded their say.

Gray wasn't sure what was happening, exactly, but his mom was even more upset than yesterday. Quick-eyes and Onyx took turns staring at Gray as if they wanted to eat him. Overbiter was busy gnawing on his own tail fin. He used to be second in the Line years ago and sometimes didn't remember he wasn't a member of the council anymore. Atlas and the rest never said anything and let him stay. Supposedly he had been a great warrior long ago. Yeah, right.

Shocks sent a weak bolt of electricity arcing into the water, calling everyone in the area to attention. Gray had never seen so many dweller leaders gathered at one time! There were all kinds of fish; tangs, grouper, lantern fish, angelfish, hatchet fish, clown fish, puffers, wrasse, frog fish, sunfish, doctor, and surgeonfish. Every other non-fish dweller seemed to be here too: big and small rays, eels of all sizes and colors, anemones, urchins, shellheads, turtles, and many, many others.

This would be really neat if I wasn't the reason they were here, Gray thought as he floated above the flat stone that was traditionally known as Speakers Rock. It didn't seem like he would get to speak, but there was no good area for everyone to see him otherwise, so Atlas allowed it.

Barkley was asked questions by the manta rays, their pilot fish nearby. Some of these rays were wider than Gray, and their larger cousins, the giants, were bigger in all ways. Supposedly rays were distant cousins of sharkkind from prehistore times. He didn't really believe it as they weren't very good hunters, living mostly on floating greenie, krill, and shellheads. They did have really cool stingers, but didn't use them for hunting. What a waste!

Gray watched his mother become more and more agitated as Prime Minister Shocks spoke with her. Gray wished he could hear, but they were in a place where the currents masked their conversation. The other dwellers who could listen in seemed satisfied, though. Suddenly the current shifted, and Gray could hear parts of what his mom and Shocks were talking about.

"You know what's out there!" his mother said. "Battle shivers are on the move! The Indi King's armada—"

The tide shifted, and Gray could only hear Shock's reply in bits, " ... are only rumors!"

Battle shivers? That was the kind of intensely interesting stuff Gray always wanted to hear about— the stuff adults whispered and then stopped discussing whenever he or Barkley got close. For a moment Gray thought his mother was going to bite the distinguished eel. Shocks spoke to the next group of dwellers, and pretty soon everyone *except* Gray knew what was happening.

Come on!

Atlas and the other sharkkind in the Line tried to calm his mom, but it wasn't working. Gray felt awful. Why do I keep disappointing her? She broke free and swam toward him. Prime Minster Shocks tried to get ahead of her, but she left the eel tumbling in her wake with a furious tail stroke. "That's totally out of order, Sandy!" he harrumphed.

"I want a minute with my son!" she yelled, close to tears, her barbels quivering. After a stare down, Shocks gave her a curt nod. She approached Gray and said, "Just tell the truth, okay? We'll get through this."

Get through what? he wondered. Gray was becoming irritated. A growing shark has to eat! They couldn't punish him for that. But a creeping feeling in his belly told him that they could.

Prime Minister Shocks let off another low-voltage attention grabber that quieted everyone. "Gray, please swim over here so everyone can listen to you answer my questions."

"Umm, sure." Gray moved to the area where the current would catch his words and broadcast them.

"Why did you leave the reef homewaters last night?" Shocks asked.

Everyone was listening and watching intently and Gray became nervous. "I, umm, I mean, we—" He looked over at Barkley. "We saw some fish and got hungry. They were mixed with shrimp, very delicious, by the way, and also—"

The gathered dwellers' whispering rose in volume as Shocks cut him off. "But wasn't it *you* who convinced your friend to go? In fact, didn't he say that you shouldn't leave the reef?"

"Well, yeah. But he's always trying to keep me from doing fun stuff—" Gray stopped in confusion as the murmurs from the dwellers got louder, in some cases surging to outright yelling. Except for his mother. She was crying now. Atlas glared again. Gray continued with his point, speaking over the crowd so he would be heard. "Hey, I was hungry!" For some reason this made things much worse.

Shocks zapped the water with a heavy charge to quiet the crowd enough so he could speak. "ORDER!" he yelled. "I will have order!" The eel turned to Gray.

"Is that why you left the reef and drew the attention of a tiger shark, who was himself a member of a shiver? Because you were hungry?"

"Umm, well, I didn't go out there with the intention of meeting anyone, but, yes, I was hungry."

"So you put your hunger ahead of the safety of everyone on the reef. Is that right? I hope you're at least full!"

It took a moment for Gray to realize what he was being asked. Unfortunately, his mouth was already speaking. "I'm still a little hungry but—wait—what?"

The gathered dwellers exploded, everyone shouting, clacking their claws, basically making any loud noise they could as a sign of their anger. Prime Minster Shocks futilely shot electrical charges into the water. He needed to call the rest of his eel friends to raise the voltage before he got everyone's attention and order was restored.

"Mom!" said Gray as she swam close to him. "I'm really sorry! I'm—"

She cut him off with a slash of her tail. "I know you are, Gray. Look, there's something I haven't told you. You're going to have a brother and a sister. "

"What?!"

His mother was much sadder than he would expect her to be as she told him the news. "You're going to be a big brother. Oh, Gray, I'm so sorry." She sobbed.

"Why are you sorry? Why are you crying?" he asked.

"This is great! I've always wanted brothers and sisters!" Then Gray grew confused. "I really am happy, but why are you telling me now? I don't exactly get it."

There were tears in his mother's eyes as she said, "Because that's the reason I can't go with you!"

"Go with me? Where?"

Sandy was led away by Atlas and the other sharks in the Coral Shiver Line. "Meet me at the Tuna Run! Prove yourself as a strong and good hunter and they'll take you back!" The noise grew so loud that Gray could no longer hear his mother.

The Tuna Run! He was allowed to go! But what did she mean by take him back?

He grew cold and afraid as Prime Minister Shocks swam near Speakers Rock directly in front of Gray. It was then he noticed that Barkley was also blubbering. This isn't going to be good, he thought.

Shocks cleared his throat to speak. There was absolute silence now. "Gray, you've endangered the shiver because of your own selfish desires. If this was the first time you needed to be disciplined it might be different. But it isn't, so . . . " Shocks looked at him sadly but pronounced the sentence in a clear voice. "You are hereby banished from Coral Shiver!"

INTO
THE
BIG
BLUE

CHAPTER 7

THE WORD ECHOED IN GRAY'S EARS LIKE THE TIDES.

Banished.

Prime Minister Shock's word was law by the reef, and even though Gray was a big fish, the sentence would be carried out. The octos from the octopus clan were waiting with their foul jets of black ink if he didn't obey. And the seedier bottom feeders who lived on the dark side of the reef—Orin the scorpion fish and his friends came to mind—were poison-ous enough to send even Gray to the Sparkle Blue if he caused trouble. Aside from his mom and Bar-kley, Gray's only ally was Yappy! And that was only because Yappy's family couldn't *stop* him from talk-ing. Not until they caught him, anyway.

For a moment Gray almost chuckled at the thought of Yappy zipping around, with so many others chasing him and yelling, "This is a slippery slope! What will you do when they come for you? Slippery slope! Slippery slope!" But Gray sobered quickly, remembering how Barkley's family ushered him away before he had the chance to react at all. That was probably a good thing. The dogfish could get emotional sometimes.

"At least I didn't give them the satisfaction of throwing me out," Gray muttered. He swam out, head high, on his own. Truthfully, the reef and Coral Shiver homewaters were too small for a fin like him. Gray needed space if he was going to live it up. Maybe Prime Minister Shocks had done him a big, fat favor.

It sure didn't really feel that way, though.

Gray almost began to sob but stopped when he saw a giant sea turtle staring as it leisurely floated by. "What you lookin' at, shellback? You want a piece of me?" The turtle churned its stubby legs a little faster. For their kind this was the equivalent of a panicked rush. Gray was satisfied with the reaction, so he didn't go ram the turtle. "You better not tell anyone I was crying!" he yelled at the turtle's receding figure. "Because I'm not!"

Gray had traveled for three entire days, near as he could figure. When he was near the reef, he could sense the depth of the water and didn't need to open his eyes to tell if it was day or night. In this open water, Gray stayed near the surface to keep himself oriented.

Not that he was afraid to go deeper, of course. He just didn't want to go deeper *right* now. "At least the sun shines into the water the same way," he said aloud. But it was colder and the current stronger. Not like home at all. What I'd give to be grounded by the reef again, he thought sadly.

Gray looked down to where the water darkened. Although he could sense the bottom was there, he couldn't see it. How did dwellers there even know what time it was? It was even colder than the water around him. And always black as night. Gray's stomach churned. He was hungry, but the ocean seemed absolutely empty! It was eerie. And when there were fish, they came and went so fast he actually missed with his strikes. Compared to the ones by the reef, these fish were bigger, stronger, and faster. Gray's stomach growled again, and he grew scared. Maybe he'd just starve in the open waters.

"Hey, Gray!" Gray almost jumped out of his skin. It was Barkley!

"Would you stop doing that?" Gray sputtered, momentarily forgetting his situation. But *only* for a moment. They were a very long distance from the reef. "What are you doing here?"

Barkley was uncharacteristically tongue-tied for a moment. "Umm, nothing. Just stretching the ol' fins. You know me, always trying to broaden my horizons."

"Go home."

Barkley made a rude noise. "Who do you think you are, ordering me around? Takiza the magical fighting fish?"

Gray chuckled despite the situation. Takiza was a legendary fish who supposedly could conjure whirlpools and underwater lightning with magic. There were lots of fantastic stories about Takiza, who went by lots of different names depending on whom you asked. One time he supposedly fought ten great whites, the meanest of all sharkkind, and beat them easily when they threatened a baby dolphin. It was a fantastic tale and obviously just for amusement. "Be a good shark or Takiza will come and put you in your place!" The worst part of it was that Barkley's dumb comment reminded him of the reef and his mom telling him stories about Takiza, which made him even more homesick.

Gray sighed. Even though he was arguing with Barkley, the truth was that he *wanted* his friend to stay. But that was wrong. Gray was exiled and Barkley wasn't. His home was by the reef, and Gray couldn't let him throw that away. "I know what you're doing, but you should turn around."

"And I know what you're doing, Gray. But we've been friends since you were born—I was born first, so of course I remember—and I *want* to come along. I was going to sign up for Miss Lamprey's migration class this year, anyway. This'll be like that, only better! Besides, you think I'm going to let you hoard all the adventure like some adventure-hoarding hermit crab?"

Gray replied with a subdued "Okay, then." It was all he could do not to burst into tears. Tough fin you are, he thought to himself.

They found a swift current, which pulled them deeper and deeper into the open waters of the Big Blue. Gray enjoyed the silence for a time. But with Barkley being Barkley, silence never lasted too long.

"So, where we going?"

"Umm, into the open ocean," Gray answered with as much confidence as he could muster.

Barkley sighed. "Yes, I'm aware of that—being here and all. We're into the Atlantis Ocean now, North Atlantis, by the way. But where do you want to end up?"

"I don't know. I started swimming in this direction after they kicked me out. I didn't have some big exile plan ready to go. You know, you can get annoying in a fin flick!" But Gray wasn't really mad at Barkley. He was mad at himself. He was so upset after being banished that he had started swimming without even thinking about where he was going. He certainly didn't want to end up in the Arktik where he heard the very water froze, forming jagged masses that could crush a shark!

Barkley flexed his flukes at Gray in irritation. "I'm hungry. How about we find some food?"

Finally, something they could agree on. It took a while, but they did find, and more importantly, *catch* some food. First Gray chased a small horde of cod toward

Barkley, who picked a few off. It was either a horde or upper drove. The dogfish thought it was an upper drove of eight or nine hundred. Gray didn't care as he was unable to catch even one since the small horde or upper drove was fast-moving and left the area quickly. But Barkley returned the favor by finding a lower cluster of sailfish. One muscular game fish didn't know what hit it as Gray pounced from below, taking most of it down with an enormous bite.

"Any cod left?" Gray asked after he'd finished off the last of the sailfish.

"You know, sailfish work out constantly. They think their bodies are temples. You might learn from that kind of thinking," Barkley told Gray while jabbing Gray's stomach with his tail.

"Hey, I'm big cartilaged!"

Barkley swam away, leading Gray in a slightly different direction. What was he doing?

"By the way, I'll pick the way we're heading, since it's my exile!" Gray told his friend, perhaps a little too vehemently, as he corrected their course.

"Right. What grade did you get in navigation class again?" Barkley asked innocently.

Oh, now he was playing dirty. Gray had taken the navigation test immediately after eating a puffer fish which had *not* gone down well. It felt as if the fish were inflating in his stomach, which cramped violently the entire day. The galling part was that he got *lost* during the exam! Miss Lamprey knew Gray was sick, which she took into account, but he got a poor grade that cycle.

The truth was Gray didn't know where he was going. For the first time in his life, he was swimming without a purpose. That scared him. Before, if he was unsure of what to do, he'd ask his mom. But he couldn't do that anymore. He was about to confess this to Barkley when the dogfish whispered a fearful "Uh-oh."

There were four sharks swimming in a tight pack; a thresher, a bull, a sawfish, and a great white. Miss Lamprey said great whites should be left alone in the open ocean. She said they hunted other sharkkind, even when they weren't hungry. For fun.

"Umm, Gray? How about we make like a sea frog and scoot?" suggested Barkley.

It was a good idea. But too late.

The four sharks fanned out and swam toward them.

CHAPTER 8

THE SHARKS WEREN'T ATTACKING. YET. THEY were in a strong defensive position, though.

"Oh, I don't like this one bit. We're jelly drifters here!" Barkley exclaimed. Gray and Barkley began swimming in a slow figure-eight pattern that would let them speed away in case trouble started. Gray was larger than any of the four by a few tail-tips, but the biggest fish wasn't always the winner in the Big Blue. That much even he knew.

The four sharkkind slowed their advance and hovered against the current. They were barely five tail strokes away. For a moment the only sound was the slow current swishing past their flanks.

"So," said the great white. "Any luck hunting?"

Barkley jumped in before Gray could reply, "Nope. Just seeing the sights. We're moving through. Sorry if this is your territory."

"Oh, it's not!" piped in the sawfish. He stopped talking when the white gave him a look. The great white was definitely the leader. Now that the group was so close, Gray could see they were pups like he and Barkley. If any were older than their twelve summers, it wasn't by much. An uncomfortable silence descended on them all. The thresher girl, who seemed nice, gave a worried look to the great white and indicated they should leave. He nodded and the four were about to turn.

For some reason Gray didn't want them to go. "So, what are your names? This is my friend Barkley and I'm Gray."

"I'm Snork!" replied the sawfish shark, a little too eagerly for anyone in either group. He was about to swim forward, maybe in greeting, but maybe for a sneak attack.

"Whoa, whoa, whoa! Snork, is it? Keep your distance, okay?" Barkley told the sawfish, whose nose looked sharp and deadly, chock-full of pointy spikes on either edge. Neither of them wanted to be filleted, so caution was a good thing.

The girl thresher didn't like this one bit. "You seem kind of rude, Barkley—is it?" she asked sarcastically, saying "is it" just like Barkley had, mocking him. This made Gray smile, which she saw and continued, "Snork's just being friendly, you know."

"Yeah," Gray piled on, "Snork's just being friendly."

Wow, if looks could send you to the Sparkle Blue,

Gray would have begun his eternal swim on the spot.

It turned out that Barkley's venomous stare was hilarious to the four sharks from the other group, and they laughed. "Oh, so now I'm the big flipper?" Barkley asked everyone. "I'm just being safe, you know!" For some reason this struck everyone as even funnier.

"You're hilarious!" exclaimed Snork, snorting as he laughed, making Barkley and Gray chortle along with everyone else. Pretty soon Gray's sides hurt he was laughing so much. It took a moment for everyone to catch their breath and introduce themselves properly.

Aside from Snork, the great white leader was Striiker, Shell was the big bull shark, and then there was Mari, who seemed pretty interested in Gray when he said he was a reef shark, but that could have been his imagination. Mari had that really cool thresher's tail, bent back at an angle that just looked awesome. Gray wondered if it made her faster.

"You're really a reef shark?" Mari asked.

"That's what my mom tells me," he joked. Of course he was a reef shark. What else would he be?

"They must grow them real big by that reef of yours," commented Shell. The bull was quieter than the rest. He seemed okay, though.

Barkley grew suspicious. "Enough about our reef. Where do you live?"

Now Striiker gave Barkley the stink eye. "Why do you want to know where we live?"

"Just making conversation." Barkley swished his tail in a way that told Gray he was agitated. "Any reason you're so nervous?"

"I'm not nervous. Any reason *you're* so nervous?" Striiker shot right back.

Mari swam between them, taking position by Gray's right. "Okay you two, enough," she said. "We're not part of any shiver, if that's what you're thinking. We're four friends who swim together because it's safer here if you do that."

"So, you're like a rogue quad?" Gray asked. Barkley waved his tail for him to stop.

Striiker was genuinely puzzled. "Rogue quad? Is that even a thing?"

"I love it!" Snork exclaimed.

Gray explained, "Barkley told this shark we were a rogue pair when he got flustered."

"Aww, did you have to go there?" Barkley said, flipping his fins in embarrassment. "I thought that giant tiger was going to kill us! A flipper named Thrash."

There was an immediate chill in the water. Their new acquaintances moved back a couple of tail strokes from Barkley and Gray. "You know Thrash? Are you friends with Thrash?" Striiker asked evenly.

Gray answered, "Like Barkley said, he attacked us. So, no, we're not friends." He proceeded to tell the entire story of their meeting with Thrash.

Barkley added a lot of description to the fight. Gray wasn't sure it was all true, but it sure sounded good. He ended with, " . . . and then that muck-sucker asked us to be a part of his gang, and I was like, 'no way, lagoon scum, we're a rogue pair and way too cool for your dumb shiver!' And we let him see our tails when we left." Barkley waved his tail in a derisive manner. It was kind of embarrassing. Almost no one believed that's what happened. Almost.

"You may be the coolest sharks, ever," Snork whispered in wonder.

Striiker shook his head. "And on that note . . . " He rolled a slow turn, beckoning Mari and the other three sharks away from Gray and Barkley. Mari didn't move, sizing them up, instead.

"They did fight Thrash, and they're still here," Mari told Striiker, who turned around. He didn't seem happy.

The bull shark agreed. "And they're not with Goblin."

Striiker glared at Snork before he could add anything, then frowned at both Mari and Shell. "We just met them today! How do we know they can be trusted?"

"How do we know *you* can be trusted?" Barkley huffed. "By the way, what are we talking about?"

Gray had a pretty good idea and nodded to Mari to continue.

"The reason they're still swimming the Big Blue is because there were two of them against Thrash. The reason we're still around is because we four look out for each other. I think six would be better than four," Mari explained.

Shell nodded in agreement. Barkley wasn't so sure. Striiker seemed annoyed but not totally against the idea. And Snork? Well, Snork was being friendly again. "Come on! With six sharks we could be a real shiver! A leader with Five in the Line!" he said.

The great white shook his head. "If we wanted that we could have all stayed in our shivers. Mostly." Striiker gave a guilty glance to Shell, who for some reason looked away. He continued, "The one reason we like each other is because we aren't in shivers, which we know from experience is bad!"

"Hey, not all shivers are bad," Barkley protested.

"Yeah, we came from a great shiver," Gray told the four.

"The six of us could be a good shiver! A great shiver, even!" Snork almost bounced in the water as he got more and more excited, flexing his flippers back and forth. "And I have the perfect name! Rogue Shiver!"

And so, on the swim to their new homewaters, Rogue Shiver was born.

CHAPTER 9

THE PALE MOON'S GLOW LIT THE WATERS WITH a soft and eerie light. Gray sped toward the drove of snapper, slowing just enough to let them see him streaking their way. The group of fish angled away from his open maw—right between the walls of a cramped canyon where Rogue Shiver was waiting! The plan worked to perfection once again, and Gray was able to munch his share of snapper as they fled in the return direction after the rest caught theirs.

"We are getting so good at this!" Barkley remarked, finishing off a plump and juicy fish.

Gray nodded. Who would have thought that what had started out with the worst day of his life would turn into the best time of his life? It had been two weeks since Gray and Barkley formed Rogue Shiver with their new friends. After some initial wariness, mostly from Striiker, the group now mixed easily. They learned many things about each other, except for the whale in the water. The one topic nobody brought up was why each was swimming the Big Blue and not in another shiver.

"I'm stuffed," said Snork. "We never ate this well when there were just four of us!" It turned out Snork was nearly thirteen and a half, the oldest of the group by six months, although he didn't act like it. Striiker and Mari were twelve like Gray and Barkley, and Shell had turned thirteen just last month.

"It's probably a good time for hunting or something," Gray said.

Striiker harrumphed. "Let's go home. We don't want to be seen by Goblin Shiver's patrols." For some reason, if anything was more annoying to the great white than having his leadership questioned, it was Gray being nice to him.

"Their name was much cooler when it was Riptide Shiver," remarked Snork as he followed. "Since Goblin changed it, now *we* have the best shiver name in the whole Big Blue."

They actually had performed a shiver creation ceremony. Snork insisted. Even Striiker went along with it, probably because he got to be leader. The others voted themselves in the order they had been subconsciously swimming in. Mari was elected first, Shell second, and Snork third. Gray was chosen as fourth in the Line. Mari wanted to vote Gray higher, much higher in fact, but he wouldn't hear of it. It did seem pretty funny that Snork—

now that he knew Snork—was technically supposed to be tougher than him. Gray let it slide. He hadn't been in the open ocean for even one moon, and he knew the others were better suited toward making decisions.

Besides, Gray was happy to wait until the Tuna Run when he would rejoin his mother and Coral Shiver. Gray wanted to ask his new friends to come to the reef but hadn't found the right time. He didn't tell this to anyone, though, because he hadn't mentioned it to Barkley yet. The dogfish's mood was *not* good when he was chosen as Rogue Shiver's fifth.

"Are you kidding me?" his friend wailed. "There are only six of us, total! That's just embarrassing!" But when Mari asked whether he would rather be fifth in the Line or the only general member of Rogue Shiver, Barkley grumbled "Fine. Fifth. Great," and swam away. It took an entire day to calm the dogfish down.

Their new home was only a short swim away and well hidden. Towering brown and blue-greenie waved majestically, forming a wall that made everyone feel safe. You could enter unseen by swimming beneath a short tunnel formed by a fallen cliff. And there was the perfect hiding spot. It was an old landshark ship, *really* old from what Barkley told them. And big!

The ship had three levels, and when it had ridden the chop-chop, humans used wooden planks called "oars" to move the bulky thing through the water! Aside from a large crack in the bottom of the ship now, it was through these oar openings that a nice current flowed, allowing easy breathing. This was much better than sleeping in open water where you could be spotted, or down in the greenie where you could get something in your gills. There was plenty of space inside, although one room on the end was filled with shiny yellow disks that spilled everywhere because the wooden boxes they were packed into had rotted through. No one liked that area, as the moldy boxes left a tang in the water you could taste, unlike the rest of the ship.

Even though the ship lay three times the depth of the reef, there was still good light from the sun and moon. But it wasn't like the reef where other dwellers would talk with the shiver. Here the shellheads, lumos, fish, and urchins stayed out of the way when Rogue Shiver was around. Gray tried to ask a sea dragon if she knew Yappy, but the little dweller slalomed into the greenie without saying a word. He hadn't thought he'd miss speaking with other dwellers, but he did.

Only when Gray and his new shiver were by the wreck did they relax completely. It had been a good day. No, a great day. Gray found himself staring at Mari's sleek thresher tail as they went inside the landshark ship.

Unfortunately, Barkley saw this and whispered, "Mari cuts a nice wake, eh?"

He felt his face color. "She's okay, I guess."

They hung around the main cabin, enjoying the cool current streaming through the ship. Gray decided on the spot. It was finally time to tell the rest of Rogue Shiver how he got here.

"You've all heard of the Tuna Run?" he asked.

Striiker snorted. "I've been there twice!" Others in the group rolled their eyes. Apparently the great white spoke about this a little too often.

"Well, I think I should tell you how I got here and why I'm mentioning it now," Gray told everyone.

"Everyone's tired, Gray." Barkley swished his tail furiously. "We don't need to hear any of your long, boring stories." But Gray was determined and told the entire tale. After he was finished, Mari, Striiker, Shell, and Snork stared at Barkley with a newfound respect.

The dogfish misread the situation. "What? Is there snapper between my teeth?" he asked, genuinely clueless.

Snork tapped his saw bill on Barkley's head. "You are the best friend a fin could have!"

Even the normally quiet Shell remarked, "Not many sharkkind would leave their home like that."

Gray never thought he'd see the day when Barkley was speechless, but that day had come. The dogfish stuttered, actually embarrassed by the attention. "Yeah well, that's the way I roll. Anyway, we're talking about Gray who still hasn't said what any of this has to do with Tuna Run! So?" Barkley gave Gray a friendly bump in the flank with his snout.

"My mom wants me to find her at the Tuna Run. If I can prove I'm a good hunter, they'll let me back in."

The reaction wasn't what Gray expected.

"You're leaving?" asked Mari.

"I knew they were just acting like our friends!" huffed Striiker. "They only needed a place to stay for a while."

Shell stared at both of them as Snork said in a trembling voice, "Is that true, Gray?"

Gray had enough of Striiker. "You know, you're a real tail bender! I've been nothing but nice, and you just think the worst of me!"

"Tell me I'm wrong!" roared Striiker

Gray was ready to rumble, butting Striiker against the hull of the landshark ship. "If you'd let me finish, I was going to say you could all come back to the reef and be a part of Coral Shiver, you great, big krillhead!"

Striiker was speechless for a moment. "You'd do that for us?" he asked in wonder. "For me, even?"

Gray was taken aback by the vulnerability of the great white. "If you promised not to be such a flipper, then yes."

"But if you think you'd be leading, or even in the Line, you'd be wrong," said Barkley a little too loudly. He had taken up position above Gray and was still amped up and ready to fight the great white. "I mean, maybe one day, maybe. But you know how it is with new members. Take it from your fifth." This got a chuckle from Striiker, which released all the tension among them. Pretty soon everyone was chattering excitedly, with Barkley telling the other four all the great things about Coral Shiver's reef.

But everything took an odd turn when Shell asked, "So it was still there when you guys went back?"

"Went back when?" asked Gray.

"The day when Barkley was named fifth and swam off," the bull shark answered. "We thought you went for a visit or something. Some of us do that, from time to time. We didn't know you had been banished."

"No, our home is farther than that," Gray told him.

"And the reef's been there since Tyro swam past it," Barkley guffawed. "Why wouldn't it still be there?"

Everyone grew quiet. A bad feeling prickled up Gray's spine. He looked at Mari for an explanation, but she shook her head and didn't say anything.

Striiker swam forward a bit. "You mentioned you were in a shiver by a reef when you fought Thrash. You shouldn't have done that."

Barkley shook his head. "Gray didn't say *where* our homewaters were."

"They found mine," Snork whispered in a haunted voice. The happy-go-lucky sawfish was trembling. "They find every shiver they hear about."

"Mostly, we're from shivers that Goblin found," said Shell sadly. "He's at war with my old shiver, Razor Shiver. The only reason we're still alive is because we have more mariners than Goblin. Not because he doesn't want to destroy those homewaters."

Mari was upset and didn't seem to want to speak, but Gray motioned her to tell him what she was thinking.

"Thrash is dumb, but if he told Goblin you were from a reef where he could find new recruits, he *will* find your reef."

"Then what?" Gray asked, growing frantic. "What would he do?"

Snork's voice was faraway and reedy when he broke the silence. He whispered, "They eat anyone who doesn't join."

CHAPTER 10

GRAY AND BARKLEY LEFT IMMEDIATELY FOR THE reef and didn't speak, conserving their energy on the long trip. After two nonstop days swimming with no food or rest, they finally reached the Coral Shiver home-waters. Gray saw that the greenie path into the reef was intact.

But it was quiet. Very quiet.

There was usually noise by the reef. Keen shark senses picked up the sounds and disturbances caused by dwellers and other sharkkind talking or swimming. When you weren't hunting, you'd ignore these as background noise. Now all Gray felt, all he heard, was the gentle tide swishing the greenie back and forth. There were no snatches of conversation, or shouting, or tail strokes from any ocean dweller. It set him on edge. Gray's heart was pounding so hard, it felt as if it would hammer its way out of his body.

"Follow me," he whispered.

The entire reef was still and silent. When he got closer, he noticed there were a few tiny, darting fish about, but not many. The larger dwellers had been scared away. Or eaten. He could smell the faint scent of blood everywhere. The beautiful corals and greenie were gouged and torn, as if hit by a mighty undersea storm. A few urchins and anemones were there, but faded their colors into muted browns and grays, the better to hide themselves. For a moment neither Gray nor Barkley said anything, hushed by the devastation around them. Gray had expected the worst, but it still didn't prepare him for this. The reef was totally destroyed.

"Do you think everyone..." Barkley left the question hanging in the water.

"Mom! Mom!" yelled Gray, startling the dogfish. No one answered, though.

"All of them?" Barkley asked himself in a dazed voice. "How can ... how?

"NO!" Gray sped around the entire reef but it was the same everywhere. Desolation and stillness. Gray and Barkley cried by the edge of the reef, where they had gone after the drove of bluefin. It was quite some time before either could speak.

"This is my fault," Gray told Barkley.

"Gray—"

He cut his friend off. "If I had listened to you none of this would have happened! If I had listened to Mom! If I—"

Barkley gave him a sudden stinging tail slap to the flank. "You didn't do this! You. Did. Not."

This didn't make Gray feel any better. He knew deep inside that this was his burden to carry. I'm sorry, Mom, he thought silently as the slow tide carried his tears away.

"Gray? Barkley?" asked a small voice. They looked to where a few sad strands of greenie were still in place. There! Something moved. Gray and Barkley tensed, scared and alert.

Out poked Yappy's head. "Is it really you?"

Barkley exhaled loudly. "Yappy! You nearly scared us to death!"

Gray quickly swam up to Yappy and asked loudly, "Who did this? Have you seen my mother? Where is everyone?"

The little sea dragon zipped back into the greenie. "Stop yelling at me!" he squeaked.

Barkley nipped at Gray's tail, almost getting bitten as a result. The dogfish couldn't believe it and yelled, "What's wrong with you? Yappy's our friend." Gray saw the look in Barkley's eyes and was ashamed.

Yappy poked his head out of the greenie again. "Really, Barkley? I always thought you didn't like me!"

"No, Yappy. Sometimes I get annoyed and take stuff out on you. Sorry," said the dogfish. "Do you know where our families are and what happened?"

"I don't know where your cousins are, Barkley. They were on the other side of the reef, so I didn't see. The shiver, they tried to fight. They tried. But there were so many. So many."

"My mom?" asked Gray fearfully.

"I'm not sure." The little sea dragon choked back a sob. "I ran and hid! I'm a coward!"

"You're not a coward!" Barkley told him. "The shiver—were they taken?"

"No! They got away!" Yappy told them. Gray's heart leapt as Yappy continued. "Atlas was shouting, 'Go! Go! We'll meet at the Tuna Run!'" The sea dragon brightened a little. "You shoulda seen Atlas! He wanted everyone to leave, but Overbiter stayed with him, flank to flank! They held them off as Quickeyes and Onyx led everyone away! Sent at least three of them to the Sparkle Blue! But then..." Sadness returned to Yappy's eyes.

Gray couldn't speak, so Barkley prodded in a low voice, "Then?"

"They both were eaten."

Gray felt a hotness growing inside him. A reddish haze descended over his eyes as he thought of someone eating sharks from his shiver family. "Who did that?" Gray asked in a deathly quiet voice.

The little sea dragon's eyes grew misty. "They came at high moon when everybody was resting. But not me. I saw them. I saw ..."

"Yappy! Saw who?" Gray asked his voice rising, Barkley gave him a look when the sea dragon cringed.

"Saw who?" the dogfish asked in a soothing tone.

The sea dragon answered in a shaky whisper, "Bull sharks. They were bulls."

Barkley was struck dumb with a look of disbelief. Gray swam over, but not too fast or close this time. He kept his voice low so he wouldn't scare the sea dragon off. "Yappy, this is no time for stories. Who really did this?"

"STORIES?" he yelled into Gray's face. "Look around, you big lumpfish! Two of my sisters were eaten!" Gray actually backed away from the tiny sea dragon's rage and grief. Yappy got hold of himself. "I'm sorry I yelled. But they were definitely bull sharks. The one who ate Paxson had a weird scar on his snout. Looked like a clam shell."

Paxson was the sea dragon's oldest sister. She had always made fun of her brother for talking with Gray and Barkley. Now she was gone.

"Do you want to come with us?" Barkley asked. "We have another place."

The sea dragon shook his head. "My family's leaving. We have cousins in the Dark Blue. We'll stay with them for a while." Yappy's eyes grew hard for a moment. "When we find those bulls, we'll get them. You'll see." The diminutive sea dragon flicked his flippers in a wave good-bye and left. "See you around. Maybe."

Barkley shook his head. "Yappy and his giant cousins getting revenge on a shiver of bulls. If it wasn't today that would be funny."

"But it is today," said Gray. "And it's a good idea. We'll find who did this and somehow, someway—"

Barkley flicked a fin at Gray. "Whoa, whoa," he said. "Didn't you hear the good news? Yappy didn't see our families get taken or eaten. He said the shiver escaped! We'll go to the Tuna Run and find them." Gray was about to ask if Barkley really believed that everyone was still alive and there would be a big, happy reunion at the Tuna Run. His friend saw the question in his eyes and answered before Gray could say anything. "I have to believe that," he said. "We both do."

Barkley was right. No matter what, their families would be at the Tuna Run.

They would find them. Or swim the Sparkle Blue trying.

GOBLIN
SHIVER

CHAPTER 11

THE SWIM BACK WAS QUIET. GRAY WAS WORRIED sick about his mother. But there was another thought that cut through this sadness, and he was ashamed that it terrified him more than anything else. Gray was homeless now. Barkley was also, of course. And the dogfish was certainly worried about his family. But Gray's overriding feeling wasn't sadness, anger, or confusion. It was fear that he had no place to go. And this made him feel awful because he was only thinking about himself. Again.

Before this, after his banishment was over, Gray's exile would have turned into an adventure he'd tell stories about around the reef. But now his mother was missing, and there was no Coral Shiver reef to go back to and he was petrified.

Gray could feel that Barkley was also scared, but grief was the biggest sensation coming from him right now. He grew mortified when he realized that his friend could probably feel his state of mind, too. "I'm the worst shark ever," Gray muttered.

They reached the edge of the Rogue Shiver homewaters, where they were met by Mari. Her silhouette was easy to spot with the sun shining overhead. She raced over. "Are you okay?" Then she saw the looks on their faces and knew everything wasn't okay. "I'm so sorry. I hate Goblin!"

"It wasn't him," Barkley told her. "They were bulls."

"Oh, no! Please don't tell Shell that!"

Gray was going to ask why, when the big bull steamed toward them. "Striiker saw Thrash on patrol! We should get back to the wreck and hover low."

They began swimming, picking up their pace with steady, powerful tail strokes. They were nearly home when they saw Striiker and Snork. They were being circled by at least ten other sharks!

"Goblin Shiver!" Mari exclaimed.

There was no trouble picking Goblin out of the pack. He was as large as Gray, but all muscle, his teeth flashing in a harsh grin. Striiker and Snork had nowhere to run. The seabed was clearly in sight, and the greenie and rock formations in the area were too sparse to hide in.

"We can make it home without being seen if we stay away," whispered Shell.

"Shell's making some very good sense," said Barkley, tapping Gray's side with his tail.

Mari bristled. "We can't just leave them!"

Then they heard sharks laughing and Goblin's booming voice carrying through the current. "If you don't join us, we'll rip your pointy-nosed friend to pieces in front of you!"

That did it. "You guys can go. I'm not." Gray swam toward Goblin, who taunted the sawfish by nipping at his tail as his other shiver sharks laughed.

Gray picked up his pace by ferociously whipping his tail back and forth. He lost speed blasting two whitetips out of his way. Gray hit the great white in the side, doing no real damage but forcing him from Snork. There was yelling and screaming and total confusion for a few seconds. Gray saw that Barkley, Mari, and Shell had followed him into the melee! His heart pounded with pride and fear as the two shivers faced one another, ready to fight. Rogue was outnumbered about three to one, but at least they weren't surrounded anymore.

"Who the heck are you?" shouted Goblin.

"Come find out!" Gray yelled back.

It seemed like the shiver leader would surely attack, but a mako got his attention and whispered something only he could hear. The mako was black as night with eyes even blacker. She stared at Gray as if she was looking inside him. Inwardly Gray shivered and wondered why he was doing so. Goblin calmed down, curiously looking him over from snout to tail tip.

"Told ya he was different," said Thrash, off to

one side. Goblin silenced him with a hard look. Gray watched Goblin, who was distracted by the mako speaking low and urgently to him. Gray probably would have been distracted, too. Even in this life-threatening situation, he couldn't help but notice that the mako was stunningly beautiful. Every now and again her sleek, black upper half would reflect the sunlight from above, making her skin shimmer with color like a rainbow.

"All right, all right," Goblin told the mako, irritated. He swirled his fins and made an incredibly quick turn to face Gray. This great white was much faster than Striiker! Gray was lucky he'd caught the big fish by surprise, or he might have ended up swimming the Sparkle Blue. "So, how's your day been? Good?"

The change in tone caught everyone by surprise. Gray didn't have the first clue what to say. Striiker shoved in front of him. "Like I told you, we were just leaving, Goblin."

"I wasn't talking to you, flipper," the larger great white told him. He flicked his tail dismissively at Striiker, who gritted his teeth at the insult. Goblin looked right at Gray. "You! Who are you and what are you doing here?"

"Don't be a turtle. Say something," Barkley whispered to Gray, who slapped him quiet with his tail. He didn't need the dogfish's special brand of humor right now.

"I was—" as Gray spoke he was reminded that he had

just come from his destroyed home and missing mother. He was nearly overcome with emotion. I'm going to bawl like a pup in front of everyone, Gray thought. Way to make a tough impression.

Mari, sensing his hesitation, took over the conversation. "He's lost his home and family, Goblin. He and the dogfish were passing through when we found them."

The mako swam smoothly in front of Goblin and gently scraped against Gray's side. It felt wonderful. "You poor fin," she said. "You must feel so alone. I'm Velenka, by the way."

Mari stared daggers at the mako and gave her a quick slap with the elongated upper lobe of her tail. "He's not alone, Velenka. He's with us!" She stared defiantly. That was odd. Mari seemed to know both Velenka and Goblin.

Snork chose this time to exclaim, "You attacked his family just like you attacked mine!"

Goblin struggled to keep his temper. "I asked you to join us and your leader said no. That was his choice, not mine."

"You're a murderer!" cried Snork.

"A realist," Goblin insisted. "I won't let my shiver starve, and I won't share what little food there is in these waters. Your leadership failed you." The great white was very much in control as he stared down the sawfish.

"Rogue Shiver forever!" Snork yelled.

Goblin chuckled, joined by everyone else on his side. "Rogue Shiver?" The great white shook his head at Mari.

"I should have known you were involved when the reports came in of sharks hunting in our territory without permission, Mari."

Barkley and Gray looked at each other. Goblin *did* know Mari!

That wasn't the end of the surprises, not by a long shot. It turned out both Striiker and Mari were former members of Riptide Shiver and had left after Goblin became the leader. In fact, they'd left right when he renamed the shiver after himself. Mari's mother and father were members too, before they died. She blamed Goblin for the loss of many shark lives, including her father's.

The big great white was offended. "That wasn't my fault," he said in a quiet voice. "Your father was on a patrol, and Razor Shiver attacked us. I'm sorry about him, just like I'm sorry when we lose anyone from the shiver!"

Goblin seemed genuinely upset, which confused Gray. He expected the great white to be evil and nothing more. Certainly not a fin with feelings. Velenka saw his reaction. "I see you've heard Mari's lies about our shiver," she remarked. The mako moved closer, as if to stroke Gray's flank, but stopped when Mari glared. "Goblin Shiver is about family. We protect our friends and our hunting grounds. Is there anything wrong with that?" Velenka asked Gray, her big black eyes boring into him. He couldn't find anything wrong with it.

Gray turned to Mari. "So Razor Shiver sent your father to Sparkle Blue?"

"Goblin and Razor have been fighting for years. They won't stop until everyone's dead!"

"But the bulls did that. Just like they did to Coral Shiver," said Gray.

Goblin shook his head at Gray. "Mari needed someone to blame, so I let her blame me. Should we leave our territory and wander the Big Blue homeless? No. We stand and fight."

Velenka looked pointedly at Gray. "Don't you want revenge on the ones who destroyed your home?"

"I do."

Barkley grew alarmed. "Gray, no! We'll meet our families at the Tuna Run!"

"If they're alive," he answered. "But we need to survive until then."

Goblin smiled a toothy smile. "Then come with us. But I won't let you hunt in our territory. You join the shiver or leave the area."

"Oh, really?" Striiker asked sarcastically. "You'll just forgive and forget? You must be pretty desperate."

Goblin's eyes flared with anger, but his answer came calmly as he looked at Mari and Striiker. "We need to band together and put aside our differences, so I forgive you both." Next he flicked his tail at Snork. "I'm sorry I threatened you. It was Striiker who made me angry. You can leave here in peace or come along. Your choice."

Barkley looked absolutely pained. "Gray, this is crazy."

"It gives us the best chance to get to the Tuna Run and find everyone," he told his friend. "And I want to fight the bulls. Sorry, Barkley."

Shell, who was a bull himself, had been silent for the entire exchange. Now he asked, "What about me? Can I join?"

Mari looked horrified.

Goblin swam around the bull, taking his measure. "I recognize you. You've battled against us." Shell gave a terse nod. "You'd fight your own shiver? Why?"

There was a long silence. "You don't need to know why. You just need to know I'd fight against Razor and anyone who swims at his flank."

The great white nodded. "That's good enough for me."

CHAPTER 12

THE FORMER MEMBERS OF ROGUE SHIVER SWAM into their new homewaters at moonrise. It wasn't like the Coral Shiver reef or the landshark ship, which relied on greenie to hide their location. This wasn't hidden at all. Since ancient times this shiver had been an unquestioned power in the North Atlantis, and their location was well-known in the Big Blue. Gray wondered aloud why the shiver didn't just move if they were being attacked.

"So we can move from one place to the next like jelly drifters?" Goblin asked, shaking his massive head from side to side. "My shiver has claimed this territory from the time of Tyro. We're going nowhere."

"That's truer than you know," muttered Mari. Both Striiker and Barkley stifled their snorts.

Goblin didn't hear, or he pretended not to hear, and continued, "Besides, don't you think this place is worth fighting for?" The great white said the last as they swam over the crest of a hill, which revealed a massive, sloping cliff face that glittered with different colored greenie, each on a separate terrace. The greenie was grown and tended this way! Incredible! The entire Coral Shiver reef could have easily fit inside a small portion of this place. At the floor of the cliff, long greenie grew in thick strands that were forever scrubbing the lower crags, flowing back and forth with the currents. The expanse in front of the cliffs where the shiver-gathering area was located was even larger, with huge pylons of rock and coral. There were whales here! And schools of giant manta rays! Both Gray and Barkley's mouths hung open in wonder.

"I think I just swallowed a tooth," Barkley whispered.

Gray nodded to his friend. "You and me both."

"Wow," said Snork, waggling his serrated nose as he looked this way and that. Barkley dodged the dangerous snout and decided to move a body length away. The sawfish had ended up coming with them. Gray was glad for that. Snork was a genuinely good fish. Striiker and Mari, having seen the shiver homewaters before, didn't react much.

Goblin proudly swished his tail as if he'd personally carved out the cliffs and planted the terraced greenie himself. "This is my home. Our home."

Velenka swam over. "Now, I don't know about where you lived before, but there are a few rules we follow."

"Hmph!" Goblin grumbled. "We do it to make the dwellers feel like they have a say, but sharkkind run things around here."

"Of course we do," the mako said before turning to Gray and Barkley. "In this area we don't hunt. It's a safe zone for everyone."

"Sure," Barkley agreed. "That's how it was where we lived."

Goblin jumped back into the conversation. "Ah, but if a dweller leaves this area you can take it as a meal if you're hungry." The great white ground his triangular teeth together and smiled.

"Really?" Gray asked. This sounded a bit awful. How could you talk to someone one minute and eat him or her the next?

Mari knew what he was thinking and said to everyone, "Yup! You can be having a perfectly nice conversation with a dweller, and if it drifts outside the magical marker, you can have it for lunch! Literally. Isn't Goblin Shiver nice?"

"We aren't supposed to be nice!" Goblin answered sharply. "Nice fish get eaten! We're only as strong as our mariners, and they need to be fed."

While Gray liked Mari, he thought Goblin made a good point. If Coral Shiver had been stronger, maybe it would still exist. He pushed the thought from his head.

The rest of the day was spent on a tour with Goblin and Velenka. There certainly was a lot to see. Thrash went out on patrol with four other shiver sharks. They met other members of Goblin's Line returning from another patrol: Streak, Churn, and Ripper. Ripper was a giant hammerhead and Goblin's first. He had so many scars it was hard to find a section of his massive body that was unmarred. Streak, a shiny blue shark that seemed really angry, was third in the Line. Mari told him that Streak acted that way all the time. But she said it very quietly, so the blue wouldn't hear. Fourth was Churn, a whitetip who said, "Learn to love patrolling, pups," and laughed as he passed.

"You've been scratched," Goblin told Gray. "Looks like my hide has some bite of its own, eh?" Gray looked at his flank down by the tail. It was gashed slightly, blood seeping from the wound. At the reef he would have let it heal on its own.

But Goblin said, "Go with Velenka and get that fixed."

Mari immediately said, "I'll swim him over there."

But the great white shook his head. "No, you won't."

The thresher glared but bobbed her head to the shiver leader and obeyed. Velenka flicked her tail for Gray to follow. With a last look at Barkley, he went.

"You have no clue what getting a scratch *fixed* means, do you?" she asked with a chuckle. Gray didn't but wasn't about to let the mako know that. He swam past a small reef almost entirely covered by starfish. There must have been thousands in a pile, and these stars were much bigger than the ones at the reef. Everything was bigger! It took real effort for Gray not to gawk like a pup at all they passed. She continued, "By treaty, any dweller who dies in the area is given to the bottom feeders, including shark-kind. Waste not, want not." The rule was the same in his homewaters, but it always made Gray a little queasy. He knew the muck-suckers were just doing their job clean-ing the Big Blue. And he guessed it was better than seeing the carcass of one of your shivermates slowly decay into nothingness. But it was still creepy. "In return, they do things for us."

They swam over to an area where there were many fish, urchins, and crabs. There also seemed to be a few recently injured fish, but amazingly, their wounds had been *repaired* somehow. Gray had never seen anything like it before.

"The shiver requests help!" she announced loudly before turning to him. "I have to go find payment. Be back soon."

A large yellow surgeonfish came over and swam around Gray's cut. "Ah, not too bad," she said. "We'll have you in and out in no time. I need a doctor here!" A doctor fish joined them and began nibbling on the edge of his wound.

"Hey! What's the big idea?" Gray shouted.

The surgeonfish swam in front of his left eye. "My name is Oceana, and I'm your surgeonfish. Hold still. We can't fix this if you move around."

Oceana flicked out razor-sharp spines from the

back of her tail and gently cut the ragged edge of Gray's wound. Another doctor fish joined the first and ate the remains. Gray tried not to move as this tickled a little. It was also kind of disgusting.

"We have surgeon and doctor fish at the reef. *Had,* I mean," Gray said. "But I've never seen any do this!"

Oceana chuckled. "Not every surgeon or doctor fish can. You have to be trained, usually in an ancient shiver's homewaters. The best are the shivers that allied with humans in the olden days."

"You mean landsharks?" Gray asked. "Sharks and landsharks were friends?"

The surgeonfish nodded at his amazement. "*Landshark.* Such a rustic term. Anyway, we have the finest treatment for wounded sharkkind and dwellers in all the Atlantis. This is literally cutting edge, and you wouldn't see it if you grew up in some out of the way backwater. What we're doing is clearing away the dead and infected skin so we can suture the cut. Hold still." Gray didn't want to ask any more questions, as he already felt like a jelly-brain, but *suture* the cut? What did that word even mean?

He watched and found out. When the gash was cleaned, it did seem to feel better. An old sea turtle swam up carrying a crab on its back. The turtle hovered as the shellhead, with amazing dexterity, inserted and tied off several urchin spines, knitting both sides of the cut together. It was amazing!

In a moment Velenka came back with a fat haddock in her mouth. She chewed it several times and let it sink to the rock bottom as the crab finished its work. The doctor fish nibbled on the edges of the knitted wound, smoothing them. After they finished, the dwellers descended on the fresh fish.

"Paid in full," Velenka told Oceana and her assistants. The mako tapped the urchin spines in Gray's flank. "Those will work their way out, or you can come back and have them removed. But then you owe them a fish."

"Thanks," he said. The wound felt better, and the oozing blood had completely stopped.

"Come on," Velenka said to Gray. "Let me show you some of the shorter patrol routes. If you feel well enough, that is."

"Do I!" he told the mako. Gray wanted to see everything! Luckily, it seemed Mari and Striiker were completely wrong about Goblin Shiver.

CHAPTER 13

THE MOON HAD GONE THROUGH AN ENTIRE
cycle since Rogue Shiver had joined Goblin Shiver. Most
days were spent patrolling their territory and hunting.
All the sharks from the shiver took turns swimming
patrol routes, but there was always a large group protecting the homewaters. Other than a few probing patrols
of their own, there was little sign of Razor Shiver. Gray
hadn't seen a single bull.

"You think maybe the war is over?" he asked Barkley.
"It has been very quiet." This was Gray's first time
patrolling with the dogfish. He had been looking
forward to it all week. His friends hadn't adapted
to their new lives as well as Gray had to his. Mari
and Striiker both seemed edgy or irritated most of
the time. Other than a few meetings by the Speakers
Rock for announcements or speeches by Goblin, Gray

really didn't see his ex-shivermates at all. It seemed as though they were being intentionally kept apart.

"No, it's not over," answered Barkley, "and this isn't a war. It's more like a turf battle, which is why we didn't know anything about it. If there was a war—a real war—we would have heard something, even by the reef." The dogfish snapped up a mackerel that passed close to his mouth. "I think we should leave. I hear the Sific Ocean is nice. Goblin would never follow us all the way there," he told Gray while he munched on the fish.

"And what about your cousins?" Gray asked. "And my mom?"

"Easy. We sneak back through the territory when the time for the Tuna Run comes."

Gray could see Streak and Ripper in the distance, waiting to continue their patrol. "Let's talk about this some other time," he told the dogfish.

"Sure, Gray. Whatever." Barkley swam away without another word.

"Any trouble?" Streak asked.

"All quiet," Gray replied. The blue nodded, and the pair swam out.

"Well, well, well!" said Goblin, appearing from nowhere. "How's everything going?"

"Fine, Goblin." Gray grew wary. The shiver leader hadn't ever stopped to chat before.

"Follow me," the great white told him. They went to the edge of the central area and then a little farther. Suddenly Goblin turned and attacked! It was all Gray could do to evade his initial rush. Then they both spun a tight turn and rammed each other. Gray was dazed, then Goblin started laughing. "You don't know your own strength. For a young pup, you hit like Ripper!"

Gray was confused but couldn't help but puff with pride at the compliment. Ripper was a warrior, a true mariner. That much he knew from his short time here. "Umm, thanks."

"You've been with us a month now," Goblin said. "Are you getting your sea legs?"

"Sea *legs*'?"

The great white chuckled. "Right, you're from the boonie-greenie." Gray was about to ask where the boonie-greenie was but thought better of it. "'Sea legs' is a landshark saying for getting used to the ocean. Humans sometimes get sick on their boats when the chop-chop is rough. When they get used to the waves, they say their landshark legs have turned into 'sea legs.' Get it?"

Gray understood very little of what Goblin was saying. Barkley would have definitely known. Maybe he should have paid a little more attention in Miss Lamprey's classes. In any case, an answer wasn't required.

"Did you know sharkkind used to talk with the humans? They even use some of our words!"

"Aww, come on," Gray said before he could stop himself.

But Goblin didn't get angry. "No, really. These home-waters have been led by great whites for thousands of years." Goblin thumped him on the head with his tail in a joking way. Gray didn't mind, though, as the shiver leader was talking and listening to him. That was some-thing that Atlas never did. "In those days the entire Atlantis Ocean was part of an empire that ruled with an iron fin over all the seven seas."

Gray was fascinated. He listened as Goblin told him that an evil and corrupt mako empress by the name of Silander ruled everything from her giant kingdom in the Sific Ocean, which was a hundred times larger than Goblin Shivers homewaters. She ordered her brutal, armored *squaline*, which meant "fish soldier" in an ancient landshark language called Latin, to collect food from the shivers until everyone was starving. "*Squaline* is also where the concept of the Line comes from," Goblin noted. "But good shark-kind in the Indi, Arktik, and Atlantis oceans rose up against her empire. Riptide was formed back then, and it teamed with tattooed Indi Shiver to strike the first blow in a long war."

Gray was hesitant to interrupt but asked, "Tattooed Indi Shiver?"

"No, they're called Indi Shiver, *and* they have tat-toos." Goblin saw that Gray didn't understand and explained further. "They mark themselves with designs on their bodies by having urchins crawl along their skin and release acid."

How cool was that? It was the most interesting story ever! Gray listened, totally captivated as Goblin described the pitched battle between *armadas* of shark-kind and dwellers on each side in the South Atlantis that broke Silander's power. It was fittingly called the Battle of Silander's End. After she lost, her own Line sent her to the Sparkle Blue. Then those sharkkind fought among themselves over who would lead, and the empire crumbled, never to rise again.

Gray just gaped. He couldn't believe he had never heard of this before. What kind of school was Miss Lamprey leading? They spent a month studying plankton! But Gray knew it wasn't her fault. The Caribbi sea was off the beaten path, and she probably didn't know anything about the Battle of Silander's End. Or maybe he wasn't paying attention that day in class. It was definitely one or the other.

"So, are there still big battle shivers with armadas of sharkkind?" Gray asked.

"No, they all splintered into smaller ones like here in the Atlantis. Some say Indi Shiver has a new pup king who wants to be emperor of the Big Blue. They say he's already taken over the Arktik."

Gray gasped. "Is it true?"

The great white chuckled. "No. These stories bubble

up every now and again. Ten years ago, a South Sific shiver was supposedly conquering everything. Somewhere far away, there's probably a story about me wanting to be emperor."

"Do you?"

The great white waggled a fin, pointing. "Can you guess how this part of the Big Blue got its name?" Goblin asked. Gray didn't know, and the story the great white told seemed even more unbelievable and made him forget his question. The Atlantis Ocean wasn't named after sharkkind after all. It was named for landsharks who called themselves Atlanteans! They lived on a faraway island. All the shivers, even when they fought each other, would protect Atlanteans if their ships sank in storms. In return, these landsharks taught them things, just like Oceana told him.

The Atlanteans were the ones who showed sharkkind how to repair battle wounds and even cure fever from the poisonous stings of urchins and jellies with algae and mosses from the ocean. They forged metal armor for sharkkind, with razor edges to cover fins, a spike for the tail, and protective plating for the flanks. Sometimes humans even swam into battle with sharks, protecting their dorsal topside while breathing air from a bladder made of animal skin! The humans who lived on Europa got jealous of the Atlanteans as they became more and more powerful and finally sank their island. They killed many sharks while doing that. Because of this treachery, all sharkkind vowed never to treat with humans ever again. Now any landsharks that came into the Big Blue were fair game.

"Although they're not really worth it, even the fatter ones," said Goblin as he made a face. "They're bony and don't taste good at all."

Goblin also told Gray about the measurements landsharks used. These measurements did seem useful, especially when comparing them against the mako standard of flippers and body lengths. It would be easier to tell someone that a drove of halibut was a thousand feet down than to describe it in tip-to-tails. Gray wondered how the landsharks could be so smart and so stupid at the same time. After generations and generations of sailing on the Big Blue, they still can't swim better than a turtle!

"Why are you telling me all this?" Gray asked.

Goblin smiled. "I see potential in you. Who knows, maybe one day you could be in the Line. Maybe even my first." The initial emotion that hit Gray wasn't pride— that would come later. His first emotion was fear, the image of the ferocious, giant Ripper coming to his mind. Ripper wouldn't like being displaced. Not at all. Goblin seemed to know what he was thinking. "Don't worry, I'm not asking you to fight anyone today. You're not ready yet. And besides, we don't battle for position much anymore. Sharks die often enough without wasting lives."

"I—I don't know what to say," Gray stumbled over his words. "It's so . . . umm . . . weird."

"Weird to be appreciated?" Goblin nodded. "I get it. Sometimes when you grow up in a shiver where it's quiet, the sharks in the Line only see you as the pup they scared in the greenie for a joke that one time."

"Or when you got your head stuck in a bucket," Gray added.

"What's that now?" asked Goblin.

Gray coughed. "Nothing. You were saying?"

"What I see is a big fin with lots of potential. That's why you're going to the Tuna Run with me and the rest of the shiver."

"You mean it?" Gray fairly shouted. He was being invited as a *hunter*! His own shiver didn't even want him as a member. Or they hadn't, until. . . . Suddenly Gray could only think about his mother. Goblin saw his sadness and bumped him.

"None of that now," he told Gray. "You're going to the Tuna Run, pup. And if you find your family, they'll see what a great hunter you've become. But you need to practice first."

"Practice for the Tuna Run? How can you do that?"

Goblin just smiled his toothy smile. "You'll see."

CHAPTER 14

THE GAME WAS CALLED TUNA ROLL. "IT'S NOTHING like the actual Tuna Run, but it'll help you work on your quickness and side-to-side movement. That's a good thing to have at Tuna Run and anywhere else in the Big Blue," Goblin told Gray.

"Sounds like fun!" said Snork. The sawfish had regained some of his cheery nature since Gray saw him last.

Streak jabbed Ripper in the flank with her snout. "He'll be swimming the Sparkle Blue in the first five minutes of a real run."

"Yeah, he's chum," Ripper agreed in his gravelly voice.

"Quiet down, you two," Goblin told them. He explained the game, which actually seemed fairly simple. There were two teams of six, symbolizing a leader and their Five in the Line. Both teams faced the same way. Gray, Barkley, and the other former members of

Rogue Shiver were one team and hovered farther back. Goblin and his Line took their places closest to the starting end of the field of play.

Gray's team was about twenty good tail strokes, or a hundred yards, away from Goblin and near the end line of the field. He taught the landshark measuring system to Barkley, who found it to be both fascinating and useful. In the game, a single drove of exactly one hundred fish would try to zip by both teams. For every fish Goblin's group caught they received one point; any that Gray's team caught were worth two points, as the fish would have time to gain speed in the water between the two teams. Neither team could swim outside their own zone, marked by glowing lumos. "The object is to make quick decisions and catch some fish!"

"Wait, wait," said Barkley, looking absolutely confused. "Are you forcing some poor dwellers to play a *game* in which they get eaten?" This struck Goblin and his team as hilarious. They laughed so hard they could barely breathe. Striiker and Mari also chuckled. Snork joined in, too, but Gray was pretty sure the sawfish didn't know why he was laughing.

"Forcing them?" Thrash could barely speak he was laughing so hard. "He thinks we're forcing them!"

"Like he's going to catch one anyway!" yelled Streak. Barkley gave her a glare, and she burst into another giggle fit.

"Wisko! Get out here!" yelled Goblin. A fish that Gray

had never seen before streaked forward and stopped between the two groups. This fish knifed through the water with ease! It shined silver and was shaped like a long, thin spine with jagged fins pressed close to its body. "This is Wisko, the wahoo. She's been in charge of our Tuna Roll for the last three years."

"She *what*?" Barkley asked, now even more confused.

"Watchu want, Goblin pup?" Wisko danced in front of the great white, tapping him on his head with her tail. For some reason this didn't bother Goblin at all, and he playfully snapped at the fish. "What's the hold up? Wahoo! We going or what? Or you too turtle to play today? Wa-hoo!"

"The dogfish is afraid we're *forcing* you to Tuna Roll with us," Goblin said dryly.

"Who? Who said that? Him?" After Goblin nodded, Wisko jetted over to Barkley, hitting him in the face with a tremendous tail slap.

"Hey!" yelped Barkley. "I'm making sure you're not being abused! You obviously aren't a dumb grouping fish."

"We invented Tuna Roll, dog breath!" said Wisko. "We play by different rules than the rest of the dwellers in the Big Blue. Hey, did you know you're named after a dumb land animal called a *dog*, which eats its own poo?"

"We're *not* named after it," huffed Barkley. "It's named after us!"

"So you admit you eat your own poo? Ha ha!" said Wisko as she finned Barkley's snout with another blazing fast pass. "Wa-hoo!" Barkley got angry and darted after the wahoo, but never came close to catching her. She taunted him as he flailed about. "Over here! No, here! Too slow!"

"Only the fastest wahoo are chosen for the Tuna Roll by their leader—that's Wisko. It's a great honor for them to test themselves against us," Velenka told everyone. "They're actually faster than the tuna we'll hunt at the run."

"Waaay faster! Wa-hoo!" exclaimed Wisko, a flash of silver as she pirouetted in the water. "We are the fastest of the fast, the quickest of the quick! So quick, it'll make ya sick!" She flashed by Barkley again, making him duck. "We're also the best tasting fish in the sea, pups!"

Velenka continued, "Tonight we have to bring dinner to the wahoo who get by us. As you can see, they are insufferable winners. If they get eaten, that's also an honor. They call it the Way of the Wahoo." The mako rolled her eyes as if she didn't totally get the Way of the Wahoo either.

"Wa-hoo! It sure is!" Wisko told everyone. "Getting old and slow is no way to go! So we dancin' or what, sharkkind?"

All thoughts of how the wahoo might be mistreated went totally out of Barkley's mind. He stared menacingly at the fish. Well, as menacingly as Barkley could stare, which wasn't very. "Then I'd love to 'honor' you, Wisko."

This comment got the dogfish another slap on the snout. "You'll be feeding me tonight, dog breath! Wahoo!" The fish twisted and swam back to the starting line, moving to a quirky beat in the tides only she heard.

"That is one odd fish," Shell said.

"Odd or not, it's so on!" Barkley muttered to himself as he ground his teeth in annoyance.

"Ready!" yelled Goblin, and his entire team swum into a ragged formation. When he bellowed "SET!" the line moved into a perfect two-tiered V-formation with Streak and Churn hovering topside.

Gray's senses went into overdrive. He hadn't noticed before, but there were loads of dwellers around. Squid, eels, octopi, crabs, and other bottom dwellers gathered to watch near or on the craggy rock wall facing the field. Fish of all sorts and colors hovered with the tide; smallest in the front, largest in the back. There were even a few whales in the distance, although they'd need very good eyesight to see the game. All of this was interrupted by Goblin shouting, "ROLL!"

A hundred shining wahoo cried in unison, "WA-HOO!" and accelerated past the start line the instant after Wisko snapped her tail as the signal to move. Goblin's team stayed in their formation until the last second, then blasted out every which way. Streak, a very fast blue shark, got one. All in all, only two or three wahoo were caught.

"Stay together until they're right on us, then break!" yelled Mari.

But Gray's team couldn't hold their formation like Goblin's, and the fish were past them in a fin flick. It would have been nice to know that teams did that before the game, he thought sourly. The wahoo easily avoided them. In fact Gray was pretty sure Wisko herself shouted "Wa-hoo!" into his ear and gave him a slap on the snout as she whizzed by. While the wahoo were amusing earlier when they were having fun with Barkley, now they were super annoying to Gray.

Goblin's team was in stitches, laughing so hard they had to call a time-out.

"Did you see the look on Gray's face?!" yelled Churn.

"Nothing compared to doggie!" agreed Streak, still gnashing her teeth from her meal.

Goblin and Velenka explained the rules more fully between rolls, which referred to the rounds of wahoo swimming through the field. There were ten rolls to a game, and each team got to be up front for five of them. "Ohh, you're taking too long," Goblin told everyone. "Now you're gonna get it."

Goblin pointed with his fin as Velenka added, "Tyro had an off day when he created the wahoo."

The ninety-seven wahoo who made it across the line in the first roll were still slapping fins with each other and hurling insults at the sharkkind. But when Wisko snapped her tail, they swam into a tight formation.

"WHO-ARE-WE?!" she shouted, each word more of an exclamation than a question. The entire formation of wahoo began doing the same slow fin moves: three strokes one way, then a tail clap with the wahoo on their left, then three strokes to the right and a tail clap to the nearest wahoo the other way. They moved together perfectly in this massed victory swim, and *sang* in time to their tail claps!

We are the wahoo, the speedy, speedy
wahoo!
WA! HOO!
You are the drifters, the jelly, jelly,
drifters!
SO! SLOW!
We are the wahoo, the speedy, speedy
wahoo!
WA! HOO!
You are the drifters, the jelly, jelly,
drifters!
SO! SLOW!

"What the heck are they doing?" Snork asked.

"Right now? Insulting us," snorted Striiker.

"Don't let it get to you," said Mari. "Huddle up!"

Mari tried to explain the strategy for the game, but Gray couldn't hear her at all. It turned out that the gathered dwellers were cheering as loud as they could for the wahoo! The entire bowl-shaped stadium was alive with their energy. A school of glowing lantern fish circled the edge and all the dwellers rose when they went by—even the bottom feeders who couldn't swim raised a claw or tentacle—which made it look like there was an undersea wave rolling around the edge of the field! And lumos of all sorts were blinking together forming pictures in the shape of a wahoo!

Shell nodded. "Yeah, the dwellers always root for the fish."

Tuna Roll was incredibly fun and exciting! How could anything else compare? After Gray caught his first wahoo, Tuna Roll immediately became his favorite thing ever. First, wahoo were delicious, just as Wisko said they would be. And second, after having been so embarrassed by the fish, it felt absolutely wonderful to catch one! The game ran for four more rolls, with Goblin's team in front. After taking a small break, they switched positions and went five rolls with Gray's team in front. At the end of all ten, whichever team had the highest total score won. And flip, Rogue was getting killed! The score was twenty-one to seven heading into the last roll. Goblin accounted for eight points on his own!

Cheers from the dwellers rose as Gray began what was called the "sound off." "Ready! Set! ROLL!" he shouted.

The wahoo streaked past their line with a swimming start. Wisko was playing again! She angled the cluster of a hundred wahoo to the right. Gray was at the *diamond head* of the formation—there were so many cool terms in this game—and moved to intercept. Wisko was the fastest of the wahoo and blew by them. But the stragglers, if any fish so fast could be deemed a straggler, were forced to change direction. Striiker ate one wahoo in a single bite. Mari and Gray each struck home as Barkley just missed. Both Goblin and Ripper were successful, though, further increasing their team's score. Gray's team lost but, wow, this game was fun!

"What a beat down!" yelled Streak as Goblin and the rest joined them.

"Ah, they didn't do too bad," commented Velenka. "Especially with a rookie at diamond head." The mako brushed her tail against Gray's flank, earning a scowl from Mari.

Wisko led the other wahoo through a song that started out sad but ended with a rousing chorus, commemorating the wahoo who were eaten during the game. They finished by shouting, "On your way to the Sparkle Blue! WA! HOO!" After the song ended, Wisko brought all the remaining wahoo to Goblin. "Time for the losers—that's you—to feed the winners—that's us. See you at Slaggernack's."

"We'll be there," Goblin told her.

The rest of the wahoo swam by, bumping fins with sharks who'd done well.

Wisko passed him and said, "Not bad for a pup."

Barkley hadn't caught a wahoo. Not even close. He wasn't feeling good about himself and began to swim away.

"Hey, dog breath," yelled Thrash. "Not so fast."

"What? It's over, right?" asked Barkley.

"Oh, you wish!" Streak told him.

CHAPTER 15

IF THE GAME WAS GREAT, THE CAMARADERIE after Tuna Roll was even better. Everyone gathered in a series of coral formations and caves called Slaggernacks a short swim off the East side of the homewaters, which was named after a giant crab who had lived years ago. His massive exoskeleton stood there on display as if guarding the place. Everyone who entered slapped a fin on Slaggernack's giant claw for luck before moving between jagged outcroppings of coral that were covered with glowing anemones and dwellers of all types. Even though the place was dark—with just a sliver moon above—and mostly enclosed by rock and greenie, lumos provided a great deal of their own light to brighten the place. There was also a small vent that blew warm water upward toward everyone's belly. Velenka said it was prehistore water from the Dark Blue that was warmed by volcanoes far below the ocean floor. It felt very pleasant.

Thrash explained that Slaggernacks was a free zone, meaning anyone could come, even competing shivers like Razor's, and there was absolutely no fighting allowed. "You mean if Goblin and Razor came in here at the same time, they wouldn't attack each other?" Gray asked.

"Nope. They wouldn't," the big tiger shark said before gulping down another seasoned halibut. Apparently you could get fish with mosses, planketon, krill, and other *seasonings*—a landshark word— made by the crab *chefs* here at Slaggernacks. That was one of the reasons the place was a gathering spot. Gray nearly threw up when he tried a piece. It was horrible! Whatever the shellheads put on the fish made him feel like something exploded inside his mouth. The flavor was everywhere—and strong! Thrash called it an acquired taste. Maybe it was, if by "acquired" he meant disgusting. The tiger motioned with a fin toward the urchins lying inside of Slaggernack's skeletal remains. "Those urchins are part of Gafin's crew. He owns the place.

"Gafin?"

Thrash shook his head. "I keep forgetting you're from the boonie-greenie." The tiger chuckled. "Gafin is the king of the urchins. He does business with lionfish, stonefish, scorpion fish, and any other poisonous dweller you've heard about. And a bunch you haven't."

"*King* of the urchins? Are you yanking my tail, Thrash?"

"No, I'm totally serious," the Tiger told him. "His territory actually covers most of the North Atlantis, including both Goblin and Razor shiver homewaters."

"Oh, so that's why Goblin and Razor can't fight here," Gray said, realizing this.

Thrash nodded. "Exactly. No one wants to be on Gafin's bad side. You can kill one urchin or stonefish. But sometime, somewhere, you *will* get stung." The tiger took a dainty bite from a seasoned fish and caught Gray chuckling. "You're supposed to *savor* the flavor, not just gulp it down like—oh, forget it. Fine dining is wasted on you."

Gray pointed a fin at the urchins clinging in and around Slaggernack's skeleton. "So, which one is Gafin?"

"I don't know. Go stick your snout in there if you wanna find out." Thrash called over a few spiny shrimp to drop the last small bit of his meal in his mouth and ordered another dish—haddock this time. Apparently the tiger would have to catch many fish, four to one, to pay for this meal. It was quite a deal for Gafin, king of the urchins. Before the spiny shrimp swam their way up to his mouth, Thrash told Gray, "By the way that's a joke. Don't stick your nose in Gafin's business. Ever."

Barkley, Snork, Shell, and Churn returned with fish for the wahoo. The losing team's three lowest point scorers and the low *roller* on the winning team were charged with getting the fish. It was called wahoo work. Gray had heard this term from sharkkind in Goblin Shiver but never knew what it meant until now. Wahoo work was any menial, embarrassing job. Ha!

The wahoo divided up the meal and took positions of honor above the sharks. They then proceeded to critique the two teams' performances in the Tuna Roll from best to worst. This they called rolling abuse. Not all of it was abuse.

"Still the baddest fin in Atlantis! Wa-hoo!" was how Wisko led off Goblin's rave review to the fin-slapping applause of the rest of the wahoo. Ripper, Velenka, and Streak were also praised. Thrash got angry at his so-so grading and needed calming by Goblin, who reminded him it was just a game. Churn received some razzing but took it in stride. The whitetip still scored more points than any of the Rogue team members besides Gray.

Wisko gave Gray a tail slap to the flank to begin his heckling. "Wide load here had the best showing by a rookie I've ever seen in my life! Wa-hoo!"

Gray wasn't sure he liked the "wide load" comment but knew it was said in a spirit of friendship, though Barkley was laughing a little more than necessary.

Another wahoo commented, "You've got yourself a keeper there, Goblin!"

Striiker and Mari were made fun of, but their performances were pretty good. Shell ate a wahoo during the roll, so even though he got an earful, he didn't mind.

"This sawfish bit me and *still* couldn't slow me down!" said another wahoo. "Laaaame!" He proudly showed a small divot taken out of his tail. Snork chuckled, a little embarrassed.

Gray was sure there were more comments to come about Snork, but Barkley interrupted. "Why don't you quit picking on him and shut up?" said the dogfish. Bad move. Everyone's attention turned completely to him.

"Look who suddenly got his big fins!" said Wisko. "Dog breath, the world's *worst* Tuna Roller!"

The rest of the wahoo joined in. "Bark for us, dog breath! That's what doggies do! Bark! Bark!" Soon the entire pack of fish were *barking*—they were making some kind of noise anyhow; Gray wasn't sure if it was actually how a landshark dog sounded or not.

"You're not even a real shark, doggie fish!" yelled another. And those were some of the nicer comments. It got worse when Thrash joined in.

"Maybe we should make him wear one of those, what is it—a *collar*—around his neck like those landshark things!" added the tiger very unhelpfully. "Wisko and the others can trade off on taking him for a swim!"

Goblin and his Line laughed right along with the wahoo. The rest of Rogue struggled not to laugh, except for Mari. She was genuinely upset at the treatment Barkley was receiving and glared at anyone from Rogue who was laughing.

Gray felt ashamed for his friend, but a chuckle escaped his teeth before he could stop it. It was an accident, but Barkley saw. The look in his eyes told Gray that he had totally betrayed him with that snicker. "You're a krill-faced whale!" the dogfish yelled, close to tears.

"Hey, you didn't mind laughing it up when they called me 'wide load'!" Gray was getting annoyed now. Barkley was always running his mouth about things he could do well at, like school, and making fun of others who weren't good at it. "You can fin it out but you sure can't take it, huh?"

Barkley rushed him. For a moment Gray thought he might take a chunk out of his side, but the dogfish whooshed out of Slaggernack's to the derisive hoots of Goblin Shiver. Led by Wisko, the wahoo sang a mocking song about dogfish. Gray later learned that they had a song about *everything*.

"You all suck algae!" Barkley yelled on his way out as the wahoo began barking a chorus in their song. Wow. Gray wanted to go after Barkley and make things better. He really did. To his mind, though, the dogfish was being thin-skinned again. How could anyone be angry here? This place was so cool!

But Gray decided to follow him, anyway. After all, Barkley was his friend. Gray was about to leave when

Goblin came over with Velenka. "Don't worry about your friend," the pretty mako told Gray. "Streak will teach him a couple of moves, and he'll catch a wahoo next time."

"Ripper used to be terrible, but now, watch out," Goblin said.

Gray considered. "I really should check up on him."

"Give him time to cool off," the great white told him. "You're just going to make it worse, and besides it'd be rude to leave so soon. Wisko named you rookie of the year!"

"Barkley will be fine," Velenka reassured him, her eyes hypnotizing him with their sheer blackness.

"Okay," agreed Gray. "You're right."

"Or he's not tough enough," Goblin mused. "And that's not your problem."

Gray disagreed and shook his snout side-to-side. "I'll help him toughen up."

Suddenly a peculiar wailing interrupted their conversation, and for a moment everyone stopped. "Oh, the entertainment's starting!" Velenka exclaimed.

An old gray whale and a few dolphins hovered on the edge of the cove. They were singing a strange yet uplifting song. "There's usually music after a Roll," Velenka explained. "We provide them with the entertainment of watching the game, and they do this for us in return."

Amazing! This day kept getting better and better. Gray knew he should go see if Barkley was all right.

And he would. In another hour or so. It would be rude to leave while the whales and dolphins were singing. He couldn't just take off. After all, he was rookie of the year!

Gray was so absorbed he didn't notice Mari motion to Striiker, Shell, and Snork. The former members of Rogue Shiver quietly slipped away, one by one.

THE
CURRENT
QUICKENS

CHAPTER 16

BARKLEY CHURNED FURIOUSLY THROUGH THE dark waters. The homewaters of the Goblin Shiver, and more importantly, Slaggernacks Cove, were now behind him. "Stupid wahoo and their stupid game!" he muttered to himself. Barkley couldn't believe Gray had laughed with all the others. Sure, Gray was better than he was at Tuna Roll, but that was no reason to make fun of your best friend. I'll bet plenty sharks aren't good at it, he thought. Although, even Snork had gotten closer than he had to catching a wahoo. How could they be so fast? Oh, how Barkley would have loved to have seen the surprised look on Wisko's face if he'd caught her! "The honor is all mine," he'd tell her and then, crunch! Barkley shook his head. Keep dreaming, doggie breath.

He was wandering aimlessly when the others found him. Gray wasn't with them.

"Are you okay?" Mari asked, concerned.

"You kind of expect it from the wahoos; they're weird. But from your own shiver? That's cold," added Shell as Striiker nodded in agreement behind him.

Snork patted Barkley on the back with his fin. "Thanks for sticking up for me."

Barkley was so grateful for his new friends that he felt as though he was going to tear up. It was bad enough everyone saw him cry on his way out of Slaggernack's. "You guys are the best," he croaked, trying to make sure his voice didn't crack too much. "I wish we'd never been caught by Goblin. And not just because of today." Barkley sniffled. "I think it was much better when we were Rogue Shiver." Where was Gray? How could he not be here?

"You and me both, Barkley," said Striiker. "So what are we going to do about it?" He gave a pointed look at Mari.

"You're serious?" she asked. "Goblin will never let us leave."

"I'm not saying we should ask for permission," Striiker told the thresher. "Do you all still accept me as your leader?" Barkley didn't quite know what was going on. But if he was going to be led, he'd rather Striiker do it than Goblin.

They all nodded, Mari hesitantly. "Why are you asking?"

"I'll challenge him."

"Are you crazy?!" Snork blurted out.

Shell agreed. "Why are you so anxious to swim the Sparkle Blue?"

Striiker stubbornly whipped his tail back and forth. "I can take him."

Barkley shook his head. "Look, no one wants to leave more than me, but why fight at all? Why not just go?"

"Where?" Striiker asked. "The Sific? It's a long trip."

"And it could be worse than here," added Mari. "No, if we're going to do anything, we should go back to our old place at the landshark wreck. They don't know where it is."

"But," Shell said, "they'd find us." The group knew this was true. If they left the shiver without permission and were caught again, it would be certain death.

"Let's not do anything hasty," Barkley said. "No fighting. No leaving. Who knows, maybe Goblin will go to the Sparkle Blue at the Tuna Run."

"Now that's a thought," Striiker mused, a faraway look in his eyes.

Mari got in Striiker's face. "Don't do anything stupid! Do. Not." She stared at the great white until he nodded.

"Someone will have to stand up to Goblin one day," he told Mari. "We're just putting it off."

Barkley didn't want to fight the great white or his shiver. That wasn't the way to find his family, if they were still alive. It wasn't a way to remain alive, either. "Look, we all know I didn't eat during the game, so I'm going to take a swim and hunt," Barkley said. "Thanks for coming, all of you. I'll meet you later. You're good friends."

"Unlike Gray," Striiker said under his breath. But everyone heard. The four swam back to the Goblin Shiver homewaters.

A short time later Barkley spied a few fat mackerel feeding on sardines. He zoomed in and caught one, picturing Wisko instead. "Oh, please, Barkley, your teeth are so sharp!" he imagined the wahoo crying. That would serve her right. He pursued another mackerel into the low greenie but lost the fish.

Keep dreaming about catching a wahoo, dog breath, he told himslef. You can't even catch a stupid mackerel.

It was then he heard voices. Barkley moved forward slowly, not disturbing the sand or leaving a trail as he swam through the kelp bed. He peered through the feathery strands of blue and red greenie while hovering with the tide.

"You like how I piled on?" the voice asked. Barkley stalked forward to get a better look but remained well-hidden. It was Thrash.

Then a female voice sighed, irritated, "Fine, it was funny. But we have more important things to do."

"Like that little muck-sucker didn't deserve it!" Thrash huffed. "He's always looking down on me, like he thinks I'm stupid or something." Barkley's eyes popped open in surprise as he hadn't given Thrash credit for being smart enough to *know* he thought that. Apparently he was mistaken and had made a large tiger shark into an angry enemy.

"We have to get along for now," the female voice said. The tide pushed Barkley ever so slightly. Instead of correcting, he let it ease him sideways. This gave him a different angle which revealed—Velenka! The mako continued, "You can annoy his friends, but don't hurt them."

So the whole thing was a setup? Were the wahoo in on it, too? No, Barkley thought, he was just really bad at Tuna Roll. But what was the rest about?

"I don't know why we're going through all this trouble just to get some fat pup on our side," Thrash said. "I think we should just eat them instead."

"You're not supposed to *think* about anything; you do what I tell you to do!"

Barkley got very worried. The fat pup was Gray! Not that he was fat, of course—just big cartilaged. They were planning to use his friend in some scheme! He strained to listen as the tide shifted, carrying their voices away.

Thrash looked confused. "You mean I should do what *Goblin* tells *you* to tell *me* to do, right?"

The pretty mako became all sweetness and light. "Of course. And you're doing a great job. You'll be first in the Line for sure. But for now we've got to keep this a secret. So, did you pass the message to Kilo?"

"Yeah, I did. Streak would blow her top if she knew we were dealing with the bulls," he said. "This deal is rotten."

Velenka looked as if she wanted to eat the tiger's liver. She kept her temper under control, but her tail twitched with a lethal anger. "Don't talk about the deal, Thrash. Ever."

The tiger shark edged away. Even he was smart enough to be wary. "Sure, sure, Velenka. Whatever you say." The pair swam off in different directions, Thrash toward the homewaters and Velenka away from them.

What was Goblin up to? Was Velenka playing her own game? How was Gray involved? All of these questions and a dozen others rolled through Barkley's mind as he slowly made his way back into what he now considered an enemy camp.

"How did it go?" asked Goblin.

Velenka nodded, smiling as she swam over. "It's done."

They swam the open waters in silence for a while. The mako knew not to speak just now. Goblin was irritated, and when he was irritated, he was liable to lash out at anyone. "It feels like I'm betraying everything the shiver stands for," he said quietly. "My mother would have never have agreed to this. Neither would Hawley."

This needed to be handled gently. Ever since Hawley's

death, it was Velenka's duty to be Goblin's confidante. This was exactly the way she wanted it. Velenka was glad Hawley swam the Sparkle Blue. What would Goblin do if he ever found out that she had helped him get there?

A thrill ran down Velenka's spine at the thought of the thin current she was swimming. Everything was in her reach. Everything! "Your mother was a great shark," she began. "She led us well for years. And Hawley was a great friend."

"You got that right," Goblin replied.

Velenka stroked his back with her tail. "But times are different. You know that."

"Stupid landsharks and their giant nets," Goblin grumbled. "They sweep the Big Blue clear, and we're left to fight for scraps."

"And that's why what you're doing is right. You're leading us to victory." Velenka scraped against his flank the way he liked. "When the bulls are under your control, think how many more territories you can conquer!" Velenka saw that the thought appealed to him, but then his mood darkened once more.

"I'd rather it be a stand-up fight," Goblin told her.

Not this again! "We don't have the strength."

The big white whirled. "Then Razor and I, one-on-one, like the old days! There's honor in that!" Velenka was silent for a fin flick too long.

"You don't think I can beat him? Is that it?"

"Of course I do," she soothed. "But what if you were injured during your noble fight? What if he gets lucky and takes a piece of your tail?"

"I wouldn't be able to lead. Ripper or someone else would come at me for being weak," he agreed grudgingly.

"And your plans—who would see them through?" Velenka asked with all the sincerity she could muster. Pfah! She hated playing fawning fish to his "great leader." But for now, it had to be done.

"Many of them were your ideas, Velenka," he growled.

Did he suspect? No, this was a lucky strike. "I only agreed with what was on your mind, Goblin," she told him with a smile. "Can anyone really make you do something you don't want to?"

Now the great white laughed. "Not likely!"

The tension in her spine released with an almost audible whoosh in her ears. She could always count on Goblin's opinion of himself being very high. They swam onward, and she was forced to listen to him prattle on. For now.

CHAPTER 17

GRAY HEADED TOWARD THE AREA INSIDE THE homewaters where many of the shiver sharks slept. It had a nice current that allowed you to easily hover and doze. He felt guilty about having such a good time at Slaggernacks. He hadn't even seen Mari and the others leave. "What's so bad about the place, anyway?" he muttered.

Just then, Barkley streamed into view. Gray was glad for a chance to talk with him alone. It might get awkward after the dogfish rightly apologized for being such a little puffer. Barkley could be such an emotional shark.

"Gray! Gray!" he panted. "I'm so glad I found you."

"It's okay, Barkley," Gray told him. "I forgive you."

"What? You forgive me?" The dogfish slowed sharply. "*You* forgive *me* for being such a total flipper?"

"You weren't a *total* flipper."

"I'm not talking about me, jelly-brain!" the dogfish shouted.

Gray didn't say anything. He wasn't going to get into another fight with his friend tonight. Instead, he swam by without saying a word.

Barkley caught up with him. "Okay, we can figure out who was the bigger flipper later. I have something very important to tell you!"

Gray stopped. He was still miffed but would hear the dogfish out. "Go on."

The tone Gray used irritated Barkley for some reason, but he shook it off. "You're in danger! Goblin and Velenka are planning something."

"Planning what?"

"I don't know. She didn't come out and say it, but they want to use you somehow."

"She and Goblin?" Gray asked.

"No, she was talking to Thrash."

Gray looked at Barkley incredulously. "So now Goblin, Velenka, *and* Thrash are plotting against me? What about Ripper, Streak, and Churn? Won't they feel left out?"

"Please take this seriously, Gray! They're planning something that involves you, and it didn't sound good!" The dogfish hovered, gills pumping furiously, waiting for his reply. "Well?"

Gray shook his head. "Barkley, you sound like Yappy with his crazy stories."

The dogfish bumped him hard. "I'm trying to save your life!"

"It was only a game," Gray told him. "I can teach you."

Barkley swam in a furious circle, talking to himself. "Tyro's tail! He thinks this is about Tuna Roll! What am I going to do?"

"Calm down."

Barkley yelled toward the surface, "ARRGH!"

"What are you two doing?" asked Mari. "Half the homewaters can hear you." The rest of Rogue Shiver came through a nearby curtain of kelp, watching curiously.

Barkley told everyone, "While I was out hunting, I overheard Velenka and Thrash talking about some plan of Goblin's. It doesn't sound good."

Mari, Shell, and Striiker looked to Gray for an explanation. He shook his head and rolled his eyes. "I have no idea what he's talking about."

Snork finally said, "We're going to need more information, Barkley." The group gathered by a coral tower, instinctively moving behind it so they couldn't be seen from the homewaters.

"I know it's not much to go on," the dogfish began, lowering his voice for some reason. "But Velenka was talking about an alliance with the bulls. And Thrash didn't like that."

Shell looked dubious. "Goblin and the bulls? Unlikely."

"Could you have misunderstood?" Mari asked uncertainly.

Barkley shook his head. "No. And also, Gray's part of their plan. Somehow."

"Of course he is," Striiker said sarcastically. "He's the center of attention in *every* ocean."

"I am not!" Gray exclaimed. "This is all in Barkley's jelly head. If anything's in there at all! He's mad that Goblin and Thrash gave him a hard time. And what's so wrong with that, Barkley? I'm saying this as your friend, but you need a little toughening up."

For a moment it was so quiet that Gray could easily hear a single sardine swimming in the distance, its tiny flippers making a *switswitswit* sound as it passed.

Then the dogfish exploded, slapping his tail against the coral spire with a CRACK! "It's not about being tough!" he yelled. "It's about looking out for your friends!"

Striiker swam over to Barkley, getting his attention. "I'm sorry I have to ask this just to be sure—this has *nothing* to do with your really bad day at Tuna Roll?"

The dogfish gave Striiker a death stare and said nothing, though his gills pumped furiously. Barkley swam in front of Gray. "One more time—please believe me when I say that I'm trying to help you! Goblin has a plan and it involves you!"

"Of course I do!" Everyone spun around to see Goblin grinning, accompanied by Velenka. "I have a plan for all of you, and it involves being good members of this shiver."

"There, see?" Gray said to Barkley.

"What about the bulls? What about Gray?" the dogfish accused.

Velenka swam very close to Goblin, rubbing his flank. She spoke so low only he could hear. Though Goblin was perfectly motionless, it seemed as if he wanted to rush forward and swallow Barkley whole. "My plan with the bulls is to rip them to shreds," Goblin spit. "My plan for Gray is to let him help. Something wrong with that?"

"Unless you don't think you're up to it," Velenka remarked to Gray.

"I'm more than up to it!" Gray countered.

Goblin sighed. "If the rest of you want to leave, then go. I've got bigger fish to hunt." As if to prove his point, the great white snapped up an unlucky sea trout that swam a hair too close to his massive jaws.

Mari swam over to Velenka, eye to eye. "Just like that?"

"Just like that," Velenka told her. "You don't deserve to be a part of this shiver, you ungrateful turtle!" Mari rushed the mako, but Velenka did a nifty turn and slammed her in the side. "Like you could ever be my match!"

Striiker and Shell blocked Mari from making another sprint at Velenka.

"Go!" said Goblin in a commanding voice. "All of you leave this place. You can stay until we go to Tuna Run. If you're hunting in my territory after that, you'll swim the Sparkle Blue." Barkley stared at the great white, probably a little longer than he should have. "What, doggie? What now?"

"And Gray?" asked Barkley. "Can he leave with us, too?"

"Sure," Goblin told them. "None of you are worth the distractions you're causing."

Striiker looked very unsure of himself as he said, "Then, we'll do that." He, Snork, Mari, and Shell withdrew, swimming away from the Goblin Shiver homewaters, looking back from time to time. Almost automatically they headed in the direction of the land-shark wreck.

Gray felt torn. He didn't want to see his friends leave. "Mari, you really want to go?"

"I do."

Barkley stared straight at him. "Are you coming?"

Gray looked first at Goblin and Velenka, then at Barkley and the rest of Rogue Shiver.

"No. I'm staying."

CHAPTER 18

GOBLIN RIPPED AND TORE AT THE GREENIE, shredding the strands between his razor-sharp teeth and imagining the dogfish as his victim. But Barkley wouldn't go straight to the Sparkle Blue. Oh, no. Goblin would make sure his last moments alive were painful. Then he would eat every last morsel of the ungrateful little flipper.

"I want to kill them all!" Goblin yelled loudly. Velenka's eyes seemed to grow larger, if that were even possible. She had big eyes for a shark. It was part of her beauty, he supposed. They were well away from anyone who could hear, near a roaring volcanic vent, which added a constant hiss and rumble to the water. If you weren't directly in front of the shark you were talking to, your words were lost in the noise.

"How would that look to Kilo?" she yelled back, although not with anger, but just to be heard over the noise. Velenka knew better. The fish he chewed and spit out did nothing to relieve his temper and neither did the greenie.

"I've wanted to deal with Mari and Striiker since they ran away! And the others were feeding in my territory! *My* territory!" Goblin began taking massive hunks out of a hard coral bed, destroying an entire section. He might lose a few teeth but it made him feel better. "They'll swim free when we leave for Tuna Run! And they deserve to swim the Sparkle Blue!" he yelled.

"What if I could keep them from escaping?" Velenka mused. "Put them somewhere to wait for your justice?"

Goblin stopped. "'To wait for my justice.' I like the sound of that." If anyone could, Velenka would find some underhanded way to stop them. This wasn't how he'd normally deal with a problem; it wasn't in his nature to slink around like a mako, the sneakiest of sharks. He confronted problems head-on, with a snap of his powerful jaws. But they couldn't do that right now. Not in his shiver's weakened state. Not with Razor waiting to attack.

"What about Gray?" he asked. "Why are you so interested in keeping him in the shiver? He's just a pup."

"Exactly," she answered.

The vague response infuriated Goblin, but he wasn't about to let on he was bothered. Velenka constantly spoke in riddles and double-talk, never getting directly to the point unless forced. "So?"

"Have you been to the prehistore vault lately?" she asked.

"Not since I was a pup myself. Get on with it."

"You really should visit again," Velenka continued. "There's a legend among the mako about a shark who will unite the shivers of the Big Blue."

"Yeah, every sharkkind has a legend where they'll be the ones to end up on top," Goblin said dismissively. "Bunch of wishy-washy mush."

"That's mostly true," she agreed, "but in this case, *you* can be that shark."

He laughed, his anger momentarily subsiding. "That's crazy talk. After we get Razor's territory, maybe we'll conquer a few more. But the entire Big Blue? Impossible."

"Not for a great leader such as yourself." Velenka rubbed against him and whispered in his ear. "That is, a leader who has a megalodon in his Line and obeying his orders."

He chuckled. "That would be nice, Velenka. Now find me one."

"I already have," she said smugly. "His name is Gray."

Goblin was thinking of tail-slapping that smug smile off her face when he stopped cold. Velenka was right! The sameness of the teeth and the overall shape—how had he not noticed that? Goblin himself was huge for his kind, bigger than all but a few he'd ever met in the Big Blue. But the prehistore skeleton in the vault was gigantic! It could finish *him* in two bites, its mouth was that large. That's what Gray, the big reef shark *really* was—a megalodon! And the pup didn't even know it!

"With him in the Line, you'd be invincible," the mako whispered in his ear.

With a megalodon in his shiver—maybe as his first— Goblin *would* be unbeatable.

Goblin saw Velenka smile and something struck him as little off. He would have to swim carefully into this particular greenie.

Very carefully.

CHAPTER 19

GRAY LEFT SLAGGERNACKS AS THE SUN ROSE and shined into the Big Blue. He hadn't meant to be out so late, but patrol was boring with no sign of anything anywhere, and Thrash convinced him to stay. He and the tiger ended up having a great time, but now Gray was exhausted, having gotten no sleep. He and Thrash had spent countless hours flank to flank in the last few weeks. He could tell at first that the tiger wasn't too fond of him, and the feeling was mutual. He had attacked Gray when they'd first met, after all. But keeping up a dislike for one another was a miserable way to spend time. So, grudgingly, they began to talk and Gray grew used to most of Thrash's quirks and now thought the shark was all right. The tiger was kind of a braggart, and there was always some commotion when he was around, but Gray wasn't perfect, either.

"Ocean Spray really brought it tonight, eh?" Thrash said as he nudged Gray. Ocean Spray was a musical group consisting of a baby whale singer, two bottlenose dolphins backing him up, and an entire dance troupe of singing sea horses. They were pretty impressive. "That whale pup would make good eating, huh?"

"Isn't there a treaty with the whales to not do that?" Gray asked. The idea of feeding on the sweet-faced, adorable calf horrified Gray.

"Right, the treaty. How could I forget? I love the treaty!" Thrash said loudly as a group of dolphins passed. Then he lowered his voice to a whisper. "But if you're on deep patrol and find a lost pup? Well, the Big Blue can be a dangerous place."

Gray was okay with Thrash most of the time, but this was getting to be one of those times he wasn't. He yawned exaggeratedly. "I'm beat. Heading home now."

"Come on," Thrash prodded, "we aren't patrolling today. Let's get a bite."

Gray was hungry. And he didn't like sleeping with an empty stomach, which rumbled just thinking about food, in fact. Since Barkley and the rest of Rogue left Goblin Shiver over a month ago, he had grown longer by another foot at least, as well as gained a good deal of weight. I'm going to be the fattest shark ever, Gray thought. As if on cue, his stomach grumbled so loud even Thrash could hear it.

They went to an area by the North edge of the home-waters. There was a carpet of high greenie nicknamed Hydenseek. You could always find a snack at Hydenseek if you nosed around a little. Today it didn't take long at all, and soon they were both satisfied.

"That was another good idea," Gray told the tiger as he playfully bumped flanks with him. "You're just full of them today."

Thrash swished a fin, signaling for quiet. "Look there," he whispered. They watched as a turtle led her young toward the greenie field.

"Hey, turtles aren't dumb fish. We can't eat them!" Gray said.

Thrash stared at him and snorted. "Says who?"

"You know. Everyone," Gray replied. "And we just ate, remember?"

"Things that talk get eaten all the time in the Big Blue, you know." Thrash took a couple of lazy tail strokes in the reptiles' direction. "Let's scare them."

Gray was uncomfortable. He liked turtles. The ones at the reef had always been polite and even nice to him. "I'm really tired, Thrash."

"Do what you want," said the tiger as he swam toward the turtles. "I'm going to have me some fun!"

Gray didn't want to leave Thrash alone with the turtles, although he didn't know what he'd do if the tiger wanted to do more than scare them. He reluctantly followed. The female turtle—the mother, as the hatchlings were undoubtedly hers—had no chance of escaping. She motioned for her young to head into the greenie. Gray could hear her voice pitch into a squeak, crying, "Swim and hide! Swim and hide, children!" But the hatchlings were so scared, they just crowded closer to their mother.

Thrash glided after her slowly, but still much faster than the turtle could manage, and said things like, "I'm in the mood for turtle pups!" and "Here comes a big, bad shaaark!" He lazily slid with the current so he was now facing the turtles and blocking them from the safety of the greenie. He gnashed his teeth together. "Just swim inside! You won't feel a thing!" Thrash laughed; a deep, mocking rumble.

The mother turtle panicked and began screaming, "Heeeelllp! Someone help me!" She was surprisingly loud for such a small dweller. This scared the hatchlings so much that they froze and echoed the mother, screaming the same thing, "Heeeelllp! Someone help me!" in their own tiny voices.

The tiger laughed at the turtle family's distress. He looked over at Gray. "You just going to hover there like a bump on a reef? Get in here and have some fun!"

"I, umm, you seem to have it, umm, covered."

Thrash shook his head. "You're soft! I always knew you weren't as tough as you acted!"

"I am too! I am!" Gray protested.

The tiger laughed, this time at Gray. "Well, I don't see you doing anything to show it."

"Please let us go!" shrieked the mother turtle as her scared hatchlings hovered behind her tail.

The wailing of the turtles, the uncomfortable feeling in the pit of his stomach, the lack of sleep, and above it all, Thrash's laughing, pressed against Gray, somehow inside his head. He needed to make it stop.

"I'll show you who's tough!" Gray streaked forward.

He blazed past Thrash and scooped every turtle hatchling into his mouth. He would have gotten the mother too, but Thrash's bulk blocked him just enough.

"Now that's more like it!" yelled the tiger. "How's the shellback today?"

Gray slung himself down in the greenie. Using the sandy bottom he skidded to a halt, ejecting the hatchlings from his mouth. Luckily, they were so shocked at still being alive they stayed mute. "Shhh, be quiet or I'll eat you for real!" Gray hissed to the little turtles before turning to Thrash. "Yuck, they were awful! All shell, no meat. I'd find a fat fish if I was you."

"Suppose you're right, but I can't let you be tougher than me, hatchling-eater!" Thrash laughed and then opened his mouth to bite the momma turtle in half with his jagged teeth. She screeched in fear, a cry somehow even higher pitched than before and so piteous it broke Gray's heart. He was about to say something when—

"Tiger, tiger, full of spite. Tiger, tiger, not so bright."

Thrash whirled and shouted, "Who said that?" Gray

also turned toward the voice but saw nothing. Apparently Thrash knew this insult and didn't like it one bit. "Come on out! I'll show you who's not bright!"

Now the voice came again. It spoke with an odd lilt like nothing Gray had heard before. "But I'm right before you, silly tiger!" And it was! There, in front of Thrash's snout, floated one of the oddest fish Gray had ever seen.

It ruffled its frilly fins and announced, "My name is Takiza and I do not suffer fools. So you, sir, would be wise to move along."

CHAPTER 20

GRAY'S MOUTH HUNG OPEN IN DISBELIEF. *Takiza was real?* Impossible! Gray didn't know what was going to happen next, but he wouldn't have missed this for all the tuna in the Big Blue! Takiza, if this was really Takiza—it couldn't be!—wasn't running from Thrash. Exactly the opposite! He was preening, right in front of the giant tiger shark! Takiza's huge, delicate fins were bright red and white, fluttering like greenie in the tide. How could this fish even swim with fins that looked so fragile—as if they could be ripped from its tiny body by a strong current? They were so frilly!

For some reason Gray remembered one of Miss Lamprey's lessons about the landshark world. There was an animal called a *peacock* that supposedly strutted around in ritual dances, showing off its bright, long feathers. This fish, whatever it was, was definitely the ocean version of that animal.

Thrash took one look and roared with laughter. "Did

you hear this flipper? He thinks he's Takiza! Looks like a piece of greenie I got stuck between my teeth!" Gray chuckled at the comment. It was kind of funny.

"You have the manners of a blob fish, and you smell like algae on the seashore!" This caused Thrash to have another fit of laughter. Gray too, truth be told. And the funny, ruffled fish wasn't done. "You will leave this area now. Be on your way, and perhaps I won't give you the beating you so richly deserve!"

Gray was sure the female turtle and her hatchlings were safely hidden in the kelp and wouldn't be found. But there was absolutely nothing he could say to stop Thrash from sending this crazy fish to the Sparkle Blue. That jelly had already drifted away with the current.

"How is it that tigers are always such unthinking brutes?" Takiza asked. "If your elders would spend more time learning how to be vital dwellers of the Big Blue, instead of muscle-headed bullies, the seven seas would be much more harmonious."

Thrash nodded, as if taking the fish's words seriously, moving closer and closer. "Wow, you're right. I should give that some thought. The next time I'm at a meeting with the elders, I'll be sure and bring that to their—" Quicker than a sea snake, the tiger lunged at Takiza and his teeth smashed together onto the fish. "Ha!" exclaimed Thrash proudly, "how do you like me now, *Takiza*?" The tiger began doing a little shimmy that made Gray chuckle. But then—

"Whether you are dumber or *slower* is a question to

baffle the wisest in the Big Blue." The frilly fish was now hovering over Thrash's head, but directly between his eyes where the tiger couldn't see him.

"Wazzit?! Where is he? Where?"

Gray couldn't help but snort in surprise. "Right over your head!" Thrash moved one way and then the other, but the odd fish moved *perfectly* with him! It was the most amazing display of swimming ever. "Still there," Gray told the tiger.

"Are you yanking my tail?" asked Thrash.

"I'm not," Gray told him. "He's right over your head."

Thrash quickly barrel-rolled, trying to get a look. Still, without seeming to put forth any effort at all, the fish that called himself Takiza stayed between Thrash's eyes, just over his head! Gray's mouth opened in disbelief. It was impossible!

"He can't be still there!" yelled Thrash. "And if you're joking with me, pup—"

Gray could only shake his head and gesture with a fin as Takiza swam slightly away so that he came into Thrash's view, but upside down, so that he was eye to eye with the tiger. Or rather Tazika, being much smaller, stared into one of Thrash's much larger eyes.

"Is it your first day with those clumsy fins?" asked the fish calmly. "I've seen starfish missing legs swim better than you do." Thrash's mouth opened in shock as Takiza continued, "And to have poor eyesight as well? It seems you have received none of Ramtail's gifts. Are you sure you're a tiger shark at all?"

Then the little fish caught Thrash by the tip of his tail with its frilly fins and somehow swung him in circles! And fast! It was unbelievable! All the tiger could do was let out a high-pitched scream as he was whipped through the water. The little fish then threw Thrash into the distance, several body lengths away. "A wise dweller knows when he's outclassed. I give you the chance to exhibit wisdom and leave this instant."

Thrash got his fins underneath him. "I don't know what just happened, but you're going to be chowder! You hear me? Chowder!"

Gray was pretty sure that asking Thrash if he needed any help fighting the little fish would get him bitten, so he stayed quiet. The frilly sea peacock didn't, however. "Unfortunately I do," he answered. "Your voice is like the baying of an injured sea cow and hurts my ears."

Thrash was so angry he couldn't even respond in words. He trembled with rage and shouted an unintelligible "Gonnakillyerraggh!" before charging. The laughably small fish stayed where it was until the tiger opened his mouth to swallow him whole.

And then . . . *something* happened.

Gray wasn't really sure what, it happened so fast. He caught just the briefest flash of the colorful fish zipping forward and snapping a ruffled fin into Thrash's flank. The tiger grew quiet, still moving, but not swimming— his enraged features frozen.

Then, he started to sink!

Gray swam over to him, concerned. "Thrash! Thrash?" he yelled. "You okay?" But the tiger didn't answer.

"The oaf will be fine after a few moments," said the little fish, now hovering in front of Gray's left eye. "I am a practitioner of the noble art of Shar-kata, a peaceful form of self-defense, which does not send anyone to the Sparkle Blue so lightly." Gray struggled to keep Thrash from sinking, but it wasn't easy to remain underneath him.

"Who are you? Really?" Gray asked, amazed.

"Excellent! You have manners enough to ask for an introduction," the fish told him. "I am a Siamese fighting fish, or betta." His frilly fins caught the tide and expanded to their full length. "My given name is Takiza Jaelynn Betta vam Delacrest Waveland ka Boom Boom." The fish gave Gray a flowery nod. "You may call me Takiza for short."

For a minute Gray didn't know what to do. He looked at Thrash, who stirred and mumbled, "Ma, is that you? Don't wanna go to class." Gray let the tiger settle into the sand and greenie.

"You're actually Takiza? You're real?"

Takiza moved his fins in another flourish. "I am."

"You know, I should eat you for doing this to my friend," Gray told the betta.

"You may try. But is he really your friend?"

"What? Of course he's my friend," Gray sputtered.

"He is an evil shark," Takiza said matter-of-factly. "Perhaps you should find better friends. Now, may I ask a question of you?"

"I guess so."

"Do you know yourself?" The little betta cocked his head and waited for an answer.

"I don't understand."

"Inside you, I see a shark who swims with one fin in the light and the other in darkness. Peace or anger? Only you can decide the current you shall swim, so which will it be?"

Gray couldn't for the life of him figure out what the betta was talking about. "What does that even mean?"

"If you do not know the answer then that *is* the answer for now." The betta shook his delicate fins and swam off. "Perhaps we shall speak again." And with that Takiza disappeared into the Big Blue.

Thrash twitched, sending a cloud of sand blooming off the seabed. "Huh? What happened?" He swam up to Gray. "Where is that little piece of krill?"

"Umm, you scared him off," Gray answered. He was pretty sure the tiger wouldn't want the exact truth. Thrash seemed dazed, as though he didn't remember everything.

"I sure showed him, didn't I?"

Gray nodded. "Yeah, that was...something, all right."

After Thrash gathered his senses, the two of them swam back to the shiver homewaters. Gray was dead tired when he got to the resting area, but couldn't sleep a wink.

All he could think about was Takiza Jaelynn Betta vam Delacrest Waveland ka Boom Boom.

BLOOD
IN THE
WATER

CHAPTER 21

GRAY SWAM ANOTHER MOON PATROL ON THE East side of shiver territory with Goblin, Ripper, and Churn. It was his fifth patrol in force this week, which meant that the group consisted of at least five sharkkind. Velenka, Thrash, and Streak led another down the Western ridge. The homewaters were tense these days as Razor Shiver sharks were spotted close by several times.

Goblin was also taking an increased interest in Gray, even scheduling one-on-one combat lessons. It was so much more than just ramming and biting! Strength and size were important, but real fighting was about tactics. What to do in a given battle depended on the particulars of the situation. Were you fighting alone or with other sharks? Were the numbers in your favor? Did you have the element of surprise? Were you swimming with or against the current? It was how you answered these questions, and many others, that would prove if you were a true mariner, or just another brawling sharkkind.

Goblin said that in the old days of the empire, some sharkkind battles involved armadas of sharks and dwellers that fought in formation, with the opposing forces clashing at different points on what they called the *battle waters*. Apparently humans did the same thing when fighting on land and in their ships on top of the ocean. Sharkkind had given the humans the idea of massed battle formations, but of course the landsharks said it was the other way around. As if . . .

In their last single-combat practice, Gray fought Goblin to a standstill. He thought the shiver leader was going to bite him in anger, but the great white laughed instead. "Now you're doing it!" he told Gray. "You're getting tough!" In the Big Blue that was the only way to survive.

But Gray had been troubled since his meeting with Takiza. A week had passed, and he still hadn't told anyone about it. Thrash was quiet about it too, but that was likely because he may have finally remembered the frilly fish beating the stuffing out of him. Somehow Gray knew the betta swam the Big Blue without concern, without constant fear or anger. What would it be like to live that way?

"You're quiet today," said Goblin. "Anything the matter?"

"Nothing," Gray began, but then he said, "You ever think if all the shivers stopped the patrols and stopped trying to take territory from each other that maybe things would be better?"

"You mean in a perfect ocean? Where there's enough food for everyone?" Goblin asked sarcastically. "Where magical sea horses pull us around so we don't have to swim?"

Gray nodded. "I guess you're right. Too good to be true, huh?"

"You know it. What brought this on?"

"I met this little fish, a betta, named—"

"Takiza." Goblin almost choked on the name. "The *peace-loving* Siamese fighting fish."

"You know him?" Gray asked, surprised.

"Don't know him, know *of* him," answered Goblin. "There are stories about Takiza all around the Big Blue. Crazy stuff about how he's invincible. He's more than five hundred years old—if you believe it." Goblin cast a sidelong glance toward him. "Did you fight him?"

"No, just talked," Gray said. He wouldn't tell Goblin about Thrash's beating. The great white would definitely make fun of the tiger and that would be trouble for everyone.

"Peace and love makes the current go around, eh?" The great white shook his head. "But that little flipper supposedly kicks some serious tail. So you tell me, why is such a nonviolent fish so good at fighting?"

"I'm not sure."

"Because he's not peace-loving," Goblin continued, "Why would you learn to fight so well if you
believed that peace and harmony is the way to go?
No, no, he learned how to fight so he can crush anyone he meets."

This was an excellent point. Why would a fish who
preached the evils of violence be so good at finning it out
himself? It should have stopped the nagging thoughts in
Gray's mind, but somehow made them worse.

Suddenly Churn cried, "Razor Shiver!"

Eight bull sharks were resting on the other side
of an immense field of glowing coral. The coral was
beautiful to Gray's eyes, different spires casting eerie
light everywhere: pink, red, blue, green, and yellow.
Everything was lit by the ethereal glow of moonlight
from above the chop-chop. But no one stopped to
admire this.

Without a word the bulls sped up, and the two shivers clashed over the shimmering coral field. Though
everything was in a frenzy of commotion, time slowed
for Gray. The cries of bloody victory and death receded
until he only heard his heartbeat and the water whisking past his gills. Gray rammed one attacking bull hard,
sending it spinning away just before it could bite Thrash.
In doing so, though, Gray dazed himself. His vision
blurred, and the rigid coral spires seemed to sway like
greenie in the tide.

"Thanks," Thrash mouthed. Maybe he said that aloud, even yelled it, but Gray didn't hear anything. The big tiger flashed away, avoiding a dorsal attack from another bull. Gray hovered and watched. Something crashed into him.

"Move it, pup!" Gray blinked at the shark in front of him, sensing that he should know who it was. There was a high-pitched whine filling Gray's ears, and whoever was speaking sounded very far away. "Can you hear me? Snap out of it!" The large great white whirled and slapped Gray across the face with his tail, and suddenly he could hear again. "STAY WITH ME IF YOU CAN!"

"Right, right!" Gray heard himself yelling over the sound and fury as everything came into deafening focus. Goblin battered a blue shark away from Churn, then bit the dorsal fin off another. Gray rammed his way through an attack. He knew his side should hurt, but it didn't right now. That shark was replaced by another, faster one. This bull did a series of tight turns, trying to get behind him, and succeeded in separating him from Goblin. Gray recognized this move, called the Sea Horse Circles. The tight, attacking maneuver could rip his tail off if it succeeded. To protect against this, Gray switched into Manta Ray Rising, a series of counter turns.

As he was swimming for his life, Gray caught only flashes of the continuing battle. Ripper took a massive chunk out of a bull, and a cloud of blood fogged everything, adding to the confusion. Churn was being attacked by two sharks and was trying to defend himself, but Gray couldn't get away to help the whitetip. If he stopped turning, he would lose his tail! Goblin narrowly avoided having his flank opened, then killed his attacker with a bite clean through its head.

Another bull streaked to join his shivermate behind Gray. Gray executed a violent downward power thrust to get out of the way, letting his second attacker accidentally ram his pursuer, who had almost closed to striking distance. In a moment they would turn and attack him from both sides at once and send Gray to the Sparkle Blue! There was no choice. Gray tore the flipper off the first bull, sending him spiraling to the bottom of the ocean, then charged the second bull. That attacker beat a hasty retreat now that it wasn't two against one, *and* Gray had the current flowing in his favor. Then, as fast as the battle had begun, it was over. The bulls were nowhere to be seen. All that remained was a red haze, already thinning. Soon it would be as if nothing happened at all.

Ripper bumped him from behind and Gray nearly jumped out of his skin. "Nice work, fin," the hammerhead grunted. "Goblin, you okay?" he called over Gray's flank. Goblin was facing away from them and didn't turn. Both went to where the great white hovered. Blood bloomed in the water around him. Gray got worried. With that much blood gushing from his body, the great white would swim the Sparkle Blue in minutes. But it wasn't Goblin who was bleeding.

It was Churn.

The whitetip had received two massive bites, one in the side and one in the back. "Did—did we win?" he asked.

"Yeah," Goblin told him with sadness in his eyes. "We won." And with that Churn's gills stopped moving and he sank to the seabed.

Gray wanted to throw up. "This is winning?" he asked in a shaky voice.

Goblin turned, but not in anger. "Yes, and it's not pretty. If the bulls have their way, we'll all be just like that." The great white pointed a fin at Churn's carcass. "*That's* what Takiza's mumbo jumbo gets you! A place right next to Churn."

Gray looked at the unmoving whitetip lying on the coral. Already, crabs and small fish were gathering to eat.

CHAPTER 22

BARKLEY WAITED IN THE THICK BLUE-GREENIE for his prey. He'll never know what hit him, he thought. He was careful to let the target swim past his hiding place before rushing out to attack.

"Gotcha!" Barkley yelled as he scraped Striiker's flank, but not hard enough to cause a gash.

As the great white groused, Mari, Snork, and Shell joined them from where they had been watching. "Your angle was all wrong! You should strike a fin or the tail if you've got a chance like that."

The dogfish's flippers drooped. "Oh. That *would* have been better."

Mari gave him a playful slap with her tail. "But your stalking was excellent! You were so far into the greenie that I didn't see you at all."

"Yeah," said Snork. "You're really good at sneaking."

"Thanks. I think," replied Barkley.

Shell shook his head. "How can you deal with all that greenie? Being inside the thick stuff gives me the willies. Like it's going to strangle me."

"If you go slow it slides right by," Barkley told the bull. "Just don't charge through it and you'll be fine." Barkley felt a little better now. He definitely wasn't the toughest fin around, but with Rogue Shiver's help, he felt a little more at ease in the open waters of the Big Blue.

They were practicing—Striiker refused to call it play-ing—for when trouble came. The great white was sure it was on the way and only a matter of time before it would show up. He didn't trust Goblin any further than he could drag him onto shore. Barkley hoped Striiker was wrong, but practicing was a wise precaution. Still it would take a long time, if ever, to change Barkley into a relentless, steely-eyed mariner.

It was just like old times after they got back to the landshark shipwreck. They were careful not to hunt anywhere near the patrolled areas of Goblin Shiver's territory. After the second close call, Barkley took it upon himself to monitor when and where the patrols went. Luckily, these were on a fairly regular schedule. Whoever was in charge of organizing the patrols, prob-ably Ripper or Thrash, wasn't devoting enough thought to the task. Velenka definitely wasn't in charge. What was she planning? Barkley didn't have a clue what she was up to, and it worried him.

One time he caught sight of Gray patrolling with

Thrash. Obviously Barkley didn't pop out from his hiding spot to say hello because the big tiger was there. But he wondered whether he would have come out even if Gray had been alone. This made him sad. They had been such close friends. And now? Barkley wasn't so sure.

Striiker was muttering and looking at him. "Barkley, you've got to get better at this. If we get into trouble, we're going to need everyone." The young great white was always so serious!

"Why don't you leave him alone?" said Snork, coming to Barkley's defense. He and Snork were now fast friends. Barkley liked Mari, of course. Everyone did. And Shell seemed okay, but distant. Even Striiker, though annoying sometimes with his short temper, was a good fin. But Snork seemed like the brother Barkley had never had.

Striiker was about to start a full-blown argument when Mari stepped in. "He's getting better every day. We all are! And we have you to thank for that."

"I just hope there are enough days to practice before we leave for the Sific," he answered. "It's a long trip and there are plenty of territories to swim through."

"Or we could *sneak* through them. And Barkley's great at that!" Snork said proudly. "He'll be leading us forward some of the time, you'll see."

Before Striiker could get angry, Shell interrupted. "All this practice made me hungry. How about we hunt?"

Striiker looked Barkley's way. "Patrols?" he asked.

Barkley shook his head. "We should be clear on the

Western side of the wreck. But like you always say, let's be careful."

"Finally," the young great white said, "some sense." Striiker never could let anyone have the last word. Barkley wondered if this was a great white thing, or if all shiver leaders were like this.

The group swam to the area past the Western reaches of Goblin Shiver's homewaters. There was usually good hunting there, and this day looked to be no different. Though there weren't any large clusters or droves, the fish were plenty.

Barkley's stomach rumbled. He was about to launch himself toward his prey when Mari whispered an urgent "Wait!" She motioned into the distance with her snout.

For a moment Barkley didn't see anything, but suddenly a shark materialized in the distance. And then another, and another, and more and more. It wasn't a patrol in force like Goblin Shiver was using lately. This was different. There were pups and older sharks. Some were trailing streams of blood.

"So many," whispered Snork fearfully.

"I don't recognize anyone," Shell said in a low voice.

Striiker agreed. "It's not Goblin Shiver."

"Then who are they?" asked Barkley.

No matter what Striiker thought they should do, he always looked to Mari before deciding anything important. This was one of the things that, to Barkley, counted very much in his favor as Rogue Shiver's leader. Striiker knew Mari was smart, and even though he was bigger and tougher than she was, the great white valued her opinion.

Striiker looked at Mari now, and she said, "I think we should talk with them."

Striiker nodded in agreement. "Let's swim in slowly so we don't scare them into attacking."

"And what if they *do* attack?" asked Snork, his eyes very wide.

"Swim away if you can, fight if you have to. And don't head straight for the wreck, circle wide." All of this was very good advice. Striiker had his moments.

Barkley followed as Striiker and Shell took the lead. Mari formed a second level above them, with Snork protecting the pair's topside. As they rose from the greenie and revealed themselves, the ragged group stopped and quickly formed a defensive position with the more mature sharks on the outside. Barkley saw that these sharks were wounded. All of them. The pups in the group wailed from underneath their mothers' bellies as Rogue Shiver slowed to a stop, barely a few tail strokes away. Barkley was horrified to see that some of the *pups* were also injured!

A scarred, old thresher swam out in front of the pack. "We're not here for trouble," he said. "Just passing through. We won't hunt in your territory."

"That's fine," Striiker replied. "Can you tell us what happened?"

The thresher spoke in low tones to a couple of other sharks. He definitely looked like their leader and was probably consulting with what was left of his Line. He faced Striiker and said, "We're called Jetty Shiver. Our homewaters are about a day away in the direction we came from, a nice little reef." The thresher stopped, overcome for a moment, but the fin was a mariner and kept his emotions under control. "We were attacked by sharkkind from Goblin Shiver. We had heard of them but didn't think they'd come so far East. They took some of us to be recruits and killed others who said they wouldn't go. We're what's left."

Barkley felt sick to his stomach. Goblin was an evil shark!

"We're sorry for your losses," Snork said. The sawfish was tearing up. Strangely, this seemed to dispel any tension between the two groups. Snork was the best.

"You're sure it was Goblin Shiver?" Shell asked. "Maybe it was bull sharks from Razor Shiver?"

A small hammerhead answered, "No bull sharks were there. The leader of the raiders was a big tiger. A mean blue shark was giving orders, too. They said they were Goblin Shiver. Was it someone else?"

"No," Striiker told them. "That's Goblin Shiver."

Barkley nodded to himself. The tiger was Thrash and Streak was the blue.

"If you swim another quarter day to the West, you should be able to hunt there for the rest of the sun,"

Barkley told the thresher. "But Goblin Shiver will send a patrol through there by moonrise."

The thresher nodded. "We thank you and hope to repay the kindness." Their group began to move again. They could only swim as fast as their slowest member, though, so it wasn't very fast.

Barkley's mind raced. Was Gray with Ripper when they did this? Could *he* have been a part of the attack on Jetty Shiver? Attacking pups? No! Barkley could see that Mari was asking herself the same questions. He needed to know! "Excuse me!" he yelled to the thresher, who turned. Barkley's voice caught in his throat as he asked, "Was there a big, young pup with them? Kinda like a reef shark, but not?"

The thresher shook his head. "Nothing like that." And then the group swam onward. No one spoke as the refugees receded into the Big Blue.

"At least it wasn't Gray," Barkley told Mari.

Striiker got furious! "'At least it wasn't Gray'? I got news for you, dogfish! He's a member of Goblin Shiver! He's probably okay with what happened!"

"Striiker, you're not being fair!" Mari protested.

"Maybe he was there and they didn't see him!" the great white continued. "Maybe he was busy gutting some-one's mother!"

Barkley had had enough. "Come on, Striiker! I don't know why you don't like Gray, but I can tell you he would not kill *anyone's* mother! Not possible!"

"You're right." Striiker calmed. "But are you absolutely sure he won't be part of the next raid on some poor shiver if Goblin orders it?" Striiker whirled and left everyone in his wake. Mari, Shell, and Snork slowly followed him toward the landshark wreck.

Barkley grew cold when he realized that deep down, he wasn't absolutely sure what Gray would actually do.

CHAPTER 23

GRAY WAS STUNNED. FOR A MOMENT HE couldn't speak at all. Velenka, Ripper, and Streak looked on from their favored positions above him and the other full members of the shiver not in the Line. Goblin wore an amused expression, hovering highest of all above the Speakers Rock.

"Snapper got your tongue, Gray?" the big great white joked. "You have to actually answer the call."

"Of course, I mean—yes!" Gray said loudly so everyone watching could hear. "I accept the position of fifth in the Line!"

Then there was whooping and hollering. Goblin came over and bumped him, then Ripper, and then Thrash. Gray lost track after that as *everyone* was bumping and finning him. It was all in good sport, though. Moments before Gray's appointment, Velenka had received the same treatment when she ascended to fourth in the Line.

174

Later Gray found out that in the old days sharkkind actually drew blood in this part of the ceremony by biting the newly ranked shark, becoming family in the tasting of their blood. But there were times that the celebration got out of hand, and the promoted shark died from his wounds, so the practice was wisely stopped.

Gray couldn't believe it when Goblin offered him fifth! He didn't have a clue that it was about to happen. Everyone was congratulating Velenka—he was right next to her—and Goblin said in a loud voice from his position above Speakers Rock, "I now name Gray as my fifth. Does any full member want to contest my decision and fight him in mortal combat for the right to his rank?" Gray didn't want to be in the Line if it meant fighting, especially when there were so many sharkkind who had been members for so much longer. He was about to open his mouth when Velenka stopped him.

"It's just old-timey language," she told him. "No one will go against Goblin's wishes, and he wants you!" And she was right. After a bumping and jostling melee, the great white made introductions to everyone Gray hadn't met, and even a few important dwellers in the homewaters. Then the party began.

The celebration lasted all night long. A trio of whales sang songs while a school of lantern fish swam around the shiver area, brightening the place with their colored lights. Very festive! It felt good to flick his tail back and relax after the previous few days. Gray was still shaken by Churn's death and the ferocity of the fight against the bulls. True, Gray hadn't known Churn that long, but he had been a shivermate, and they had gone patrolling together once. Even though they hadn't said two words to each other, in Gray's mind, it still counted for something.

The weird thing was that Gray found something enticing about the battle after it was over. He'd felt horrible *right* afterward, of course. He'd sent a bull to the Sparkle Blue and watched Churn die. There was no way that wouldn't jolt even the toughest shark to his core. Gray had been so shaken, in fact, that he'd actually thrown up on the way home. Oddly, this broke the pall hanging over the survivors, who'd swam in silence until that point. Goblin and Ripper laughed, along with everyone else, and confessed that they did the same thing after their first battles.

The remarkable thing was that after the immediate, horrible blackness of terror and death subsided, there was something else. After you battled for your life—and won—it was incredible! He felt the bond he had with both Ripper and Goblin *change*. The huge hammerhead had pretty much been a rude and icy fish to Gray before that day. But since he and Rip (the hammerhead said to call him Rip!) had fought flank to flank, they talked often, Rip even divulging little secrets now and then. Who knew Rip had sea horse friends? Not that Gray was going to tell anyone about that. And Goblin? Gray would go into the blackness of the Dark Blue for Goblin. They were brothers now. They had fought together and survived.

And then to hear that Thrash's patrol was attacked by another shiver that same day! Thankfully they didn't lose anyone to this Jetty Shiver. Apparently their leader was so crazy that a bunch of their shark-kind decided to leave him and join Goblin Shiver. That was good! There was strength in numbers, just like the great white said. They would need every shark they could muster if they were going to avenge the death these bulls were causing.

Velenka glided over, her shapely form moving through the crowd like a sea wraith. "I need a little clear water," she told him, scraping against his flank. "Would the new fifth like to take a swim with the new fourth?" Her big, black eyes bored into him.

The mako occasionally made Gray nervous and this was one of those times. She seemed so sure of herself. He took a quick glance over at Goblin who was furiously pushing against Ripper in a test of strength. Whoever was moved over a glowing line of coral underneath them would lose. It was all in good fun, though. Goblin would probably get the best of the hammerhead, but not for a while.

"Sure," Gray told her. They swam from the raucous crowd. But Velenka didn't appear to be going for an aimless swim.

"Where are we going?" he asked.

"I want to show you something. Something special." The mako smiled and flicked her tail for him to follow.

They headed into a cave mouth. It was dark inside. "In there?"

Velenka chuckled. "You're not afraid, are you?"

Gray flicked his tail. "Of course not. I just don't want to get stuck." The cave looked creepy as all flip, but he wasn't a pup to be scared of the dark and followed her.

"Don't worry," Velenka answered. "It opens up into a cavern after a bit."

As soon as they entered the cave mouth, a few body lengths in, it was absolutely black. Luckily, Gray had a keen sense of direction, even though he couldn't see a thing. The water got much colder as they angled down, down, down. After a long stretch Gray thought he saw a faint, white glow. Were his eyes playing tricks on him? No, something was definitely glowing, and it was getting brighter. After another turn, it got *really* bright. Gray slowed to let his eyes adjust.

"Come on," Velenka prodded. "Just a little farther!"

Gray emerged from the tunnel into an underground cavern. It was immense. There was even a surface to the water above him, meaning there was an air pocket. How strange! The walls above and below the surface glowed pale white like the moon. Now that Gray's eyes had adjusted, he could see it wasn't algae or lumos, but the rock itself that was glowing.

"So, is it worth it?" Velenka asked as she flicked her fin at—

"Tyro's tail!" Gray gasped. "*What* is that?"

There, at the wall of the cave, half covered by rock sediment, was a giant skeleton of a shark. You could tell it was sharkkind from its curved, dagger teeth. But it was the size of a whale!

"We call this the prehistore cave," Velenka began. "This is a megalodon. They were the rulers of the Big Blue when the oceans were young. Some think that Tyro was a megalodon."

"No way!"

"It's true," she told him. "Why? What type of shark did you think he was?"

"Hmm, guess I never pictured him as anything. He's the first fish, so he's kind of like all fish, I suppose." Gray learned about prehistore sharkkind in Miss Lamprey's class. It was one of the few times he paid attention, because it was so cool. But she only described how they looked. It was one thing to be told that sharks were the size of whales but quite another to see it in real life! One time they took a class trip to a rock tower, where Miss Lamprey showed them a rib bone of something she said was a prehistore sea dragon. Yappy got really annoyed when Barkley said he thought it was just a whale rib. That trip was a disappointment. But this! This was incredible!

"It's huge!" Gray exclaimed. "What a monster!" He drifted over to the skeleton's rib cage. Gray could fit inside the beast's stomach with room to spare. He swam around the megalodon and stopped in front of its awe-inspiring jaws, frozen open as if striking at some other giant fish. Its teeth were at least three times the size of his own. "Wow. This is great." Some of the meg's skeletal teeth shined reflectively because of a silvery mineral coating. It was so smooth Gray could see himself, a rare occurrence. The last time he got a good look at himself was a year ago when he was near the surface of the water and the sun was shining at just the right angle. Today, however, he wasn't pleased with what he saw. "Flip, I'm really fat!" he whispered to himself.

"What did you say?" Velenka asked.

"Nothing, nothing." Gray looked deeply into the reflective surface of the petrified teeth. He smiled and gnashed his teeth, making a scary face into the silvered surface. He was pretty fierce, indeed. Gray looked closer as something caught his attention. His teeth were smaller than those of the giant prehistore skeleton, but they were shaped *exactly* the same. Exactly.

How could he have the same teeth—it was then he realized the truth. A cold prickle danced down his spine, and he unconsciously whispered, "I'm not a reef shark at all."

He turned to find Velenka staring at him, the blackness of her eyes like two holes in the ocean. "I don't think so, either," she said.

"You knew?"

"I suspected."

Gray shook his head from side to side. "No, it's impossible. Even I know these things lived a really long time ago!" he told her. "They're all swimming the Sparkle Blue."

"Yes," the mako said nonchalantly. "Except you."

"You're yanking my tail, right?" asked Gray. "This is some sort of new fin in the Line joke, right?"

"No," Velenka said matter-of-factly.

"How?" was all he could think to say.

"That I don't know."

What did this mean? How would others react? "It can't be! It just can't!"

Velenka swam over, scraping against him. "It'll be all right."

"I'm a monster!" Gray yelled. "How's that going to be all right?"

"Accept it. You're a megalodon, or at least a cousin of one. I think it's fantastic."

Gray looked at the meg's teeth again, hoping to see some difference he could point out to Velenka. But they were the same, which practically guaranteed that nothing in Gray's life would be the same after today. He wanted to scuttle underneath a rock like a crab. "I'm here to help you through this," Velenka said as she slid her tail underneath his belly.

"Thanks," he told the mako. His mind whirled. Why would his mother keep this from him? Is this why she never spoke of his father? Did she know? Maybe she didn't. But if so, where did he come from? How could it be possible?

A nagging feeling whirled inside his stomach when Velenka smiled at Gray. It was probably the combination of such a huge, life changing discovery and this creepy cavern.

Probably. But in any case, Gray was now much more worried than when he first swam inside.

CHAPTER 24

THE MESSAGE WAS MYSTERIOUS AND THE lionfish rude. Barkley was hiding in the thick greenie, watching the Goblin Shiver homewaters. The patrol routes and patterns had changed, and he was determined to make sure he knew the schedules. Even Goblin wasn't so thick as to not make a few adjustments after his attack on Jetty Shiver. Probably afraid someone will come looking for him, thought Barkley just before the arrival of his strange messenger.

"Hey, dogfish," the lionfish said after swimming around him once. "Your name Barkley?"

On the whole, lionfish were impressive fish, and this one was no different, having neat, two-toned brown stripes separated by white ones. Its fins were almost featherlike (he knew about feathers from seeing landshark birds hunt in the ocean) and stuck out everywhere in a dazzling display. But lionfish were also deadly, having poisonous spines in those feathery fins.

Barkley backed from the fish slowly, ready to streak away. "Maybe. Who wants to know?"

"I do. That's why I asked."

"Why don't you introduce yourself first?" Barkley said. This was a mistake.

The lionfish's spikes went rigid. He fluttered them menacingly and said, "That's on a need-to-know basis. AND YOU DON'T NEED TO KNOW!" He went on in a quieter tone. "What *I* need to know is, are you or are you not Barkley? And since I asked first ... SPIT IT OUT!"

"Fine, yes, I'm Barkley."

"Good, because I was looking for you."

"Yeah, I figured as much."

The lionfish stretched his spiky fins menacingly before continuing. "I have a message for you from a shark, big fin who calls himself Gray." This definitely got Barkley's attention, and he swam closer to the lionfish.

"What did he say?"

"He wants to talk with you. And he wants you to ask everyone if he can come back."

"Gray said that?"

"Are you slow or something?" the lionfish asked. "I wouldn't say it IF HE DIDN'T TELL ME TO SAY IT! He says meet him by the half-moon rock North of the homewaters at high sun." The lionfish came closer to Barkley and whispered, "And he says to come alone."

And that was exactly how Barkley told the rest of Rogue Shiver.

"Never believe a lionfish," said Striiker. "Anything poisonous is a liar."

Snork nodded seriously. "I've heard that, too."

"Why would he lie?" asked Barkley. "Maybe Gray's in trouble."

"Goblin and the shiver will be leaving for the Tuna Run soon," commented Shell. "It would be a good time to sneak away. But why trust a lionfish with such an important message?"

Mari nodded and swished her tail in thought. "Did Gray use to talk with dwellers at your reef?"

"Yeah," Barkley told her. "Not a lot, but sometimes."

Striiker harrumphed. "If you ask me, I'd say he's been poisoned by Goblin first, and by the lionfish second. We can't trust him."

Barkley shook his head. Striiker had never been warm to Gray, but now it was even worse. Mari looked thoughtfully at the greenie swaying in the current. Barkley knew she was smart, so he asked her, "What do you think?"

"It's odd he told you to come alone," she said. "We should go with you in case it's a trap." Barkley didn't like not trusting Gray, but this seemed like a good precaution.

Striiker spun in a quick, angry circle. "Do not tell me you are actually thinking of going! It's too dangerous!"

"He was our friend," said Snork in a quiet voice, not wanting to anger Striiker.

"*Was* is the key word there!" yelled the great white. "I've never trusted him!"

Mari swished her tail in agitation. "And that's part of the problem! But if he's in trouble, shouldn't we help? Shouldn't we get him away from Goblin?"

Shell had been very undecided until this. Now he nodded to himself. "I'll go."

"Well, I won't!" shouted Striiker. "You guys go ahead and talk with that big, ungrateful flipper if you want! Not me!" And with that, he swam away.

Barkley and the others did go to the appointed place after the sun rose. He insisted on getting there early so they could pick a good spot to secretly survey the area. They saw nothing suspicious, so they went forward. The half-moon rock was so named because of its crescent-moon shape. The area surrounding the rock was flat, barren sand, with no greenie. And no place to hide.

Was Gray afraid that Striiker would attack him? Possibly, which didn't make Barkley feel any better about exposing himself and the rest of the group. But if there was a chance Gray was in trouble, Barkley owed it to his friend to show up.

The time of high sun came and went and shadows began to lengthen by the crescent-shaped rock. Barkley's spine tickled the way it did when he became anxious. He definitely didn't like being out in the open even though this area was beyond the patrol routes of Goblin Shiver.

"Maybe he's not coming," Mari said.

"Or couldn't get away without being seen?" added the sawfish in a whisper.

Both of those statements could be true. But waiting around any longer would be foolish. Barkley was about to say as much when he heard a voice come from behind the other side of the half-moon rock.

"What do we have here?"

Barkley grew cold. He knew that voice.

"A cluster of traitors!" said Thrash triumphantly as he glided from behind the wider edge of the rock formation. Streak and Ripper were with him.

It was a trap!

Streak's eyes blazed. "I hate traitors," the sleek blue shark growled. There was a meanness about her that Barkley had never liked. Ripper just grunted menacingly.

"Swim!" cried Mari. The group tried to dart away in different directions, but Shell bumped Snork, slowing them both down. Mari swam right into five more sharks from Goblin Shiver. Barkley turned in the direction they'd come from, but ten other sharkkind hemmed him in. Others were descending fast from above. There was nowhere to go!

Ripper barreled into Shell, knocking him senseless. Snork was so scared, he tried to burrow into the ground.

The shiver sharks all laughed as they rammed the sawfish.

"I'm going to enjoy this!" said Thrash, zooming toward Barkley.

Barkley didn't even feel the tiger's impact on his side. Suddenly he felt the water cool and sweet, and he was floating by the Coral Shiver reef.

"How did I get back *here*?" he wondered.

CHAPTER 25

GRAY FINISHED DOING DRILLS WITH HIS shivermates and was ravenously hungry again. Combat drills had been ramped up since their battle with the bull sharks, and everyone took their bumps and bruises willingly. Gray was bigger, faster, and stronger, but he was also becoming very good at fighting both alone and in tandem with others. Goblin supervised the drills while Thrash and Ripper led them. Gray could usually beat Thrash, but the massive hammerhead still gave him problems. Rip was smart when it came to fighting and owned a lifetime of battle scars to prove his experience. Because of the T-shape of his head, the hammerhead had no blind spots in his vision, so it was very hard to get after his tail or attack him from above.

Gray's ego wasn't getting too big, though. Streak fought with such ferocity that she beat him in a one-on-one battle. He thought that Thrash would laugh at him, losing to the much smaller shark, but Streak had earned the respect of everyone long ago. And the fact that she also beat Thrash the same day certainly helped.

Gray enjoyed the battle drills, which kept his mind off unwelcome thoughts and feelings. He now knew he wasn't a reef shark and was actively hiding that. Where did he come from? Did his mother know he wasn't a reef shark? If so, why hadn't she told him? Gray missed having Barkley and the rest of Rogue Shiver around. Sometimes he was angry that his friends had chosen to leave; other times ashamed he hadn't gone with them, and still other times he was happy he had stayed. And always there was the uncertainty and sadness about not knowing if his mother were alive. Those thoughts swam around inside his head and threatened to over-whelm him.

Gray was just leaving the homewaters when Velenka joined him. "You're getting very good," she said with a toothy smile. "Thrash was really annoyed."

Gray grinned back. He had beaten the big tiger badly today.

"Aside from getting my tail kicked by Streak, it was okay," he said. "Who knew there was so much more to fighting than ramming and biting?"

"Those are two very important parts, though." She chuckled and nudged him in the direction of a secluded area. It wasn't good territory for hunting, but he allowed the mako to lead him. Sometimes Velenka seemed like she genuinely cared about him. But other times it seemed like she was *studying* him. She thought it would be best to keep his secret about being a megalodon from everyone for now, which was actually a huge relief. Gray was still new to the shiver and getting his fins underneath him. He didn't need to be known as Gray the megalodon-monster freak while trying to earn the shiver's respect as their fifth in the Line.

"If you were a leader, what would you do?"

"Umm, I don't know." Gray was tired from the drills. And hungry. And Velenka was forcing him to answer questions when all he wanted was a nice, fat fish. "Help the shiver be the best shiver it can be?" There was a flash of irritation in the mako's eyes, but it was quickly replaced by a look of deep sadness. He couldn't help but ask, "What's the matter?"

"Have I ever told you how I joined the shiver?" She put an odd, distasteful emphasis on the word *joined*.

"No." Gray would have certainly remembered if she had. Now that he thought about it, Velenka never shared anything personal about her life with him.

"I was just a pup when Riptide Shiver came," she began. It seemed hard for her to go on, but she did. "Goblin's mother led, with him as first. It was one of their last long swims into the Sific, which is where I was born. They destroyed my home. They took me prisoner."

Gray tried to comfort her but couldn't think of anything to say. He hoped there was more to the story, but there wasn't. "I thought you liked Goblin. Liked the shiver," he sputtered. "How can you stand it?"

"That's what life in the Big Blue is about: choices," she said curtly. "I could choose to live or die."

"Why are you telling me this?"

Suddenly she was snout to snout with him. "Because you can change things!" she said with fervor in her eyes. "You could be the one to lead us into a new current, a new age!"

"Goblin is our leader!" Gray shot back without thinking. This felt all wrong! "You're his fourth! What are you talking about?"

The mako bumped him in the snout with steel in her eyes. "Under Goblin's leadership we've taken loss after loss! It's an endless cycle of death that won't stop until he's gone."

"Velenka, I lost my mother, my friends, and my home," Gray told her. "But you're not making sense. I'm not going to fight Goblin."

The mako sensed his agitation. Her eyes became calmer. She sighed. "Of course not," she told him. "Sending a leader to the Sparkle Blue to take his place would be wrong."

"That's more like it," Gray said. "Did you eat a bad fish or something?"

Velenka snapped her tail, slapping him in the belly hard. "No, I did not 'eat a bad fish'!" She calmed, again. "I'd like you to think about the future, Gray. Goblin will fight against Razor until one of them is dead. If he loses, can I count on you to step up and lead the shiver?"

"I don't know how to lead! Besides, Ripper is the first!"

The mako cut him off. "It's your destiny! Do you really want Ripper making decisions for everyone? He's strong, but stupid. I wouldn't put him in charge of a clam shell." Maybe she had a point. "Or Thrash? Or, Machiakelpi's fin, do you want to put Streak on the Speakers Rock?"

Gray nodded. Thrash would be worse than Ripper, much more unpredictable. And Streak seemed scared, somehow. Who knew what either would do if they were leader? "What about you, Velenka?" he asked. "You're the smartest fin I know. And you're tough!"

Now the mako smiled a smile that lit up the ocean around Gray. "Thanks for the compliment, but I like staying behind the scenes. A shiver leader needs to be imposing and strong. You're made for it!" Velenka scraped against his flank. "I suppose I could advise you, though." The light hit her black top half just so, and a rainbow rippled across her graceful form.

"Umm, *if* anything should happen to Goblin," Gray stammered. "If . . . " He looked around to make sure no one was hearing this very dangerous conversation. And no one was. Not even a single bottom-feeding dweller. It was odd. Absolutely nothing lived here. The entire area was a dead zone for some reason. They were in the perfect spot for the conversation to remain private.

Had Velenka planned this? Gray couldn't be sure, but it seemed possible. "But you'll be the first if I'm leading. That's unless Razor Shiver doesn't send me to the Sparkle Blue. Or Ripper, Thrash, or Streak. Or if something else doesn't kill me before that." Gray chuckled, bumping Velenka to join in his laughter, which she did eventually. "I'm hungry. Want to come along?"

The mako shook her head. "No, I have things to do." Velenka swam off. Gray sincerely hoped none of those things she had to do were related to this conversation. He wanted to make sure but found to his dismay she was already gone.

CHAPTER 26

IT WAS A PERFECT SUNNY MORNING IN THE WARM waters off the reef and there were fish everywhere! "What a great time to be a fin in the Big Blue!" Barkley exclaimed, the water whisking past his gills. Suddenly, there was Yappy, right in front of him. Oh, the little flipper was such a talker, but Barkley didn't even care! "Isn't it great to be alive?" he said to the sea dragon.

"Snap out of it, already!" Yappy yelled. Well, that was rude! And then the colorful sea dragon slapped Barkley in the face with his tail. And the slap was really hard! Much harder than Yappy's little tail should be able to deliver, anyway.

"Yappy, what are you doing?" he asked as the sea dragon began to fade away like a ghost. "Hey! Where are you going?" But the sea dragon was gone and the reef disappeared, too.

"Who the heck is Yappy?" Shell asked Snork as he

hovered nearby, a look of concern on his face. The bull slapped Barkley again with his tail.

"Okay, stop it," Mari told Shell. "He's awake."

"I think he deserves another couple whacks for getting us into this mess!"

Barkley wasn't at the reef at all. It all came rushing back to him. The ambush! The fight! And now they were—where?

"They put us in a cage!" said Snork before he could ask. Barkley looked around. It *was* a cage of sorts, made out of a whale skeleton attached to a coral reef. The ribs were the main bars, but razor-sharp coral grew between the large gaps, forming smaller ones. Even Yappy wouldn't have been able to wriggle through, although there was room for water to circulate so they could breath. No way the coral was accidental! It had been put there on purpose and then cemented in place to make the spaces between the whale ribs smaller. How would a shiver make a deal with crabs, mollusks, and whatever else, to do this? That was a question for another time. Right now they were prisoners.

"Is everyone okay?" Barkley asked.

"We've all got bumps and bruises, but nothing too bad," Mari answered. She hesitated for a moment, and then asked, "Do you think that Gray was a part of this?"

Barkley answered instinctively, "No."

Gray couldn't. He wouldn't!

Would he?

Mari saw the doubt on his face and got worried.

Snork trembled. "I'm scared." Barkley patted him on the flank but didn't say anything. He was scared, too.

"Okay, I'm getting us out of here!" Shell told everyone. The big bull furiously churned his tail back and forth to gain speed and rammed one of the smaller ribs of the cage. It did nothing except cause him to yelp "Oww!"

"Think you're going to bust your way out, eh?" came a voice from below. A lichen-covered rock separated from a wall to which the whale skeleton was anchored. But it wasn't a rock at all! It was some sort of fish that looked like a rock! It said, "Not likely. Not likely at all."

This scared the kelp out of Snork. "Talking rock! Talking rock!" he shouted, jamming himself behind everyone.

It was without a doubt the ugliest fish Barkley had ever seen in his young life. Did they live at the reef, too? If they had, he would never have noticed! The fish was dirty, with thin strands of moss and greenie waving from its mottled brownish hide. Its scales, if they could be called scales, were malformed; some bumpy, others wispy. It actually looked like something that swam the Sparkle Blue for a while and came back to life after not liking it. The entire group backed away from the fish, which was only as big as Shell's front flipper.

This was ridiculous. It was just a fish, after all.

Barkley swam forward and Shell shouted, "Watch it,

Barkley! That's a stonefish. It's the lionfish's uglier and even more poisonous cousin."

Stonefish? Well, the name was right on, Barkley mused.

The dweller took offense. "Who you calling ugly, krillface? I'll slice you good!"

"You're calling me krillface? I'll grind you up!" sputtered the bull.

"Just try it, bullhead!"

"No one is slicing or grinding anyone!" Mari said forcefully. "Let's all calm down." She introduced herself and the group, then asked the fish its name.

The stonefish used its stubby fins to flutter slowly in a circle. "Guess it don't matter much since we're all goners anyway. I'm Trank." He shook his head. "Youse fins got yourselves in way outta your depth, huh?" The stonefish spoke with a weird accent. "That Velenka's a piece o' work, eh?"

"What do you mean by that?" asked Barkley.

"Only Velenka and Goblin know about this cage," Trank told them. "And Goblin don't use the cage. Goblin eats youse if he's gotta problem with youse. He's a direct flipper, if youse know what I mean."

Even though the situation was dire, Barkley became a little happier. Gray didn't do it! It was the sneaky mako who was behind this. "Velenka! I knew it!" he said. "And how did you get in here?" Barkley asked Trank.

Trank hemmed and hawed. He didn't want to say

anything until Mari reminded him, "Like you said, it doesn't matter, right?"

The stonefish nodded. "I'm in here because I know too much," he said. "Gafin loaned me out on a job. I'm his best hitter, see?"

"What?" asked Barkley, not understanding.

Mari told him, "Trank's an assassin."

Barkley opened his mouth wide, but nothing came out. An assassin?

The stonefish laughed. "At least yer not all from the boonie-greenie. Anyway, she makes a deal with Gafin for me to do one thing, then changes her mind and wants me to take out the fifth in the Line, name of Hawley. Well, that's not how it works, and besides, Hawley was a good fin." Trank shook himself and a cloud of dirt fell away, floating down to the sand. "She put me here and got someone else to do the job instead."

Barkley's mind spun from the sheer deviousness of it. He had heard about the mysterious death of Hawley when he was in Goblin Shiver. Velenka got rid of Goblin's best friend and put herself in the Line to be his adviser! And now she was holding on to him and the rest of Rogue Shiver in case Gray didn't do whatever she wanted.

Trank continued, more to himself, "Gafin's gonna be one angry urchin if he ever finds out. Not that he'll get a chance, though. Once the Tuna Run's done, she'll kill him, too."

"What's happening at the Tuna Run?" Barkley asked.

"The Run is where *everything* is gonna go down! That's where she makes her move on both Goblin and Razor and takes everything for herself." Trank chuckled. "After that, youse, me, and every dweller she doesn't like is chum. Come to think of it, she and Gafin would make a nice couple, if youse know what I mean."

CHAPTER 27

GRAY GULPED DOWN THE LAST OF THE ALBACORE. He could have caught more but wasn't in the mood. This was one of the rare times he remembered not having an appetite. He swam farther out than normal to hunt, wanting to get away from the feverish preparations Goblin was making for the Tuna Run. They Tuna Rolled constantly, even in the dark of a moonless night, which made it much harder, but Gray was proud to catch more than his share.

After one game where he landed three wahoo in a single heat from the back half position, Wisko gave him such a joyous slap of celebration that he almost ate her in self-defense. Wahoo were strange fish. For some reason his conversations with Velenka and Takiza kept bumping around in his head, mixing together. Since the day Gray was banished from Coral Shiver, he'd felt adrift, cut off from family and home. What would he do with his life? What kind of shark would he become? That was the question that would be answered by his time in the open waters, in the wild Big Blue.

The current Velenka was asking him to swim seemed to be a dark one. There was something hidden in the mako's black eyes, and Gray couldn't figure out just what it was. But Velenka was a shivermate and the same couldn't be said of Takiza. Did Gray really owe the odd little betta anything? Takiza seemingly swam the Big Blue with no ties to anyone. No loyalty to any fin or dweller but himself. How could that be swimming a good current? Yet, the little fish fought a tiger shark to protect a family of turtles. Who else would do that? Gray grew hot with shame when he realized he wasn't sure he would have stopped Thrash. He'd tried to guide the situation, but there was no way he would have thrown away his relationship with a fellow shiver shark over a bunch of turtles.

"Did you do it?"

Gray turned around as the troubling thoughts thankfully slipped from his mind and Striiker slid into view around a patch of waving greenie.

For some reason Gray's heart leapt. It was Striiker! "Hi! Where's everyone else?" he asked.

"Like you don't know!" the great white seethed. "What did Goblin give you to betray us?"

Same old Striiker. Gray was in the mood to fight, but he realized it was his own thoughts and deeds that made him angry, not Striiker being his usual abrasive self. Gray wasn't going to compound the situation by doing something else to regret. He shook his head and swam away. "I don't have time for this. Say hi to everyone."

Luckily Gray didn't let Striiker out of his sight.

"Make time!" the great white yelled and charged straight at him!

Gray's training kicked in and he performed a half-circle dive, easily avoiding the rush. "Look, Striiker, I've got a lot of things on my mind! You don't want to make me angry!" If his goal was to calm the great white by saying this, Gray failed spectacularly.

"Oh, *I* don't want *you* to get angry, huh?" Striiker came after him even harder.

But Gray was bigger, faster, and better trained now. And he *did* want to fight. "Let's dance!" Gray had learned that the landsharks called single combat *dancing*, which was also a thing they did when they were happy and to attract mates. He liked the term, and Ripper and Streak, in particular, would always show their teeth in a wicked, toothy smile and say, "Let's dance," before single combat drills. It sent chills down your spine. Gray had started doing it too because he thought it was cool.

Gray rammed Striiker right in the gills with his snout. That'd teach him! Striiker slowed, wheezing, and hovered in a defensive position. "Why did you betray them?" he asked, gasping a bit. "They were your friends!"

"What are you talking about, jelly-brain?" Gray

shouted. "You came out of the greenie and attacked me for no reason! Where's everyone else? Where's Barkley? And Mari? Answer before I make you my lunch!" The last words leapt out of Gray's mouth before he realized it. He would *never* eat another shark.

Would he?

In any case, an uncomfortable silence descended. Striiker was definitely freaked out and seemed to grow less sure of himself. "They were ambushed coming to see you."

"WHAT?"

"A lionfish told Barkley that you wanted to come back to Rogue Shiver," Striiker said.

Gray shook his head in disbelief. "I don't know any lionfish! Are they okay?" The questions came out in a rush. Striiker told him the entire story. He even seemed a little ashamed that he hadn't gone with the group. He felt guilty that they had been ambushed, but not about not helping Gray. He went out of his way to make that clear. Same old Striiker.

Striiker told Gray about how he had searched for days and finally saw Streak going out from the homewaters alone. He followed the blue shark and found where the group was being held. "It's usually one from the Line and a couple of shiver sharks guarding the cage," he explained.

Gray was dazed. His shivermates were holding his friends captive. Could this be happening? "Maybe

Goblin doesn't know?" Gray asked.

"Oh, grow up!" Striiker yelled angrily, "Of course he knows!"

"But he gave his word!"

"His word means nothing! All he wants is power!" Striiker swished his tail furiously. "And he doesn't care who he has to hurt. Believe me. That's why Mari and I left in the first place."

"This can't be happening . . ." Gray whispered as his insides grew cold.

"I can't get them out of there alone," Striiker told him. The great white was absolutely pained by what he forced himself to say next: "Will you help me?"

"Of course!"

Striiker winced from his bruised gills but got in Gray's face. "But don't think this means we're best fins or anything. After we get them, we're going to the Sific. That's *my* plan. You do whatever you want. Like always."

Gray whirled and gave Striiker a tremendous tail slap to the face. Gray actually felt it all the way up his spine. "Keep running your mouth and see what happens, Striiker. And here's *my* plan: You show me where they are right now, or I'll beat the chowder out of you again."

The great white was shocked. Then slowly, he started swimming.

Though he didn't feel proud of it, Gray had finally gotten the last word with Striiker.

CHAPTER 28

GRAY PEERED THOUGH THE RED AND GOLD greenie as Striiker watched their tails. There they were! Barkley, Mari, Shell, and Snork! How could someone be so cruel as to jam them together like that? To lock them where they couldn't flex their fins properly? He grew angry. How could sharkkind treat other sharks this way? Or any dweller for that matter? This was wrong! Whatever loyalty he felt toward Goblin and his shiver was carried away by the current.

"The coast seems clear," Gray whispered, more to himself as he and Striiker hadn't exchanged a word during the swim over.

"Look again," Striiker replied, flicking a fin toward a rocky outcropping several lengths away from the cage. Sure enough, there was Thrash. He was talking with two more shiver sharks. Gray's emotions clashed. Thrash was a battle brother to Gray! How could he, of all fins, do this? And all the while the tiger had smiled and laughed with him when they were in the homewaters and on patrol. "We should go in hard and fast," Striiker said. "Scare them off."

Gray shook his head. "They may scatter at first, but they'll turn back in an attack formation." He couldn't see any way to get to the cage and free his friends without sending Thrash to the Sparkle Blue. And even now, Gray didn't want to do that. "Let me talk with him," he told Striiker.

"Look, I don't want to argue over who's leading who here, but are you out of your mind?"

"Maybe I am, but why don't you listen to me for a change?"

After Gray told Striiker what he was planning, the great white gave him a begrudging nod. "Nice plan," Striiker said as he went away, low, and in the greenie so as not to be seen. Gray waited for him to get into position and then simply swam into view.

To say Thrash was surprised was an understatement. "What the—Gray, hey, pal!" the tiger sputtered. "What are you doing here? I think Goblin needs you back at the homewaters."

Gray acted as surprised as he could. He didn't look at the cage, pretending not to see it. "I was chasing a lower drove of grouper but lost them. You see where they went?"

As Thrash was forming an answer, Striiker whizzed in from above and speared one of the two other shiver sharks in the side, sending it spinning to the sand. The other, a small mako, raced upward and out of sight.

Thrash knew he had been tricked and launched himself at Gray, who barely missed losing his left fin. He jammed Thrash as he passed flankside with his dorsal fin, raking the tiger. Both turned in counterpoint, but Gray was the quicker one. He could stun Thrash without killing him. Striiker was behind the tiger, blocking his escape angle.

Suddenly, Snork yelled from the cage, "Look out! Above you!"

Streaking back into the fight, the forgotten mako was now in perfect position to mortally wound Striiker. Gray gave up his attack on Thrash and used his speed to collide with the attacking shark, knocking it away just in time to save Striiker. Now Thrash turned. If it wasn't for Striiker slashing toward the fin to distract the attacking tiger, Gray would have been killed for sure.

With the great white now chasing Thrash's tail, Gray made a quick half loop to gather speed for the downward attack called Orca Bears Down and slammed into Thrash. Striiker was about to tear out Thrash's gills when Gray yelled, "Stop!" The great white crashed into the tiger but didn't bite him.

"You've made a big mistake!" shrieked Thrash, protecting his injured side. "Goblin will kill you all!"

"Like he wasn't planning to do that, anyway!" Striiker answered.

Gray shook his head sadly at the tiger. "Thrash, how could you do this?"

"NO! How could you betray us?" the tiger yelled. "I'm under orders! What's your excuse?"

"I'm not an evil shark, that's my excuse."

The other two shiver sharks got their fins under them and shakily joined Thrash. None was in any condition to fight, so they swam for the homewaters. "Tell Goblin I resign as his fifth," Gray said.

Thrash laughed as he left. "You can tell him yourself. Just before he guts you!"

Gray looked at Striiker, who gave him a bump on the flank with his fin. They had saved each other's lives in mortal combat. Like it or not, they were battle brothers now, and the great white knew it. Gray wanted to say something and so did Striiker, but neither could find the words. Then Barkley kind of ruined everything when he shouted, "Hey, I hate to interrupt your tender moment, but could you guys get us out of here?" Relieved from having to say anything, Gray and Striiker swam to the cage.

"I can't believe you just did that!" Mari exclaimed. "Goblin will explode like an underwater volcano!"

Shell looked at Striiker from inside the whalebone cage. "So do we like Gray again?"

Striiker told the group, "He didn't have anything to do with you guys being ambushed."

"Like I told youse," Trank said.

"Who's that?"

"That's Trank!" Snork explained.

That didn't really answer anything, but Gray was busy figuring out the locking device on the cage. It was cunningly made. You needed to disengage two bars that meshed perfectly together. Perhaps if Striiker or Gray had small fins they could have opened it by pressing down, but both were too big. And the area in front of the door had a pylon blocking the way. You couldn't take a swimming start to crash through it.

The great white figured the same thing and shook his head. "No way. Our fins are too big and those whale bones are too tough to ram through."

Gray got himself into a position hovering in front of the door. Striiker figured out what he thought Gray was about to do and said, "Did you hear me? You can't break those! Not enough room to speed up."

"I'm not going to ram it," Gray said. "I'm going to bite through."

"I'm pulling for you," Barkley said. "But are you sure that's a good idea?"

Gray got himself directly in front of the locking bars. "We'll see!" he said and then opened his mouth as wide as it would go. At first the petrified whalebone didn't give an inch. And for a heart-stopping second, he thought his jaws had locked in the painful position. Then his razor sharp teeth cut into the bars. With one last, loud, crunch! The door was ripped out.

After Gray spit the large bones out of his mouth, Striiker said, "Now *that* was impressive."

"It feels good to get some fresh water pumping through these gills!" said Barkley. He bumped Gray. "I knew you'd help us. I mean, I was pretty sure."

"Let's get swimming," Gray told the group. "Striiker said he knows the way to the Sific. That is, if you're okay with me coming along."

"Well, you're good in a fight, so that might be useful." And that was that. Gray was about to follow when he noticed the rest of the group wasn't moving.

Striiker got annoyed, of course. "You have to move your tails back and forth if you want to go forward," he sarcastically told them.

"We can't leave," Barkley said.

The great white sighed. "Why?" Striiker flexed his flippers as if he'd like nothing better than to ram Barkley.

"I'll let Trank tell you," the dogfish said. "Trank?" But the stonefish was nowhere to be seen. So Barkley and Mari explained everything they'd heard from him. When they were finished, there wasn't a doubt in anyone's mind where they were going.

Rogue Shiver was going to the Tuna Run.

CHAPTER 29

THE FINAL PREPARATIONS FOR THE TUNA RUN were being made when Velenka returned from her meeting with Kilo and his most trusted bull sharks. Goblin thought she went to make sure everything go as planned. Well, all would go as planned all right. Just not *his* plan, Velenka thought. *Mine.*

After sending Razor to the Sparkle Blue, Kilo and his followers would then turn on Goblin. Ripper and Thrash would be dealt with also. She had convinced Streak to join her, and the blue would help in the fight if needed. Kilo thought he would be Valenka's first, but he too was in for a surprise. A giant megalodon of a surprise! If she could just control Gray, and making him her first was her preferred way of doing this, she would be fine. But if Gray placed a fin out of line, he'd swim the Sparkle Blue with the others! Velenka would combine both Razor and Goblin shivers into a new, improved Riptide Shiver. She wouldn't be merely a shiver leader, but queen of the entire North Atlantis!

Velenka was so excited that she could hardly keep a toothy smile from stretching across her lips. Her plan was a thing of beauty. Machiakelpi himself would be proud! Unfortunately, she hadn't noticed when the bruised Thrash swam into the homewaters and began blubbering to Goblin until it was too late.

"WHAT?!" Goblin roared, which got Velenka's attention. She swam over as fast as possible. Ripper and Streak were already there. They were all in uproar but none more so than Goblin. "I'll eat them all!"

"What's going on?" she yelled, trying to get the furious great white to focus on her.

"I'll deal with them if it's the last thing I do!" Goblin shouted.

Velenka looked around for answers and noticed that Thrash looked battered as if from a recent fight. She went cold even before he spoke to her. "Gray jumped us. He freed the Rogue flippers."

"I told you we should have killed them!" Goblin yelled at her. "This was your idea!"

Of course it was her idea. Everything was her idea! But now Gray was a liability. Her plan could still work, but she'd have to deal with Kilo on her own. Velenka couldn't show weakness in front of Goblin, especially when everyone she would eventually rule over was watching. No one would follow a turtle.

Velenka steeled herself and looked Goblin right in the eyes. "This changes nothing!" she said. "Nothing!" She swam up close to—but not on—the Speakers Rock. "Everything you planned is finally in place! It would be nice to deal with those traitors, but if they run, which they most likely will, they're still gone for good."

Goblin calmed. "And if they show up at the Tuna Run looking for their families?"

"Or trouble?" added Thrash.

"Then you eat them," Velenka told the huge great white coldly. "But focus on what's important and get that done first. We're—I mean, *you're* so close!"

Goblin nodded, then yelled at the sharks who were watching and listening, "What are you looking at? Get ready to swim for the Tuna Run!" Activity started up immediately, no one wanting to arouse the shiver leader's temper by being anywhere near him. Goblin took out his temper on Thrash with a tremendous tail slap to the head. "And you! You're demoted to fifth! Ripper, Streak—come with me!" Streak gave Velenka a subtle nod and swam away with the others. But before they left, Goblin told her in a low, menacing tone, "When this is over, you and I will talk."

Velenka exhaled. She was in control of the situation. Everything was still moving forward with the current. Slowly, the warm excited feeling in her stomach returned.

"When this is over, you'll be dead," she whispered at the great white's receding figure.

TUNA
RUN

CHAPTER 30

GRAY WAS EXHAUSTED. THEY'D BEEN SWIMMING nonstop for days, eating only when they could do so while moving. Striiker led them toward the deepest of the Big Blue. With every tail stroke, Rogue Shiver moved closer to the middle of the North Atlantis and the Atlantis Spine, the undersea mountain range the bluefin followed for the Tuna Run. Gray and Barkley hoped it would lead them to their families and friends from the reef. But as important as finding their loved ones was, they knew that Velenka's plan must be stopped. If it wasn't, no one would be safe.

"You know," Barkley gasped through labored breaths, "It won't do any good if we go belly up before we get there!"

"It's just ahead!" Striiker shouted through the current. "Toughen up!"

Barkley grumbled but kept swimming. Gray sped up

so he could get a better look. He bumped into Striiker's tail when he saw the range.

Snork gave out a squeak and even Mari said, "Whoa." Everyone else was shocked into silence.

Gray had heard that in the landshark world there were huge mountains that stretched into the sky, much larger than any by the Caribbi reef where he was born. But they couldn't be larger than these! The immense, jagged mountain range rose from the Dark Blue as though it were the ocean's spine. Its depths were said to be deeper than any shark could swim and inhabited by monsters. Gray always thought those stories were something to scare pups, but seeing the blackness below, he shivered.

"So Striiker, you've been here," Mari began.

"Twice!" added Striiker.

The thresher rolled her eyes. "Right. So what happens? Tell us what to expect."

"The shivers take up positions either by the edge of the mountainside or away from it on the water side. I like the water side because you can be swept away if the tuna swerve too near to the rockside depending on if a legion or siege comes through. It's best to hunt from above or below the main body. If you get too deep inside the run you'll be battered. These dummies may be smaller than us, but get hit by a few hundred, and you'll swim the Sparkle Blue." Indeed, Gray could see most of the shivers that were already here set up to feed a good distance away from the jagged walls of the rockside. There were a good number of smaller shivers that couldn't get a good spot, though. Once again, Gray saw how it was an advantage to be the strongest shiver.

Barkley was becoming more nervous by the minute. "Good tip," he said as his voice cracked. "Don't get killed by our dinner."

Suddenly a swarming mass of bluefin swept through the area. Snork cried, "Look! We're missing it!"

"That's a shimmer at best," Striiker told the sawfish. Gray hid his embarrassment. He had almost launched himself toward the tuna but now saw the great white's count was accurate. "These are the shimmers and shoals that swim in front of the main Run. You can feed on them if you like, but most wait. It's tradition."

Barkley wasn't in favor of this. "Forget that," he said. "Let's feed now and stop Goblin's plan on a full stomach."

"You don't want to fight with a full stomach," Shell said. "Slows you down."

This made the dogfish sick with worry. "Oh, right," he answered in a quiet voice.

"If what you say is true, why's Razor Shiver on the rockside?" Mari asked.

"Because even though it is rockside, that particular spot is the best spot there is!" Striiker told the thresher and everyone else. "See how they're protected by the wall behind them?" Gray took note of the bulls in front of a jutting outcropping rearing from the mountainside. This formed an area where the current would be slower and they'd be protected as the tuna would undoubtedly swing wide to avoid running into the cliff wall. This way they could hunt the inner edge at their leisure. Tuna were dumb fish, but not even they were dumb enough to swim straight into the mountain.

"There's Goblin!" Shell said, pointing a fin. "Hmm, I was here last year with Razor, and they didn't set up there."

Striiker also looked perplexed. "Yeah, that's not their spot at all. They take the best water-side spot. That's not even a good spot. The current is really strong near the spine."

Gray couldn't figure out why Goblin would want to be on the rockside wall in front of the bulls. It seemed dangerous. Another shimmer, maybe even a double shimmer, roared through. A few sharks did catch a straggler or two, but not many.

Mari was trying to figure it out, too. "Striiker, what would happen if Razor and his shiver came out from that area protected by the wall?"

"They would never do that," he told her. "You'd take the brunt of the Run right in the face."

"But what if they were *pushed*?" she asked.

The bull shook its head at Mari. "Nah, it's very defensible," Shell said. "Razor's pretty smart. The shiver feeds in shifts, and there's always a group of sharks guarding their tails that would outnumber two to one anything Goblin could use to attack. If they tried anything from where they're set now, Goblin Shiver would get shoved into the Run because of the current and Razor Shiver."

Barkley swam in a quick circle. "Unless they were betrayed by bulls in their own shiver! That's it!" The dog-fish explained: "Kilo and his fins will join Goblin Shiver while Razor and his Line are feeding! What Goblin doesn't know is that he's on the menu, too!"

"Kilo!" Shell growled the name. "I never liked that flipper. Too bad the giant clam didn't snap his face just a little tighter. Left a nice mark, though."

"WHAT?" Gray yelled so loudly Shell started.

The bull was taken aback. "Umm, when Kilo was a pup, he almost got eaten by a giant clam. The thing clamped onto his face—what does this have to do with anything?"

"Did it leave a scar like a clam shell?" Barkley asked, almost as wound up as Gray.

"Yeah," the bull said. "It sure did."

It all came together in Gray's mind. Barkley knew too, but neither could speak they were so overcome by emotion.

Finally the dogfish looked at him and said, "Tyro's tail. She's evil." Gray couldn't have agreed more.

Mari told the rest of the group, "Kilo led the bulls who destroyed their reef."

"So it wasn't Razor who ordered that. It was Goblin

and Velenka, after they learned about Coral Shiver's reef from Thrash!" said Barkley bitterly.

Gray could feel himself trembling with fury. All this time Goblin had stoked Gray's rage against Razor Shiver, when he was the one who had caused everything!

Barkley was angry but controlled it. "Gray, we're not here for revenge—"

"Speak for yourself!"

The dogfish bumped Gray hard in the flank. "You're not an evil shark!"

"Oh, come on, Barkley," said an exasperated Striiker. "If anyone deserves to swim the Sparkle Blue, it's Goblin!"

"I'm afraid I agree," Mari added.

Barkley shook his snout side-to-side "No! All we'll do is get ourselves killed. How does that help anything?" This gave everyone pause.

"Whatever you decide, I'll help," Snork said in a squeaky voice. "Or, I'll try my best. But how can we beat them all?"

"We don't have to," Barkley told him. "We can hurt Goblin *and* Velenka. It'll be worse than sending them to the Sparkle Blue."

"And how do we do that?" asked Shell.

"By spoiling their plans," Barkley answered with a grim smile. "By spoiling their plans."

Just then, a long, soulful whale call pierced the water around them. Then another and another! A thin, dense stream of bluefin tuna spilled into view. It was the Tuna Run! The fish were blue on top with silvered bellies that caught the sun rays and caused a million flashes of light, resembling the landshark fireworks Gray and Barkley once saw near the reef. They were so fast! Maybe not as fast as the speedy, speedy wahoo, but the difference wasn't enough to bet your life on. Their torpedo-shaped bodies shot through the water as their crescent tails churned, moving them faster and faster as they mindlessly swam to who knew where. The tuna Gray had caught on hunting trips by the reef were half this size. These were open-ocean bluefin, twice as long as the wahoo, weighing four and five times as much!

The dogfish spoke for everyone when he said, "Wow."

"It's beginning," Striiker told everyone. "If we get caught in the middle when the main mass comes through we won't make it to the other side."

Even now the stream of fish was getting thicker and more dense. "Then let's go," Gray shouted. The noise of bluefin tails churning caused a constant buzz even from this distance.

So Rogue Shiver swam into the Tuna Run to do battle and meet their destiny.

CHAPTER 31

"PEEL AWAY WHEN YOU'RE OVER RAZOR SHIVER!" Striiker yelled. "Don't get turned around and definitely don't get pushed inward! If we do that we can surprise Goblin!"

"And Kilo," muttered Gray darkly as he increased the pace of his tail strokes. The shark who had destroyed Gray's home finally had a name. The current was fast and made even more deadly by the bluefin who tore through the water as if they had been ordered to do so. Many shivers whizzed by, arrayed in loose groups, now readying to feed. There were so many!

One particular group caught Gray's eye. They weren't creeping up to feed like the others. They hovered in a perfect formation of three precisely stacked rows. And they were all marked. *Tattooed*, if Gray remembered the word correctly. What were sharks from Indi Shiver doing here?

Gray's thoughts were interrupted by a panicked Snork shouting, "I think we need to go faster!" as he struggled to keep up. The sawfish wasn't built for speed, swimming and hunting near the seabed where his long nose was an asset. If they went any faster, they would lose him entirely. They'd need everyone before this was over, though. Gray turned to see what had him so spooked.

Oh, no!

The main body of the Tuna Run rushed toward them like an undersea tidal wave of fish! It was a siege. At least! Maybe a double siege!

"Must swim faster! Everyone must swim faster!" shouted Barkley as he pushed Snork from behind.

Gray quickened his pace and swam for his life. The rock face to his right faded into a blur with glowing patches of distorted light from lumo clusters whizzing by at a terrifying pace. But they still weren't fast enough! The siege engulfed them, and everyone was battered from side to side. If they hadn't been swimming with the current, they would have undoubtedly been swept away to the Sparkle Blue.

"Go straight! Don't turn!" he heard Mari shout. She was only a body length away from him, but Gray couldn't see her at all, so thick were the bluefin. Then Gray saw another tattooed shark. But it wasn't someone from Indi Shiver.

It was Onyx! Gray hadn't put two and two together until this moment, but those really cool markings on Onyx were *Indi Shiver tattoos*!

And next to Onyx was Gray's mother! "Mom!" he shouted. "MOM!" He peeled off from the group.

"Are you crazy?!" shouted Striiker.

Mari yelled, "Gray, what are you doing?"

He took a look to see if Barkley was following, but the dogfish wasn't there.

His mother saw Gray and flicked her tail in a motion that indicated for him to stay away. She shouted, "It's too dangerous!"

Gray kept himself flowing with the tuna but was getting thumped more and more, glancing blows that threatened to turn him over. "WHERE CAN I FIND YOU?" he shouted. His mom answered, but Gray couldn't hear. There were too many bluefin whizzing by. "WHERE?" he shouted again as he was driven farther away by the mass of fish. Finally, Gray couldn't hold out and was pushed away from his mother. "I WILL FIND YOU!" he shouted. "I WILL FIND YOU!"

Then Gray was past them in an instant. She might have heard him. Were there others from the reef? Was that Quickeyes next to her? Gray was so focused on his mother he didn't know. But she was alive! His mother was alive! There was no going back, no fighting the siege while in the thick of it. Now, even glancing backward might get him killed. Gray would find her later, but there were things that needed to be done first. Besides, he couldn't have stopped if he wanted to.

Gray covered the distance left between himself and Razor Shiver in an eel strike. It took all his strength to muscle his way from the grip of the current and the running siege. He hoped the others had done the same.

Earlier, Gray held visions of skidding to a stop on a clam shell in front of Goblin, revealing his evil plan, and looking good doing it. That wasn't going to happen. As he forced his way sideways toward the rock face, he was rammed in the flank by a massive bluefin. Boom! Boom! Boom! Gray was smashed by three more and flipped over. Soon four- and five-hundred-pound fish were buffeting him from every angle. It was like being caught in the turbulence of a tidal wave and forced through a maze of coral, but a hundred times worse. Somehow Gray was ejected from the mass. He hit the wall sideways above Razor Shiver. Shell was already there, shaking his head, dazed.

"You all right?" Gray yelled over the noise of the siege. Luckily both of them were only bruised. The bull waggled his fins, indicating he was okay. As Gray got his fins working again, he saw that Striiker and Mari were much farther away, too distant to join with them for a while. They'd have to fight their way against the current to where he and Shell were. Gray looked for Barkley and Snork, but there was no sign of either. If they were gone there would be time to grieve later. The coup was happening now!

Razor and his shiver sharks hunted the edge of the Run as it continued roaring past. But he didn't see Kilo and ten other bulls swim into an attack formation with Goblin, and twenty other sharkkind. Razor and his Line would be shoved into the Tuna Run and never seen again!

It was all happening so fast! Gray needed to do something right now! He pumped his tail ferociously, fighting the current, but couldn't reach Goblin in time to stop the attack. The great white bore down on Razor and the bull didn't see him.

Just then, by skill or crazy luck—probably crazy luck—Barkley shot out of the siege of bluefin. He was spinning with tremendous speed and hit Thrash, who then knocked into Goblin, Streak, and Ripper, sending them all plunging beyond Razor. Even though it was only a short distance, it was strategically huge because now they needed to fight the current to regain position.

But before Goblin could get back into position to attack, Razor saw him swimming with Kilo and other sharks from his shiver. He understood instantly, and shouted, "Traitors!"

Every bull with Razor—easily forty—charged the outnumbered Goblin Shiver and the disloyal bulls. It was chaos! Razor swam at the head of his phalanx of sharks in a tight formation. They let themselves be carried toward Goblin and his allies, who barely avoided being swept away. The two shivers met near the edge of the safe area by the rock wall with a crash loud enough to be heard over the roar of the bluefin—and now Gray and Shell were in the middle of the battle!

"You!" shouted Goblin when he saw Gray. Anger and hate shined in his eyes. The big great white would have gone straight for him if there weren't so many bulls streaking in every direction. Gray swam away from Goblin Shiver, avoiding raking attacks from Streak and another shiver shark, a thresher. Shell and Gray were then spotted by Razor. Razor thought they, too, were with Goblin!

Gray and Shell fought their way through Razor Shiver while staying in front of Goblin and his forces. They swam full-speed ahead, flank to flank, so tightly an urchin spine couldn't have fit between them. Everything was flashing teeth, blood, confusion, and above all, the thunderous din of the bluefin siege flashing by, a relentless, speeding, silvery mass. Gray didn't want to kill anyone, but he defended himself fiercely. He butted two attacking bulls off the safe area, and both were sucked into the Run as if jerked away by a giant octopus tentacle.

While Gray and Shell were handling anything coming snout to snout, swimming fast enough to keep Goblin Shiver from biting their tails, neither was defended from above.

That's exactly where Velenka and three others attacked from.

They streaked downward, and there was nothing Gray or Shell could do. If they stopped churning forward, Goblin Shiver would catch them. If they stopped defending from the bulls attacking head-on, they were also done.

"Get away from them!" came a shout.

It was Mari! And Striiker! They had fought the current and bluefin to make it back when it mattered most. Mari would have taken Velenka's dorsal if she hadn't peeled off her attack, which saved Gray. Striiker smashed into Shell's pursuer, biting him in the gills and forcing the dying shark into the current. All of the attackers were swept away by the Tuna Run. Now Gray, Shell, Striiker, and Mari were up current from both shivers, which were busy fighting with each other.

"What took you so long?" Gray shouted to Striiker and Mari over the noise of the swimming tuna.

"Just doing a little sightseeing," the great white replied with a grin.

Everyone was catching their breath when Snork made his appearance. He was scratched and bruised, but otherwise okay. "Sorry I'm late," he told everyone.

But where was Barkley?

The area cleared as the siege moved itself farther away from the rock face. Gray could now see the battle clearly. Both shivers lost many sharks, but Razor's fins still outnumbered Goblin's. Razor's first said something to him and the bull leader nodded. He yelled, "I'll deal with you all later!" Razor and his shiver caught the current and disappeared with the thinning bluefin.

They had done it! They'd stopped Goblin and Velenka's plan!

This triumphant feeling was short-lived as Gray saw their situation. The Tuna Run tapered to a thin flow of stragglers and older fish. The current also lessened, as it had been partly driven by the bluefin themselves, and there weren't so many now. Goblin and his forces formed a massive attack formation. There were at least twenty-five Goblin Shiver sharkkind in three levels along with the remaining bulls.

Velenka stared at Gray and the others hatefully. "Kill them, Goblin! Eat them alive!"

As if Goblin needed any goading. There was no way the five sharks of Rogue Shiver could win this fight. Shell and Striiker were too injured to swim away. Snork wasn't fast enough. And Gray wouldn't leave his friends behind.

Not now, or ever again.

At least Goblin and his shiver sharks were slowed by their own injuries. It wouldn't help for long, but it didn't allow Goblin and his force to charge right away. "What are you waiting for?" cried Velenka from a distance.

Goblin panted for a moment, but that was all the time his hate would allow him to rest. "ATTACK!" he cried and rushed Gray and his friends, intent on eating them all.

But Goblin Shiver was exhausted from the fight with Razor. Struggling against even the weakened current, they seemed as if they were swimming in slow motion. Gray got in front of Mari, while Striiker and Shell swam to either side of Gray to protect his flanks. It looked like Snork was running away, but instead he made a vertical half loop and took position hovering topside. Gray was so proud of his friends. But he suspected that their formation wouldn't last more than a few seconds after the battle began.

"I see you've found better fins to call friends!" said Takiza, hovering next to Gray's left eye.

"I guess so." If Gray had had any strength left at all, he would have been more surprised to see Takiza. But he was too tired to be surprised. The betta didn't seem to be affected by the currents whipsawing around them. His frilly fins waved gently as if he was in a much calmer ocean. "How have you been, otherwise?"

Gray was utterly worn out and sure he'd heard Takiza wrong. "You may want to leave now!" he yelled over the dull roar of the bluefin passing. "Goblin wants to eat us!"

"No. We have much to discuss," said the colorful betta. "I'd like you to become my apprentice! Do you agree?"

Gray blinked at the smiling betta. The frilly fish was mad! "Fine," Gray told him. "If we live through this, I'll be your apprentice."

"Excellent!"

The appearance of the betta caused Goblin to slow down. It seemed he feared the tiny, ruffled fish. "This has nothing to do with you, Takiza!" the great white growled.

"You have the manners of a lumpfish and the odor of sea kelp baking in the sun," the betta told him. "Go now or I will become annoyed!"

Striiker's eyes popped open. "Who's this, now?"

"Shh!" Shell hissed.

Mari agreed. "Yeah, I wanna see this."

Goblin didn't take it well, that's for sure. "You'll grow annoyed? You—*you*? Will . . . be . . . *annoyed*?!" he sputtered. "I'll show you annoy—"

That's as far as the great white got.

Takiza fluttered his frilly fins and did a slow barrel roll, and a whirling mass of glowing water grew in the middle of the Goblin Shiver, sucking them inside while it expanded. Velenka was so shocked that she just stared at the betta as she was pulled into it, not swimming against the force even a little.

Goblin did, though. And mightily.

It was impressive how the infuriated great white kept himself outside the whirling maelstrom for a while, even though his tail was caught. "This isn't over!" he shouted. Gray didn't know if he was talking to him or to Takiza, but was too tired to care. "This isn't over, I tell you!" Then Goblin was hauled into the roiling, shining, water ball.

The sharkkind inside were spinning at a tremendous speed. It wasn't hurting them, Gray saw, but they'd be dizzy for a week. With a flick of Takiza's tail, the ball moved into the current and was carried away into the distance. The betta snapped his frilly fins and the glowing ball disappeared. Goblin and everyone else tumbled away with the current.

Takiza passed Striiker, Mari, Shell, and Snork, giving them all polite nods. Nobody returned the greeting, mainly because they were so awed and dumbfounded. The siamese fighting fish stopped in front of Gray to say, "I'll tell you when your training is to begin. Until then, I bid you good day." And with that Takiza Jaelynn Betta vam Delacrest Waveland ka Boom Boom swam away, humming a sprightly tune.

"Seriously, who is that?" asked Snork.

Just then, Barkley appeared. Gray's heart leapt when he saw his friend. The dogfish had a giant lump on his head and was swimming at an angle.

"What happened?" he asked. "Did I miss anything?"

Everyone hooted with laughter. Barkley looked at them, perplexed. "What?" he asked, which made everyone laugh even harder.

CHAPTER 32

BECAUSE OF HIS SIZE, GRAY COULD NO LONGER use the crack in the hull of the tri-level landshark wreck to get inside, so his friends widened a back entrance that was rotting away.

"Don't take this question as an insult," Barkley said after they were inside, "but how much more do you think you're going to grow?"

"And less fatty fish taste almost as good as the, umm, fatty ones," Mari added.

"Not really," Shell said.

"Yeah, about that," Gray began. "I don't know how much bigger I'll get, because I'm not a reef shark."

"What do you mean?" asked Striiker. "You said you were."

"Because that's what I thought. I'm actually . . . I might be . . . wow, this sounds crazy—"

Barkley slapped him on the flank with his tail. "Spit it out!"

"I'm a megalodon."

There was silence. They all just stared at him. "Velenka took me into the prehistore cave, where there was this skeleton. . . . My teeth matched . . . and, uh, I actually kinda look like it."

"That's so cool!" said Snork. "I thought all megalodons were extinct, though."

"They are extinct!" said Striiker. "But I've been to that cave, and I gotta say there is a resemblance. Gray is definitely as ugly as that thing." The great white gave him a good-natured smile. "Maybe even uglier!"

Mari swam close, looking into his mouth. "Open," she instructed, and he did. Pretty soon everyone was crowding around for a better look. "Wider!" Now Gray couldn't close his mouth because Mari's snout was actually in there.

"His teeth do match. They're smaller, but they're the same curved shape," the thresher told everyone. "I love the prehistore cave. I've been in there twenty times."

"By the way, you have a bluefin head stuck in your back row," Snork told him.

"Even if him being a megalodon is true," Shell began, "how *can* it be true?"

"Umm, hahh-loww?" Gray said as best he could while the others held a conversation practically *inside* of his mouth. "Could ya pluhs back awahhhh?" They did, and he closed his mouth. "Private space, anyone?"

Barkley was the only one who hadn't said anything. Gray could see the look on his face. He got that expression when he was thinking hard about something. Then the dogfish nodded to himself and broke his silence. "This makes sense. It really does."

"Please, enlighten us," Striiker said sarcastically.

"Velenka knew it. Knew it right away, somehow," Barkley explained. "She wanted Gray all along. She pulled the strings to get Goblin to find the reef, to make sure we were homeless, everything."

"So Velenka's smart," the sawfish said, "but in a really bad way."

"That's exactly right, Snork. And Gray," the dogfish said evenly, "I don't think she's done with you."

"Neither is Goblin," Striiker added quietly.

"Then I'll leave. It'll be safer for all of you."

"No, Gray," Mari said. "Striiker means Goblin isn't done with any of us. Neither is Razor, for that matter." Gray looked over at the great white, and he nodded, agreeing with the thresher.

"Another one of your jelly-brained ideas," Barkley said with a chuckle. "But we have a better plan."

Striiker moved to the front of the pack. "You should lead us."

"No," Gray said. "This is your shiver. I couldn't."

"You can and you will. What you did at the Tuna Run

showed me how much I have to learn about being a real leader."

Gray looked at Barkley, Mari, Shell, and Snork. They were all in on it. Gray was touched. He'd told them he was a megalodon and they didn't think he was a monster. They still wanted him as their friend. And they trusted him to lead them.

"Would you be my first?" Gray asked the great white. Striiker grinned.

"Can you two fight or yell at each other now?" Barkley asked. "I liked it better when you were fighting." This brought out a round of good-natured laughter—something they all needed.

Rogue Shiver was reborn! There were many problems, to be sure, but for some reason Gray felt hopeful.

"Group rub!" Snork shouted. Soon they were all yelling, laughing, and scraping against each other. It was a great ending to an absolutely terrifying day. But not perfect. On the way back from the Tuna Run, Barkley and Gray had talked. Neither had seen any sign of his mother or anyone else from Coral Shiver.

Or Indi Shiver, which also bothered Gray for some nagging reason. And what was Onyx's connection to a shiver from another ocean? That was a question to be answered later. For now they could take comfort in the fact that Coral Shiver was alive. They were out there somewhere. Gray would never stop searching until he found them. Barkley and the rest of his new friends would help. All in all, it was the best Gray could hope for right now. Tomorrow was another day to find the answers he was looking for. And his mom.

No one noticed Takiza smile and swim away from the greenie-covered porthole.

EPILOGUE

VELENKA STILL COULDN'T BELIEVE WHAT HAD happened. The little betta had tossed the combined might of Goblin Shiver aside with no effort at all. She'd heard stories when she was a pup about the magical fighting fish but had never believed them. All her carefully laid plans had been swept aside by his frilly fins! How could she harness Takiza's power for her own desires? How indeed?

"We will find them," Goblin growled while hovering over Speakers Rock. "We'll defeat all our enemies!" The ceremony to make Kilo his third was over. Velenka thought that elevating the bull into the Line wasn't a good idea, especially after Kilo's efforts brought nothing. But Velenka couldn't talk Goblin into anything right now. As it was, Streak wasn't pleased by being passed over by a traitor, and Ripper didn't like the ex-Razor Shiver bull, either.

At least she was able to soothe Thrash's bruised ego. She stepped aside, rather than fighting him for fourth in the Line. Not that she thought she could beat him in a fair fight, anyway. Goblin wasn't happy. He was in the mood for blood. The great white would be even less pleased if he found out that Velenka had *told* Thrash to challenge her, and that she wouldn't stand in his way.

"They won't leave the Atlantis. I can feel it. And when we find them, there will be blood!" Goblin roared to the approval of the gathered shiver sharks.

But whose? Velenka thought silently as she nodded and gnashed her teeth in support. Was tiny Rogue Shiver under the protection of Takiza? And even if it wasn't, Gray was a megalodon. That was a definite problem. He needed to be converted to her cause or killed before he got too powerful. She would have to think carefully about her next move.

"Who will swim by my flank and send the traitors to the Sparkle Blue?" yelled Goblin to the shiver. Everyone answered with a rousing roar.

Velenka made sure she cheered the loudest.

For Mom and Dad

EJ ALTBACKER

THE
Battle OF
Riptide

RAZORBILL

RAZORBILL

An Imprint of Penguin Random House LLC
Penguin.com

RAZORBILL & colophon is a registered trademark
of Penguin Random House LLC.

First published in the United States of America by Razorbill,
an imprint of Penguin Random House LLC, 2011

LIBRARY OF CONGRESS CATALOGING-IN-PUBLICATION DATA IS AVAILABLE

Razorbill ISBN 9781595143778
This omnibus edition ISBN 9781984836212

Printed in the United States of America

1 3 5 7 9 10 8 6 4 2

This is a work of fiction. Names, characters, places, and incidents either
are the product of the author's imagination or are used fictitiously, and any
resemblance to actual persons, living or dead, businesses, companies, events,
or locales is entirely coincidental.

THE GATHERING STORM

CHAPTER 1

IT FELT LIKE A STORM WAS COMING. THE CURRENT had gotten colder and faster in the last hour, the way it did in the Big Blue when a squall gathered in the skies above the chop-chop. With all the silt and sand churned from the seabed, it was difficult to see or smell anything from a distance. Gray crept along the side of a massive clump of brain coral and surveyed the area as the others hovered behind him.

"I don't see anything," he said in a low voice, nervously gnashing his dagger teeth.

"I told Snork not to go patrolling by himself," hissed Barkley. The dogfish had been Gray's best friend since he was a pup and had become a trusted voice in Rogue Shiver.

The other members of the Rogue Line present—Striiker, the great white; Mari, the thresher; and Shell, the bull shark—waited uncertainly. Everyone was worried about Snork, who had gone missing. It wasn't like the sawfish to leave without telling the rest of the group. No one had seen him for hours.

Fish and other dwellers had cleared the area as the storm neared, leaving it eerily empty. The only sound was the cold water whisking through the foreboding canyons of rock.

"Maybe he just got lost!" Striiker said, a little too loudly.

Mari cut her long thresher tail through the water to quiet him. "Keep your voice down."

"Yeah," Shell added, watching the water above them. "Goblin may not run many patrols through here, but Razor does."

They were in an area off to the side of both the Goblin and Razor Shivers' homewaters. The hunting wasn't especially inviting in these sharp and craggy rock formations, not when there were much better feeding territories in each shiver's own homewaters. Mainly, Goblin and Razor both claimed the territory so the other wouldn't have it.

Since the Tuna Run though, the two warring shivers did share one goal: to *eat* Gray and every member of Rogue Shiver alive. Goblin wanted revenge on them for spoiling his plans against Razor. Fortunately, Goblin didn't have time to search for Gray or anyone else because Razor, the leader of Razor Shiver, was thirsting for Goblin's blood. Razor barely escaped with his life when he was attacked at the Tuna Run. Now the bull shark leader struck at Goblin Shiver every chance he got. But given that both Goblin and Razor wanted Gray and the rest of Rogue Shiver dead, it made swimming here foolish . . . and awfully dangerous.

"Why would Snork even come here?" Gray muttered to himself.

Barkley fidgeted. "I *may* have said it was a good area to practice stalking."

"You and your big mouth," Striiker said.

The great white and Barkley didn't get along well but pulled together when it was important. Gray didn't want to listen to them argue back and forth for five minutes before agreeing *this* was important. He bumped the dog-fish to stop his snotty reply before it happened.

"Here's what we're going to do," Gray told everyone. He was the leader of Rogue Shiver, so it was up to him to decide the course of action. "Striiker and Mari go to the left side and start searching inward. Shell and Barkley, you go to the right side and do the same. I'll head to the middle and hunt outward in a circle pattern."

"What if there's trouble?" demanded Striiker. "What's the plan then?" The great white was first in the Rogue Line, so it was his right to ask. Most of the time, Striiker was a good first: strong and dependable. But he could wear your teeth down with his attitude.

"Signal everyone, then swim and hide. Fight only if you have no other option," Gray answered.

"Let's not waste any more time with dumb questions," Mari said, swimming off to the left.

Striiker grumbled but followed. Mari was Gray's second in Line: smart, capable, and levelheaded. Barkley gave Gray a nod before leaving with Shell, who was third in Line.

The Five in the Line was an ancient sharkkind invention. Basically, whoever was chosen to lead a shiver of sharks would pick five others to take over if he or she was injured or killed. It was dangerous in the open waters of the Big Blue. Even a fifth could become leader overnight to hundreds of sharkkind in a shiver's general membership. Rogue Shiver was unusual in that there were only six of them total, Gray as leader and the Five in the Line. They were a bunch of castoffs and castaways, which was why they had named themselves Rogue Shiver.

Gray caught a descending current into a field of ropy green-greenie so he could swim somewhat unseen toward the center area of the maze of rock and coral formations. While the green-greenie would easily hide Barkley, Snork, or even a thresher like Mari, the disturbance Gray made plowing through the field negated most of the stealth benefit. If someone from Razor or Goblin Shiver were looking, Gray knew he would definitely be noticed. Since Tuna Run, he had grown even more, becoming longer and wider than Goblin himself, the former biggest fin around.

"Because you're a freak," whispered a voice inside Gray's head.

He shook his snout, clearing away the negative thought. In a way, Gray was an oddity: the only megalodon swimming the Big Blue in a million years. The members of Rogue Shiver knew he was a meg but still swam with him, flank to flank. Everyone said it made him *special*. Gray chuckled to himself. He used to dream about being the baddest shark in the ocean. Now, when he thought about being *so* different from everyone else, it sent a chill down his spine.

Today Gray would give *anything* to be just another shark in the Big Blue. But he wasn't and never would be.

Gray moved from coral spire to spire. Being in front of a tower of light green coral didn't seem especially smart, so he swam behind a dark blue one. That was more his color. "Should have been called Blue," he muttered as he began searching the area in the middle of the other two teams.

Nothing stirred except the greenie, bent at an angle by the increasing current. There must be one heck of a storm above, Gray thought.

But otherwise it was quiet. Too quiet.

Gray strained to hear anything out of the ordinary and was rewarded when he detected the muted thrashing of a larger fin nearby. Gray swam in low and fast before gliding to a stop.

It was Snork! The sawfish was trapped underneath a fallen piece of coral, caught by his long serrated nose, which he used to dig for shellheads and other smaller dwellers. "Snork, are you all right?"

"I can't get my bill free!"

"Don't worry," Gray told the frightened sawfish. "I'll have you out in a fin flick!"

"LOOK OUT!" cried Striiker as he hurtled out of nowhere and speared a streaking bull shark in the flank, butting it away from biting Gray.

Razor Shiver!

Barkley took on another bull as Shell rammed a third. It was a melee!

Gray was about to accelerate into an attacking sprint when Shell shouted, "Free Snork! We'll hold them off!"

"Mari, cover my topside!" Gray yelled. The thresher did so, and it was a good thing. She deflected an attack at his dorsal fin with some help from Striiker, who was all flashing teeth and spitting anger.

"Come on, you flippers!" the great white shouted. "Who wants a piece of me?"

Gray got into position to move the large chunk of coral that was pinning Snork. He churned against it with all his might. The coral moved, but not enough for the sawfish to get free. Instead, he yelped in pain.

"Sorry, Snork!"

"It's okay," the sawfish replied, crying a little. "Just get me out of here!"

Gray heard Mari's tail strokes suddenly falter above him. "You've got to hurry!" she told him.

"I am!"

"I mean it!" she urged. "I see twenty more bulls coming!"

Twenty more! Gray and his friends would be torn to pieces!

"Fins up! We've got to move, move, move!" bellowed Striiker as the three attacking bulls were finally scattered. He, too, had seen the other bull sharks coming.

Gray did a lightning quick circle and sped into an attacking sprint. This is going to hurt, he thought, just before ramming the coral that was trapping Snork. Gray could taste his own blood, but the coral snapped into three smaller pieces.

Snork swam off the seabed as Barkley motioned with a fin. "This way!" No one knew the area better than the dogfish, so Gray signaled for everyone to follow.

The group darted into a crack in the ocean floor, probably caused by a seaquake years ago. It was wide enough to swim in, but not by much. Thankfully, it was sufficiently deep that the Razor Shiver sharks couldn't see them for a crucial few seconds.

Everything blurred as they sped through the tight turns inside the crevice, zigging and zagging in silence while putting distance between themselves and the dangerous bulls. After a few minutes, they were in the clear.

"Wow, they don't get much closer than that," commented Shell when they were safely away from the area.

Striiker flicked his fins in annoyance. "We shouldn't

have even been in that situation! Snork, if you do something that chowderheaded again, I'll bite you myself!"

The sawfish dipped his long nose. "I'm sorry. I just wanted to help you spy on Goblin and Razor's patrols."

"It's okay, Snork," Gray said. "But next time, go with Barkley. He's an excellent teacher. And very sneaky."

"I'll help, too," added Mari with a toothy smile. "But let's hope that's the last we see of Goblin or Razor Shivers."

The gang headed into the hidden greenie path leading to the landshark wreck they used as their home and hideout. Gray paused before he joined his friends inside. Night had fallen, and the storm overhead arrived with a vengeance. Gray could feel the vibrations of thunder above the chop-chop. He could see bursts of bright lightning, which caused his skin to tingle each time it struck the water. It was the fiercest type of storm; one they called a flashnboomer.

Gray hoped that Mari was right. He hoped that he and his friends wouldn't see either Goblin or Razor ever again. But Gray couldn't shake the feeling that, like the storm above, the one in their watery world was just getting started.

CHAPTER 2

TAKIZA JAELYNN BETTA VAM DELACREST Waveland ka Boom Boom shook his fins from side to side to get some feeling back into them. With his powers, in his youth, he could circle the entire world in a little over a moon, or a month, as the humans called it. But that was many, many years ago. Now, even a fraction of that effort was a chore. Yet when he received word of what had happened from a quickfin messenger, he knew he must come.

Quickfin was the exclusive news and messaging service for the Big Blue. It was usually reserved for communications and diplomacy between the ancient shivers. Because Takiza shared a long and colorful history with many of these great shivers, he was one of those who received word of the major happenings in the seas.

And make no mistake, the destruction of a royal shiver like AuzyAuzy was a major event.

Takiza had decided to begin training his new apprentice, an interesting young sharkkind named Gray. He was a mere pup, large and inexperienced, only now coming into focus. It would take much effort to mold him into a fin of worth. Sometimes Takiza wondered why he even bothered attempting to pass on his knowledge of shar-kata. Apprentices were forever whining and exclaiming things like, "That's not possible!" or "You want me to do *what*?" and even "But that could kill me!"

So immature.

Using shar-kata, Takiza was able to harness the power in the tides and currents to swim at a rate others might call magical. It wasn't, of course. Mastery of the upper levels of shar-kata bestowed these gifts on the few who could master the supreme effort and concentration required. Thankfully, Takiza hadn't lost his abilities just yet, despite his age. He swam down the Atlantis and crossed the canal the humans dug as a shortcut to the Sific Ocean. Humans had a few good ideas—the canal between oceans being one of them. After braving the foul-tasting waters behind a massive ship, Takiza caught a swift current that took him into the South Sific, past the Australia landmass, and into Oceania where the AuzyAuzy homewaters were.

Were. But not anymore.

The light green-greenie swayed in the slow, warm current as the surviving dwellers drifted in a fearful daze. Unspeakable evil had been done here. From what Takiza could gather, AuzyAuzy had been destroyed by Indi Shiver, another ancient and royal power, originating from the Indi Ocean. King Lochlan I, leader of AuzyAuzy, now swam the Sparkle Blue, having been killed in the attack. What had possessed these two regal shivers to fight like the brawling gangs that now inhabited the Atlantis? Takiza needed answers.

Not wanting to cause a commotion, he decided to speak with the king's son alone. Slipping by the guards and into the cave was easy for him. "Greetings, Prince Lochlan boola Naka Fiji," said Takiza.

To his credit the prince—now the new king—did not start, though Takiza had swum up to him unannounced and undetected. This frightened most sharkkind, who thought their senses fine-tuned.

"Takiza?" The massive great white turned so they could speak face-to-face. Lochlan II projected both grace and power. He was the perfect representation of his kind and the spitting image of his father as a young shark, complete with the telltale golden hue that marked him as AuzyAuzy royalty.

"Your manners are impeccable, young one. But tell me, how are you?"

"Been better." The words hung there. Lochlan's stunning gold skintone sparkled, even in the dim light. The coloring was unique to his great white family and gave the shiver its nickname, the Golden Rush. "You know

Father is dead? The homewaters smashed? Of course, you know. You know everything."

"Not everything," Takiza replied.

Lochlan launched into the story without emotion. "Finnivus came with his floating court. I should have noticed there were too many. We went to hunt off the edge of our homewaters, and they turned on us. Their entire armada was waiting. There were just too many."

Takiza pretended not to notice the tears leaking from Lochlan's eyes. It wasn't his intention to shame the fin. "It is your right to grieve, Lochlan."

"NO!" the golden great white roared. A sleek whitetip reef shark poked her head through the greenie curtain that Takiza had snuck through, and he yelled, "I'm all right! Privacy, please!"

She darted away and Lochlan went on in a lower voice. "Finnivus and Indi Shiver have to pay! I can get in touch with my feelings later."

"Blood for blood only serves to foul the water," Takiza said. "Your father knew that."

So this was Finnivus's doing. The tiger shark King Finnivus was vain and cruel. That Lochlan had bested him in every contest and hunt the few times they had met when they were pups was a sore point with the Indi tiger. Takiza had hoped Finnivus would grow out of such stupidity and become a good leader. The cold feeling in the pit of his stomach told him this hope was now dead.

Lochlan ground his triangular teeth. "Will you help us? We attack tomorrow."

Takiza winced inside as he saw a sizable gash on the golden great white's side, most likely from the battle. It had been expertly stitched by a doctor and surgeon fish from Lochlan's shiver.

"Absolutely not," Takiza answered with a shake of his gauzy fins. Lochlan stiffened until Takiza added, "But only because you will lose if you act so soon."

"Then we go down fighting. That's the way Father would have—"

Takiza slashed his fins in front of Lochlan's left eye so the great white would be sure to see. "Do not put words in your father's mouth he would *not* actually say! Your father would want you to protect your shivermates, not lead them to their deaths!"

Lochlan quieted and after a moment asked, "What would you have me do?"

"Leave the Sific."

"WHAT?" Lochlan yelled so loudly that the whitetip reef shark poked her head inside once more.

"Is everything—"

"Kendra! Please!" exclaimed Lochlan, and she left quickly. "My first," he told Takiza, which was explanation enough. The new king sighed. "Okay, swim that by me again."

"I would like you to leave this ocean for now. You are the rightful king of the Sific and cannot throw your life away."

Lochlan churned his tail from side to side in agitation. "Do *not* call me that! My father was the king."

"As you wish," Takiza told him.

"I won't swim away from my problems, Takiza. I won't. Finnivus ate my father after the attack. Thank Tyro Mum wasn't alive to see that. You ask too much."

Finnivus *ate* Lochlan I! Takiza's mind reeled. It was something out of the barbarian age. He struggled to hold his own emotions in check. "I am not asking you to swim *away* from your problems. I am asking you to swim *toward* an opportunity. Leave your forces behind and come with a select few."

"Will this opportunity involve a chance to take a fin from that vain and evil fish Finnivus?"

Takiza sighed. "Unfortunately, yes. I believe so."

With that, Lochlan nodded grimly. He swam out of the cave and began giving orders.

CHAPTER 3

"YOUR PRIVATE CAVE IS READY," SAID THE LIONFISH, one of the hosts for Slaggernacks. Even for a lionfish, she was stunning with her vibrant purple-and-blue stripes. But underneath those colorful fins were razor-sharp spines that could inject poison into an unsuspecting victim. "Do you have something for me?" she asked.

Gray was carrying a bonefish he had caught earlier, and now he ejected it from his mouth. This one was barely two feet long, but bonefish were highly prized and could be seasoned well, which is what they did at Slaggernacks. The place could earn up to six or even eight fish from someone who had a craving for bonefish but was too slow to catch one. That was how Slaggernacks made a profit and kept themselves fed.

"Very nice," said the hostess as she looked over the bonefish. "There's a swell band playing tonight if you're staying around."

"Why don't you show us to our cave?" asked Mari pointedly.

The hostess sniffed but did as requested. After the lionfish left them at the cave entrance, Mari grumbled, "I really hate this place." She swished her long thresher's tail in annoyance and caught Gray watching. "What?" she asked.

Gray completely lost his current of thought. "Um, other than searching the entire Big Blue, there's no better place to find information about Coral Shiver, and that's why we're here." His mother, Sandy, was the third in Line for Coral, so she would be with the shiver. Or someone from the shiver would know if . . . Gray shook the thought from his mind.

When he had last seen his mother, she was alive and well, and there was no reason to think otherwise. Gray missed her terribly. Frustratingly, neither Barkley nor he had seen a single sign of anyone from Coral Shiver since their epic fight with Goblin Shiver at the Tuna Run.

As if reading his mind, Mari said, "If Goblin, Razor, or someone from their shivers, sees us . . ." she trailed off, not needing to say anything else.

Their miraculous escape from Goblin and Razor Shivers at the Tuna Run was now the stuff of legends in the North Atlantis. Of course, that would be the case when the mythic Siamese fighting fish Takiza showed up and caused some sort of glowing whirlpool disturbance to suck up Goblin and his shiver, tossing them away like minnows in a strong current.

"That's why we're using the back area of Slaggernacks," Gray told her. "So we won't be seen."

There were several private caves set apart from the greenie-covered main area. That area was more of a *restaurant*—that was a landshark word—with plenty of areas to hover and eat seasoned fish. When Gray had first tried seasoned fish, he'd hated it, but now he enjoyed it more and more. And there was entertainment from various dweller singing groups. The best ones featured whales and dolphins, although there was a sea horse chorus called *Sea Horsing Around* that Gray liked very much. Gray wondered again how Gafin had thought up the idea for creating Slaggernacks.

Gafin was the king of the sea urchins and used Slaggernacks as his home base of operations for his tidal pool of murky dealings. It was hard to picture entire shivers of sharkkind listening to a sea urchin, but Gafin controlled thousands of poisonous dwellers. The toxic gang included stonefish, octos, lionfish, jellies, and many others who could send even the biggest fin to the Sparkle Blue. After all, you couldn't be on guard every second of every day.

Although no one ever actually saw Gafin, both Razor and Goblin Shivers respected the truce he demanded from anyone who swam in his territory.

This particular back cave had a crisp and cold current

that made it easy to breathe. The secluded greenie-hidden back caves were guarded by poisonous dwellers who protected the safety of those inside and guaranteed their privacy. Supposedly.

"Oww!" Gray muttered under his breath. He had hit his head on the roof of the entrance to the cave. Barkley would have told him his head was getting fatter for sure. Would he ever stop growing? Mari pretended not to notice his embarrassment. Gray liked that about her.

"The dwellers here can't be trusted," Mari said. "What if someone tells Goblin we're here? Or Velenka?"

Gray's mind involuntarily pictured the beautiful and sinister mako shark.

Velenka...

She was Goblin's fifth, guiding his fins as if she were swimming for him. She was the one who had told Gray he was a megalodon. She wanted Gray to rule as a figurehead after getting rid of Goblin and Razor. In fact, Goblin still didn't know that Velenka had planned to betray him right after she had dealt with Razor. Gray was certain he would have been the next to swim the Sparkle Blue after those two.

"Youse wouldn't be meanin' me, would youse?" A random rock in the cave floated off the fine-grained sandy bottom. It wasn't a rock, of course. It was a stonefish named Trank. Mari involuntarily recoiled and moved back. The urge to get away from the poisonous fish was strong in the enclosed cave, even for a shark.

Trank worked for Gafin, but would never point him out. "Gafin likes to keep a low profile," was the greenie-covered fish's standard answer.

"Of course not, Trank," Mari answered. "You're the most trustworthy stonefish I know."

"Well, thanks—hey, wait a second, how many stonefish do youse know?"

Gray waved a fin at the stonefish. "That's not important."

"It is to me!" huffed Trank. "Us stonefish are very loyal. We stick by our deals, unlike youse sharkkind." The stonefish gave them a knowing look. Velenka had double-crossed Trank and put him in prison with Barkley, Mari, Shell, and Snork. That was how they'd met in the first place.

"Unbelievable!" Mari said, swishing her tail back and forth. "Well, I'm not sticking up for Velenka, so you have me there."

"There you go," Gray told the stonefish. "She admits you're more trustworthy than Velenka."

"That's *not* what I meant," grumbled Mari.

"No take backs!" Trank shouted and whirled his fins in a way to signal the end of this particular current in the conversation. Mari wanted to continue her argument with the cantankerous fish, but Gray gave her a pleading look and she quieted.

"What have you found out?"

Now Trank seemed embarrassed. Mari leapt into the silence. "Nothing! Again."

The stonefish's small fins circled furiously but then drooped. "You're right. And when you're right, you're right. And you're right."

"Coral Shiver was at the Tuna Run," Gray told the stonefish, his voice rising a little as he slapped the rough wall of the cavern with his tail. "How can no one know anything about an entire shiver?"

"The shiver youse came from was small, and the Big Blue's mighty big—hence the qualifying first part of its name, which is *big*."

"Now's not the time for joking," Mari scolded.

"Who's joking?" Trank replied. "Gafin takes a contract seriously. We're tracking down leads but comin' up empty. I actually think that's a good thing."

"How would that be a good thing?" asked Gray, a bit annoyed. He had been dropping off a steady stream of fish at Slaggernacks for payment and was tired from hunting around the clock to both feed himself and pay the huge number of fish that Gafin demanded in exchange for his help finding Coral Shiver.

"If we can't find 'em, neither can anyone else," Trank told Gray. "They're smart enough to keep their snouts in the greenie while Razor and Goblin fight it out."

Gray flicked his pectoral fins in frustration. The stonefish did have a point, but it didn't make him feel any better.

Trank chewed on a piece of greenie hanging off his upper lip. He really did look like a sandy stone come to life. "Look, Gafin told me to tell youse he's sorry and youse can ease up on the fish for a while. We'll keep looking, free of charge."

"Really?" Mari asked in wonder.

"Youse don't have to say it that way," Trank replied. "Makes us look bad not being able to find a shiver from the boonie-greenie. Why, just yesterday, I swam twenty miles to personally track down a lead I knew was a bunch of chowder, but I went anyway. I mean, whoever heard of a sea dragon named Yappy who never stops talkin' and brags about giant cousins who live down in the Dark Blue?"

CHAPTER 4

IT WAS A WARM NIGHT WITH GENTLE TIDES AS Gray waited for Barkley to get back. His friend was patrolling again, keeping a sharp eye on both Goblin and Razor Shivers. The exhausted and hungry dogfish finally returned to Rogue's three-level landshark wreck after the moon rose, its glow casting the swaying greenie field around the wreck in an eerie half-light.

Shell, the bull shark, was nice enough to catch an extra, very fat tunny and save it for Barkley. "This is delicious," the dogfish said between ravenous bites. "I don't know how I missed every fish in the ocean on my way back, but I saw nothing but a couple of wrasse." Wrasse were colorful and smart fish—not like the dumb fish Gray and Barkley were taught to hunt when they were growing up in the Caribbi Sea. Gray had heard wrasse weren't very tasty, anyway.

The rest of the Line in Rogue Shiver—Mari, Striiker,

and Snork, in addition to Shell—also hovered in the lichen-covered lower level of the ancient sunken ship. "Yeah, you being such a great hunter, it's practically impossible for you *not* to catch a fish whenever you want," Striiker said, bumping Barkley with his pointy great white snout. In the old days there would have been a sting to his words, but now Striiker gave Barkley a good-natured toothy grin.

"Aww, that's not nice," said Snork, waving his long serrated bill with a frown.

"I was only kidding," Striiker explained. "Did everyone get that I was kidding?"

"I got it, I got it," said Barkley. "Good one. I know I'm not the best hunter, but this was different. Never seen anything like it. It was like something chased every fish in the Atlantis away." The dogfish turned to Striiker with a grin. "But we know that since you weren't there, the fish didn't run away from your ugly krillface, so it must have been something else!" Barkley gave the great white a confident tail slap.

Gray marveled at the change in his friend since they first swam into the Big Blue as scared pups. Barkley had followed him out of loyalty and friendship after Gray had been banished from Coral Shiver. They'd gone through some tough times. At one point, they were so angry with each other they didn't speak at all. But even when they were fighting, Barkley could always be counted on.

One of the small things Gray appreciated was that Barkley had insisted on being fifth in his Line. After their victory over Goblin at the Tuna Run, Rogue Shiver had made Gray their leader. He'd appointed Striiker as his first but wanted Barkley to be second. "A tiny dogfish as your second?" Barkley had said sarcastically. "Are you out of your jelly-brained mind? Do you want to get Rogue Shiver laughed out of the Big Blue?"

Gray grinned at the memory as he tapped his tail against the side of the landshark boat, making an impatient thumping noise. Mari shook her head. "Why don't you just tell him?"

"He's eating," Gray said. "Don't want to interrupt."

"Tell me what?" asked the dogfish, his mouth full.

"Trank gave me some interesting information—"

"Awww, Gray. Not the stonefish again." Barkley gnashed his teeth as if he had tasted a bitter mackerel. He didn't like anyone from Slaggernacks, but especially not Trank.

"Wait, listen," Gray told him. "Trank said he heard about a sea dragon who tells wild stories about his huge cousins in the Dark Blue."

"Yappy!" exclaimed Barkley.

"Do *you* think there might be more than one Yappy?" Gray asked.

Barkley shook his head. "No way. Who would have thought his nonstop talking would actually work in our favor?" He flicked his fins up and down in excitement. "So, go on. Where are they? Is everyone okay?"

"Well, that was kind of it," Gray replied.

"What do you mean, 'kind of it'?" asked Shell. "Didn't that muck-sucking stonefish actually *find* this sea dragon for you?"

Striiker joined in. "Seems like with all the fish you've been bringing to Slaggernacks, they might actually do some work." The great white churned his tail so hard it caused loose greenie to fly everywhere. He didn't like Trank much, either.

"Trank did try and find him," Mari told everyone. She swished her shapely thresher tail in a figure eight, signaling everyone to calm themselves. "But Yappy wasn't there. Neither was anyone else from Coral Shiver."

"So they've moved on," Striiker said, nodding to himself. "Smart."

"Could be," Gray answered the great white. "Or maybe not!" He flexed his tail, full of nervous energy.

Barkley looked at him. "Why are you so happy?"

"Because Coral Shiver was always good at hiding."

"You think they're still around?" Barkley got a little more excited when Gray smiled. "You think they're still around! Somewhere between here and our old reef! Of course! Close enough where it feels like home, but far enough to get lost!"

"So?" asked Shell. "So what? Does anyone else get this?"

"The thing you don't understand is that *nothing* can stop Yappy from talking," Gray said as Barkley nodded in agreement. "If they were just moving from place to place like drifters, we would've picked up their trail."

"How do you know they didn't just leave the area entirely?" Shell asked. The big bull shark rubbed his rough hide on one of the broken beams of the land-shark ship, clouding the water with a mist of tiny wood particles.

Striiker sneezed and glared. "How many times have I told you not to do that?"

"But my flank itches!"

Gray slapped the great white with his tail, stopping the argument before it began. "Coral Shiver wouldn't have gone off to the Sific or someplace on the other side of the Big Blue."

"How do you know that?" asked Striiker. "We were ready to go to the Sific to hide from Goblin."

Mari swirled her long tail as she did when thinking intently. "But we didn't. Once sharks find a place that feels like homewaters, we do like to stay there."

"That's true!" said Snork. "I don't want to leave here because I like it!"

"Look, I know you think you're good at sneaking around—" Striiker began, but Barkley cut him off.

"I *am* good at sneaking around," the dogfish said. "But I know what you're worried about. We'd have to skirt the edge of Goblin's patrols and go through part of

Razor Shiver's territory. But it's not like I haven't done it before, you know, like just before I got back tonight."

"But you weren't leading Gray," Shell commented. This did quiet Barkley as it was true. It was also the main reason why Gray didn't go searching for his mother and Coral Shiver in the open waters with his friend. Gray was too large not to be noticed on a long swim. But this time he wouldn't stay behind.

"I'm not sticking my snout in the sand and going turtle while you swim into danger," Gray said, smacking his tail against the hull of the landshark boat with a BOOM! "I'm coming with you and that's that."

Barkley gave Gray a little snout bump and asked, "So when do we leave, big fin?"

The answer turned out to be immediately. Gray wanted to wait until Barkley got some rest, but the dogfish wouldn't hear of it. The journey from the North Atlantis to the edge of the Caribbi Sea took nearly two days. Not because it was that far, but because Barkley insisted he lead the way and swam so *slooowly* it was unbelievable. He knew the patrol routes of Goblin Shiver by heart. That was the easy part. It was after that, when they got to Razor Shiver territory, where things really slowed down. The dogfish took Gray through thick green-greenie and tight lava canyons whenever he could.

"Sharkkind hate swimming through areas like this," Barkley whispered while heading into yet another field of thick-beyond-belief blue-greenie.

"Add me to the list because I hate it, too," Gray answered quietly. It was awful. This type of greenie felt like it would catch in his gills or wrap around his tail and send him to the Sparkle Blue. There were stories of haunted greenie that would reach out and snare you if you weren't careful. If a shark couldn't swim, he couldn't breathe. This wasn't that type of greenie, though. It was, however, a kind that tickled Gray's snout unmercifully.

The dogfish seemed to have no trouble whatsoever moving through it, which made Gray simultaneously proud of his friend and annoyed with himself. But he was four times Barkley's size, and that probably had something to do with his own lack of stealth.

"Move a little slower," Barkley suggested. "You're ... causing the greenie to sway, umm, more noticeably than the tide moves it naturally."

"Just say I'm fat," Gray told him, whispering a little louder.

"Hey, I didn't—"

"I can tell you're thinking it!" Gray shot back.

Barkley motioned at him with a fin. "Maybe you're *supposed* to be fat!"

Gray was caught by surprise. Could that be true? Was he supposed to be fat? Barkley knew he was a mega-lodon, though neither talked about it for fear of someone, even a dweller, overhearing. He shook his head at Barkley. "Nope. I'm just big cartilaged. And you better not share your theory on my fatness with Striiker or anyone else from Rogue, or I'll—"

"*Shhh!*" Barkley hissed, making a chopping motion with his fin.

Gray immediately quieted and strained to listen. He heard the tide moving the greenie all around him, a few shellbacks scuttling in the sand below, and smaller fish swimming by. Nothing large was in the immediate vicinity of Gray's sharp senses. And thankfully, there weren't the telltale chopping tail strokes of a bull from Razor Shiver speeding up to attack.

But farther away…there was something. Gray could smell the drifting scent of a group of sharkkind. It was too distant to identify what type of sharks, but there was a large gathering somewhere. Gray's nose tingled as he focused on the scents in the water; fear, anger, and excitement. It was like a growing storm. Barkley sensed the same and began picking a path leading away from whatever was going on. Gray stopped him. "Maybe it's Coral Shiver."

"Much more likely it's Razor Shiver." That was true. They were near Razor's homewaters. If there were more than ten sharks in one place, they would probably be shiver sharks.

"Barkley, we have to see. For my mom—and your cousins. We have to be sure they're not in danger."

The dogfish nodded and led them slowly through the greenie and toward a low rock formation where they would be able to see upward while remaining hidden themselves. Gray followed, letting Barkley find their way. The dogfish really was very good at stalking around unseen.

Gray copied the way Barkley moved, alternately shimmying or drifting depending on the current. He found that by doing this he caused less disturbance in the greenie and moved more silently. He was about to compliment Barkley when suddenly the dogfish's tail jerked as if he'd been shocked by an eel. "Back, back, back," his friend whispered urgently.

Gray lowered himself onto the seabed, trying to become a part of it. "What did you see?"

"Razor Shiver."

"How many?" asked Gray.

"All of them, I think."

Gray's heart thudded in his chest as he looked upward, the sun shining dimly into the ocean from its place high above the chop-chop. There they were! Razor Shiver! He could see their outlines clearly. At least a hundred bull sharks. More, even! They were arranged in loose rows, hovering at the ready.

"What are they doing?" Barkley whispered.

"That's a battle formation," Gray told him quietly. "But the better question is, 'Who are those sharks they're about to fight?'" Gray pointed a fin across the waters to more than four hundred sharkkind lined up against Razor Shiver.

"*Whoa*," Barkley breathed in a raspy whisper.

CHAPTER 5

"PLEASE DON'T LET MY MOM AND CORAL SHIVER be a part of this!" Gray thought as his stomach heaved. The sharkkind facing Razor Shiver weren't just a shiver—they were a *battle* shiver! Goblin had told Gray those didn't even exist anymore. The strange mariners had markings on their flanks that didn't look natural. They were tattoos! That meant these sharkkind were Indi Shiver!

What were they doing so far from their home-waters? Here they were, perfectly ordered and facing off with Razor Shiver. They hovered motionlessly in the strong current as Razor and his shiver sharks struggled to maintain their own formation. Thankfully, Gray saw no one from Coral Shiver. His concentration was so complete he didn't hear Barkley until his friend brushed against him.

"Sink and hide!" the dogfish whispered urgently.

It was then Gray noticed *another* group of sharkkind. These were in no hurry at all and glided on the lazy current. This wasn't a battle formation as these hundred or so sharks were definitely not ready for a fight.

They were here to *watch*.

Gray took a moment to figure out that these sharks were a royal court, like the ones he'd heard stories about in Miss Lamprey's class in school. While the sharks in the Indi battle shiver all had the same tattoo—a series of never-ending black waves running down each flank—these sharkkind's markings were different and much more intricate.

The young tiger shark leader was the most decorated of all. His tattoos were thin lines forming whirls and swirls, like stormy ocean waters. These covered the white of his belly and the underside of his fins along with most of his flanks. Gray thought the marks looked kind of ugly, even though they were colorful. The sleek tiger shark had a wild look in his eyes and lounged on top of a blue whale, which acted as kind of a mobile throne. Gray looked around and saw there were actually multiple whales, each with a Speakers Rock somehow pressed in its back. When one whale needed to swim to the surface to breathe, another smoothly slipped in, so the royal fish didn't have to flick a fin. Usually a Speakers Rock would be located in a shiver's homewaters, so it was odd. Did Indi Shiver think they had a right to all the water in the Big Blue?

The current flowed just so, and Gray could hear the tiger shark leader perfectly as he giggled a high-pitched titter. "I'll bet my new herald gets eaten! Anyone want to wager the seasoned head of their first in the Line he gets eaten?" Gray's stomach involuntarily clenched in horror. Was the wild-eyed leader joking?

"What do you think, Tydal?" the royal asked, showing off the tattooed underside of his fins.

A brightly colored brown-and-yellow epaulette shark answered. "King Finnivus, this lowly court shark would never presume to know!"

So the leader was a king and his name was Finnivus. Gray wasn't impressed. He would have been far more interested to meet Tydal, the epaulette shark, because his bright brown-and-yellow markings were fascinating.

"Watch this! Watch what happens!" yelled King Finnivus, his tail swishing with a weird, stuttering excitement. The herald was saying something to Razor. After a moment, Razor's eyes widened in surprise, then anger. He roared and took the herald's dorsal fin with one clean bite.

Finnivus cackled from the back of the blue whale. "Looks like I'm going to need a new herald! Again!"

"Yes, Your Magnificence!" answered Tydal, the court shark. "I'll see to it at once!"

"Mariner Prime, have my armada attack!" Finnivus told a battle-scarred tiger shark, who was hovering by an odd device containing lantern fish. The lantern fish inside were kept perfectly still by a metallic grate holding them gently in place. If Gray had to guess, this device was something made by landsharks. The lantern fish flashed a series of colored patterns. Once they were done flashing, the entire armada attacked. Gray marveled. Indi Shiver was using the lantern fish as a signaling device!

There was loud yelling by the bulls of Razor Shiver. Gray recognized this for what it was: fear. The attackers didn't waste valuable energy yelling, and this made their silent, whooshing charge all the more terrifying. Next to the discipline of Indi's battle shiver, Razor's mariners were about as dangerous as a drove of tuna. And their fates would be similar.

The attackers charged toward the already disorganized resistance. Gray could see that most of the younger sharks in Razor Shiver weren't holding their place in formation—some even bolted the opposite way, swimming into their shivermates and causing confusion.

Gray looked over at Indi Shiver's commander, who was signaling to the armada with the lantern fish device. His five-layer formation broke off into three columns that twisted and turned like sea snakes. The first column was made of heavy sharkkind to batter the enemy: great whites, tigers, and, of course, hammerheads. They swam in snout to snout, mauling the defenders.

The second-battle fin was organized for endurance; threshers and bull sharks would feint an attack, but then draw back. Being the best swimmers, they wouldn't tire easily. When they did attack, it was usually from behind as they possessed the strength to swim around the entire battle waters and still make a concentrated strike. The third-battle fin included the fastest sharkkind: blues, spinners, and makos. When they joined the battle, they widened the cracks in the Razor Shiver's defensive formation caused by the other two battle fins.

After only a few fin flicks, there was blood everywhere. Razor Shiver's formation was compacted into a tight ball, useless for either defense or offense. It was a slaughter. Then two Indi Shiver sharks—a blue shark and a mako—struck at Razor himself, one mauling his dorsal, the other taking his right fin.

Razor was finished!

Gray couldn't believe it. All this time, Goblin could never beat Razor, and now Razor was swimming the Sparkle Blue just like that! His large shiver, one that Gray and all of Rogue Shiver constantly feared being discovered by, had been destroyed in less time than it took to eat a bluefin tuna!

The armada ceased its attack and circled what was left of the terrified Razor Shiver. "Whalem, destroy them to the last!" King Finnivus yelled.

"My king, their leader is dead," the mariner prime said. "These remaining bulls could become valuable additions to your armada with proper training."

"They are a disorganized mess!" Finnivus screeched. "Kill them all!"

"King Finnivus, your father would offer mercy."

For a moment, it seemed as if even the noise of the injured and terrified bulls from Razor Shiver subsided. The sharks in the royal court held their breath. Apparently, questioning the cruel king's orders was not done.

Finnivus smiled, showing his notched and pointed tiger shark teeth. "Of course, you're right!" he exclaimed. "My father put you in charge of the armada those many years ago because of your experience, so I should listen to what you think!"

The commander was wise enough to say nothing as Finnivus went on with his mocking praise. "Who am I to disagree with your considerable age, Whalem? Mercy for those who stop fighting, but any who flee must die! Now, forward! I need my rest. Conquering the Big Blue is very tiring!"

And so King Finnivus and his court swam into the heart of Razor Shiver territory and made themselves at home.

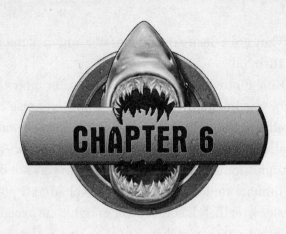

CHAPTER 6

A LITTLE BLOOD IN THE WATER WOULD NORMALLY sharpen a shark's appetite.

Not today, though.

Gray wanted to throw up. He gaped at the carnage, never having seen anything like it. Torn bull sharks from Razor Shiver littered the ocean floor. A few dying, finless torsos even crashed into the greenie field he and Barkley were hiding in. These sharks didn't need to be mauled further and were allowed to drift from the fight. Their piteous wails were unnerving but there was nothing to be done. If you lost a fin, the only place you'd swim was the Sparkle Blue.

Gray was cold inside. He waggled his fins just to feel himself move. Nothing he'd learned from Goblin about battle shivers and fighting in formation covered what had just happened. Had Indi Shiver found Coral Shiver and done *this* to it already? Was his mother ... gone?

"Razor's dead," Barkley whispered in wonder. "Do you think any of his Line is alive?" The remaining bull mariners, less than half, were divided into small groups. They would become Indi Shiver sharks or else. Join or die.

"I vote we not stick around to find out," Gray told his friend.

Barkley nodded and began picking his way through the greenie. They were some distance from the battle waters when Gray felt a prickle run down his spine and recognized it for what it was—danger!

"Swim!" he shouted to Barkley. The dogfish made a crazy turn just as a mako crashed into the seabed where he was an instant before, getting a mouthful of sand for his trouble.

Gray managed to shift to his left before a blue shark struck in an equally vicious manner. The slight move was enough to cause the attacking shark to miss his dorsal. But only barely!

Gray couldn't believe that these two sharks, not much bigger than Barkley, would come after a shark his size. But whatever they lacked in size, these mariners more than made up for in speed and cunning. The two swam in tandem, weaving and switching position like greenie in a strong tide. They turned and came again.

"What do we do? What do we do?" cried Barkley, hysteria creeping into his voice.

Gray gave him a tail slap to the flank. "Get above me and stay there!" Luckily Barkley was good at close-order swimming. Gray could feel the dogfish right above his dorsal. When Gray became leader of Rogue, he'd ramped up the training a few notches. Striiker loved it, but the rest of the shiver had grumbled. Despite all his considerable complaining, Barkley had learned a few things since Tuna Run.

"Make sure they don't peel you away!" Gray reminded.

"Right!" Barkley answered in a hiccupping voice, switching his tail back and forth to gather speed. "I got it." The dogfish needed to protect Gray's topside from attack if they were going to survive.

"You can swim, but you can't hide!" yelled the mako as the pair came forward in a rush. The two sharkkind performed an attack Gray recognized as Hake Sideslip, with both doing the move in its mirror opposite as they constantly swapped positions. It was incredible. If he survived the next minute, Gray would have to rethink all the moves he'd learned from Goblin.

The Hake Sideslip faked a snout-to-snout ram, but then rolled into a sideways attack on a back fin. Since the two sharks were doing the move together, Gray couldn't counter with Waving Greenie as he was taught.

If Gray did that, one of the two attackers would have an easy strike on Gray's left or right pectoral fin as both couldn't be defended at the same time.

Instead, Gray did a rolling turn and angled away in a very common move called Grouper Swims Away. Usually shortened to Swim Away, this was basically the same as fleeing. The important thing was to not swim in terror. You needed to keep looking for a way to turn the situation to your advantage and go back on offense.

"So even though you're swimming from a fight, you're swimming away with *purpose*!" Goblin had told him, before saying that he himself would never, ever, use such a cowardly move. Here, though, there was no choice. Gray wasn't experienced enough to match himself against the two well-trained mariners and protect Barkley. He needed to use his size and strength to his advantage. But how?

Gray slipped into a falling current of colder water and plunged downward into a thick kelp bed. He felt the green-greenie scrape past his flanks. Strands even got caught in his mouth, but he plowed forward anyway. The Indi mariners closed the distance. They weren't afraid of a little seaweed, either, and this was what Gray was counting on. He hoped Barkley would understand what he was doing. Yelling directions would defeat the purpose.

Gray found a coral pillar that was big enough. He

accelerated, whipping his tail back and forth, then cut a turn completely around the coral. The move was called Sea Snake Protects Its Tail. Some of the combat moves Gray had been taught were named in confusing ways, but this one was easy. Every shark made the mistake of trying to catch a sea snake by the tail when they were young. What that got you was a bite on the snout!

When Gray emerged from behind the pillar of coral, he was zooming straight at his two attackers. Surprise! Gray smashed into the mako, snout to snout. He weighed much, much more than that shark and heard its spine audibly snap. It sank, a surprised look frozen on its face.

The blue shark was thrown off and lost its forward speed. Before it could do anything, Barkley bit it in the gills—a small bite, but lethal. The blue shark keeled over and sank, warm blood rising from the wound.

"Oh, no," Barkley said. "What did I do?" Then the dogfish threw up.

Gray heard other patrols in the area and didn't know what his next move should be. They had beaten their attackers with a combination of luck and skill. If they met another pair of Indi mariners, their luck would end for sure. Most likely with their lives.

"Keep down!" hissed an urgent voice. "Get low, or you'll be seen!"

Gray turned to the voice and couldn't believe his

eyes. "Onyx!" he whispered. The blacktip was a member of Coral Shiver's Line.

"Is he really here?" Barkley asked in a dulled voice. "Or are we dead?"

"We're not dead," replied Onyx. "But we will be if you don't stay quiet!"

REUNIONS

CHAPTER 7

"SWIM LOW AND SLOW," ONYX TOLD THEM. "Don't churn up any sand, or they'll see us. You think you two can do that?"

Gray was flabbergasted! Even though he and Barkley were searching for *anyone* from Coral Shiver, it was still a shock to see Onyx. Was Gray's mother nearby, too? Was she all right? There were so many questions to ask, but they couldn't stop and talk. They were in serious danger.

"We can do it," Gray said, pushing the shocked Barkley forward. "Nice and easy."

"Always were a load of trouble," Onyx muttered under his breath. The blacktip led them through algae-covered canyons of rock. Luckily there was plenty of waving greenie floating up from the bottom to hide their movements, as Barkley wasn't swimming at his sneaky best. Gray risked taking a peek at the sun-mottled water above and breathed a sigh of relief when he saw no sharkkind.

After another quarter-mile, they came to a sheltered area surrounded by colorful coral. Gray's heart thudded louder and louder as Onyx guided them through a hidden swimming lane. It blocked the views from above and to the sides—just like the one leading into Coral Shiver's old homewaters.

The swimming lane jogged back and forth. It would be easy to lose your way, and that was the point. Gray's mind raced as the path finally opened into a large central area.

"Where are we? What is this place?" Barkley whispered. He was still stunned from the fight.

Gray's heart leapt when he saw Prime Minister Shocks, the old moray eel who had been the leader of the Coral Shiver dwellers since Gray was a pup. Morrison, the crusty old crab, was busy arguing with Timmons, the sea snail! Aqualina, the red tang, was speaking with Dundee, the sunfish! And there were others, too! Shocks saw Gray, and the eel stopped the conversation he was having with Kanter, the sea horse leader. Soon everyone was staring. It got so still and quiet, Gray heard the water whisking past the algae-slick rocks around them.

"Hi, everyone," Gray said in a soft voice.

The silence remained deafening. Gray was about to say something else when he saw her. There, hovering off to the side by a blue coral spire covered with lumos, was his mother. She had been blocked earlier by the same pillar of coral. Now she stared at him as if she couldn't believe her eyes.

"Gray?" she asked, her voice catching in her throat.

Her mouth and nose barbels vibrated so much, he could feel the movement in the still water. It tickled a little, like when he was a pup.

"Mom!" He swam to his mother, bumping her a little harder than he meant to. She skidded sideways and scattered a colorful group of tangs. "Mom, Mom, Mom!" he yelled. "You're here! You're actually here! I—I missed you so much!"

"*Shhh*, it's okay, Gray," Sandy told him, rubbing his back with her tail.

Gray felt tears well up in his eyes. "I can't believe it's you! I can't believe I finally found you!"

Onyx swam up to them both. "So, I picked up this wayward shark for you to question."

Sandy chuckled, crying freely. "Thank you, Onyx."

"Like a bad clamshell, this one," the blacktip said with a grin. "I guess we can't get rid of him. And maybe that's not so bad." Onyx looked over Gray from snout to tail tip. "He's grown. Again. And learned how to fight."

Sandy grew concerned. "What do you mean?" she asked. Gray's mom looked at him crossly, her barbels now pulsing as they did when she was mad. "What happened?"

"I—we—didn't want to. . . ." Shame reddened Gray's

49

face and his tail drooped. He had just sent another shark to the Sparkle Blue. It would have been unimaginable when he was a pup.

"They had no choice, Sandy," Onyx told her. "I was watching the Indi patrol and saw them dive and attack. I figured it was Razor Shiver survivors—Razor's gone, by the way—and then I saw these two." Onyx flipped his tail in frustration and spoke to Gray. "I would have helped, but you were too far away. Where did you learn that move? Both of you fought well."

Gray looked over his shoulder at Barkley. Some of the dogfish's color seemed to have returned, but he was still shaky, listing to the side a little.

"I—I feel sick again," Barkley muttered.

Onyx tapped the dogfish's flank with his tail to steady him. "It was him or you, Barkley. Did you want it to be you?"

"We wouldn't want that!"

Barkley turned and saw his cousins. They were all there! Barkley started crying his eyes out as his family enveloped him. Seeing his friend flank to flank with his loved ones got Gray welling up again. Pretty soon he gave himself over to laughing and crying and rubbing against his mom. But he didn't care. It felt so good!

He even met his new brother and sister, Riprap and Ebbie. They were little nurse shark pups who couldn't speak yet and mostly hid in the greenie, but they smiled at Gray. Both had the cutest little barbels of their own, just like their mother. He immediately loved them. What an overwhelming joy that his family was safe and sound!

They talked for hours, catching up. Gray and Barkley didn't get all the details of the attack by Razor Shiver that had destroyed Coral Shiver's reef, but they didn't really want them. Even now, it was obvious that most of the sharks and dwellers here were still dealing with the currents from that terrible day.

It turned out no one in Coral Shiver knew the attack was really the work of Goblin and Velenka. Quickeyes, who had been first but was now leader of Coral Shiver because of Atlas's death in the attack, wanted every bit of information. After the story, he looked to Sandy (who was now second in the Line) and Onyx (first) and said in a low voice, "One day, maybe we'll get a chance to talk with those two."

Everyone in the circle knew that there would be no conversation involved. Gray hoped Quickeyes wouldn't go looking for trouble. Even though the thresher was a strong shark, fighting Goblin wasn't a smart thing.

Gray and Barkley recounted all their adventures. Sandy puffed with pride when Barkley told them Gray was the leader of Rogue Shiver. She gave her tail a swirl and smiled as she had when he'd gotten a good grade in class. For his part, Gray was totally embarrassed. He blurted out, "It's a really small shiver, though!"

After a while, he noticed that everyone was listening—really listening. Quickeyes and Onyx were asking for Gray and Barkley's opinions, weighing their words as if they were real shiver sharks. There was actual respect in their eyes when Barkley told everyone about stopping Goblin's plan to take over the North Atlantis at the Tuna Run.

After Barkley was finished, Gray asked, "Why choose this place? Why settle so close to Razor Shiver?"

"It wasn't planned," Sandy answered. "We swam away as fast as we could, and this was where we stopped to rest. It's hidden and can be defended, two things that were very important right then."

"Yes," agreed Quickeyes. "It was the best we could hope for under the circumstances."

"Goblin once told me about sharks with markings called tattoos. They were named Indi Shiver, from the Indi Ocean. The sharkkind that fought Razor Shiver had those. Could it be them? The Indi Ocean is so far away."

"Yup," Onyx said. "They're Indi Shiver."

"How can you be so sure?" asked Barkley.

"Because," Onyx told them, as he turned and showed his own tattoos, "I used to be a member."

CHAPTER 8

EVERYONE SETTLED INTO THE MAIN AREA OF the new Coral Shiver homewaters to listen. There the spires of rock and coral were covered by yellow and green moss, trailing long strips of greenie as the current moved through the shelter. Onyx had quite a tale to tell. His own shiver had been conquered by Indi when he was just a pup, but it hadn't been bloody.

"Their king at the time was Finnivus's father, Romulus," Onyx told everyone. "He was a good and wise king who took in our wandering shiver, which was searching for better feeding grounds."

King Romulus let them become part of Indi, and Onyx was put to work as a hunter when he was barely older than Gray was now. Later, Onyx became an Indi mariner and swam with the armada, which was nicknamed the Black Wave. "That's how I got my tattoos," the blacktip said. He showed the markings that Gray and Barkley had long ago thought were just odd but natural—and totally gilly. But now that Gray had seen the black wave pattern up close, as well as in battle, he didn't think they were cool at all.

"So you know them?" asked Gray. "You know Finnivus?"

"I saw him many times while he was growing up. He's a couple years older than you. Since he was the prince, I tried not to go anywhere near him. He was a spoiled brat."

"Obviously, he's gotten worse," Sandy remarked.

This was an understatement, of course. "One day, I was hunting with King Romulus and the royal court, including Finnivus. We both went after the same fish. I was young and jelly-brained. I should have let the prince have the strike, but I beat him to it. Finnivus got mad and ordered my death."

"What kind of shiver is this?" Gray asked incredulously. "It was a *fish*!"

"They have their own rules, and I dishonored the prince," Onyx replied. "Their laws may be harsh to us, but according to them I was wrong."

"But you're still around," Barkley said, pointing with his fin. He seemed to be doing better since their escape earlier in the day. "What happened?"

"King Romulus would never disgrace his son by taking my side in front of the royal court. He told a commander to carry out the prince's order. Maybe Romulus knew he wouldn't do it, maybe not. But the commander swam me out of sight and let me go. He said to never come back. So you see, Gray, you're not the only one who's been banished."

"Tell them about the commander," said Quickeyes.

"Ah, here's where it gets interesting. That commander's name was Whalem."

"That's the name of the shark Finnivus called the mariner prime," Gray said thoughtfully.

Onyx nodded and swished his tail. "Exactly. They are one and the same."

"You're sure?" Barkley asked. "Are you positive?"

Onyx nodded. "You don't forget the shark who spared your life."

"Do you think you could talk with him? Make the mariner prime get Finnivus to change his ways?" asked Barkley.

Onyx shook his snout back and forth. "Whalem would never disobey his king."

Barkley whipped his tail through the water. "He spared your life, didn't he? Isn't that disobeying?"

"Or, was he obeying a king who secretly told him to let me go? I don't know."

"You were a member of the armada," Gray said. "Do you know how they fight? What their weaknesses are?"

"Sure, I know their formations, but that's not enough. Their mariners are well-trained, and in the hands of a good mariner prime, which Whalem is, they are unbeatable."

The group spoke for another hour, before everyone drifted apart. Gray and his mother went off alone. The day had brought one huge surprise after another. Gray wondered if he could bear one more, but knew he must take up the subject. He pointed at Riprap and Ebbie, still hiding in the greenie. They were intensely interested in their giant big brother but too shy to swim up close.

"Riprap and Ebbie are so cute," he told his mom.

"Aren't they?"

"Much cuter than I am," Gray said evenly. He didn't want to upset his mother, but he had to continue. "They have barbels, just like you, and fan-shaped teeth, just like you. I don't have those...."

His mother's barbels twitched in a way that Gray had never seen. He didn't know if she was angry or hurt or thinking. Then she finally said, "I've been waiting for this day. In some ways, I hoped it would never come."

Gray forced himself to be patient while his mother gathered her thoughts. It was obviously hard for her.

"The truth is I found you, alone and scared in the ocean far, far away."

The words passed momentarily without Gray realizing what they meant. But then he did. "So...you're not my mother?"

Sandy rubbed his belly with her tail. "Of course

I am, Gray. I raised you and fed you and loved you. I'll always love you. I'm just not your birth mother." Tears leaked from the corners of her eyes and were carried away by the tide.

It felt like the Big Blue was spinning round and round, and Gray was tumbling tail over snout.

"I know this is hard, but I love you. You can tell me anything, Gray. Even if you're mad at me, it's okay."

"I'm not mad, Mom. I just have so many questions," he hiccupped.

"I know," she soothed. "I'll answer what I can."

"Did you know I'm a megalodon?"

Sandy's mouth hung open in surprise. Her barbels moved left and right as she shook her head in wonder. "I didn't. But I knew you were special."

Special. There it was again. Only this time it just added to the storm of confused feelings Gray was having. He was beginning to hate being *special.* "Where do I come from?"

"The place I found you was almost in the Dark Blue. It was deep and ancient. The very mountains shifted, and there was a huge volcanic eruption. It became so bright, it was like a red sun had fallen into the ocean. I almost died. And there, in the dark, with the water tasting of sulfur—I found you. That's why I named you Gray. The entire Big Blue seemed gray that day."

He couldn't help it and laughed. "You named me Gray because the water was mucky and stank?"

His mom gave him a little tail slap to the flank. "That is not the reason." She grew quiet before continuing. "It seemed like the ocean itself *changed* so it could have you swimming in it. It was incredible and terrifying. But most of all, it was a day unlike any I've lived in my life. I knew right then it was my job to take care of you."

Gray hugged Sandy with his tail for a long time. But then he asked his last question. "So my parents could be alive?" Gray wasn't sure which answer he wanted to hear.

Sandy shook her head. "I'm sorry, but I don't think so. If there was another megalodon in the ocean looking for you, I would have heard about it. And I stayed in the area for a long time to make sure. I think your parents died saving you. You see, they must have also known you were special." This time the word didn't feel so bad.

Gray asked his mother not to tell anyone about his being a megalodon, and she agreed that keeping the secret was a wise thing for now. That was a mystery for another day. Right now, Finnivus was threatening everyone Gray cared about. That problem demanded all his attention.

But there was one more thing. . . .

"Can I still call you Mom?"

"Of course, you can!" Sandy said, her eyes leaking tears. "Always and forever, Gray."

CHAPTER 9

WHALEM WATCHED AS THE RAZOR SHIVER prisoners were herded from their homewaters, each bull between two armada sharkkind for the long swim to the Indi Ocean. There they would be broken down before being raised up into Indi Shiver mariners. Right now, the prisoners' fins drooped, and they swam listlessly, having been easily taken apart in battle. Of course they lost. This *shiver* was no more than a gang of thugs. And to only allow one type of sharkkind into membership? That was foolish.

Whalem had once tried to get Finnivus's father King Romulus to allow dwellers into the Indi armada as equals. That was the one time there was a total disagreement between them. Romulus thought that only sharkkind should be allowed into his glorious armada. Dwellers could serve in different ways, as the blue whales or lantern fish did, but could not be Indi armada mariners. Whalem thought the advantages that a swarm of eels would provide far outweighed the fact that they weren't sharkkind.

"Mariner Prime, you called?" asked one of Whalem's commanders, a bull shark. A commander led each of the four battle fins of the armada, but this was the only bull among them.

"I'd like you to talk to the prisoners," Whalem told him. "Calm them. Make sure they don't do anything stupid or Finnivus will have them for lunch."

"He might, anyway."

Whalem let his commanders speak on even terms when they weren't in official settings. He believed the sharks who fought flank to flank with him deserved this measure of respect. But it wasn't the time for this sort of talk in the ranks. "What do you mean by that, commander?"

"I—I . . ."

"Surely you aren't suggesting that the king would dishonor Indi Shiver by harming surrendered prisoners?"

The bull cast his eyes downward, dipping both head and tail. "No, Mariner Prime! I misspoke."

"Plainly, you're tired from the battle."

"Yes, Mariner Prime!"

"I don't want you saying any such thing to the other commanders, is that clear?" Whalem said, making his eyes like volcanic rock. He could not afford to let rot like this begin. Once started, it was impossible to stop.

"Yes, Mariner Prime!" the commander answered, dipping his head once more.

"Now, see to the bulls," Whalem told him. "I'm sending you because you are a bull yourself. So it's up to you. Will you help me save their lives by making sure they join Indi Shiver happily and without reservation?"

"Yes, Mariner Prime!" he exclaimed. "I live to serve you! I mean—I live to serve the king! It seems I am very tired, Mariner Prime, forgive me."

"On your way, then." Whalem shook his head after the commander left. Some in the armada probably did have more loyalty to him personally than to Finnivus, even though it had been five years now since Romulus swam to the Sparkle Blue. But Whalem would not use that loyalty, as some had asked him to. He could no more betray Romulus's wishes now than when they'd been young. And Romulus had always wanted his son to be king. "Now if only Finnivus would believe that," he muttered silently into the current. Whalem thought the young king was going to have him seasoned and served for lunch for disagreeing with him earlier. That the young pup would even think about bloodying the waters further after their crushing victory made Whalem's stomach turn. And this was also after the disgrace they had committed against AuzyAuzy Shiver!

AuzyAuzy was the only shiver that could have given the Indi armada a tough time. Finnivus had never liked

Prince Lochlan, or his father. He was jealous of Auzy-Auzy Shiver and its reputation in the Big Blue as the most honored shiver. And golden-hued Prince Lochlan was loved and respected by everyone. While the body of his father, King Lochlan, had been found, the prince's had not. So many sharkkind had been killed in the frenzy during and after the battle that Finnivus was sure the golden great white was swimming the Sparkle Blue. That was the reason behind Finnivus's attack—he hated Prince Lochlan. Well, that and the fact that Finnivus was a power-hungry fish who wanted every sharkkind and dweller in the ocean to bow before him. Whalem felt his stomach turn. Such dishonor! Such disgrace! He would never feel clean again after witnessing the horrors Finnivus had wreaked upon AuzyAuzy.

Finnivus had none of his father's mercy, grace, or intelligence. Indi Shiver needed replacements for its mariners who had died, were injured, or grew too old to fight. Killing a group of disorganized and terrified enemy sharks when a battle's outcome was decided was a strategic blunder that showed bad leadership. The best way to turn a beaten shiver into loyal Indi mariners wasn't to terrify them with cruelty.

If only the battle had ended just a bit earlier! thought Whalem. Every fin flick the king delayed had put more blood in the water, which every Razor Shiver shark would remember. Swimming to the royal court, Whalem sighed. Such a waste.

Finnivus watched as the decorator crabs and fish wove Indi Shiver symbols into the greenie which grew in the area. "Pfah!" the king grumbled. "What a low and lowly place this is! Isn't that right, Tydal?"

"No place in all the Big Blue is as glorious as your own Indi homewaters, Magnificence," answered the brown-and-yellow court fish. "But we do try."

"Try harder," was the king's bored reply.

"Immediately, Your Highness!"

Finnivus gave a noncommittal grunt. Whalem suppressed a smile as he thought of Tydal's nickname among some of the armada: First Court Toady. The epaulette shark was required to see to every tiny detail that tradition dictated. He did his work well.

Whalem nodded at the king's Line, all friends of Finnivus. Their parents were Indi royalty, as evidenced by their intricate tattoos. The young sharks had been secretly against Finnivus taking his rightful place on the throne, but now hovered under his belly like remora. Five years ago, these supposed friends thought Whalem should take the throne when Romulus died.

Whalem knew this wasn't because of their tremendous respect for him as their first in the Line. No, it was because he was more than seventy summers old and had no children. If he became king, one of them would rule within a few years. Thankfully, the others of Romulus's old Line sided with Whalem and voted to make Finnivus king. They weren't here anymore, though. Whalem was the last of the old guard, kept in position because he remained undefeated in battle, and Finnivus was a superstitious fin.

"Three cheers for King Finnivus!" yelled the second in the Line, a tiger.

"Finnivus Victor once again victorious!" the third cried immediately afterward.

Whalem especially disliked it when they did that: one yelling something, followed by another emphasizing the point in a different way. They were being sucker fish! But Finnivus didn't seem to notice. The king flicked his pectorals, preening. "Oh, please! I—I mean, *we*—only do what *we* are meant to!"

Finnivus *loved* the royal *we*, but didn't always use it correctly.

Whalem sighed as his eyes slid to the now nearly invisible Tydal. The brightly colored court shark could hover perfectly still and seemed to disappear through sheer motionlessness. Probably a good trait to have for a court fish when Finnivus got angry, Whalem thought.

Finnivus slapped his tail enthusiastically against the Speakers Rock as the seasoned head of Razor Shiver's leader was brought to him on the back of a sea turtle. Whalem used the tide to drift farther away from the meal. It turned his stomach. Though Indi Shiver had a past tradition of eating an enemy shiver's leader, Romulus had never, ever honored it. But Finnivus brought the ritual back. Whalem shuddered as Finnivus ate with gusto.

"Oh, this is delicious! I can't wait to see who I'll get to eat next!"

A prickle of fear marched down Whalem's spine. Had he made the wrong choice when he refused to be king of Indi Shiver? One poor decision, one tail stroke out of place, and it could be his head on that dining platter. Whalem shivered.

"GRAY, THIS IS ABSOLUTELY THE WORST IDEA you've *ever* come up with," Barkley said as they waited in a thick kelp bed outside of Slaggernacks. It had taken most of the day to carefully creep through the greenie from Coral Shiver's hiding place and skirt Goblin's territory to get safely into the neutral area around Slaggernacks.

"Quiet," Gray whispered.

"I didn't think you could top your other classics," the dogfish went on. "You know, like when you got banished from Coral Shiver? Or when you decided joining Goblin Shiver was a good idea? Or when you listened to Velenka instead of me? How about when you—"

"*Shhh!*" Gray said as he bumped Barkley in the side. "Quit being such a tail bender, will you? We have to do this."

"Why? Why do we have to?"

Gray looked at Barkley. "Because it's the right thing. And you know it."

"Doesn't mean I have to like it," the dogfish grumbled.

"Could you at least be more quiet in your dislike?" Barkley made a face that Gray pretended not to notice. "There they are." Sure enough, Goblin and Velenka were swimming into the back cave at Slaggernacks. "Don't forget the fish," Gray told Barkley as he left the greenie.

The dogfish shook his head and muttered, "This is so dumb," before grabbing the huge sea bass. Barkley was right. This wasn't smart. But it was a calculated risk that Gray hoped would work out.

Barkley dumped the plump bass by the door. Trank gave him a nod and led them inside as a large octopus dragged the tasty fish away.

The dogfish shook his head and waggled his fins nervously. "Such a bad idea."

When they got to the cave where Goblin and Velenka were, the reaction was immediate. "WHAT ARE THEY DOING HERE?" shouted the furious great white. He gnashed his teeth so hard that one cracked off.

Velenka was just as agitated when she saw Trank. She had double-crossed and imprisoned the stonefish.

"Relax, Velenka. This isn't what youse think. And youse, too, Goblin," Trank said.

Goblin glared balefully at Gray. "Didn't I teach you

anything?" he seethed. "At least challenge me to a snout-to-snout fight."

"Some other time," Gray told them. "Razor's dead."

"What?"

"Are you hard of hearing?" Barkley asked sarcastically.

"One day I'll eat you, doggie!"

"Like you wouldn't for no reason at all," the dogfish replied, churning the water with his tail. "Suck algae, you big bully."

Trank swam between them, little fins turning dainty circles as dust and debris fell from his upper body. "No one is doing anything to anyone in Slaggernacks unless Gafin says so! Youse get me?"

Goblin leered at the small fish. "Think you can slow me down if I wanted to do something?"

Trank motioned upward with a fin. "Not me, personally. But it just so happens it's not just me, personally, that's here."

Everyone looked up. Hundreds of urchins and poisonous dwellers including blue-ringed octopi and stingrays hung on the ceiling of the cave. If Goblin attacked, there was no way he'd get out of the cave without being stung many, many times.

The tension in the room vibrated in Gray's lateral line and spine, but the great white didn't charge. He motioned to Velenka and she broke the silence. "How do you know Razor's dead?"

"I saw it," Gray told the mako, her blacker-than-black eyes boring into him. "Half his shiver went to the Sparkle Blue. The rest were taken."

"Taken by whom? Why should I believe anything you say?" snorted Goblin. "What kind of game are you playing?"

Barkley shook his head. "You should have just let them drift right into that whirlpool."

"They call themselves Indi Shiver," Gray persisted.

Goblin snickered. "Indi's homewaters are halfway around the Big Blue!"

"They fight in coordinated formations and would take your mariners apart in a fin flick," Barkley said. "Turns out your little playtime practice drills are good for nothing!"

Gray slapped the dogfish with his tail. "Barkley! You're not helping." He turned to Goblin. "But he's right. Even at our best—with ten times our numbers—the fight would be over in minutes."

"What do you mean by *our* best?" the great white sneered, showing his teeth again.

"What *do* you mean by that?" asked Barkley.

Gray smiled at both of them, a little embarrassed. "I, umm, didn't mean that, I guess." He looked at Goblin and Velenka. "But I know what your shiver can and can't do. And what Indi Shiver did to Razor and his bulls was nothing short of . . . horrifying."

Goblin chuckled. It started as a slow rumble but

then grew and grew. "Only a turtle like you would say that Razor being eaten was *horrifying*."

Velenka gave Goblin a calculating look. When she saw Gray watching, it vanished. "Maybe we should listen to the meal of the message. Razor and his bulls were smashed by some shiver."

"Right. By *Indi Shiver*."

"Whoever they might be," Velenka told him.

"Why are you really here, pup?" Goblin snapped his jaws, his triangular teeth scraping their serrated edges together. "You want to make nice so I forgive you?"

Barkley shook his head and muttered, "Such a bad idea."

"I'm here because you did teach me a few things, and for that I'm grateful," Gray said to the barrel-shaped great white. "I'm here because your shiver sharks aren't evil and don't need to die. But lastly, I'm here because I think no one, not even you, deserves what happened to Razor and his shiver."

Goblin's gills pumped in and out, hate making his eyes glow in the darkness of the cavern. While Gray hadn't been expecting the great white to get all weepy and say everything between them was okay, this wasn't the reaction he'd envisioned.

"I told you once, pup, our homewaters are worth fighting for. If you don't understand that, I never taught you anything. Come on, Velenka." Goblin swam past

Gray brusquely, his crescent-shaped tail slapping Barkley in the face on the way out. The dogfish took it in silence.

When Velenka left, Gray asked her, "Will you talk with him?"

"I'll try," the mako replied. "It's good to see you."

"Feel free to keep moving, sister," Barkley told her.

"How do you know we won't wait for you outside?" she said to Barkley with menace in her voice, her pitch-black eyes boring into him.

Barkley just smiled. "Because I made a deal with Gafin and your friend Trank. If I go missing, you get a visit when you least expect it. So you better hope I stay healthy."

Velenka glanced warily at Trank, who was speaking with some other stonefish on the far side of the cave.

"Did you really do that?" Gray asked Barkley after the mako had gone.

"Of course not!"

Trank swam over to them. "If I knew the meeting was gonna be *that* tense, I woulda charged youse more."

Gray and Barkley swam out of Slaggernacks soon afterward. They scooted into the cover of the greenie and made their way to the landshark wreck. "That didn't exactly work out," Barkley commented.

"I did what I had to," Gray told him.

"So, what's next?"

"I think it's time we make the introductions between Rogue and Coral."

"Finally." Barkley gave Gray a stinging tail slap to his belly. "An idea I can really get behind." The dogfish tore through the greenie as fast as he could.

Gray gave chase, the tension of the meeting melting in the crisp current. "Oh, you better swim!"

CHAPTER 11

BECAUSE GRAY HAD BEEN THERE BEFORE, HE was able to lead his friends to Coral Shiver's new homewaters even though the entrance was well-hidden. The trick was to approach from the east and look for the rock formation shaped like an upside-down lobster tail someone had named Rock Lobster. Once they got there, a shiver shark Gray didn't know led them into the hidden swimming lane and through the long fronds of green-greenie. Barkley and the other Rogue members followed single file until the path widened into the secluded reef. The shiver shark told them to wait there until Quickeyes was informed of their arrival.

Shell tapped Striiker with his flipper. "Hey, do I look okay?"

"What do you mean?" the great white asked, genuinely confused. "You look like you always do."

"You're sure? Do I have a mackerel head in my teeth or anything?"

Striiker sighed and didn't answer, flicking his tail instead.

"You've been edgy all day," Barkley told Shell. "Don't worry. These fish are family."

"But my ex-family attacked your family," Shell replied, his tail switching right and left. That was true. Goblin had used sharkkind from Razor Shiver to do his dirty work.

"We've been through this," Gray said. He knew his mother wouldn't blame Shell for Razor Shiver's actions, but to be safe he'd sent word that they would be coming with an ex–Razor Shiver bull shark before their visit. He couldn't be absolutely sure how everyone else would react, and he didn't want any surprises. "It wasn't your fault, Shell."

Quickeyes and Onyx swam over with Gray's mother. There were introductions all around, and then Rogue Shiver toured the reef. It had interesting coral formations that shined with ghostly yellow and blue hues. The sea moss covering the rocks underneath was light green and fluffy as it waved back and forth in the current. It wasn't their old reef in the Caribbi Sea, but it was nice.

They heard Yappy before seeing him. The little sea dragon came tearing through the greenie where he'd been hunting, shouting, "It's Gray and Barkley! It's Barkley and Gray!"

"Not again," muttered Onyx to Quickeyes at the same exact time Barkley said it to Gray. This made everyone chuckle as the little dweller zipped between Gray and Barkley.

"I knew it was you two when I heard your voices, on the account of it *is* actually you two!" Yappy exclaimed. "Have you guys seen the coral on the other side? It's pretty gilly, all right! Pretty *and* gilly, I mean! How do you think coral got its name? I mean, what if we called it *gracklenut*? I supposed coral sounds better than gracklenut, though."

Snork, the sawfish, chimed in. "Gracklenut sounds more like that rough kind of orange-greenie. Maybe we could start calling *that* gracklenut!"

"That's a great idea!" said Yappy, his attention now thankfully focused on Snork. "Who are you? Have you named many other things?"

"My name's Snork," he answered. "I've always wanted to name things, but never got around to it."

"You definitely should find the time. I can tell you'd be good at it. Why, I'll bet we could go around the reef, and you would name three of four things right now. Do you want to?"

"That sounds like fun," Snork replied. The pair swam off to the amusement of everyone else.

"So that's Yappy," Mari remarked.

"Yep," Gray said, nodding.

Barkley motioned with his tail at the retreating

figures. "That's a dangerous combination." When every-one laughed, he added, "I'm serious. Those two? They might never stop talking. Ever."

"Snork seems like a good fin," Quickeyes told Gray. "Like the rest of your new friends." After that, the discussion grew more serious. Onyx took Shell off to the side, and they spoke intently by themselves, probably about Shell's history with Razor Shiver. When they returned, the blacktip seemed at ease with the big bull shark.

For some reason, Gray's mom and Mari were talking. A lot. After every other sentence, they glanced Gray's way and chuckled.

A horrible thought hit him. The bucket story! What if his mom told Mari the bucket story? When Gray had been a young pup, he'd explored a galleon—a different kind of landshark ship than the one Rogue Shiver lived in now—and gotten his head stuck in a bucket. It was wedged on so tightly Prime Minister Shocks had to get help from the octopus clan to pull it off. Everyone had called Gray *buckethead* for a long time after that. His mother and Mari laughed again, but louder. "Not the bucket story, Mom," Gray muttered to himself.

"So, what do you think?" Quickeyes asked Gray. "Will you and Barkley join our Line? You'll be third, he'll be fourth."

Gray was dumbfounded. He just clicked his teeth,

not knowing how to answer. Barkley came tearing over and gave Gray a fin bump. He had obviously been told.

The news traveled fast, and pretty soon everyone, even Snork and Yappy, were back. The colorful sea dragon was actually silent for once.

"Are you surprised?" Sandy asked Gray.

"Definitely, Mom. Definitely." Gray wanted to accept Quickeyes's offer, but something nagged at him.

It was Striiker who brought what was troubling him into focus. "I'm happy for you," the large great white began, "but right now, with everything that's going on, you can't be a member of two Lines! Your loyalty has to be to just one."

"Your friend is right," said Quickeyes. "I wish he wasn't. But it's your choice."

"Rogue will respect whatever decision you make," Mari added.

Sandy swirled her tail to get everyone's attention and announced, "Either way, Coral and Rogue should be allies. If any of you are in trouble, you can always come here."

"Are you serious?" Shell asked. "Really?"

Onyx gave the bull shark a slap on his flank. "Any friend of Gray and Barkley's is a friend of ours."

"Well?" asked Barkley.

Gray wanted to say yes. He really did. But Goblin was still out there. If Gray joined Coral Shiver, the evil shark might attack his family again. Gray wouldn't take that chance. But before he could tell everyone someone else spoke.

"He cannot!" said an oddly accented voice. "He promised himself to me."

Everyone started as Takiza seemingly appeared from nowhere and settled into the center of the council discussion. It was a moment before anyone could speak.

"And who are you, exactly?" Quickeyes asked.

The tiny fighting fish ruffled his fins with a flourish. "I am, exactly, Takiza Jaelynn Betta vam Delacrest Waveland ka Boom Boom."

"Huh. I pictured him bigger," Onyx mused. Takiza featured prominently in the story of how Rogue Shiver had stopped Goblin and Velenka's plan at the Tuna Run. When Gray had told the story, he could see that the members of Coral Shiver didn't totally believe him. Now their disbelief was replaced by amazement.

Quickeyes swam up to Takiza. "You're really him? The same Takiza who Gray said saved a family of turtles? The Takiza who saved a whale calf from fifty makos when my father's father was a pup? The same Takiza who stopped a tidal wave from washing away an entire reef between the AuzyAuzy and Zeeland land masses? You're *that* Takiza?"

The little betta bobbed his head and snapped his filmy fins straight out for a moment. "The same."

"Why do you want my son?" Sandy asked, her nose and chin barbels vibrating.

"He is my apprentice. He must come with me for training."

"Training for what?" Mari prodded.

"Why, to defeat Finnivus Victor," Takiza said matter-of-factly. "After Finnivus declares himself emperor, of course."

VELENKA STRIKES

CHAPTER 12

VELENKA TRIED TO CONVINCE GOBLIN THREE times that they couldn't hope to survive an Indi Shiver assault fighting snout to snout. A scouting party had confirmed the armada was camped at Razor Shiver's old homewaters. Of course they were. Ever since the Tuna Run, it seemed as if Goblin Shiver had been caught in a whirlpool of misfortune. First, their plan to get rid of Razor was blocked by Gray and Rogue Shiver. After the Tuna Run, Razor Shiver had launched a series of successful attacks against them. And now that Razor and his bulls were gone, a new and much more powerful force—the Indi armada led by King Finnivus—had taken their place and threatened to annihilate Goblin Shiver. Indi continued to send out large patrols from their new homewaters, but they were content to stay close to that area. For now.

"Ha!" Goblin had snorted. "They're scared to come out!"

Velenka knew why Indi Shiver wasn't interested in probing their defenses. Indi could crush them anytime. When Goblin had ordered an ill-advised ambush, the outnumbered Indi patrol didn't even pursue after absolutely mauling Goblin's forces. The tattooed mariners hadn't been surprised for more than an instant. Their defensive formations and light-ning-quick counterattacks easily won the battle. Ten Goblin Shiver sharkkind had been killed, with just six getting back to safety.

If only Goblin hadn't made it back, Velenka thought. But he had and insisted on getting ready for the *father of all battles*, as he called it. The situation was hopeless.

"Where are we going?" Goblin asked.

"Hydenseek," she answered. Hydenseek was an area inside Goblin Shiver territory just off their homewaters where big fish hunted the small fish that gathered in and around a thick field of blue and green-greenie.

"Pfaf!" he snorted. "If I wanted seaweed, I'd order it at Slaggernacks. Let's hunt the open waters."

"You go if you want." Velenka gave him a smile and a friendly swish of her tail. Encouraging him to go was taking a gamble, but she didn't want to reveal that she had an agenda, so she acted nonchalant. If Goblin left right now, Velenka would have to come up with a different plan. As it was, she'd waited two nerve-jangling days for everything to click into place.

Indi might come for them tomorrow, so she had to act today!

Thankfully, the great white flicked his crescent tail in annoyance but followed. Velenka led him into Hydenseek where the greenie grew denser and denser.

"So, you might as well start," Goblin said.

"Start what?" Velenka asked.

"Talking me out of what I'm planning," Goblin grumbled.

The last time she'd tried to do that, Velenka thought the angry great white would send her to the Sparkle Blue. "I'm done with that," she said. "Swim your current. I know I won't change your mind."

"Finally!" He laughed. "I've worn you down." He snapped up a fat mackerel that was too slow in recognizing the danger Goblin represented.

Velenka wasn't going to end up like that mackerel. "Something like that," she told him as she angled in a slightly different direction.

"Where are you going?" he asked. "The greenie's too thick there."

"I think this way is going to be lucky for me," she replied. "But if you're scared, I'll meet you later."

The great white followed, of course. He was so predictable.

It was only a few tail strokes later that she heard Goblin grunt in pain. Velenka turned and saw he didn't realize what was happening. Finally, the great white recognized the blue-ringed octo hanging on to his tail, bending it back onto itself.

"Can you believe this?" he said. "The little flipper is attacking me! *Me!*"

Velenka remained silent as the octo hung onto Goblin's tail, injecting him with its poisons.

"Krillfaced coward!" Goblin shouted. He slammed his tail against the nearest rock. One octo, even a blue-ringed octo, wasn't enough to kill most full-grown sharks. Certainly not one as big as Goblin. No, it would take more than that.

So Velenka had arranged for more.

A dozen stonefish floated up from their hiding places in the moss-covered rocks below where they had been waiting for days. The toxic dwellers stung Goblin on his belly and by the bends of his fins.

Goblin screamed in frustration as the stonefish kept low and underneath him. He mashed a few with his serrated, triangle teeth. He received a huge sting in the gums when he scored one bite. "Oww!" he yelped. "This is why I never come here!"

Velenka realized she should have been saying encouraging things. Or acted scared for him. Velenka was doing neither—because she was the one behind the attack.

And with one look into her black eyes, Goblin knew it, too.

"Traitor!" he shouted. The great white darted forward, but she was quicker, avoiding his lunge. The poison was working. And with the octo entangling his tail, bending the top half downward, Goblin couldn't swim at full speed. But his rage provided a momentary edge. He almost caught Velenka with a quick rolling turn, but she dove underneath a coral lattice, and he got a mouthful of rock for his efforts.

"I'll ki-ki-kill you," he slurred. The poison was working. But she hadn't left anything to chance.

The delicate box jellyfish floated eerily through the water toward Goblin. How it moved, she didn't really know. This cube-shaped jelly was the most toxic predator in all the Big Blue. Goblin stiffened as if he had swum into an invisible wall when the jellyfish stung him in the gills. The stonefish below his belly struck at will—Goblin's futile snaps no longer worried them.

The box jelly continued stinging, now floating over Goblin, attached to him by more than twenty translucent tendrils. It was a terrible sight, but Velenka couldn't look away. She had never heard of jellies dealing with sharkkind or dweller, even in ancient times. That Gafin could offer its services was remarkable. She would have to be careful in dealing with the urchin king.

With a last audible hiss, Goblin rolled belly up. The great white was paralyzed and dying but stared hatefully as Velenka glided toward him.

"I tried to tell you," she said. "But you wouldn't listen. Do you think everyone is so eager to die for your *honor*? No, we're not."

Then Velenka bit Goblin in the gills.

As she swam away, small fish and crabs gathered to eat.

CHAPTER 13

IT HAD BEEN THREE DAYS SINCE THE SPIRITED discussion with Takiza at the Coral Shiver homewaters. The ancient betta insisted Gray come with him right that minute. He wasn't big on explaining anything to Striiker, whom he called "a shark with chowder for brains," or even to Quickeyes, the Coral leader.

But Takiza *did* answer questions from Gray's mother. Through her, the little betta had managed to convince everyone it was a good idea for him and Gray to swim off together. Gray believed it was a good idea, too. He had been so excited to train with the mysterious and powerful Takiza—fish of legend! What an honor! Gray thought he would travel with his new teacher for a few days, all the while learning cool, mysterious secrets!

That was then. Now, he was miserable.

"Again!" Takiza bellowed. Gray followed the light- ning quick Siamese fighting fish through a forest of razor sharp coral spires. "Faster!" The spires, while colorful, were hidden by curtains of greenie growing from the ocean floor. Takiza was training Gray in waters much deeper than he usually swam. They were in an area two days east of Goblin Shiver territory, almost smack in the middle of the North Atlantis Ocean. If they continued a few more days, they would reach the lower edge of the Atlantis Spine, the huge mountain range that formed the guiding landmark of the Tuna Run. If they went a few days farther than that, they would be hovering where the tuna actually swam.

The Big Blue was very deep here, almost at the point where it became known as the Dark Blue. But even at this depth, which Takiza said definitely wasn't the Dark Blue, it was uncomfortable and gave Gray the shivers. He wasn't sure whether that was from the colder temperature, the eerie darkness, or the water that physically pressed against him. Gray hadn't believed that the water was *actually* squeezing him until Takiza explained that the weight of all the water above them caused that feeling.

And yet this depth was nothing, apparently. Gray could see the ledge underneath his right flank fall away into total blackness. Takiza told him that this giant hole in the ocean floor was called the Maw. It did kind of look like a huge mouth that would eat you if you were foolish enough to swim there. Inside the Maw was where the

Dark Blue actually began. Supposedly, only prehistore nightmares lived in the Dark Blue.

Gray hoped Takiza wasn't going to make him go any lower—or especially into the Maw. The blackness terrified him. As it was, the sun was only a pale afterthought, a wan light far above the chop-chop that he felt more than actually saw.

Gray heard a muffled crack as he was shoved by the fierce current into a coral spire, snapping it in two. He winced as Takiza glided over.

"No, no, no!" Takiza yelled in a surprisingly strong voice. "Why must you swim like a pregnant sea cow? You are sharkkind, so swim like sharkkind!"

Gray could barely speak at this depth because of the strain against his throat. Mostly, he just took the abuse in silence. But there were times, such as now, when he got frustrated. Gray wanted to shout, roar even, but the best he could do was whine in a high voice. "I'm trying!" he squeaked. The pressure also made him light-headed and loopy, which was one of the reasons he kept running into things.

"Make your way *around* the coral—not through it! Takiza scolded. "These spires take centuries to grow, and you are wrecking them in a single day as you bumble this way and that! Why, Lochlan didn't snap this much coral in an entire year!"

Gray ground his teeth together. Takiza had brought up the name Lochlan *many* times since his training began. Apparently, Lochlan had been a favorite student of Takiza's and was now the leader of AuzyAuzy Shiver. Takiza even called him "*my golden apprentice!*" Though he had never met the shark, Gray couldn't help disliking him. Muck-sucking teacher's pet, he thought.

"Again, Nulo!"

"Yes, Shiro!" Gray answered. "Shiro" meant *teacher* and *master* in some ancient language. Takiza insisted being called this when they were training. Gray was "Nulo," which was a combination of *student* and *nothing*. He began swimming the course again.

On the second day of training, Gray pitched a fit and tried to leave. Takiza didn't let him. "You gave your word to me," the betta told him. "Once accepted, it is not yours to take back!" Gray would never fight the little fish—Takiza had saved everyone's life at the Tuna Run—but instead he started swimming away.

Big mistake.

Takiza dragged him back by the tail, commenting, "This is for your own good. It hurts me much more than you!" Somehow Gray doubted that. When he made the mistake of struggling, Takiza spun him around until he threw up! That was the last of Gray's rebellions.

"Can't we take a little break?" Gray asked now. "I'm tired."

"No, you are not. Megalodon do not tire so easily."

Gray stopped, flabbergasted. "You know I'm a megalodon?"

The betta flicked his fins in annoyance but answered, "It's as plain as the overly large snout on your face. I also know you were put in the Big Blue as a force of change. You are special, but if you rely on your gifts without seeking to improve yourself, you will fail. And you cannot fail!"

"Put here by who? Do you know my parents? What gifts do I have? And why can't I fail?"

"No questions, Nulo! They are unimportant at this moment! What *is* important is obeying what I tell you to do!"

Gray felt his voice go up, and he whined, "But I'm hungry and scraped by the coral, Takiza—I mean, Shiro. I don't want to be special. All I want to do is eat and sleep!"

The betta flicked his fins again as his eyes blazed. "You complain endlessly! You are soft and coddled, whining like a vain puffer fish at the merest discomfort. And you have no idea whatsoever of your true potential. Now swim the course or I will once again thrash you!"

Gray forced his aching tail to stroke left and right. He wouldn't get any answers right now, and he didn't want to be spun around again. Gaining speed, Gray used the wickedly cold and fast currents to his advantage just like the betta had showed him the day before.

These currents had a heaviness the ones above lacked. It was tougher to get in or out of these as the water flowed through the coral spire field and fell downward toward the Dark Blue. Takiza told him this was because water heading down had an entirely different weight and thickness. Lighter and thinner currents moved upward, while the heavier ones traveled downward. Takiza also said that all currents, no matter if they felt level or not, moved in one direction or the other, rising or falling. This was how the Big Blue cleansed itself, apparently.

Gray only knew it was hard to swim here.

Coral spires whizzed by on the left and right. Gray twisted and turned, instinctively leaving a heavy current that was rushing too fast over the edge and sliding into a slower one to brake himself without actually using his fins or tail.

"Excellent!" Takiza said, swimming upside down in front of his left eye. "Use your lateral line to feel the obstacles in your path."

The lateral line was another amazing thing Takiza had taught him. It was that buzzing feeling Gray got inside his head when he couldn't see but knew something was there. Sharkkind used it instinctively to hunt, Takiza had said. But to truly master it, you needed to practice and exercise its power.

"Don't rely on your eyes or your nose! Both can be fooled," the betta commented as he deftly dodged a thick rope of greenie. Gray's weight snapped it, and Takiza shook his head. "Never swim through things you can avoid."

"But, Shiro," Gray said, panting. The water felt thick pumping through his gills. "If I can go *through* something, isn't it faster because I'm swimming in a straight line?"

The frilly fish nodded, thinking. "That is true, except for . . ." Takiza trailed off as he adjusted his position upward.

"Except for what?" Gray wheezed, just before smashing snout first into a giant coral spire, which didn't give at all. For a second, he was paralyzed with pain, the current pushing his back and tail up against the coral.

Takiza shook his head and nudged Gray's stunned body into an area where the current wasn't about to sweep him off the ledge and into the Maw. "*Except for* the inevitable fact you will lose any time you have saved when striking an object thicker than even your very thick head, Nulo!"

Gray saw glowing motes swimming and winking everywhere. "Pretty," he mumbled, before taking a much-needed nap.

CHAPTER 14

THE CURRENT FLOWED BRISKLY ACROSS THE battle waters, which were very clear today. Whalem gave the orders for the armada to make the last of its preparations. Indi's mariners were massed on the south side of the Riptide territory. Apparently, the leader here had renamed the ancient shiver after himself, but that didn't matter. According to Indi Shiver, these were the Riptide homewaters. The terraced area, full of different single-colored greenie, was in the distance with Riptide Shiver sharks in a loose battle formation in front of that. Whalem could see their mariners were nervous, fins flicking and tails swishing. His stomach turned, sensing another oncoming slaughter. There was no glory in this. None at all.

Whalem noticed the industrious court shark Tydal making his own preparations in the floating royal court. Whalem disliked the court with all its pomp and vanity, but after this victory Finnivus could rightly call himself emperor of the seven seas. The arrogant tiger would want an elaborate ceremony, of course, hence Tydal's activity.

The past year was wearing on Whalem. Seeing Finnivus grow more capricious and cruel with each victory sickened his stomach. He hoped his nausea was due to the slightly different fish of the Atlantis, but doubted it. Maybe, just maybe, after Finnivus conquered everything he would calm down and rule well. Whalem felt a wave of despair as a small voice inside him whispered, "That won't happen. He'll become a monster."

"Why the long faces?" Finnivus boomed.

Whalem snapped to attention at his position by the lantern fish signaler and was relieved to find he wasn't the focus of the king's attention. It was a couple of young sharks from the Line. "This is my day! Everyone should be as happy, but never happier, than us!" Finnivus laughed his grating, high-pitched, and ridiculous laugh.

A couple of the younglings had asked Finnivus if *they* could command the armada for the final battle instead of Whalem, but they were denied. That was the reason for their sour mood. Whalem didn't actually care and took the insulting request in stride. He could have asked for single combat as was his right, but he had tired of all the blood being spilled. The more Whalem thought about the request, the more he realized it was a carefully laid trap. He was fifty summers older than the pups who'd challenged him. Victory would have been no sure thing, even with his combat experience. In any case, Finnivus was superstitious and insisted that everything stay the same.

Of course, the new royal herald would be the first to approach the other shiver. Finnivus cackled as the poor shark made what would in all likelihood be his last few tail strokes across the empty expanse between the mighty Indi armada and its pitiful opponents. Riptide had barely a hundred sharkkind.

Finnivus motioned at the herald with a fin and told the court, "He's going to say that their leader has to admit he is a jelly-brained turtle next to my glorious magnificence! Ha!" More high-pitched laughing.

Whalem, in his position off to the side, could not hear the herald as he delivered the message and waited for what he knew was certain death. Heralds weren't allowed to defend themselves. Their job was to wait for a reply. That the reply could be—today more than ever—a bite to the gills was beside the point.

Curiously, the mako leader of Riptide Shiver listened to everything and didn't attack the herald, which would have undoubtedly begun the battle. Indeed, she—the leader looked female even from this distance—seemed to be answering. After a moment, the herald swam back toward the king's court!

What was this?

"Tydal!" shouted Finnivus. "Why aren't we fighting?

Why is there no killing?" The king adjusted himself on one of his blue whales.

"I'm—I'm not sure, Your Magnificence," the epaulette shark stammered. Tydal's fins seemed to move in opposite directions and with crossed purposes.

"Find out this instant!" Finnivus yelled.

Tydal swam as fast as he could from his position in the court to the approaching herald. Whalem followed. He could signal his lantern fish and have the Indi armada in action at a moment's notice, but he wanted to hear this.

"I greet you, First Court Fish—" the herald began. The official greeting between them would last far too long and Tydal knew it.

"Forget all that!" the epaulette whispered urgently. "What's happening?"

"She agreed."

"By Tyro's tail, make sense!" Tydal urged, his own tail twitching as if he were being shocked by an eel.

"Their leader wants me to deliver a message to the king that she'll do everything he demands," the herald told him.

Whalem's heart leapt. Could the day end with *none* of his mariners swimming the Sparkle Blue? It seemed too good to be true. Tydal was caught open-mouthed, gills pumping spastically. All he could do was ask, "Really?"

"What's happening, Tydal?" shouted Finnivus from his throne. "We grow agitated and not amused!"

A split-second decision was needed. In the deadly world of royal mood swings, it could mean Tydal's life. "Deliver the message," he heard the court shark say.

This was about to get interesting. Tydal took his place in the court as the herald explained. It was for the king's ears only, so no one else could hear. Heralds were taught this skill; they could speak loudly enough for thousands to hear, or quietly enough so only one would, even in a crowd.

After listening, Finnivus laughed with glee, bouncing himself on the back of the blue whale underneath him. For once, Whalem thought, the ridiculous laugh was the most welcome sound in all the Big Blue. "Excellent! Bring their leader to me this instant!"

The commander of the *squaline* ordered the king's personal guards to form a defensive line. Another complement of mariners circled above the king, protecting his dorsal. These armored guards were faster than all but a few unarmored sharks, which was why they'd been chosen for this duty.

The prisoner swam up slowly, pressed flank to flank between two massive great white *squaline*, so she couldn't streak into an attack. The mako leader of Riptide Shiver was beautiful, there was no denying that.

"I'm honored to hover in the presence of the wise and mighty Finnivus Victor," she said, loud enough for everyone in the royal court to hear. "I'll happily swim to the Sparkle Blue today because I've met the greatest shark in all the oceans and seas!" She smiled and showed her thin and pointed teeth in a friendly way.

"And what do they call you?" asked Finnivus.

"My name is Velenka, Your Magnificence."

Finnivus smiled at the court, which hung on his every word. "She certainly is well-mannered for an uncultured fish." He tittered at his own joke, immediately joined by everyone else.

Velenka then said, "Your Majesty's laugh is a most beautiful music."

Whalem's opinion of the Riptide leader changed immediately. This shark *was* a threat, but not to him or Finnivus. She was a threat to anyone in court who would fight for rank with her.

One youngling in the Line realized this immediately, too. "Make her wish come true, Majesty!" he yelled. "Feast on her! The leader of the last ancient shiver in the Big Blue would make a fitting meal to announce the age of *Emperor* Finnivus!"

Finnivus preened for the mako and made a show of thinking about this. But Whalem knew she was too beautiful and too interesting for the king to resist. Finnivus clicked his notched teeth together. "I really should eat you. If there isn't going to be a battle for my amusement, then I should have you for dinner to celebrate. My fourth is right about that."

"An emperor does what he wants," Velenka said calmly. "In the end his word is law, no matter what anyone else thinks."

Whalem almost shook his head in amazement. What an answer! Now if Finnivus were to order the mako's death, it would seem based on someone else's advice, which would make him look weak.

Amazingly, he seemed even more interested. "But surely blood must be spilled on our glorious day!" Finnivus replied. "What would you have me do?"

Whalem almost spun around in surprise. Finnivus was asking someone else for an opinion!

The mako performed a graceful bow and cast her eyes downward. It was as if she'd been born at court. "Emperor, Riptide Shiver is no more. Every sharkkind formerly a part of it is yours to do with as you wish."

"Oh, I'd like to destroy every one of your puny mariners, but undoubtedly Whalem would feel terrible about it." The gathered court fins laughed. Finnivus continued, "But you've been so charming, it would be a shame to eat you. How about your Line? Will you feast on them with me and prove your loyalty?"

The sunlight caught Velenka's pitch-black upper half, and a rainbow reflected from it. "They are as loyal to me as I will be to you, Emperor. My Line would be honored to sacrifice themselves for your celebration."

"Then come, let's go for a swim while the royal sea-soners do their work, then. You can show me around my newest homewaters."

"I am honored," she told Finnivus.

Whalem swam off, as his part in the day was over. And honored or not, there was a good deal of scream-ing when it became clear to the sharkkind in the Riptide Line what was in store for them.

CHAPTER 15

VELENKA SWAM THROUGH THE RIPTIDE homewaters at the flank of the soon-to-be emperor of the Big Blue. He was at least five or six seasons younger than she was. Velenka could only dream of having the power he was born into. The way was now clear for him to impose his will on all the seven seas. She knew there was a whale of a difference between a regular shiver and a royal shiver, and she struggled to remember her lessons on the subject. She adjusted her position so that her snout wouldn't surpass the tiger's front flipper. Position and appearances were *everything* in a royal court. *That* she did remember.

"I see that this shiver did a little seascaping," Finnivus told her. "It's nothing like my, umm, *our* homewaters, but it's the best we've seen in the Atlantis."

Velenka almost laughed at the pup king's mistakes using the royal *we*. But laughing wouldn't have been wise. Velenka escorted him through the Riptide home-waters proper, and he wasn't entirely disdainful, especially after he saw the terraced greenie gardens with their bright, bright colors.

"Not terrible," he commented.

Velenka risked a sidelong peek at the tiger. Was Finnivus a conqueror supreme? Or a spoiled brat who'd gotten lucky?

"I can't take credit for the terraces," she told him. "I was only leader for a few days before you arrived."

"Really? How did that happen?"

That was an open question. A very *smart* open question. Finnivus hadn't offered a clue about what he was thinking, or what he might like her to say. The sleek tattooed tiger shark was much sharper than Goblin, that was for sure.

"Our leader went missing," Velenka said, keeping her fins perfectly still. She didn't want to seem nervous. "Either he saw your armada and swam away in fright, or . . . he died of a jellyfish sting. There are different rumors."

Finnivus laughed. The high-pitched chortle was almost comical. "He died of a jellyfish sting just before I would have eaten him? Not likely! He ran and hid like a little turtle hatchling!"

"If he *was* sent to the Sparkle Blue by a jelly, maybe the drifters also want you to be their emperor."

Finnivus fell silent. For a moment Velenka thought

that she had overplayed, but then he laughed. "Oh, that's too good!" he chortled. "*Drifters* wanting me to be emperor! You have a keen wit!"

The laughter spread to the surrounding court sharks, which once again reminded Velenka they weren't alone. Of course, royalty should have a retinue, but this was ridiculous. There were at least twenty-five sharkkind constantly within three or four tail strokes of Finnivus at all times. Plus, his personal guard was there, coated in metallic skin. They swam so quietly, it was a miracle to hear them at all. And a mere tail's length away was the first court shark, a brown-and-yellow epaulette. Velenka ignored him completely as did everyone else. Then there were the young sharkkind of the Line who eyed her balefully. There were also many other sharks and dwellers whose jobs and names she didn't know. Velenka would learn everything about them as if her life depended on it.

Which was undoubtedly truer than she knew.

"Yes, yes," Finnivus said to himself as he looked around at the colorful greenie bordering the ancient Speakers Rock at the center of the Riptide homewaters. "This place is the most worthy we've seen. Tydal, my ceremony shall be here. Make the preparations. And do tell us when our meal is ready."

The epaulette shark bobbed his head. "At once, Magnificence!" Tydal did an eel-quick turn and vanished.

Finnivus gave her a grin. "He's good at what he does."

"Oh, I'm sure he is, Your Majesty," Velenka said. "I'd only expect the most gifted sharkkind to be allowed near you."

"Yes, you'd *expect* that," he said, casting a sidelong glance at an older tiger shark with intricate tattoos. Velenka wondered if she, too, would have to get tattoos. They didn't look half bad. The black wave pattern was quite striking, but the ones the royalty wore were even better. Finnivus continued, "But sometimes you don't have a choice in the matter."

The shark in question seemed to be the mariner prime who led the battle armada. The young sharkkind in the Line joined with their king to laugh at this not-so-private joke. The older tiger, obviously not someone to be trifled with, acted as if he hadn't heard anything.

"You have proved yourself most interesting," Finnivus commented. Velenka bobbed her head and cast her eyes downward as she had seen the court shark do. How she hated scraping before anyone, even royalty. "I want you in court for my coronation ceremony."

Velenka acted flustered even though this was what she'd been hoping for secretly. "I—I don't know what to say, Your Majesty. Such an honor! You're such a kind and compassionate ruler to a poor fin you've just conquered!"

Finnivus preened as if Velenka was stroking his

underbelly. In a way, she was. It didn't matter. She needed to stay close to the pup if she were to survive.

"We are kind and compassionate to all who, umm, *we* rule."

Even more rewarding to Velenka than the invitation was the look of absolute horror on the sharks of the Line's faces. One female spinner shark even gnashed her teeth.

Velenka started when the court shark Tydal announced, "Dinner is served, Your Majesty," right behind her. Apparently, the little muck-sucker could sneak around with the best of them.

"Ah, excellent," Finnivus said. "Lead us, Tydal."

They swam back to Speakers Rock in front of the terraces of colored greenie. Already, Velenka could see that the dwellers in Indi Shiver were decorating the area in their colors for the coronation.

In all the excitement Velenka had forgotten that they would be dining on her Line. Some of it, anyway. Ripper, the battle-scarred hammerhead and the first of Goblin Shiver, hadn't returned from a long-range patrol. Maybe he'd been killed by an Indi patrol. Ripper was a lucky one, then. At least he died in battle.

Velenka looked at the faces of her ex-shivermates arranged on a rock disc carried on the backs of four sea turtles. To not eat would be counted against her. The young sharks of Indi's court certainly thought so. They dug in with Finnivus but kept looking over, eagerly waiting for Velenka to say she couldn't join them.

"Not hungry?" asked Finnivus. This was another test, of course. The young tiger was devious, all right.

"Nonsense, Your Majesty," she told Finnivus loudly enough for everyone to hear. "I'm starving!"

Halfway through the meal, Velenka discovered it wasn't so bad. In fact, Streak was kind of tasty.

CHAPTER 16

"SETTLE DOWN!" SHOUTED QUICKEYES, THE thresher leader of Coral Shiver. "I don't want to be a hard shell, but we need to stop talking over each other!" It had been six hours since Gray and the rest of Rogue Shiver had passed the Rock Lobster formation and entered Coral Shiver's hidden homewaters. He had just swum back from training with Takiza yesterday and thankfully was able to get a good sleep in before an emergency council meeting was called.

"He's right," Sandy said. "Let's weigh our options."

It suddenly became quiet enough that you could hear a couple of minnows darting around above their heads. Gray was once again awed by his mother. She stayed calm and cool when everyone else was tumbling around in the current. Coral Shiver was evenly split on whether they should stay or move because of the danger Indi Shiver posed. Solutions were scarce and the arguments on each side grew more and more heated. Since Rogue and Coral Shivers had formally agreed to join together soon after their introduction by Gray, both Lines could speak their minds. That was why this particular council meeting was so raucous. It wasn't just five opinions—it was ten!

"If we left here, where would we go?" Mari asked, loud enough to be heard. She made a circle with her long tail. "Indi Shiver's territory is now the *entire* Big Blue!"

It was a good point. There were grumbles and murmurs from both sides.

"I say we stay and fight!" Striiker announced, gnashing his triangular teeth. Of course he did. It didn't take much for the great white to get himself in an uproar. What was surprising was that Onyx completely supported him. The blacktip and Striiker had become fast friends. They were much alike, as both let their tempers sometimes get the best of them.

"He's making good sense," Onyx told everyone. "This royal brat will have to get his snout bloodied before he learns his lesson!"

"You can't be serious, Onyx," Barkley remarked, rolling his eyes. "You've seen how Indi Shiver fights. And they outnumber us at least twenty to one!"

"And that's just what's here today," Shell added. "They could bring more. A lot more."

"Yes," Quickeyes agreed. "You're probably right."

Onyx's tail drooped. He brushed the sandy bottom of the seabed, raising a cloud of sand. "Doesn't mean we have to like it." Unlike Striiker, once Onyx thought things through, he was more likely to come to a wise decision. Gray hoped the great white would learn this skill one day.

"Is there a place to go where there are less of them?" asked Snork. "A place that Indi sharks don't like?"

"If they don't like it, we probably wouldn't, either," Sandy told the sawfish. "What we have in common far outweighs our differences."

"But we're not eating the seasoned heads of everyone we meet," Shell said in his understated way.

Earlier in the day, Onyx had infiltrated Indi Shiver as a hunter. Since the blacktip wore their tattoos, he'd been able to get away with it, and even brought back a few fish. Onyx had heard many things about Finnivus. Unfortunately, none of them were good.

Gray pondered. "Maybe they'll leave soon. Like the other places you heard they conquered."

Onyx nodded. "The word around camp is that Finnivus hates everything that isn't the Indi homewaters."

"So that's good," said Mari.

"No. They'll leave a force of mariners to hold the territory," Barkley noted. "Or else what's the point of conquering anything?"

"But a holding force would be smaller and easier to avoid, or fight, than this armada," Sandy countered.

"The least dangerous course of action seems to be to hide and wait."

"Hide and wait, hide and wait," Striiker blurted. "That's all you ever want to do!"

Gray was about to come to his mother's defense, but she stopped him with the twitch of a fin. She could fight her own battles. "Sometimes that's the smart thing to do, Striiker. Never let your pride get you into a fight. Especially one you can't win."

The great white caught Gray glaring at him over his mother's dorsal and didn't argue.

"Okay, I've heard enough," said Quickeyes. The thresher looked around the gathered sharkkind. Various dwellers waited to see what, if anything, would be decided. "Coral Shiver will stay and keep our snouts in the greenie for now. If Rogue wants to leave—of course they can. We'll quietly search for other homewaters while we're waiting this out. One that's farther away from the Riptide territory and more defensible." It was easy for Quickeyes to use the name Riptide. He had never known it as Goblin Shiver.

Shell looked to Gray. "What do you think?"

As Rogue Shiver's leader, Gray had to make his thoughts known to his own Line. "It's the best plan for now. If something changes, or anyone wants to leave, come talk with me."

"And the training?" Striiker asked. Coral Shiver sharks, even pups, were being taught by Striiker and

Onyx to fight. This had never been done before, but sadly, now it was needed.

"The training should continue," Gray told everyone.

But what good would the out-of-date drills they had learned from Goblin do against Indi Shiver? Not much. Gray guessed something was better than nothing. Just not by a lot.

The shiver council meeting ended with everyone drifting off in twos and threes. Quickeyes swam over to Gray just as he was about to get a few words alone with his mother.

"You didn't say too much during the meeting," the thresher told him.

"I didn't have anything important to add," Gray answered sheepishly.

"Listening usually beats talking. Most fins don't learn that until they're much older than you." Quickeyes glanced at Striiker, who was having an energetic argument with Mari and Barkley. "Or not at all."

"Give him a chance," Gray told Coral's leader. "It takes a while to get used to his . . . let's say, colorful personality, but Striiker's loyal."

Quickeyes nodded at the comment and gave a look to Sandy. "He really has grown up and done you proud." He waggled a fin at Gray. "How's it going with Takiza?"

"You remember how mad I used to make you and everyone else? It's a good day when I only make him *that* mad."

Sandy and Quickeyes chuckled. The thresher swished his long tail once and swam off. "Please keep us informed about what you're doing."

Gray got to catch up with his mother then. For a little while, it was just the two of them and that was great. For some reason being with his mom made him feel like everything was going to turn out all right. Gray knew his feelings wouldn't do him any good in a real fight—then he'd rather have Striiker at his flank—but it was nice.

Barkley and Mari came over. Barkley gestured at Striiker talking with Onyx. "That great white chowderhead tires me out just listening. I'm so glad Quickeyes is more like you, Sandy."

"Thanks for the compliment, Barkley, but the truth is, Striiker and Onyx are right."

"What!" Barkley exclaimed a little too loudly. Striiker and Onyx stared for a moment but then went back to their energetic conversation. The dogfish lowered his voice. "You can't be serious. Their type of thinking will get us killed."

"What do you mean, Mom?" Gray asked. Mari swam closer so she could hear everything.

"We won't be able to feed the shiver with just a few of us quietly hunting," Gray's mother explained. "This type of living has a time limit. We either find a place that's safe—something that might not exist if Indi Shiver tightens their grip on the major hunting territories—or we have to face them."

"They may still go back to their own homewaters," Mari added, but without much conviction.

Barkley knew Sandy was right and was dismayed. "We can't win. I saw them fight. We can't!"

Mari bumped the dogfish's flank. "Quit bringing us down, Barkley. We're safe and all together right now. Let's be happy about that."

Barkley nodded. "You're right. And who knows? Maybe Takiza will teach Gray a few tricks, and he'll beat up their armada all by himself!"

"Yeah, right," Gray said as he gave his friend a good-natured tail slap. "Or maybe you and Yappy can just talk them to death."

"Did someone say my name?" shouted Yappy. "You guys done with your big meeting? We had one, too! During our meeting a sea cucumber scared Prime Minister Shocks. Can you believe that? They move so slowly, and still, Shocks got scared! Ha! Hey, where do you think sea cucumbers come from?"

Barkley looked at Gray with a mock-annoyed expression. "This is your fault."

Mari snorted, and Snork also came over, swimming low and digging through the greenie with his long saw bill, looking for treats. The topics of the ensuing conversation were many and varied. Gray, Barkley, Mari, and Sandy said nothing. They just relaxed, and for this night, tried to forget their troubles.

It didn't work for Gray, though. He knew that soon, someone—or more likely an armada of some-ones—would have to swim out and face Finnivus and his black wave of mariners.

THE
CORONATION

CHAPTER 17

WHALEM'S SPINE ACHED, AS IT DID FROM TIME to time. Remaining stock-still, at the hover—as Finnivus's coronation ceremony required—was the absolute worst! Bruises from battles fought in his younger days were calcifying and growing stiff with his advanced years. And performing attention hover added greatly to Whalem's spinal pain. It was difficult to execute for long periods of time, and he had ordered the armada to assume this position almost an hour ago. Whalem heard the groans of his mariners only in his mind as they were too disciplined to express their discomfort out loud. Now, what they were thinking was another matter.

There wasn't a thing to do to slow the tide of old age, but following the royal doctor fish's advice to stretch and bend each morning did help. Whalem had also used that time to ask Tyro to give Finnivus the understanding of his almost limitless power and the wisdom never to use it.

So far, either Tyro wasn't hearing him, or Finnivus wasn't listening to Tyro.

The current increased slightly. Whalem moved his tail fins in almost imperceptible strokes to hold his position stock-still in relation to Finnivus's throne. Oh, how he wished the ceremony would end!

Whalem knew it was an insult for him not to be next to the other royal sharks in the court. One of his commanders, or even a subcommander, could very ably have led the armada in attention hover. Whalem almost chuckled, picturing Finnivus trying to maintain attention hover for even five minutes. The spoiled pup had never known a day when he wasn't waited on snout and fin. If the royal seasoners didn't place food directly in his mouth, Finnivus might starve in the open ocean.

Tydal, the epaulette court shark, glided down a track of brilliant red and blue crabs underneath him. Thankfully, it seemed the ceremony was coming to its important bit. Tydal stopped smartly and began to recite the words that would make Finnivus emperor. By coincidence, a bitter cold current flowed through the area.

Staying in formation was now complete agony! Whalem willed Tydal to hurry. The little epaulette shark did do his job well. From negotiating with the nearby whales to form a choir to changing what had been Riptide Shiver's homewaters over to Indi colors, everything looked very regal.

In a steady and clear voice, Tydal began the final proclamation. Surely, the first court shark must know that the slightest mistake here would guarantee his shrieking death. But the epaulette went on, smooth and steady. "Whereas it pleased Tyro to call our glorious King Romulus Victor to the Sparkle Blue and replace him with his even more glorious son Finnivus Victor, we are awed and inspired to acknowledge that his kingly rank must be raised due to his numerous magnificent accomplishments!"

The soon-to-be emperor squealed and giggled in delight as the battles of the Indi armada now became exaggerated tall tales. For example, in the Arktik, the armada hadn't even seen a single orca, but that campaign was now called the Destruction of Icingholme Shiver Homewaters and Its Mighty Orckic Battle Pods.

Tydal went on, "So the good fins of the Big Blue acknowledge and recognize that through his mastery of the martial arts and uncountable victories, King Finnivus Victor shall be hereby and forever known as Emperor Finnivus Victor Triumphant, Conqueror of the Seven Seas and Overlord of the Four Oceans. All sharkkind and dwellers will bow before Finnivus Victor Triumphant!"

There was a muted *thwump* as every fin and dweller present did a communal head bob of deference. Whalem cast his eyes downward and looked up at the eager new emperor, swishing his tail back and forth in excitement. Tydal shouted, "I give you Emperor of all the Waters, Finnivus Triumphant! ALL HAIL THE EMPEROR!"

The gathered crowd and armada responded, "HAIL! HAIL! LONG LIVE EMPEROR FINNIVUS VICTOR TRIUMPHANT!" Whalem moved his mouth but couldn't bring himself to say the words with any conviction. But it did give him a chance to ease out of the strict attention hover. He saw the armada take the same liberty and allowed it. After a moment, everyone relaxed. Finnivus and the royals in the court no longer cared about them. The armada was only in their minds when they were in danger or needed something conquered. Otherwise, they didn't care a fin flick for any mariner's sacrifices.

Whalem had his commanders dismiss the armada. They could watch the festivities from a respectful distance or go hunt or rest. He could see that the mariners who chose hunting or sleeping far outnumbered those who wanted to watch the emperor enjoy himself. Whalem began swimming away to get some sleep, but a *squaline* intercepted him.

"Mariner Prime, you are summoned to court to congratulate the Emperor Finnivus." Whalem followed the guard to where Finnivus held court. He was made to wait by another nervous *squaline*, who mumbled, "I am sorry, Mariner Prime. Orders."

"Do your duty," Whalem replied evenly, grinding his notched teeth in annoyance. Another insult.

Tydal saw this and darted over. "What are you doing? Don't you recognize the first in the Line of Indi Shiver and mariner prime of the armada?"

"Yes, sir, I do. . . ." The guard looked over Tydal's shoulder and received a nod from the commander of the *squaline*. "Go right on through, sir. Very sorry."

Whalem swam toward Finnivus with Tydal at his side.

"I apologize Mariner Prime. I hadn't thought to check if—if something like that would happen."

"You had other things on your mind," Whalem responded.

Tydal nodded and went ahead to announce his arrival. Beside Finnivus was Velenka, the former leader of Riptide Shiver. Whalem could see the mako was already bumping snouts for position in the royal court. After Tydal spoke low to Finnivus, the emperor shouted across the homewaters, "Come, come! Whalem, my first! Where have you been?"

"With the armada, sir, as ancient protocol did dictate."

Finnivus grinned. "Oh, that! Pish-posh, you should have been here! Father would have insisted! You were friends, yes?"

Whalem's insides turned to stone. Finnivus knew

very well that he and Romulus were like brothers. "Yes," he answered. "He would have insisted."

One of the pups from the Line saw an opening and pounced. "What do you mean? Are you saying that Emperor Finnivus wronged you in some way?"

The shocking falseness of the question caught Whalem by surprise. How could anyone doubt his loyalty? He should have immediately said something—become enraged at the smart-mouthed flipper—but was stunned silent. He caught a glimpse of Finnivus, who instead of protesting the innocent mistake, *watched* Whalem like he was some sort of traitor!

"Should I have taken time on the day of my royal coronation as emperor of the entire Big Blue to make sure you came to the ceremony?" Finnivus asked mockingly, getting a laugh from the court.

"Of course not, Your Majesty," Whalem began. Then his emotions got the best of him, and he added, "But you could have sent someone." There was silence in the court.

"This is an outrage, Emperor!" someone yelled from the Line.

Finnivus looked down from his position over Speakers Rock and said, "We are not offended." But the emperor's words did not match the flat, dead look in his eyes. "You seem tired, Whalem. You are very old. Get some rest."

And there it was. He was dismissed.

As he left, Whalem caught Tydal watching. Of course, he couldn't tell what the court shark was thinking, unlike the pups of the Line who were absolutely giddy at his mistake. Whalem was mariner prime and first in the Line in name only now. How soon would his head be first in the line at the royal seasoners?

CHAPTER 18

GRAY AND TAKIZA WERE BACK AT THE TRAINING ground next to the Maw. It was pitch-black, for it was night above the chop-chop, with no moon to provide even a little light. The ancient coral spires stood, wickedly sharp and unmoving, mocking him in the darkness. The greenie harness chafed and rubbed Gray raw under his fins and belly. How Takiza had managed to weave it was a marvel. The frilly betta took a long strand of greenie in his mouth and looped through the water this way and that, almost faster than the eye could see. When it was done, Gray didn't know what to make of it. But now that the harness was on him, he knew exactly what it was—a torture device.

"Can I take a break, Shiro?"

Takiza released a frustrated whoosh of water from his gills. "You may loaf after you have mastered this exercise. Unfortunately, you have all the grace of a pregnant sea cow, and I despair of you ever completing this task."

Gray muttered underneath his breath, "I'll give you a pregnant sea cow . . ."

Takiza gave him a surprisingly strong tail slap across the snout. "What was that, Nulo?"

"Nothing, Shiro!"

"I know it was nothing. The vast majority of things you say are nothing. So stop muttering and concentrate! Now—again!"

Gray could hear the greenie in the harness stretch as he pulled the giant rock inside off the seabed. He navigated the course carefully, floating the rock between, over, and under various obstacles. "Good, feel the weight and shape of the burden you are carrying. Use your lateral line to sense it as if it were an extension of your own pudgy body," Takiza said into his ear.

"I'm not pudgy, Shiro! Mom says I'm just big cartilaged," Gray answered through clenched teeth as he strained.

Another tail slap. "Quiet, Nulo! Your mother is a gentle soul who was merely being kind! Listen and learn!"

"Yeah, right," Gray said sarcastically. "Because I'm *sooo* special. But will you tell me why I'm special? Why I have to do this stuff? *Nooo*." He looked Takiza right in the eye, something that usually made the Siamese fighting fish act like his name.

Instead, his teacher sighed. "If I tell you some small bit of what I know, will there be no more complaining for the rest of this session?"

Gray couldn't believe his luck! Maybe he'd just worn Takiza down! He found that hard to believe, but wasn't going to look a gift bluefin in the mouth. "Yes! I promise. No more complaining!"

"There is an ancient prophecy that tells of a great sharkkind leading every good fin in the ocean against an ancient evil."

"And?"

The little betta ruffled his fins. "And I have now told you one small bit of prophecy."

"But that could mean *anything*!" Gray whined. "And it could be for anyone!"

"Yes, it could. Frustrating, isn't it? That's why it's best not to put too much stock in prophecy. Now, I have kept my end of the bargain—"

"By tricking me!" Gray interrupted, whipping his tail back and forth to try and warm up.

Takiza shook his head. "Oh, if tricking you were less easy, your training would proceed much faster. I could never trick Lochlan, my golden apprentice. But you? Every time it gets easier. Come, Nulo, swim!"

Lochlan, Lochlan, Lochlan! The golden wonder shark! Gray couldn't wait to one day meet this teacher's pet and bop him right in the snout for being such a goody-goody.

Gray forced himself forward. The little betta loved talking during the training, and it usually broke Gray's concentration. Maybe that was part of the lesson. If Gray could manage to listen and understand what was being said even through a flurry of insults, then his concentration would improve.

Or maybe Takiza just liked insulting him.

"Feel the distance between the rock and the ocean floor. Feel how you are now *dragging* the rock in the sand, instead of properly floating it as I told you."

Gray strained against the harness and adjusted his depth so the rock was off the seabed. It wasn't so bad after he got going, but lifting off was tough.

"Feel the currents around you. Use them to your advantage. Work with the ocean, not against it."

"I am working with it," Gray huffed, gills pumping furiously from his efforts. "But it doesn't want to work with *me*!" Nevertheless, he floated the rock underneath the hardest portion of the course, a low ceiling formed by a fallen coral spire. One that Gray hadn't broken. It was fiendishly tricky to keep the rock moving forward as there was only a tail length between his dorsal fin and the urchin spine–sharp coral above, and an equally short distance between the seabed and the bottom of the harnessed rock below. If the rock hit the ocean floor, as it had all ten times Gray had tried today, it was impossible to get enough lift in the cramped area to get moving again. But this time, with some skill and a favorable current…

"Ha! I did it!" Gray said, swishing his tail with a flourish. "Take that, obstacle course!"

Takiza nodded. "Finally, one small victory. Of course, Lochlan did it on his first try. Have I mentioned if you could be somewhat like him, your training would go much faster?"

"You may have said that once or twice, Shiro."

"Good. Now we can practice at a greater depth, my young apprentice."

Gray groaned. He couldn't imagine carrying the rock in the harness while struggling to breathe in the Dark Blue. He was about to object when Takiza did a quick half loop and plunged into the sand.

"What have we here?" asked the betta, bouncing a large sandy rock with his gauzy tailfin. "Explain yourself this instant!"

Gray thought Takiza had gone crazy, ordering a stone to speak. Then he saw it wasn't a rock at all. "Trank! What are you doing here?"

But the stonefish didn't answer. Or move. From the shocked look in his eyes, it appeared Takiza had paralyzed him with one of his mysterious pressure-point fin touches. When Gray asked to learn the move, Takiza laughed as if it were the funniest thing he'd ever heard.

"You know this stonefish? Do you realize his kind are

quite low in character? And this particular one seems even lower than most."

"He's okay," Gray said. "Let him go."

Takiza sighed. "Very well." The frilly betta did a quick turn around the floating stonefish and touched him with a fin flick between the eyes.

Trank's fins began moving. He backed away from the betta and closer to Gray. "That's a neat trick, Takiza. It is Takiza, isn't it?"

"It is."

"I'm sure Gafin would pay if youse would teach that to a few of us."

"Gafin would, would he?" Takiza gave the stonefish a smirk. "Tell Gafin to make the offer to me in person."

"Gafin don't see no one."

"In that case we are at an impasse."

"What are you doing here, Trank?" Gray asked again.

The stonefish was still mad about being paralyzed. It took him a few seconds before he could answer. "You know you're behind on what youse owe us?"

Takiza snorted derisively.

Trank gave him a look but went on. "Gafin knows yer good for it, but keep it in mind."

"First day off I have, I promise to go to hunting for you."

"Okay, fine," the stonefish said. "Then there is one other thing." Trank paused before continuing, his eyes darting between Gray and Takiza. "Velenka wants to meet."

"No," Takiza said, shaking his head. "That one swims with Indi Shiver now."

"She does?" Gray said in surprise.

Trank eyed Takiza suspiciously. "How do youse know that?"

The frilly betta ignored the question. "It is a trap," Takiza told Gray matter-of-factly.

"Gafin gives his word for your safety inside Slagger-nacks."

"What about *outside*?" asked the betta.

"Show Gafin some respect!" the stonefish growled. "Velenka knows we can get to her if she doesn't play nice. If she and I can do business, you can, too."

"It's dangerous to trust Velenka," Gray said to himself. "And Barkley would kill me."

"Finally, you prove there is something other than chowder in that huge head of yours," Takiza commented.

Trank swam closer to Gray. "Yeah, she thought youse wouldn't just come for a snack and the band, so she said to tell youse what it's about."

"Which is?"

"It's about Coral Shiver's continued safety, she says." Takiza swam around Trank very slowly, and the stone fish began spinning as if he were caught in a whirlpool. "Hey, stop it! Stop it!"

The betta ignored Trank and spoke to Gray. "If she knew where your family was, Velenka would have already traded that information to secure her position with the emperor."

"Hey! This isn't funny!" shouted the now wildly spinning Trank.

But the way Gray saw it, there was no choice. "I can't take the chance, Shiro. I have to go."

Takiza sighed. "You are an extremely troublesome apprentice, Nulo. Not like Lochlan at all."

CHAPTER 19

IT HAD TAKEN GRAY TWO DAYS TO SWIM BACK to Coral Shiver from the training grounds because the current was running against him. He stopped by Slaggernacks and left word that he would meet with Velenka. Then, after making sure no one was following, Gray swam to Coral's temporary homewaters. The shiver was safe, and Quickeyes promised to suspend all feeding while Gray went to his meeting. Every shark in the shiver would have to ignore their rumbling bellies for a while. They couldn't take the chance of being spotted. Onyx, Barkley, Mari, and the rest would continue searching for another, more defensible, place they could move to in case they were discovered. But how many times could Coral Shiver run?

After picking off a few oily mackerel, Gray crept through the dense greenie until he got to the edge of the field and stopped. He surveyed the maze of rocky caverns, coral, and greenie, whose jumble formed Slaggernacks. How could this odd place have become so important? It was still supposedly neutral ground, but only because Emperor Finnivus and Indi Shiver didn't know it existed. Would it still be safe once they found out about it? The Indi armada was a power unlike any the Big Blue had seen in a thousand years. What were a few poisonous dwellers compared to that?

Everyone in Rogue Shiver and quite a few in Coral had offered to back up Gray for his meeting with Velenka. But Gray made the decision as Rogue Shiver leader that no one else could come, something he had never done. There was no way he wanted others risking their lives. For the safety of both Rogue and Coral Shivers, he needed to do this by himself. If Velenka's information helped, that was good. If it was a trap, well, then Gray would be the only one caught.

Trank had given his word, but was his word any good? Gray felt a cold tingle creep down his spine that had nothing to do with the coming of winter and the water cooling. He looked into the distance around Slaggernacks and saw nothing unusual. He even tried to reach out with his *other* senses that Takiza was constantly berating him to use. Sometimes when Gray used his lateral line, there was a faint electrical buzzing when he located another sharkkind or fish. But now he felt no other presence aside from the usual small dwellers going about their lives. Gnashing his teeth nervously a few times, Gray swam toward the back caverns.

Trank floated upward from a pile of rocks near some waving greenie. "Didn't know if youse would show."

Not for the first time, Gray wondered how many of the rocks near Slaggernacks were actually stonefish, or something equally venomous in disguise.

"Am I first?" he asked. He'd arrived an hour before he was supposed to so he could be in the cave before Velenka.

Gray was dismayed when Trank answered, "Youse wish. Watch your back."

"Not coming in?"

Trank shook his head, causing a cloud of dirt to fall from his seemingly malformed scales. How stonefish could live like that, Gray didn't know. "She wanted privacy and paid a large amount to get everyone out. Youse is on your own."

Gray cautiously swam into the smallish cavern. Glowing coral grew only sparsely here. Without lumos to provide light, it was nearly black. But now his lateral line buzzed. Gray could feel Velenka's position clearly. He took a quick look at the craggy ceiling of the cave and saw that it was bare; there were no poisonous urchins or octos. Like Trank had said, they were alone.

"Gray, it's good to see you," said Velenka, rolling her mako tail and giving him a smile. Her upper half almost merged with the gloom around them. Those eyes—they seemed even more disconcertingly black now. Gray shivered involuntarily. Once he had liked being around Velenka. But now, despite her beauty and brains, it was as if darkness oozed from her very being.

"What do you want, Velenka?"

The mako winced exaggeratedly. "No hello? No, 'I'm glad the emperor didn't kill you'?"

"How can you deal with being around that maniac?" Gray asked.

"Finnivus isn't a maniac! He's misunderstood!" she said with sudden intensity. "I have to get close to him."

"Convenient for you."

"Convenient for everyone!" she shouted. Her voice rang off the stone ceiling. "The emperor will destroy you if he's not managed."

"And you're just the shark to do that."

"With your help," Velenka answered quietly.

Gray couldn't believe it. She was asking him to trust her? After she betrayed him and his friends on more than one occasion? "I'll trust you—after *Goblin* tells me it's okay to do that." There were rumors that Goblin hadn't been at the face-off with Indi Shiver. It was very suspicious for the stubborn and aggressive great white leader to have disappeared so completely.

Velenka bristled. "I'm the only hope the sharkkind and dwellers around here have! That includes your mother!"

Gray rammed the mako, pinning her against the wall with his bulk. He was sure this was painful, but he didn't care. "Don't—don't you talk about my mom."

"Goblin was a fool," she hissed. "He was going to get us all killed! I had to act!"

"Tell me what you know!" Gray yelled. Then he eased up. When it came down to it, Gray couldn't just bite Velenka and send her to the Sparkle Blue.

"He's going to search the area carefully for any hidden shivers," she told him. "That's what Indi always does after they beat the main forces. They'll crush anyone they find. It teaches a lesson to everyone who might want to make trouble after they've left for their homewaters. This way Finnivus can leave a smaller force to hold this area."

"But have they found Coral Shiver yet?"

From the glint in Velenka's eye, Gray knew he'd made a mistake. His heart sank as she said, "So they *are* still here."

She hadn't known until just now, he thought. Until I opened my big, fat mouth. Gray tasted his own blood as he grated his teeth back and forth in anger.

Velenka continued, "They found a remnant of Razor Shiver and a few others. If you surrender, it'll go much easier for you."

"Velenka," Gray gasped. "Are you crazy? The emperor is insane. How do you know he won't make me eat Barkley's head to prove I'm loyal?" The mako didn't answer.

It was then that Gray understood. "You don't know what he's capable of, do you?"

"I took an awful chance coming here. This is a huge favor I'm doing for you!" She went on, either not noticing or not caring about the look of horror on his face. "You can't save everyone, Gray. If you throw yourself on the emperor's mercy, things may work out."

He shook his head in disbelief. "That's not a chance I'm willing to take, Velenka."

"Then everyone you know and care about is doomed!"

Gray backed out of the cramped cavern, not wanting to turn his back on the mako. If this was her idea of a favor, who knew what she might do if she had a chance to bite his tail?

"They won't be able to hide forever!" Velenka said, her eyes blazing with a weird intensity.

Gray slid out of the cavern—and found ten tattooed Indi shiver sharkkind waiting. His heart sank. He was able to spot Trank in the pile of rocks by the door. "I thought you guaranteed my safety. I thought we had a deal!"

Trank fluttered off the sandy bottom, turning so he could look Gray in the eyes. "Sorry, pup. He offered a better deal. One where we keep breathing." The stonefish pointed a stubby fin into the distance, where Finnivus himself hovered!

The intricately tattooed tiger shark wore a dismissive

smirk and had a cruel glint in his eye. He was carried on the back of a blue whale that hovered behind a wall of armored guards. Seemingly on their own, Gray's fins and tail churned furiously as he stared at the haughty emperor. But his insides chilled. Gray knew he could never allow this shark to decide the fate of his mother or any of his friends.

"So this is the sharkkind you spoke of?" said Finnivus. "We are not impressed."

"What's the matter with you?" Gray shouted at Finnivus. He looked over at the guards and their commander, the older shark they called the mariner prime. "And you! How can you allow him to order you to do such evil? Do you have any conscience at all?"

Finnivus's eyes blazed at Gray. "No one *allows* me to do anything! I—*we*—are the emperor of all the seven seas! None may disobey!"

Gray bristled, chopping his fins through the water. "All I see is a spoiled bully! But you won't get away with it! The good fins in the Big Blue will swim against you, you—chowderheaded flipper!"

There was an audible gasp from some of the guards. Finnivus's eyes went red, and he thrashed his tail around. "Did you just call me a chowderheaded flipper?" The emperor was maniacally angry now. "No one calls me names!" he yelled. "NO ONE!" He pointed at Gray with a trembling fin. "I—*we* want your head for dinner!"

"It didn't have to be this way," the mako told Gray sadly.

"And it's not going to be!" Gray roared, rocketing forward and catching the Indi mariners by surprise. He rammed the nearest one in the liver and ricocheted off two others.

"Seize him!" their commander shouted.

For all Gray's complaining, Takiza's training had transformed him. He was too quick for the armored guards. Other armada mariners tried to catch him. Some clenched glinting ropes in their mouths—*chains* was the landshark word that flashed through Gray's mind. He knew he couldn't let the Indi sharks entangle him with those!

He accelerated right toward Finnivus, cutting a hard turn that made his side hurt. The *squaline* adjusted their positions to block. Even wearing their metal coverings, they were so fast! But Gray wanted them to do that. This way he could go underneath the blue whale that Finnivus was riding. He finned it mercilessly in its soft underbelly.

The shock caused the whale to reflexively throw the emperor off his back and into the open waters. For any ordinary shark, this wouldn't have been a big deal, but Finnivus was no ordinary shark.

"Whalem! What's happening?" Finnivus yelled to his mariner prime, his voice cracking. Things weren't going as planned and now he was scared. Well, too bad! If things went smoothly, Gray would be eaten!

Whalem ordered, "Protect the emperor at all cost! Close ranks!"

Every armada mariner and *squaline* surrounded Finnivus immediately, which was *exactly* what Onyx had told Gray would happen.

Then members of the octopus clan, whom Gray and Barkley knew from the Coral Shiver, going all the way back to the bucket incident (and more importantly, who didn't work for Trank) rose from their hiding places on the ocean floor and squirted their black ink into the water.

Barkley had arranged for a meeting with the octos through Prime Minister Shocks while they were at Coral Shiver, and they were only too happy to help. Their ink blotted out the light from the random lumos in the area and put a putrid taste into the water. Now no one could follow him by sight or scent. Gray was going to owe them a huge thank you and a lot of fish, even though the older octos insisted on naming the plan *Operation Buckethead.* Dumb octos . . .

Gray heard Whalem shout, "Fall back! Fall back!"

Finnivus shrieked even louder, "NO! WE DO NOT RETREAT! FIND HIM! I—*WE* ORDER IT!"

Yet Gray was already swimming into the thick greenie. He had escaped, but at what price to everyone he cared about?

CHAPTER 20

TYDAL WAS AFRAID TO TWITCH A FIN. Doing so might draw unwanted attention from the emperor, who hadn't stopped raging since he returned to his newly conquered homewaters. Usually, Tydal went with Finnivus on his swims outside of the royal court in order to serve him. However, when Finnivus traveled outside of the Indi Shiver homewaters, his wants and needs were under *squaline* authority, so Tydal had been dismissed by Finnivus and told to stay and "make this sad little place more befitting of an emperor!" That turned out to be a very good thing.

The emperor's party was gone for only a little while. During that time, Tydal ordered the colorful crabs and starfish forming their pleasing patterns to move and create other hopefully *more* pleasing patterns. But Finnivus returned too soon! The dwellers weren't nearly done, and Tydal couldn't give them instructions now.

They were moving slowly—which was how all crabs and starfish moved, by the way—into the shapes he'd told them to form and, to Tydal's ears, were making too much noise! Finnivus hadn't noticed yet, so great was his anger.

"WHO IS THIS SHARK NAMED GRAY?" the emperor yelled. "Why wasn't he captured?"

None of the younglings from the Line spoke. Even Finnivus's new favorite shark, Velenka, didn't dare say anything right now. Tydal had no idea who this *Gray* was, but he did know the hunting party was supposed to capture him. Apparently, they hadn't. Finnivus hated when *anything* didn't turn out exactly the way he wanted. He just wasn't used to that.

The clicking and clacking racket made by the moving crabs and starfish was *deafening*! It would only take a moment of silence for Finnivus to hear it and be displeased. Tydal's insides rumbled, and sharp pains jolted him as if his stomach were being bitten from the inside. Perhaps the shrimp and crab here didn't agree with him.

"I've been betrayed!" Finnivus huffed. Then he caught his mistake and said, "I mean, *we've* been betrayed!"

Tydal was sure he was hearing things when a voice said, "Your majesty, no one betrayed you."

But it was real! Someone had dared to speak!

Everyone looked toward the offending fin who had interrupted the emperor's royal tantrum.

Of course, it was Whalem.

The fool was going to get himself killed! Everything went dead silent. Even the crabs and starfish had the good sense to stop moving. Finnivus looked across the court from his position atop a blue whale hovering over Riptide Shiver's conquered Speakers Rock. It was built up with bright yellow and orange starfish the way he liked, and the terraced greenie behind Finnivus framed him impressively. That fact was unimportant now, though. The emperor's mouth hung open.

Finally he asked, "What?"

Whalem sighed. Tydal could see that Whalem was going to make the horrible mistake of speaking his mind, or worse—*explaining* why Finnivus was *wrong*!

Before Tydal knew what he was doing—for he definitely would *not* dare say a word if he were thinking correctly—he blurted, "Dinner is ready, Magnificence!"

Now everyone in the royal court looked at Tydal. No one could believe he had spoken, including a very surprised Whalem. The rebuke was swift and immediate, though. Finnivus roared, "Mention dinner again, and *you'll* be the main course! DO YOU UNDERSTAND?"

Tydal thrust his face down until he was groveling in the mud like the muck-sucker most of the court thought him to be. Thankfully, Finnivus turned his attention back to his mariner prime.

"What did you say?" the emperor asked. Even

though Finnivus spoke in a whisper, everyone around the court could clearly hear him. If Whalem would only grovel a little, maybe the situation could be saved. But Whalem wasn't like Tydal. The tiger was first in the Line of Indi Shiver, mariner prime, and commander of the armada. He *never* groveled. Maybe that's why Tydal admired him.

"No one betrayed you, Finnivus. We were caught by surprise."

The beautiful mako took this as an attack and hissed, "I said, 'Be prepared'! I told you Gray was powerful and fast!"

A young spinner shark from the Line joined the fray—but carefully. "I remember Velenka saying this sharkkind was dangerous, but she didn't really make it clear just *how* dangerous. And Whalem, why didn't you take better precautions?"

It wasn't Whalem's fault, thought Tydal as he pressed his snout deeper in the mud. He'd overheard this part of the discussion before the group had left. Whalem had wanted to take a full battle fin, a hundred sharkkind, but Finnivus wouldn't hear of it. The emperor proclaimed that no one could stand against even a single Indi Shiver mariner. Then Whalem convinced Finnivus that it would be much more regal to have a cohort of *squaline* around himself to show off his greatness as well as a few dozen mariners. It was, all in all, a very skillful way of bending the emperor's will to his own. Their lack of proper guard was actually Finnivus's fault, but no one would be foolhardy enough to bring that up.

No one except Whalem, apparently. "I wanted to bring along a battle fin," the old tiger reminded the emperor, speaking to him as if he were an errant school fish!

"So you're saying I—*WE*—made a mistake?"

"How dare you, Whalem?" sputtered another pup from the Line. "How dare you accuse the emperor of such a thing?"

Whalem turned to the pup. "Shut your cod hole before I rip off your tail and feed it to you." Then he looked back at the emperor.

"Your Majesty," Whalem began. He looked tired to Tydal. "We are currently many leagues from our own Indi Ocean. We're not in our homewaters and do not know the territory. One large and fast shark-kind surprised us. When that happens it is our duty—my duty—to make sure you are protected first and foremost."

Whalem had totally ignored the emperor's question! That, in and of itself, was a grave crime. However, here was a chance for Finnivus to swim right by this whole ugly scene—if he would only take it, everything could go back to normal!

But the wicked young pups of the Line would never let an opportunity like this wriggle away from them.

One insisted, "Answer the emperor's question, Whalem! Are you saying he made a mistake?"

"Yes, answer the question!" added another.

Whalem gave the pups a look that might have killed two lesser sharks where they hovered. "No battle plans survive first contact—"

The emperor laughed in his tittering high-pitched way. "Are you saying this was a battle? One shark?"

"It turned into a battle, Finnivus."

"STOP CALLING ME FINNIVUS! I am the emperor! Emperor of the entire Big Blue! You are nothing but an old, krillfaced, jelly-brained drifter that my father should have gotten rid of a long time ago!"

Whalem's fins trembled, his rage barely under control. For a moment, he said nothing, but then he erupted, "Your father would be ashamed of you! You act like a spoiled pup! YOU'RE A DISGRACE!"

There was absolute silence.

The word *disgrace* seemed to echo through the waters of the court. No one dared move or even breathe. Tydal expected Whalem to be sent to the Sparkle Blue on the spot.

But Finnivus didn't rage. He seemed relieved. Tydal guessed it was because the emperor could finally get rid of Whalem. Regardless of the reason, Finnivus didn't yell.

"You are no longer my first, Whalem. I remove you from my Line. I strip you of command of the armada, as well as the title of mariner prime. You are nothing to me now." Finnivus settled onto Speakers Rock and ordered the commander of the *squaline*, "Take him into custody, but do not harm him. *We* will decide when royal justice shall be served."

AUZY-
AUZY
SHIVER

CHAPTER 21

"I TOLD YOU IT WAS A TRAP AND STILL, YOU WENT," Takiza huffed.

"For the tenth time—I'm sorry!" Gray said, raising his voice because he had to, not because he was being disrespectful. They were heading down into the deep open ocean, and it was hard to speak unless you yelled. The words seemed to get sucked back into Gray's throat unless he really spoke up. The fact that they were swimming away from Coral Shiver and his friends didn't help his mood.

After a few hard days of exercises and drills, Gray and Takiza swam past the Maw and toward the Atlantis Spine. To Gray's surprise, they didn't stop there but headed up and over the towering undersea mountains of the Spine. The mountains forming the Spine were awe-inspiring. Their majestic greenie-covered crags contained caverns that a fin could get lost in for days. Once over the mountain range, the two swam heading down, down, down. They were deeper than the training grounds, in an area Takiza called the Azores.

"You should strive to keep your mouth closed and listen, Nulo! It is the only way you will learn." Takiza turned to see if he would say anything. Gray was so tired he couldn't muster the effort. They had been swimming for days. Was it days? He couldn't tell. There was very little light in the depths so near the Dark Blue.

"Your indescribably bad judgment has forced us on this journey sooner than I would have liked. Sooner than you are ready. See how you gasp and struggle? This could have been avoided—had you not angered the pup emperor."

Gray mumbled, "Sorry!" once more, but the ocean depths pressed the word back into his throat.

The frilly fish continued thinking out loud to himself. "Perhaps it's time. Perhaps your bumbling foolishness is, in a way, the current of destiny moving us. Who knows? Sometimes we are carried where the water wills, no matter our wishes."

"Okay, that sounded very important," Gray said with an effort. "Can you tell me what it means?" He sounded silly shouting when the gauzy-finned betta swam just a tail length in front of him.

Takiza looked at him crossly. "Everything I say is important, Nulo, or I wouldn't bother saying it. Watch and listen. Only then can you learn."

Gray struggled as they crested the lip of the mountain range. He had to swallow several times before he could ask, "*What* is that?"

"That is the Atlantean capital, which the humans who lived there before it was sunk called Poseidous." Takiza dipped low into one of the evenly spaced valleys. These valleys weren't like the craggy areas between hills or mountains. *These* were perfectly smooth. While they were made of rock—Gray checked by slapping a tail against the one they were swimming through—the valleys were slippery to the touch. The channels *cut* into these rocks—or were the rocks piled upward to form the channels?—caught the current perfectly, and made it very easy to swim. Greenie and coral had grown everywhere, but Gray could see humans—*giant* humans—between squarish caves that might be living spaces. The large guardians stood perfectly still as if waiting for unwary prey to swim close.

At the center of the landshark homewaters, there was one immense human guiding six rearing animals, which seemed like the landshark versions of sea horses, with legs instead of fins and tails. The human held a gigantic weapon. It was much scarier than a spine shooter and had three massive prongs, each ending in barbs like the hooks he had seen humans use to catch fish. But how could the human stand so still? And how could it breathe underwater?

Gray was sure landsharks couldn't stay underwater very long without cans of air on their backs.

Takiza saw him staring and chuckled. "It's a statue. A stone carving." He pointed with his fin to another grouping of these statues. "Humans liked chipping images of themselves into rock in the old days."

"Humans were much bigger in the old days!"

Takiza laughed. "No, they made the statues bigger to scare other landsharks away."

Gray looked around at a landshark version of Speakers Rock. It was a shallow bowl with rows of ridges rising upward. The ridges were covered with greenie also, but Gray could tell there was the same type of smooth rock underneath. "How come no one ever mentioned this? I don't think Goblin knew, even though he told me stories about the Atlanteans."

"It's difficult for most sharkkind to swim this deep," Takiza told him. "It took weeks to train you, didn't it?"

Gray nodded. The landshark city was so fantastic, he had forgotten his difficulty breathing. It was hard to imagine that the same humans who flailed around in the ocean and had to use nets to catch their meals could build something like this. The humans Gray knew were dumb, fouling the very waters they fed from, but had to be respected because they were also extremely dangerous. "So why are we here?" he asked.

"Again you question me?" Takiza shook his head. He muttered to himself as he circled a thick strand of greenie and then smacked it with his fin. Gray then saw it wasn't a strand of greenie, but a landshark rope. It hit the metal surrounding it, which was in the shape of a jellyfish, and made a *BONNNNNNGGGgggggg* sound that vibrated through the water in all directions.

Gray wanted badly to ask what that strange noise-making device was but had an answer soon enough when other sharks swam into view. He remembered that the object was called a *bell*. Landsharks used it to call others or warn of danger, but sharkkind could also hear its vibrations. Many came over, including a massive great white, almost as large as Gray, who was a golden color.

Could it be? thought Gray.

The golden great white's booming voice cried out, "Takiza! What are you doing here so soon?"

The betta introduced the new shark. "He is why we are here. Gray, this is Lochlan boola Naka Fiji, leader of the AuzyAuzy Shiver and the rightful king of the Sific."

"Lochlan ..." Gray muttered with displeasure. So this was Takiza's favorite apprentice. Gray had to admit, the great white was impressive, especially with that striking coloring. He was a good four feet larger than Striiker, which made him a foot bigger than Goblin used to be. Lochlan grinned in a friendly way, but Gray wasn't feeling very pleasant remembering all the times Takiza had mentioned this shark during training.

"What's the matter?" Lochlan asked, catching the sour look on Gray's face. "Did you eat a bad haddock? Stay away from the ones with yellowy eyes."

Gray shook his head. He shouldn't prejudge this shark. "It's nothing. Nice to finally meet Takiza's favorite student."

"That will be enough speaking from you, Nulo," Takiza said.

Lochlan's eyes widened. He burst out laughing, waggling his fins up and down. "Is that what Takiza's been telling you? *I* was his favorite? Well, nice to finally do something right for once, eh?"

Takiza ruffled his own frilly fins in an odd way. Gray hadn't seen him do anything quite like it before. Then he understood the fleeting look on the betta's face. It was a touch of *embarrassment.*

"Wait a second," Gray began. "You weren't his prize student?"

This sent Lochlan into gales of laughter. "Prize student? He said I was his worst apprentice ever! He would always mention another finner named Ranier, who I absolutely *hated* after my first week! It was always, 'If only you could be more like Ranier, your training would be quicker' and 'Ranier never snapped even one coral spire,' things like that, over and over."

"Oh, *reeeeeeally,*" said Gray, giving Takiza a long look.

The little betta chopped his fins imperiously. "I only mentioned Lochlan to compare him at the *end* of his training—when I was finally able to teach him a few things—to you at the *beginning* of your training. Respectively, you two chowderheaded lumpfish are *tied* for being the *worst* apprentices I've ever had."

Both Gray and Lochlan laughed as Takiza ruffled his frilly fins again.

The massive great white nodded after catching his breath. "Gray, any friend of Takiza's is a friend of mine. And call me Loch."

"Okay, Loch," Gray answered. "Nice to meet you."

It was safe to say Gray liked Lochlan at once.

"Let me intro you to some of my Line. These are three of the fins I count on to tell me when I'm about to make a tail bender of a decision!"

"Which is often!" said a pretty whitetip reef shark. "My name is Kendra and I'm Loch's first."

Gray nodded and said hello, then found a smiling scalloped hammerhead grinning at him. "Xander del Hav'aii, call me Xander. I'm third."

Gray was slapped on the flank, hard. A small girl tiger shark said, "G'day! Name's Jaunt, and I'm fifth in Line of AuzyAuzy, which is kinda like being the smallest biter in the wet-wet. Sorry about not bringin' a prezzy, but we didn't know we wuz gonna yabber-jabber with you today."

Gray nodded nervously at Jaunt and then looked to the rest of the AuzyAuzy line, who seemed amused at his discomfort. "Umm, what language is she speaking? I understood about half."

"Too right!" yelled Lochlan as everyone laughed. "You got most of us beat, then! We hardly understand *anything* she says!"

Jaunt looked pained and flicked her tail. "Aww, come on! I'm no squiddily kelpie from the boonie-greenie! Maybe you guys should learn to speak proper like me!"

"Boonie-greenie!" Gray exclaimed. "I know that! But what's a squiddily kelpie?"

Everyone laughed again, even Jaunt this time. She slapped him on the flank and said, "*You're* a squiddily kelpie, ya big beauty!"

They spoke long into the night. Lochlan had lost his father and many friends when Finnivus had attacked. The golden great white grew sad telling the story. Lochlan's father had been a peace-loving ruler and was missed by everyone. The AuzyAuzy forces were currently scattered, but the rest were regrouping with Lochlan's second and fourth in Line until he would lead them back to their homewaters. That had been delayed when Takiza asked him to come here.

Lochlan turned to Takiza. "So why bring this one sharkkind—what kind of shark are you, anyway?

"Umm—"

"He's a rare type of reef shark," Takiza told everyone. The betta had sworn Gray to secrecy about being a megalodon. He was to tell *no one* else.

"Good on ya," Jaunt said.

Now Kendra, the whitetip, spoke. "Gray seems like

he could hold his own in a scuffle, for sure. But why just bring one fin to this fight?"

Now it was Takiza's turn to chuckle. "Oh, Gray is not here to join you," he said. "I would like *you* to join *him* and repel Finnivus from the North Atlantis."

For a moment no one said a word.

Then Jaunt gave Gray another tail slap to the flank. "Good on ya, twice!"

CHAPTER 22

MARI WATCHED AS AN INDI SHIVER PATROL worked its way through the valley. It was her turn to guard the entrance and sound an alarm if the worst should occur and they were discovered by Indi Shiver. She was determined nothing like that would happen on her watch. Deep in the greenie field, a good hundred tail strokes past the Rock Lobster mound, something caught her attention. It took a while to make sure it wasn't just a fish—or her imagination.

It was Barkley. He slowly slid through the wide and thick, blue and brown greenie stalks, almost crawling on the seabed like an octo. How he was able to move so stealthily was beyond her.

Barkley got under the entranceway to Coral Shiver, but he still didn't swim. It was a good thing he didn't. The Indi patrol had doubled back and would have seen him. The dogfish hovered, motionless, and was gently carried into the Coral Shiver homewaters by the mild current.

When he was safely underneath the canopy of greenie, Mari whispered, "You looked like you were dead, floating like that."

Barkley nodded. "And that's the point. If you stay in sync with the current, you're harder to spot. It's a sort of camouflage through movement."

Mari was impressed. Barkley was smart that way. He knew he wasn't the strongest shark in the Big Blue, so he'd learned to use anything he could to his advantage. Barkley could even follow Onyx without being seen by the cagey blacktip. Onyx was one of the best hunters she'd ever seen. Even though he was older and smaller than many shark-kind, he was almost always the first one to strike in a hunt.

She and Barkley reached the covered area of the Coral Shiver homewaters, and Onyx swam quietly to them. "How'd it go?" he asked Barkley. The dogfish shook his head. Onyx sighed. "Come on. He's going to want to hear it from you."

Onyx led Barkley and Mari to a more secluded area in the homewaters. Everyone was waiting there.

"How bad?" asked Quickeyes.

"We can't swim out of the area without being seen," Barkley told everyone. "Their patrols are thick, with no gap between them where we'd have the time to leave. And Indi varies their patrols, so there's no pattern. Or at least, none that I could figure out."

Striiker slapped Onyx's flank. "Then we fight our way out!" he whisper yelled.

In the past Barkley would have immediately put down the great white's idea. The dogfish wasn't usually diplomatic when he thought an idea was a bad one. Now he waited for someone else to do that. Striiker seemed to take having his ideas dismissed by Quickeyes, Sandy, Shell, or even Snork, better than when Barkley did it. "There may be safer options," Sandy told Quickeyes. "Waiting for the perfect time would be better than getting caught while half of us are still inside."

That was true. The same thing that made the homewaters defensible also made it hard to leave all at once— a narrow choke point was the only exit. Mari shuddered to think what the mad Emperor Finnivus would do to those who were captured.

"Starving as we wait isn't a great option," Onyx groused. Striiker agreed, of course, nodding. "The few of us that do go outside can't bring home enough fish for everyone."

"It's only a matter of time before one of us makes a mistake and tips them off, isn't it?" Snork said fearfully. "I hope it's not me."

Shell patted the sawfish on his flank. "You're one of the fins who can hunt quiet. I know you won't do anything jelly-brained."

Snork seemed to gain strength from the bull's comment. For a shark who didn't say much, when Shell did speak, his words counted.

"We'll starve!" Striiker insisted. "Quickeyes, you have to lead!"

"And I am." Quickeyes flicked his angled thresher tail into the sand, causing a muddy cloud to rise. "But we have to figure out a way to move without being eaten. When I do, you'll be the first to know."

"But—" Striiker stopped speaking when Onyx shook his head.

"What youse needs is a distraction!" exclaimed a gruff voice.

Mari was able to find its source and wasn't surprised. There was only one fish she'd ever met with that accent: Trank. She whirled. "How dare you show your little krillface in here?"

"Ay, ay—no need for personal insults. I'm here to help."

"Like you *helped* Gray by betraying him?" Striiker said, batting the much smaller fish with his tail.

Trank recovered from the disturbance caused by the swipe and glared. "Youse got no idea of the pressure Gafin's under!"

"*He's* the one?" asked Sandy, her voice rising. "This, this—little—" Sandy had been told about the stonefish's betrayal of Gray. While Trank didn't seemed worried about any of the other sharks, he backed away from Gray's mother. Smart fish.

Quickeyes swam in front of her. "Please, Sandy, don't get near it. It's a stonefish."

"We should kill it," said Onyx. "Can't let it tell Indi where we are."

"Quit callin' me *it*, sharkkind! An' like I said, I'm here to help."

Quickeyes, as leader, was about to order the stonefish's death. Barkley saw this and interrupted before he could. "Wait. If Trank's here, they've already found us. Let him talk."

"Smart fin, youse are. Found you three days ago. Gafin was deciding what to do."

"Sell us out or come here with an offer?" asked Quickeyes.

Trank shrugged. "Somethin' like that. Gafin feels bad about double-crossin' Gray. But he wants youse to know that he knew about the deal youse set up with the Coral Shiver octo clan in case Gray was trapped at Slaggernacks by Velenka and Indi Shiver. There's nothing he don't know about dwellers in the Big Blue. And he let that happen—which *let* Gray escape."

Barkley looked to Mari for her opinion. For some reason, she liked it when he did this. "He seems to be telling the truth," she told him.

"Wonder of wonders," Striiker said in his cutting way, getting a stare from Trank.

Snork shook his toothy bill from side to side. "I still don't believe him."

"Look, Gafin doesn't like this Finnivus clown fish or his crew. He'd just as soon see 'em go back where they came from."

Several of the group laughed in disbelief. "Gee, us too. Are you going to battle their armada?"

Trank smiled, his little fins moving back and forth. "Fightin' snout to snout, that not our style, see? But we can give youse a very nice edge."

"How helpful of you," said the amused Quickeyes. "But if you hadn't noticed, we're stuck here, starving, and don't have an army to fight them."

"Moving day—that's in the future," Trank told everyone. "Like I said, youse needs to figure out a distraction. As far as food, I think youse all can lose a few pounds, but I come bearing gifts—you know, to make up for what happened to Gray."

Mari's mouth began watering before she knew what was happening. Then she saw it—a giant lobster crawling up the rocks near where they were meeting. In its claws were two fat hake fish! And behind that lobster was a giant crab with a couple more fish. And another, and another, forming a line of shellheads marching on the seabed—all bringing food!

"You know, my opinion is suddenly all turned around on Trank," Striiker said as he gulped down a tasty haddock. "Still don't totally trust you, though."

"And the beauty of it is you don't have to just yet," Trank replied.

Quickeyes gave the stonefish a stare and clicked his jaws shut a few times before saying anything. "Thank you for the fish. It won't be forgotten. But we wouldn't last a minute fighting Finnivus's armada."

Trank nodded. "You'd need an army. So you couldn't beat them today, but youse never know what tomorrow brings. Or tonight, for that matter."

The stonefish turned toward the blackness of the cliff that plunged almost to the Dark Blue. Rising from the dark was a massive hammerhead, followed by another fifty sharks.

It was when she saw the scars that Mari knew who it was and gasped.

"Ripper!"

CHAPTER 23

"AGAIN!" TAKIZA YELLED FROM HIS POSITION BY a large statue in the center of the Atlantean stadium. This was the area that Gray had thought was the land-shark version of Speakers Rock. He'd been a bit mistaken. Takiza told him the large, bowl-like structure was for sports and training. This wide-space place was where landsharks would play games and others could watch. It also made a perfect practice range for Lochlan and Gray, who had grown accustomed to the depths of the Atlantean city of Poseidous. It was much easier for Gray to move and speak now.

Lochlan smiled wickedly, his golden hue noticeable even at these depths. "Would you like another shot at the title, mate?"

"Don't mind if I do," Gray answered, churning his tail and rushing the giant great white. He couldn't help but grin back. This was so fun! He was learning so much, even though he was beaten every time. It seemed Lochlan deserved every complimentary thing Takiza had ever said about him. If Gray could learn to be half as good as the great white, he'd be the best fighter in the North Atlantis.

He rocketed straight at Lochlan, performing Cuttlefish Strikes but was blocked when Lochlan countered the pectoral fin attack with Swordfish Parries. Gray feinted Sunfish Greets the Morn and seamlessly moved into the dorsal attack, Topside Rip. He was learning to proceed smoothly from one move into another, then another, rather than think of each as a single maneuver. When you strung the moves together this way, fighting was more like a dance.

Unfortunately, Lochlan wasn't fooled by the fake and was ready with a perfectly executed Orca Bears Down. He drove Gray into the seabed, causing a cloud of silt to muddy the cold water. If there were a way to beat Lochlan in single combat, Gray hadn't found it.

"Hold!" said Takiza. "I can take no more! My eyes are pained by your clumsy show. I have other matters to attend to so I will leave for a time. Keep training, for though you are both hopeless, I believe everyone you will fight against is even more pathetic than either of you." Takiza reminded them they wouldn't have time to search for food once they entered the waters patrolled by Indi Shiver. Gray got the creeping feeling that the betta was involved in many different weighty things in the Big Blue. But if this fight wasn't important enough to spend all his time on, how much trouble was the watery world in? It made him feel like a tiny guppy.

Later, as Gray finished off the last of a large cod, he said, "I thought it was bad to fight on a full stomach."

"Never stuff yourself right before a battle," Lochlan told him. "That's true enough. But we'll be swimming hard for a good while, so we need to keep up our strength." He looked at his third and gave him a nudge. "What's the matter, Xander?"

Gray was still getting used to Xander's unusual appearance—unusual compared to what he thought of as a *normal* hammerhead. Hammerheads were one of the weirder-looking sharks in the Big Blue with their heads seemingly stuck on the wrong way. Being a scalloped hammerhead, Xander had indentations on his long forehead that made him look as if he were perpetually thinking about something. But in this case, he really was. For a moment, it seemed as though he didn't want to speak.

"You know, the Line only works if you tell Loch what your problem is," Kendra said.

"I don't think we should be doing this," Xander said after a moment. He turned to Gray and added, "Sorry. No disrespect toward you or your cause."

Jaunt tail-slapped Xander on the flank. "Since when are you the sorta biter that swims away from a scrumble?"

"We're not ready for it," Xander replied. "I've gone

over this in my head a dozen times, and it always comes up the same. This is a bad call."

"How so?" asked Lochlan. The great white didn't get angry when challenged the way Goblin would have, or shout Xander down as Striiker most likely would. And Finnivus would have undoubtedly done something horrible. But Lochlan actually wanted to know why his trusted friend thought his idea was bad.

So this is what a good king is like, Gray thought.

Xander continued, "We're not prepared to face off against Indi."

Jaunt became incensed. "They deserve what's coming!"

"I'm not saying that isn't true, Jaunt," Xander answered. "But having truth and goodness on our side is no replacement for a fully loaded armada of our own. The timing is bad." Loch had mentioned that most of their forces were hiding in the Sific, far away, with only fifty sharkkind here to protect him. The hammerhead now looked to Lochlan. "We need time to get ready. And we can do that as long as Finnivus *doesn't* know we exist."

Lochlan remained silent for a moment. "You're right, Xander. But we can't just turn tail and allow Finnivus free rein to do evil. Sometimes a fin has to swim out and be counted."

"If Finnivus finds out you're alive, he'll scour the ocean for you! That mariner prime they have is no fool."

Then Xander whispered, "If the numbers are in his favor when we meet, he'll win."

Gray couldn't hover idly by any longer. "Excuse me," he began. "I really appreciate you considering helping me. But this is my fight, for my shiver and my family. I'll do the best I can with what I have. I don't want you to lose your chance of stopping Finnivus later. It might be the only real chance anyone has."

Lochlan bumped flanks with Gray. "Well said, that. But we can't allow the emperor to tighten his grip here. And we have the element of surprise. By giving him more to think about in the North Atlantis, he'll have fewer sharkkind available to control the Sific. That's good for when we make our move there." He looked at Xander. "I understand if you want to put your strength where you think it'll do the most good," Lochlan told him. "Go back to our fins in the Sific. Gather and train them."

The group waited for Xander's reply. Finally, the big hammerhead nodded. "Loch, I'd swim to the bottom of the Dark Blue and fight a prehistore monster for you. If you think this is the right move, I'm with you, flank to flank, mate."

Lochlan and Xander slapped fins.

"What are you flapping your large mouths about this time?" asked Takiza, who once again appeared out of nowhere. "You chatter like sea monkeys."

"It seems we've decided to help with Gray's fight!" Lochlan told him in a booming voice.

"It's always sensible to do what I tell you to do," Takiza responded without a hint of sarcasm.

Jaunt looked over at Gray. "Is he always like this?"

"Way worse!" he answered.

Takiza began giving orders. "Lochlan, take your sharkkind over near the Riptide Shiver homewaters and wait. Do not attack before I tell you to. I shall repeat myself, as I did countless times during your training: Do not attack before I say so."

"Easier said than done," remarked Kendra.

"I know!" Takiza exclaimed. "She is the wisest fish among you! But I have some delicate plans in place, and if you rush in and attack like some foolish rumble fish, you'll ruin everything."

"Would you like to share the reason why?" Lochlan asked, amused.

Takiza sighed as if he really didn't want to reveal anything, but then relented. "We have to save someone from Finnivus who won't want to be saved."

Kendra released a frustrated stream of bubbles from her gills. "Do you know how annoying that is? When you say something like that and don't give any specifics?"

Takiza was amused by this. "Why, yes, I do!" He grinned. "The shark we need to save is named Whalem, and until a few days ago he was the mariner prime of Finnivus's armada."

"Finnivus stripped Whalem's rank? He won't like that. He's a proud finner," Xander said with wonder.

The AuzyAuzy Line were all familiar with the old tiger. "Maybe we do have a chance."

Takiza nodded. "I only hope trusting Barkley and Onyx to sneak inside Indi's royal court to free him wasn't a fatal mistake on my part. And theirs, I suppose."

If the betta wanted Gray's total attention, he had definitely succeeded. But the frilly fish wasn't done. He turned to Gray and said, "Oh, and I need you to swim down into the Maw to get something for me."

CHAPTER 24

"STOP!" BARKLEY WHISPERED JUST LOUD ENOUGH that the light current they crawled against would bring the warning to Onyx and no one else.

The blacktip settled onto the sandy bottom without stirring a grain of sand. For someone who didn't normally sneak around, Onyx was very good at it. Neither twitched a muscle as an Indi Shiver patrol circled around the craggy shelf marking the east boundary of the Riptide homewaters and passed above where he and Onyx hid, silent as sea wraiths.

Barkley resumed moving carefully forward through the greenie, barely a flipper length off the seabed. He shuddered to think what would happen if they were caught and dragged before Finnivus.

The dogfish knew at a young age he could swim more quietly than most. It was natural that as the bullies around the reef had gotten bigger, he'd gotten better at remaining silent and safely hidden from them. Not everyone could do this. Striiker, for example, was terrible at stalking. He was a great hunter due to his strength and size but could sneak around as well as a human splashing about in the Big Blue.

Barkley signaled for Onyx to follow. When Barkley and Gray were little, they always thought of Onyx as a humorless curmudgeon. The blacktip ordered shiver sharks this way and that. But they'd never realized that whenever Onyx *did* speak, those sharks listened because he was usually right. Now, if Barkley had to pick someone for a matter of life and death, after Gray, he would choose Onyx.

He felt a nip at his tail. Barkley knew Onyx would only do that for a good reason, so he allowed his body to go limp, the tide carrying it slightly. The blacktip eased next to him. "Stay away from Speakers Rock. It's the royal court, so there'll be even more guards."

Barkley nodded. There was no need to answer with words, and it was dangerous to speak here. He adjusted his route accordingly. He and Onyx had formulated this plan after Takiza came to them with this insane idea—steal the imprisoned mariner prime of the Indi armada from under the emperor's snout. "And what else would you like us to do tonight?" Barkley had grumbled to himself.

They hugged the weedy bottom of a coral reef which gave them some cover.

They weren't even going to lead Whalem to safety tonight. Onyx was sure that if they tried to take him without his permission, the mariner prime would raise an alarm. Because of honor and royal etiquette—*pfah!*—Whalem would have to be asked first: *nicely*. As if you really needed a reason to *not* want your head served on a platter! But Whalem's honor wouldn't allow him to betray the emperor, even if Finnivus were insane. They had to convince him. That meant Barkley and Onyx needed to get close enough to talk with Whalem without being noticed. Yikes!

Luckily, Barkley knew every inch of these home-waters from his time as a member of Goblin Shiver. How small the problems they'd struggled with then seemed now. The dueling between Goblin and Razor seemed like pups fighting after school compared to what everyone faced today.

Another bump from Onyx. Barkley looked back, and the blacktip gestured to the left. Ah! There it was. The prison. The structure itself looked nothing like Barkley had ever seen in the Big Blue. That's because it was made by landsharks thousands of years ago. Onyx had told the story of how the prison was given to the first king of Indi Shiver by the Atlanteans. Barkley had no idea how they had gotten the thing here. Maybe a whale had carried it? Unlike most of the ancient landshark items Barkley had seen on the bottom of the ocean, this cage wasn't covered with barnacles and greenie. This object shined as if it were new.

The last twenty yards were the hardest. The constant patrols forced them to stop many times, and all Barkley could do was shut his eyes and will himself to be invisible. Finally, they reached the cage. So stealthy was their approach that Whalem didn't sense a thing until Onyx spoke.

"Mariner Prime, please be quiet and listen," he said. To Whalem's credit, he didn't start or twitch a muscle. His eyes focused on Onyx and widened slightly. Onyx continued, "I see you still remember me after all these years."

"Get on with it," hissed Barkley. The mariner prime heard Barkley's voice but couldn't see him in the thick greenie he was hiding in.

"I come under a term of truce and would like you to let me speak without rousing anyone. Is that acceptable?"

There was a slight nod from the ancient tiger shark.

"Takiza asks, if we can free you, would you come with us? But not only that, he asks that you help us defeat the emperor."

After a moment, Barkley saw an almost imperceptible shake of the old tiger's head.

Onyx didn't bother asking again, saying only, "Thank you for your time, sir." He bobbed his head and motioned for them to leave the way they came in.

Barkley was incensed. They had come too far at too much risk to turn around with nothing. Onyx saw his anger and started to say, "Indi Shiver is very different—" but Barkley swam past and took his spot. "What are you doing? Get back here!" the blacktip urged.

Barkley shook his head. He would have his say. The mariner prime watched in silence as Barkley waited for a group of richly tattooed mariners from the armada to swim lazily past, followed by two armored *squaline.*

"If you want to lie down on the emperor's platter, that's your choice," Barkley hissed. "But not coming with us because you think you owe crazy Finnivus your loyalty isn't honorable—it's cowardly."

Whalem's eyes blazed, but Barkley wasn't going to leave without saying everything on his mind. "You owe that flipper nothing except a good tail slap to the face. You owe it to me and everyone else in the Big Blue to help stop him—which probably isn't possible, anyway. So your honor can be served, along with our seasoned heads, when we lose."

Whalem whispered, "Who are you to talk to me this way, pup?"

"I'm Barkley. And no matter what you think, it isn't honorable to take the easy way out and leave us with this giant mess that you're at least partially responsible for! So once more, if we can get you out—which we probably can't—will you help us stop Finnivus?"

Barkley's throat was sore from speaking so quietly, yet with such hissing force. He couldn't believe no one had seen or heard anything, and he gratefully edged back into the greenie next to Onyx. The mariner prime seemed unmoved. If he was insulted, well, that was too bad. "Okay, *now* we can go," Barkley told the astonished blacktip.

It was then Onyx nudged Barkley, gesturing with a fin at the Indi armada commander.

Whalem was *grinning*.

He whispered, "All right. If you can get me out, I'll help you."

INTO THE DARK BLUE

CHAPTER 25

GRAY LOOKED DOWN FROM THE SHARP LEDGE
into the blackness of the Maw. The pressure from
these depths gave him an uncomfortable, queasy feeling. But the yawning chasm of the Maw scared Gray
to his very core.

He was wearing the greenie torture harness from
his practice session. The rock was in the harness, but at
least right now it lay on the seabed as Gray hovered near
the sand. Apparently, the rock's weight would help him
swim to the bottom of the Dark Blue.

Takiza had trained him for this very task. Gray
got chills thinking about it. Whether those chills were
about swimming down into the Maw or about Takiza
having planned for this day, Gray didn't know. He felt
ashamed that Lochlan and the sharks from AuzyAuzy
Shiver were swimming to protect his family and friends
without him. In a way, Gray envied them. Waiting on the

edge of the abyss, he discovered he would rather face the entire Indi armada than swim down into the depths of the Dark Blue.

"Shiro, I'd feel much more comfortable—"

Takiza cut Gray off. "Yes, you'd feel much more comfortable if I came with you. Perhaps I can stroke your flanks and recite a story on the way?"

"Yech!" Gray shuddered. "That image is nasty. I was going to ask if I could take the harness off for a little while. But if you do know where this glowing greenie is . . . and since you're better than I am in every way—"

"Of course, I am! Stop talking foolishness, Nulo. If I could do this, I would. But you must, and you need to succeed! Do you understand? This is the most important thing you've done in your short, pampered life! So far, anyway."

Gray nodded as if he understood the weight of the matter, but he didn't really. Takiza was such an amazing fish. There was no way that Gray could do the incredible things the little betta could. It seemed as if Takiza were sending Gray to his death. And the fact that Takiza kept saying, "I am sorry I may be sending you to your death," didn't help the situation at all.

"Again, you only have to say that one time," Gray replied when Takiza repeated it again. "I'm not going to forget."

"Then tell me again what you will do when you arrive at the seabed below," ordered the betta.

Even though it was at least the fifteenth time Gray had repeated the instructions, he got right to it. "I will descend to the bottom of the Dark Blue—" Gray quickly corrected himself: "The bottom of this particular area of the ocean and find the glowing green kelp called mared-soo, the energy plant. When I'm there, I exchange the rock for greenie and swim back to you."

Takiza grew cross and snapped his fins out. "Don't *exchange* anything. Load the greenie—but don't eat any—into the harness *before* you remove the rock. Your body will not remain at the bottom without the rock. So it's important to do it in the proper order—greenie first, *then* remove the stone. Remember, Nulo!"

"I will!" Gray shouted. "What are we waiting for? If you're not coming and time is so short, shouldn't I get going?"

Gray could see Takiza was about to explode but didn't care. He'd never felt so scared in his life—not even at Tuna Run facing off with Goblin. Here, waiting by the ever-black waters of the Maw, he felt cold and terrified. It was just too much!

But before Takiza could yell at him, a prehistore *horror* raised itself from the gloom below. It was nearly circular and had skin that was at once black, slimy, *and* pasty. Though it was tiny to Gray, it was three times Takiza's size and almost entirely composed of a giant mouth stuffed with bristling teeth. The razor-sharp needle teeth were so big, it was hard to see how the little monster could close its mouth without wounding itself. Gray tried to swim away but was stuck fast because of the rock inside his harness.

"Look out!" Gray shouted. "Behind you!"

Takiza turned, unconcerned. "Finally!" he snorted. "Have you no concept of time?"

"Ah, no actually," said the prehistore fish. "Kind of dark where we live."

"*You know this thing?*" Gray asked.

Someone said, "Hey! You better mind your mouth, or else I'm going to come over there and teach you a lesson!" But the prehistore fish's lips didn't move. In fact, this was a completely different voice. Then Gray saw there was a much tinier dweller, an even uglier fish stuck like a barnacle on the first horrible-looking fish's side. In fact, the smaller ugly fish seemed to be *feeding* on the larger one with its *fangs*.

"Oh, oh! Gross!" Gray pointed with his fin. "You have a nasty on your side! A sea tick or something! You should definitely go to a doctor fish and get that removed!"

The larger horrific-looking fish seemed put off and cocked its head to the side as it addressed Takiza. "Digging in the shallow end of the kelp bed for your apprentices these days?"

"Sadly, this is the age we live in," Takiza said, shaking his head.

"Sea tick? Did that chowderhead just call me a sea tick?" asked the smaller fish indignantly.

"Calm down, honey," said the larger ugly fish.

Finally Takiza made some introductions. "This is Briny and her husband, Hank, and I'll thank you to be respectful of them!" the betta said to Gray. "They are humpback anglerfish—"

"Devilfish!" yelled Hank, the small one.

Takiza looked at Briny curiously as Hank's face returned to press into her side, sucking blood like a leech. "I was under the impression it was rude to call you that."

"It was." Briny seemed embarrassed. "But we changed our minds. We ladies don't like talking about our humps."

"Besides, devilfish sounds way cooler!" Hank added.

With that, Takiza turned to Gray and continued, "These *devilfish* live in the depths that you fear to swim. They will lead you to the maredsoo."

Gray felt awful. "I'm sorry," he said to the pair. "I—I'm not from around here."

"We figured that out, jelly-brain!" said Hank.

Takiza shook his head in disapproval. "There is no need to race and prove yourself a bumpkin when meeting someone. They will find out soon enough. Now, lift the stone and follow them!"

"Yes, Shiro," Gray said, feeling like a total loser. With a heave and upward thrust, the rock slowly rose from the seabed. "Thank you for not making me go alone."

"Are you speaking again?" Takiza asked Gray. "Lift and swim!"

"He is a strong one," said Briny. "I'll give him that."

"That would explain the lack of brains," Hank told her. "All the big fish are dummies."

Gray looked to Takiza, who just grinned. "Oh, so you agree?"

"Come on, pup! We have a party to get to after this!" said Hank. He flapped his fins in annoyance but didn't remove his fangs from Briny's slimy side.

Gray looked down at the Maw's chasm. It was dark and terrifying. Gray shuddered, gave the wan sunlight coming from above one last look, and let the weight of the rock pull him down into the blackness.

As he was swallowed by the Dark Blue, Takiza yelled after him. "Make sure to come back, Nulo! Your training is not complete and you gave me your word!"

Gray gulped. He should have said something back, but the darkness had his total attention. Soon the pressure was squeezing him even more. The large rock nestled inside his harness pulled him down, down, down, so the water whooshed past his ears. It grew colder as it got darker. Chills, from the cold and Gray's anxiety, marched down his spine and settled in the pit of his stomach.

"You doing okay?" asked Hank after a time. "You look a little peaked."

Gray wanted to throw up. A fish the color of black slime was telling him he looked unwell. And he probably did after . . . how long had they been descending?

An hour? A day? He couldn't tell in this black vastness.

"Gray?" called out Briny. For the first part of the trip, Briny had held onto the harness with her teeth. Now she could easily swim by his side as the rock was pulling Gray more slowly. His teeth were chattering, so he couldn't answer right away. "Gray, can you hear me? Can I ask you a question?"

"Oh-oh, s-s-sure," he stuttered. The pressure from the depths was making his head swim. Were they still going down?

"Don't ask him," said Hank. "You always do this. Makes everyone uncomfortable."

"It does not," Briny answered.

"Least put your light on, so he can see you."

"Oh, you're right! Where are my manners?" A little light brightened and dangled in front of Briny's jagged rows of teeth. It took a conscious effort not to swim toward the light in this darkness. Gray realized it would be very helpful for hunting in this black place.

In the light Gray could see Briny look at him self-consciously—if a fish who looked like a prehistore nightmare could seem self-conscious—before screwing up her courage. "Does my husband make my hump look fat?"

Gray caught a look of panic from Hank before saying through chattering teeth, "N-no, B-b-b-briny. I think Hank looks sl-slimming on you."

Briny became very pleased.

Hank gave Gray a fins-up and said, "Hey, you're okay! And you'll be glad to know we're nearly halfway there already!"

"We're making very good time," said Briny matter-of-factly.

Gray's heart began thudding in terror as if it would burst out from his chest entirely. They weren't even *halfway* there yet?

CHAPTER 26

THE ROYAL COURT WAS ALL IN A BUSTLE.
Velenka heard that an intruder had been captured just
off the western edge of the heavily patrolled Riptide
homewaters. She watched Finnivus stare imperiously
from his place, high above everyone on one of his blue
whales. Framed by the terraced greenie behind him, the
young tiger shark looked royal indeed.

Then Velenka suddenly spotted the prisoner. The
battle-scarred hammerhead could be no one else:

Ripper!

So he hadn't been killed by the armada's advance
guard as she had thought. The *squaline* had secured
Ripper by looping an ancient chain through his mouth.
The ends were attached to two other armored hammerheads, so Ripper couldn't make a rush at the emperor.
There was also some sort of device in his mouth that
would prevent him from biting down all the way. The

massive hammerhead didn't struggle, allowing himself to be led down the main aisle to the foot of Finnivus's well-guarded throne. It seemed odd for a sharkkind as proud and strong as Ripper to come so easily.

"What have we here?" asked Finnivus.

"Your Magnificence," Tydal announced, "a prisoner caught by your armada mariners."

Finnivus glared at his first court shark. "Obviously, Tydal. Now tell us something we don't know."

The brown-and-yellow epaulette shark bobbed his head. "Apologies. This hammerhead, who calls himself Ripper, says he was the first in the Line for Riptide Shiver."

"Really?" Finnivus mused, looking over at Velenka. "I thought we ate those flippers."

"Ripper was Goblin's first," Velenka explained. "But Goblin left when your mighty armada arrived. I thought Ripper also turned tail and swam away." There was a bloom of anger in the hammerhead's eyes at Velenka's words, and she was glad he was bound and chained.

"Well?" Finnivus asked Ripper. "Is that true? Are you a coward?"

The device in his mouth made it difficult to speak, but not impossible. Clearly whoever made it had given some thought for this very situation. "Lies," the hammerhead spit. "And Goblin didn't leave. She killed him."

A murmur rose within the court. "I did no such

thing!" yelled Velenka, voice rising. "I worshipped my leader despite his bad decisions. But he would have swum the Sparkle Blue, anyway, because Emperor Finnivus Victor Triumphant—the rightful ruler of all the Big Blue—was coming."

Finnivus laughed his tittering laugh. "That's true, we suppose. Should we eat him and be done with it? From the looks of him, he won't be tasty no matter what the royal seasoners do."

This would solve all of Velenka's problems so she immediately agreed: "Yes, excellent idea!"

"Oh, I could give you some great advice," Ripper told everyone. The court let out a gasp. Apparently, they weren't used to anyone, especially a prisoner, talking so directly with their ruler.

Finnivus's eyes blazed. He certainly felt insulted. "And what would that be?"

"Two things. First, Coral Shiver has formed a treaty with an old friend of yours, King Lochlan boola something-or-other and his AuzyAuzy Shiver. They're gathering their forces about a day's swim from the east side of these homewaters."

"WHAAAT?" shouted Finnivus. "Impossible! I destroyed them! I destroyed *him*! That can't be true! Commander, is it true?"

The new spinner commander who had been promoted to Whalem's position was caught by surprise. "I—I—there's no sign of that from the patrols."

"YOU'RE NOT SURE? You're not sure that Lochlan isn't here with an armada! He hates me, that one! I had to strike first! But that's beside the point! The point is YOU'RE NOT SURE!"

"I am! The prisoner is lying. We haven't seen anything."

Ripper was unconcerned. "You wouldn't. They're hidden, call themselves the Golden Rush. He's coming for you." The hammerhead smiled maliciously.

Finnivus swished his tail furiously. "Take an entire battle fin and find them! But do not attack. I want to be present for my victory. And their destruction."

"Yes, Magnificence!" yelled the new commander before swimming off as fast as he could.

The emperor looked back at Ripper. "You said there were two things. What's the second? Speak. I command it."

"The second is . . . watch your tail, pal." Ripper gestured toward Velenka. The court let out another louder gasp. "If you're going to let this one near you, better watch it close."

Velenka couldn't help herself. "Kill him!" she yelped as everyone was shouting and talking at once. "He's insulting you!"

The emperor whirled. "I give the orders around here, Velenka! You do what *we* say, and *we* say . . . shut your cod hole!"

Velenka went silent and said nothing more. Unfortunately, she should have spoken up earlier. She should have listened to that nagging feeling when they had brought in Ripper without a struggle. If Velenka had thought about it more, she would have realized that the scarred hammerhead would *never* allow himself to be brought in without a fight.

Amid all the shouting and accusations, what Velenka, Finnivus, the *squaline*, and everyone else in court failed to notice was one sneaky little dogfish swimming unseen, right past their distracted snouts.

CHAPTER 27

DOWN, DOWN, DOWN, THEY WENT INTO THE blackness of the Maw. Gray's mind boggled. How could there be so much ocean? The world he swam in was just a tiny drop of water compared to the immense area below.

But who lived down here? What exactly was he passing?

Perhaps it was better to slide downward not knowing. The glimpses Gray saw were unsettling. At one point, there were a thousand tiny lights floating in the darkness, just like the stars in the sky. It was only when Gray got close that he realized that every single one of these lights belonged to a devilfish, or to their larger cousin, the deep-sea angler. That fish was like a puffer squashed flat with a wedge taken out for the mouth. In place of the missing wedge were bristling needle teeth jutting in all directions.

Gray caught glimpses of other horrors that didn't give themselves away with lumo lures. Briny and Hank pointed out the eerie black chimera, the mantis shrimp with its deadly claws, the deep sea swallower—that could eat a fish three times its own size in one gulp!—and deadly jelly fish, giant squid, and even bigger octos that dwarfed Gray as they spread their arms to embrace their lightless kingdom.

"Are-are we th-th-there yet?" Gray asked, shivering from the intense cold and pressure.

"We'll get there when we get there!" Hank grumbled. "One more word and we'll turn around!"

Gradually, Gray had to work to swim downward. The water became lighter than he was, even with the rock's added weight, something Takiza had warned him would happen. He was stiff and sore from the vicious cold that froze him inside and out. Gray panted as he fought the elements, swimming his way down, down, down.

"There it is!" said Briny as she scooted in front of Gray. The devilfish was a poor swimmer in the waters Gray called home but did just fine here. Briny shined her glowing lure and illuminated the area where the ghostly, glowing maredsoo grew. There was no other greenie or coral here. This one plant grew by itself in the desolate sand and stood alone as if waiting for Gray.

He wanted nothing more than to get the magical

greenie and head up to Takiza. Exhausted beyond belief, he tilted himself to get rid of the rock inside the harness—only to hear Hank yell, "No, no, no!"

It was then Gray remembered: Get the maredsoo first, then lose the rock. But it was too late. The stone rolled out and Gray shot upward as if he were being pulled by his tail! He was no longer heavy enough to stay at this depth!

Hank looked at Briny and said, "See? The big ones never think."

Frantically, Gray shook off his numbing terror of the blackness and cold, focusing on the glowing plant. He panted, pumping the thick water through his gills, furiously swimming for the bottom. For all his exhausting efforts, Gray only inched closer with agonizing slowness. The tail length he was short seemed like a chasm.

Gray wouldn't—no, he couldn't—fail. Not after all the training. Not after Takiza had saved the lives of Rogue Shiver at the Tuna Run. He must complete this task! With one final burst, Gray closed the distance to the maredsoo. It was like swimming through syrup. He forced himself to open his jaws—despite the pressure that wanted to slam his mouth closed—and bit! His teeth sheared off the maredsoo plant at the stalk, and somehow it floated into his harness!

But then gray saw it wasn't luck at all. Briny had pushed the plant into position. He barely had time to chatter a final, "Th-th-thank-you!" before being pulled up and away from the pair. Gray didn't know if she had turned off her dangling light lure or if he'd shot away so fast he couldn't see it anymore. By the sound of the water rushing past his ears, it could have very well been the latter. Gray's mind reeled and everything spun. He tried to make sure he wasn't actually spinning but couldn't tell. He passed an angler fish with its light lure and thankfully left it underneath him. But Gray found he *was* upside down!

Flipping himself, he saw a distant *lightness* in the blackness. It couldn't be called light, but it was a lighter shade of the total black surrounding him. That was where home was.

Heartened, Gray willed himself to swim toward the less dark darkness. He forced his tail to stroke left and right but often got this simple order wrong, which stopped his upward ascent and turned him sideways.

He kept his eyes fixed on the light. It was definitely light. He fouled up the order of his tail strokes yet again— left *then* right, what's so hard about that? At least there was no one around to see, he thought.

"Do you recall when I compared your swimming skill to that of a pregnant sea cow?"

Gray's heart leaped with relief and joy. He had never been so happy to see the little fish, no matter what insult was coming.

"Yes, Shiro."

"I am withdrawing my comment," the little betta said as he swam in front of Gray's left eye. "It's an insult to all pregnant sea cows. And you are late! Now follow me!" Takiza led Gray upward. They were only a few minutes from the ledge, which was the gateway to the Maw. When Gray crested the cliff, Takiza told him, "Rest, Nulo. You've done passably well in this task."

"Thank you," Gray answered, panting.

"Thank you—what?"

"Thank you, Shiro."

Takiza nodded and moved in a blur, taking off Gray's harness and weaving a smaller harness from it. The frilly betta turned with a flourish, wearing the new harness. He looked positively heroic carrying the glowing maredsoo greenie as his fins rippled majestically in the water. "Nulo, you will swim as fast as you can to join your friends. Remember to tell them to wait for me before they do anything."

Gray was pained. There was no way he could rush the entire distance back this instant. He felt like he wanted to sleep for a week! "I can't!"

"You can't or you won't?"

"I can't! I just swam to the bottom of the ocean!" Gray protested. "Where are you going, anyway? You're rested. Can't you do it?"

"Where I am going is none of your concern," Takiza told him.

"But—"

The betta shook his fins and cut him off. "It is of no use for anyone to know what I am doing. It is useful to remind Lochlan and your friends not to attack Finnivus before I get back! Time is short, so swim!"

Gray got himself off the seabed. It felt like he weighed less than normal, but still, he was tired. So tired.

Takiza sighed irritably. "Fine!" The betta did a quick roll, and a large leaf of the glowing greenie floated from the harness. "Eat!"

"I'm not hungry. I'm tired!"

"No talking! Only eating!"

Gray obeyed and closed his mouth on the still glowing greenie. He didn't feel the single leaf go into his mouth or down his throat. "Did I do it? Did I eat it?" he asked, puzzled.

All of a sudden it felt as though something had *bloomed* inside his stomach! Something hot! The feeling spread outward in each direction, all the way to his snout and tail. It warmed Gray's body, banishing the coldness as well as his dreary thoughts. He suddenly felt he had the strength of ten sharkkind!

"YEEEE-HAAAAA!" Gray yelled as he swam in a

tight circle so fast it spun the sand on the seabed into a whirling funnel.

"I will be there soon. Tell them to wait!" Takiza began moving his frilly fins in an odd pattern.

"What if that isn't possible?" Gray asked.

"Then be prepared to do the *im*possible!" Takiza said. The betta shot away so fast Gray only saw a churning wake in the water.

CHAPTER 28

THE MAREDSOO POWERED GRAY'S FURIOUS swim from the training grounds back home to Coral Shiver. There was a dull roar in his ears and his heart raced. But after Gray was about halfway home, the Dark Blue greenie's effects stabilized. He wasn't hungry or tired, even though he had swum at a sprinting-attack speed the whole way. Finally, he saw the Rock Lobster formation near Coral Shiver's homewaters.

A cold fear gripped Gray when he noticed a steady stream of sharkkind and dwellers leaving the hidden entrance. But then he realized it was okay. His mother and Mari were leading everyone in an organized move. Gray scanned the waters and saw nothing of Indi Shiver. Not yet, anyway. He hurried to his mom and Mari.

"What are you doing?" he asked them. "Takiza wanted you to wait."

"That would have been useful to know earlier in the day," Mari said. The thresher waved her tail for the crowd to keep moving. "Come on, come on! No time to waste!" she told everyone.

"Are you sure this is a good idea?" Gray asked his mother.

Sandy replied, "Lochlan and AuzyAuzy Shiver left early because Finnivus is going to execute the armada commander."

"Oh, no!" Gray felt his heart sink. "I've got to help! Where are they?"

Mari quickly told Gray what everyone was doing and where they most likely were, and he streaked off toward the Riptide homewaters. Luckily, Slagger-nacks was on the way, as he wanted to make a quick stop. But no one was there. The place looked like just another series of caves and greenie-covered coral.

Gray was about to leave when he reached out with his senses and found stonefish and octos hiding among the rocks. Gray was surprised he could tell which one was Trank. He glided over to what most fins and dwellers would see as an innocent pile of rocks.

"Get up, Trank," he said. Nothing moved. For a moment he felt silly. But Gray could feel the stone-fish breathing now that he was close. "Quit fooling around."

Trank didn't move, but did answer. "Wouldja keep swimmin'? Youse is attracting unwanted attention."

"You said Gafin would help, and we're going to need that help now."

"We're closed. Move along!"

Gray nudged the stonefish by swishing his large tail directly over it. "Come on!" When he tried to move the stonefish again, its spikes sprang out.

Trank turned slightly. "I told youse, we're closed."

Gray grew hot with anger. "You know what? Sharkkind say that stonefish can't be trusted. And I always stick up for you. I say, 'No, you have to get to know Trank. He's loyal.' But you're not, are you? When the current gets rough, you stick your head in the sand like a baby turtle. Well, I'm done with you. You hear that, Trank?"

But there was no answer from the stonefish. Gray shook his head, feeling more sadness than he should. The others were right: Trank wasn't to be trusted. Gray blasted away, covering the dweller with sand as he put Slaggernacks behind him.

He forced himself forward, faster and faster, trying to make up for lost time. Gray wouldn't let Lochlan and AuzyAuzy fight without him. Takiza would be angry that they hadn't waited, but it couldn't be helped. If Gray could go around to the far side of the old Goblin Shiver homewaters, he could swim into battle with the small AuzyAuzy force.

It was then he saw a hundred Indi Shiver sharkkind rise over the crest of the Riptide homewaters.

While Gray wanted to fight, he didn't want to be foolishly sent to the Sparkle Blue. He descended into the greenie and watched as the battle formation passed, leaving the homewaters. Gray counted and figured it wasn't the entire armada but about a third of it.

The odds just got a little better, he thought. But this meant two thirds of the Indi armada was still around. How could the splinter force of AuzyAuzy, along with Rogue Shiver and some sharkkind of Coral, beat Finnivus and his force of well-trained mariners? Gray had never seen the armada set a single fin out of place once they were in formation and being guided by their mariner prime.

It was then that a thought hit Gray, making him tingle all over. He hoped the tingle was because his idea was a good one, and not some funky after-effect of the maredsoo. The concept was crazy and had the longest odds of succeeding. And it would require him to wait patiently and not do anything until the *perfect* moment— something he wasn't used to doing.

But if Gray could pull it off, his friends just might have a chance against Finnivus and the Indi armada.

CHAPTER 29

"WE NEED TO MOVE SOON," ONYX WHISPERED.

They were well inside the Riptide homewaters. Barkley nodded that he understood but motioned for the blacktip to stay put. He could see the royal court and Riptide's colorful terraced greenie cliffs in the background. But there was nothing to do but be still. Usually Barkley could do this quite well. He prided himself on being able to outwait *and* outwit others. But this wasn't training or sneaking up to scare a friend or even hunting for lunch. So much was riding on this crazy mission that Barkley's patience was stretched to the breaking point.

Ripper swam by, led by two armored *squaline*. Barkley hissed softly, "Here we go." They were so close! But they had to wait for the signal. If they broke Whalem out of prison before it was time, every one of them would end up on Finnivus's dinner menu.

Barkley had taken a long look at Whalem's cage. It wasn't like the whale-skeleton prison he had been locked in by Velenka last year. This was different. There was no system of interlocking bars on the door. In fact, the front door looked much like the three other sides of the cage, although it did have a rectangular section with a hole in it. But there was no way a shark could get a fin into that small hole! How would they open it?

One *squaline* tugged on the chain that held Ripper. The scarred hammerhead glared, growling in a menacing tone, "Do that again and you'll be sorry."

The guard laughed. "The only thing I'll be sorry about is if I don't get a piece of you for dinner."

The other *squaline* added, "Or if you give the emperor gas!"

"Oh, that would be bad!" agreed the first one. "I'm on throne duty tonight!"

The first guard placed one of the links of the chain holding Ripper onto a pole in front of the cage housing Whalem. This had the effect of acting as a brake on Ripper while the other guard was still connected to him.

Whalem roused himself when he heard the clanking of the metal door. The first guard saw this. "Looks like you're getting company, *Commander.*" The *squaline* used the title as an insult. "Hope you two get along. Open the cage!"

For a moment, nothing happened, but then an octopus crawled out of its hiding place holding a shiny object in one of its suction-cup-covered tentacles. Barkley cursed to himself. How could he have been so stupid? He had *lived* in a landshark ship and knew landsharks had things called *keys* that opened doors and chests. So there wasn't a knob or lever to push and release Whalem. This cage could only be opened with a key!

And there was no way this Indi octo was going to give it to them! Barkley's mind raced as the octopus crawled its way up the bars, inserting the key into the lock. Had the octo heard them the last time they were here? If so, why hadn't he reported it? Did Trank have something to do with that? Trank had said Gafin had treaties with dwellers all over the Big Blue. But these were questions for another time. The door swung open! They *had* to act while it was open!

"Inside," the second guard ordered Ripper.

This was their chance! Just then there was a tremendous cry from the guards in the royal court. Barkley could hear, "Alarum! Alarum! We're being attacked!"

It was the signal!

Barkley streaked up and speared one of Ripper's guards in the liver. Onyx took care of the second. Being chained to Ripper, the smaller guard had no chance, and the hammerhead helped batter him into submission. Barkley let the octo scoot away. He was probably just another dweller forced to do the emperor's bidding.

Ripper saw and didn't approve. "You're still weak," he said to Barkley after spitting out the bite blocker in his mouth. "Much better," he said, gnashing his rows and rows of teeth.

Whalem crept to the edge of the cage, and Ripper moved to block the tiger. "What are you doing?" Onyx asked crossly. "We're here to get him out, not keep him in!"

"Looks like he's getting second thoughts," Ripper said. "Maybe he'd like to turn us in to prove his loyalty?"

Barkley saw that Ripper was right! There *was* doubt in the armada commander's eyes. Of course, there would be. Onyx didn't want to believe it. "That's crazy! Let him out. Sir, I am so sorry."

"Lochlan says he doesn't hold you responsible," Barkley told the tiger commander. This seemed to settle the older shark, and the look of doubt went away.

Whalem nodded at Barkley. "I still have much to apologize for, though. Lead on."

The Indi armada was being set in its battle formation, at least ten rows deep. Barkley began picking his way through the kelp field, away from the noise and bustle.

Ripper had other ideas. He zoomed back toward the royal court!

"Where are you going?" Barkley hissed.

"To deal with Velenka!" he shouted.

Before Barkley could do anything, they were spotted. "The prisoners have escaped! The prisoners have escaped!" the *squaline* shouted.

A group of ten armored guards streaked toward them.

"So much for the easy way!" Barkley shouted as he broke from cover with everyone else. "Swim for your lives!"

THE BATTLE OF RIPTIDE

CHAPTER 30

ONYX PASSED BARKLEY AS IF HE WERE ON A LAZY afternoon swim.

"Pick up the pace!" snapped Whalem, as he also flashed ahead.

Barkley tore after the two as fast as he could. Luckily, rather than pursuing them, the *squaline* broke away to defend Finnivus as Ripper shot toward him like a maniac.

Barkley saw Whalem head directly for the massive armada formation. "Follow me! I have an idea!" Whalem yelled. The old tiger swam them directly between the growing pyramid formation of sharkkind and the new mariner prime, who was busily barking orders at everyone. Barkley's group churned past, and for a moment, the new Indi commander was too shocked to do anything. He shook his head, not believing what had just happened, then shouted, "Capture them!"

The pyramid formation seemed to melt as the sharks on the top dove into a downward current straight at Whalem, Onyx, and Barkley. The armada's subcommanders, busily carrying out their last instructions, bellowed at the Indi mariners to stay in formation. The new mariner prime then realized his mistake. "No! Wait, stop! Back to your positions!" he cried. But it was too late. The formation was hopelessly disorganized. No one could swim anywhere.

"Ha!" yelled Whalem. "That new mariner prime can't hold a lantern fish to me!"

"Go, go, go!" Barkley urged.

Onyx streaked toward the area where Lochlan and AuzyAuzy Shiver were assembling, with Barkley and Whalem close behind.

"Got him," Onyx told Lochlan as he whipped into battle position facing the Indi armada.

"Good on ya," the golden great white said, nodding. "Barkley, Snork, take the commander to the safe area. We'll hold them up long enough for you to disappear."

Whalem took only a moment to size up the hourglass formation of Lochlan's forces. The AuzyAuzy mariners were mostly on the top with the Coral Shiver sharks arranged below. This would give the more experienced AuzyAuzy mariners a chance to descend from above, using the now downward-drifting currents to their advantage. With Coral Shiver's lack of training in formation fighting, they had to be protected.

Whalem looked at Lochlan and shook his head. "You'll be slaughtered."

Barkley saw the faces of the AuzyAuzy Line and knew it was true! And yet they still were willing to swim into the battle. He couldn't believe it.

"You can't do this!" Barkley told Lochlan. "You're supposed to be the shark everyone rallies around! You can't die!"

"Very touching, mate, but you've got to leave," the golden great white replied. "Whalem will lead you. He's better than I am."

The tiger commander shook his snout vigorously. "I dishonored myself! I will stay if your mariners will allow me to guide them."

"For the love of Tyro!" shouted Barkley. "Let's all just swim away!"

Lochlan told Whalem, "We don't have our dolphs to coordinate the formation, so we can only delay them."

The old tiger looked at Lochlan. "Have you studied the Battle of Silander's End?"

"Oh, you've got to be kidding," Kendra interrupted. "You want to use voice commands? From the center of the formation?"

"It would have to be a two-pronged formation," Lochlan said, a toothy grin spreading across his face.

"Exactly!" agreed Whalem. "That would negate their

speed!" The two looked at each other, and Barkley could see a mutual respect grow between the old mariner and the young king.

Lochlan nodded to the old tiger. "If you wouldn't mind commanding the second battle fin, I'd appreciate it."

"I'd be honored ... my King."

Lochlan told his Line, "Kendra, you're with me. Xander, Jaunt, you're now Whalem's subbies," meaning subcommanders.

Jaunt tail-slapped Whalem's flank. "Too right! We'll help the oldie!"

The old tiger was shocked for a moment—and then roared with laughter. Barkley supposed no one had spoken to Whalem that way for several decades.

"If today's my day to swim the Sparkle Blue, let that be the chorus of my farewell song!" Whalem called out with a smile, showing his notched teeth.

The AuzyAuzy mariners thought this was hilarious and also laughed.

Barkley turned to Snork. "Do they realize everyone might die today?"

"I think that's why they're laughing. To stop from being scared," the sawfish answered.

"Hey!" shouted Striiker. "Are we going to fight at some point? I thought you AuzyAuzy fins liked to fight, but all I see is a lot of yapping!"

Apparently Xander and Striiker were brothers at heart. Xander took his position ahead of the great white and yelled, "Soon enough, young son. Soon enough. That is if you don't talk them to death first and spoil the party!"

Then Whalem and Lochlan had a rapid conversation that Barkley barely understood.

"Watch their Topside Rip and Slide attacks," Whalem said. "They'll roll down the current with Orca Bears Down or Sea Snake Engarde."

"Should we be ready for Yellowfin Feeding on Minnows or Cuttlefish Strikes a Crab?" asked Lochlan. "Won't they be looking for a chance to end this early?"

"The new mariner prime won't be so bold. He outnumbers us four to one even without his third battle fin."

Barkley recognized the terms as fighting moves, but these two obviously knew the information on an entirely different level. As Lochlan and Whalem spoke, the AuzyAuzy subcommanders moved the formation from the shape of an X to one made up of two Vs, which then interlocked to form a W.

From his position in Lochlan's half of the formation, Barkley saw the much more massive Indi armada moving from the Riptide homewaters toward them. The armada was five levels higher than their own and in the shape of a pyramid. Barkley felt icy cold inside his stomach. How would they be able to survive Indi's attack?

"The time for chibber-chabber is done and gone!" yelled Jaunt. "Here they come!"

Both Lochlan and Whalem were well aware. "Quick

and decisive!" shouted the tiger shark commander to everyone. "That's the way to do things!"

"Agreed! Let's give 'em a good snout banging!" Lochlan exclaimed.

Lochlan and Whalem swam in the center of their respective *V* formations. From their positions, theoretically, the subcommanders would relay their shouted orders to everyone else.

In reality, though . . .

Barkley didn't understand how Lochlan and Whalem would make split-second decisions in the thick of battle while they themselves might be fighting for their lives. And even if everyone heard the commands, there was a whale-size difference between understanding an order and doing it!

Once it got moving, the massive Indi armada was a thing of deadly grace. Their sharks swam so close together and turned with such precision that the entire formation seemed like a single, monstrous predator. They shifted their ranks into other shapes, smoothly and cleanly. Lochlan and Whalem shouted countermoves, and their own ranks morphed and changed. But the combination of Auzy-Auzy, Rogue, and Coral sharks didn't blend seamlessly like the more experienced Indi armada. Their reactions were delayed, and their swimming wasn't nearly as crisp.

The Indi armada split into three battle fins of a hundred sharkkind, each one larger than the entire AuzyAuzy-Coral formation.

"Hold fast in your eights!" yelled Lochlan.

The subcommander in Barkley's section of the formation was Kendra. She translated, "Stay on my tail! Don't attack yet!"

Many sharks were out of position, and Barkley could tell some were already tired. They had none of the training or discipline of the armada.

Then Indi's second battle wing struck! At least ten sharkkind on Barkley's side were mauled and spun crazily toward the seabed below. They followed that with feinting moves by the first and third Indi battle fins, which pulled apart the AuzyAuzy-Coral ranks as they tried to counter.

Then the second Indi battle fin attacked for real and broke through, killing another fifteen of AuzyAuzy-Coral mariners. Barkley barely avoided a bite at his left fin as he struggled to keep up. He heard Lochlan yell, "Regroup! Swim through the Split S!" Kendra again translated that into something he could understand.

Barkley caught a glimpse of the flashing lantern fish device relaying signals to the Indi armada. That way of communicating was much faster. Their subcommanders didn't listen for commands but merely glanced over to *see* their orders, then acted on them. The Indi mariner prime also had the advantage of watching the entire battle waters from a safe distance. It's too much of an advantage to overcome, Barkley thought hopelessly. It's only a matter of time before they crush us.

Lochlan and Whalem *were* working miracles, though. Barkley couldn't believe how speedily their formation was reordered after their initial battering.

The first battle wing of the Indi armada did a sharp looping turn and dove from above. This time the damage was far worse. Thirty sharkkind were mortally wounded—and Indi's third battle fin, packed with heavy sharks like great whites and bulls filled the gap, preventing Lochlan and Whalem from re-forming into a single defensive formation. Blood bloomed thick in the water, causing Barkley to gag.

They were about to be eaten alive!

Barkley saw the other two Indi battle fins form a pincer move. The first did another looping attack from above. It was doubtful that the AuzyAuzy-Coral force could stop *any* of the attacks, much less all of them. Barkley glanced at the lantern fish light board and knew he had made a huge mistake. He wasn't a good mariner and never would be even if he lived to be a hundred—which definitely wouldn't happen now.

"I should be sneaking up to that signaler to destroy it! I've killed us all by not using my head," Barkley muttered through gritted teeth. The Indi armada closed in for what would be a final, decisive attack.

Just when all hope seemed to be lost, Barkley caught a glimpse of an immense shark bursting from the greenie and streaking at the lantern fish signaler.

His heart leapt. It was Gray!

CHAPTER 31

GRAY BOLTED FROM THE PATCH OF THICK greenie, very close to where the Indi mariner prime hovered. It was a miracle he had made it this far. But with Whalem escaping, the royal court being attacked by Ripper, and two armadas clashing a short distance away, it was the perfect storm. The utter panic and confusion inside the Riptide homewaters hid Gray better than even the thickest kelp field.

Much to Gray's surprise, for five whole seconds after he went into a roaring attack sprint, absolutely no one raised an alarm. Perhaps, the few sharks who saw him streak behind the throne area where Finnivus was alternately weeping and screaming had other things on their minds.

Gray could hear the new mariner prime's orders as he closed the distance between them. "Battle fin one—Sea Serpent Strikes, execute! Battle fin two ..." The richly tattooed armada commander, a young spinner shark, looked over an instant before Gray struck. The bite was clean and deep. Blood clouded the water as the spinner's eyes rolled upward to the whites.

"Look out!" cried one of the subcommanders, much too late.

Gray smashed through him, and there was a free path to the signaling device. The lantern fish inside panicked, bouncing and flashing madly, but couldn't move from the enclosed mesh pen. Gray crashed into the device, breaking it to pieces in his mouth. He whipped his head side to side, crushing the signaler further as his momentum carried him past the rim of the homewaters. Finally, Gray dropped what was left of it down a deep crevice. "Let them try and find that!"

The effect on the Indi armada was immediate. They had been doing a complex weaving maneuver with all three battle fins in motion at once. At least one battle fin took the panicked flashing of the terrified lantern fish as a real command from the now-dead mariner prime. That force went into an area where another was supposed to be. The two swam straight into each other!

The third battle fin tried to withdraw, but Gray's friends wouldn't let them. Lochlan bellowed, "Attack! Attack!" so loudly, it could clearly be heard across the battle waters. The AuzyAuzy-Coral formation struck the one Indi battle fin still in good order. Blood clouded everything in that area for a moment.

When the current whisked it away, Gray saw that Indi battle fin had lost over half of its sharkkind— more than fifty! The other two battle fins, in snarled confusion after swimming into each other, had no way to defend themselves when the entire AuzyAuzy and Coral Shiver force turned and charged them.

There was blood and chaos everywhere! The shrill, terrified shrieks chilled Gray's spine, but at least it wasn't his friends doing the screaming. If sharks had to swim to the Sparkle Blue today, thought Gray, let them be Indi mariners.

But the Black Wave armada wasn't going to swim away just yet. They were too disciplined. Their sub-commanders saw the lantern fish weren't signaling and took matters into their own fins. AuzyAuzy tried to press its momentary advantage, but their next attack was deflected without any damage done! Then the three disorganized Indi battle fins merged into two organized ones. Even with their losses, Indi still outnumbered the AuzyAuzy force by two to one!

The armada wheeled and attacked, biting deeply into the AuzyAuzy formation. Through his lessons with Takiza and Lochlan, Gray knew they wouldn't last another strike.

Gray sped up. He would fight to the finish with his friends. But suddenly, there was something in front of his eye—Gray thought it might be a bit of floating greenie, but then it spoke!

"Take them in, Nulo! And try not to be your usual clumsy self!"

"Takiza!" Gray shouted. "Take who in?"

"Always asking questions!" The little betta scooted upward and behind. When Gray looked in that direction, he didn't see Takiza—but he *did* see two hundred AuzyAuzy mariners swimming toward the battle!

That was what the maredsoo greenie was for!

Takiza swam across the entire Atlantis and into the Sific to lead the AuzyAuzy forces from there. The maredsoo had allowed them to get to Riptide in time for the battle.

The sharks of the Golden Rush, the name they used because of Lochlan's peculiar family shading, put Gray in diamond head position out in the center and near the front. Whether he wanted to or not, Gray would lead this group into battle!

"Takiza told us to follow you," said a mako with an AuzyAuzy accent. "Orders, sir!"

Gray surveyed the situation. He was deathly afraid to do the wrong thing but knew he needed to be decisive or his friends would die. They needed to stop the Indi armada's next attack! "We're going directly in!" he shouted to everyone around him. "Spearfisher Streaks by the Cliffs—execute!"

But his order wasn't shouted. It was relayed by the clicks and whistles of a dolphin swimming right above his dorsal fin. The AuzyAuzy mariners understood the dolphin's odd language and snapped into perfect formation.

Gray and the AuzyAuzy's forces caught the Indi armada unaware and unprotected. With a tremendous howl, the mariners of the Golden Rush ripped into their enemy. Indi had killed their king and attacked their home. AuzyAuzy showed no mercy. This attack broke the Indi armada.

Lochlan's formation merged with Gray's. "If you don't mind," the young king told him, "I'll take it from here!" Gray was happily relieved as Lochlan took the diamond head position with his personal guard and the dolphins now relayed his commands.

The subcommanders ordered everyone from Rogue and Coral to leave the formation. Now that Lochlan had his forces and the advantage of dolphins to relay his orders instantly, they would be much better without Gray and his untrained friends. The Auzy-Auzy mariners smoothly and cleanly re-formed and swept after the Indi armada, striking at any groups that tried to organize into a battle formation. Soon, it became a rout! The shattered Indi mariners turned tail and swam away in disarray.

In the distance, Gray saw another large group of

sharkkind had already left. It was Finnivus and his personal guard. They were retreating. Wait! Actually, they were swimming away as fast as they could!

Gray hovered in the bloody waters in numbed shock.

Somehow, they had done it. The Battle of Riptide was won.

CHAPTER 32

AN HOUR LATER, THE LAST REMNANTS OF THE Indi Shiver armada were driven from the furthest reaches of Riptide territory. Barkley, Mari, Gray's friends from Rogue and Coral Shivers, Lochlan, and all those from AuzyAuzy were talking, shouting, and singing as they grieved for their lost friends.

Even Ripper was there! How did he get out of the royal court alive?

After the initial euphoria of the moment, Gray realized the one fin he didn't see was Takiza. Where was the frilly little betta? He, most of all, deserved to be celebrating with them. Gray told everyone, "Be right back!" and quickly swam the way he'd come with the AuzyAuzy mariners. He searched and searched but found nothing. Where was Takiza?

Then Gray saw him.

But he wasn't moving.

And his gills were so still.

Gray's heart caught in his throat as he slowed himself to a hover, the little betta's body drifting with the slow current next to his left eye. For a moment the water caught Takiza's frilly fins, making them bloom splendidly, but otherwise there was no movement.

Not even a fin flick.

The eyes of Takiza Jaelynn Betta vam Delacrest Waveland ka Boom Boom stared blankly into the Big Blue.

"Takiza?" Gray said in a whisper as tears welled up in his eyes. "Takiza?"

There was no answer.

"Oh, no, no, no," was all Gray could keep repeating.

He sobbed a few times. He tried to keep his grief and pain inside, but then, like a tidal wave, everything came pouring out. How could the noble fish have sacrificed himself? For what? Finnivus was still *alive*!

Gray gave himself over to full-blown bawling for many minutes until he saw the little betta looking crossly at him, shaking his head in disapproval.

"TAKIZA!" shouted Gray.

"The first time I've slept soundly in a hundred years, and you disturb me with your hysterical sobbing!" Takiza shook himself and fluttered his gossamer fins this way and that. He grunted as if everything was to his satisfaction.

"Oh, Takiza! I—"

Gray was cut off by a sizable tail slap across the snout that made him wince. "How many times do I have to tell you to address me as Shiro?" Takiza shook his head once more. "Of all my apprentices throughout the ages, Nulo, you are truly the *most* Nulo."

"But at least I'm the *best* at being worst," Gray said, grinning. "I have that going for me, right?"

The betta snorted. He caught himself and scowled. "What am I to do with you? Keep up your training, Nulo. I must see to things much more important than listening to you weep or your pathetic attempts at humor. Do try and stay out of trouble for a little while until I return!" And with that, Takiza flared his fins once more and swam away.

Gray called after him, "I'll miss you, too, Shiro!"

Takiza didn't answer as he disappeared into the Big Blue, but somehow, Gray could tell the little betta was smiling.

EPILOGUE

"I WILL KILL THEM ALL!" SHOUTED FINNIVUS. "They have dishonored my—our!—armada! But what if they're coming after me right now? What if that evil Lochlan and his Golden Rush want to send me to the Sparkle Blue? Where are my guards? I must have more guards! I order them to protect me! And destroy the sharks responsible for this!"

Tydal watched the emperor alternate between fear and rage as what remained of their forces travelled back toward the Indi homewaters. Normally, each sharkkind in the court would fight tooth and fin to be nearest to His Highness. Not today. Most in the court stayed as far away as their rank permitted. This was a day of disaster. Tydal wouldn't be surprised if Finnivus had the whole thing wiped from the royal history. How had Whalem escaped? How had that giant hammerhead called Ripper attacked Velenka in the middle of the royal court? If it hadn't been for the quickness of the *squaline*—who had first thought Ripper was after Finnivus—she wouldn't have had a one-flippered seal's chance in a feeding frenzy of having remained with the living. As it was this aptly named Ripper had killed two of Finnivus's personal guards and *still* managed to get away!

But the most shocking thing of all was that the Indi Shiver armada had been defeated.

Tydal could only think of this in the hushed silence of his mind. The force against their mariners was smaller and not as well-trained. But they had won anyway! True, many things happened, not the least of which was a giant shark destroying the lantern fish signaler. How a fish that size managed to *sneak* into the homewaters unseen was simply baffling.

"They have not seen the last of us!" yelled Finnivus. "I am the emperor of the Big Blue, and they have rebelled from my just and gentle rule! They task me! They will pay!"

Tydal knew that once Finnivus was less panicked, he would gather his forces and bring another, far larger armada back to these waters. The tides of the entire North Atlantis would turn red with blood. How could anything stand against Finnivus's royal wrath? It was impossible.

But when Tydal had woken up this morning, he would have said any of the things that had happened today were impossible.

The armada had been defeated. Finnivus was swimming home in disgrace. There was much to think about. Tydal replayed in his mind how the emperor had shrieked when the hammerhead seemed to be hurtling toward him.

Tydal was careful not to show any emotion as he watched Finnivus sob, but inside, he laughed.

Takiza swam away with all the dignity he could muster. To be found floating in the water like a piece of drifting garbage! Absolutely galling! Little did the young pup know how close Takiza had come to swimming the Sparkle Blue. Even after giving Lochlan's mariners the maredsoo brought from the Dark Blue's depths by his increasingly capable apprentice, Takiza knew they wouldn't make it in time. He'd used his powers to speed the current, pushing it faster and faster to make up the difference.

By the time they'd arrived at the battle, Takiza could see the motes of color dancing on the edge of his vision that preceded everyone's journey into the Sparkle Blue. He allowed himself a smile. How his apprentice had led on a moment's notice! How easily Gray had filled the role of commander! Even though Takiza made sure to ask—a force as proud and capable as the Golden Rush would not blindly follow just anyone—they trusted Gray with their lives upon meeting him! It gave Takiza hope for the first time in a long time.

The Indi armada had been defeated because they had been caught by surprise.

That wouldn't be the case next time.

But these were thoughts for another day.

Takiza would go to a safe place and rest. He needed to regenerate his strength, or he would surely fail. It was such a long current to swim, and he despaired of successfully completing his journey. But he would try.

Tyro would expect nothing less.

Acknowledgments

Thanks to all the great people at Razorbill for putting up with me, but most of all Ben Schrank, who took a huge chance by choosing someone who never wrote a book before; Jessica Rothenberg, past super-editor, future super-novelist; also Gillian Levinson and Laura Arnold.

Thanks to everyone in Los Angeles who helped me over the years but especially the awesome Jim Krieg, who I met in film school and who despite that still picks up the phone when I call; John Semper, who hired me first; Mark Hoffmeier, great writer and fantasy football superstar. Also my friends from Notre Dame, Go Irish! And finally my sister Jude, who's not the most annoying sister in the world, most of the time.

Visit **www.SharkWarsSeries.com** to learn more and to play the Shark Wars game!

ERNIE "EJ" ALTBACKER is an author and screenwriter living in Redondo Beach, California. In addition to the six-book Shark Wars series, he has written animated features, such as *Justice League Dark* and *Teen Titans: The Judas Contract*, as well as several television shows, including *Niko and the Sword of Light*, *Lost in Oz*, *Justice League Action*, and the live-action *Spooksville*. He also produces the *Legend Quest* series for Netflix.

ALSO AVAILABLE NOW!